I0847071

SYMBIOTIC ASCENSION

1

Guylhann

Edited by Darien Aris Kirst
Cover Art by Fernando Granea

Published 2025 by MoonQuill®
Arlington, VA

www.moonquill.com

TABLE OF CONTENTS

Chapter 1

A BLOODY AWAKENING

Ugh... Damn, my stomach hurts like hell.

Was yesterday's takeout too much? Who can resist the temptation of a delicious three-meat taco? Wait a minute. That means I can call in absent today. Haha! In your face, Italian test! I didn't want to go to university anyway.

Crunch, slurp...

Who the hell is eating in my ear? I can't even sleep peacefully!

The first thing Glenn saw through his bleary eyes was a bald head covered in sickly black spots. The repulsive figure trembled as it shoved handfuls of unidentified food into its mouth.

I know I partied hard last night, but damn. Where the hell did I wake up? Don't tell me I went to bed with... with that!

As his senses returned ever so slowly, Glenn tried unsuccessfully to separate from the revolting head. This was a terrible hangover, even more so considering there was a particularly disgusting taste in his mouth. It was metallic. He reached for his face with a trembling hand, finding a warm, viscous liquid in a deep red color... Blood?

Did I get into a fight?

An acute pain from his belly shook his entire soul. Glenn bit down on his lips, his eyes bloodshot as he endured this awful suffering. Before he could complain, he felt a loud thump in his ears, drowning every other sound under a rhythmic beat. It took him a few seconds to realize that the noise came from his heart trying desperately to pump blood back into his body.

Beyond this dull beating were distant voices crying in anguish—trailing from far, far away. The cawing of crows accompanied the death rattles with a grotesque melody.

I... What? I'd rather take the test than endure this crap! Fucking nightmare! Let me wake up!

Glenn forced a glance downwards. He discovered two things that his mind struggled to comprehend.

First, a long, wooden spear was piercing his chest. And second, the bald figure was rummaging through his insides in search of tasty treats, devouring him like a butcher taking cuts from a pig. Trying to—no, *eating him alive*. Glenn's pupils dilated as a primordial fear entered his mind. The creature ripped off a bone covered in flesh, helping itself to the bloodiest rib—*his* rib.

Crunch, gulp...

And the worst of it? He wasn't waking up anytime soon.

What the hell is that?!

Glenn's face contorted in pain. He tried to scream, but due to blood accumulating in his throat, the result had been more of a gurgle—similar to a murloc.

He knew he was dying. Well, that he *should* be dying. Because, strangely, he didn't *sense* his life slipping away.

Each breath was the source of agony; the air scratched his insides as if it was barbed wire. He instinctively coughed, accidentally shooting the sludge over his assailant's bald head and painting it crimson with mounds of green snot.

Glenn stopped breathing, his eyes freezing in horror as the monster paused its feast. It straightened up to show a chalk-white face—featureless except for the mouth full of sharp, pointed teeth. Shreds of flesh dangled from those dagger-like fangs, swaying with each of the monster's raspy inhalations.

It twisted closer. The damned creature wasn't satisfied with his innards. Its teeth chattered, clicking and grating horribly. A guttural cry came from the otherworldly beast, its breath filled with rotten meat and death.

"Ennon ut suutrom se? Non trefer, subic cuhda se!"

Shit! What is this monster? I'm not a snack! Piss off! Didn't you have enough with half my stomach?

Horrified, Glenn's hand shot out in panic, patting the wet ground in search of a weapon until he felt a heavy weight. He caught the glint of metal, red light covering it like a mystical veil. In a desperate attempt to save himself, he pierced the sword straight through the wide-open mouth of the monster. The blade tore smoothly through its throat, poking out the other side. A cascade of black blood erupted, emitting a strange mixed scent of copper and rotten eggs.

The monster writhed with a gurgling noise and fell, slowly sliding down the sword. Its jaw rattled, making Glenn drop the weapon in horror.

Glenn's gaze froze on the monster's body, struggling to understand what had happened. He gasped for air, but nothing entered his lungs besides a lingering ache that forced him to come to his senses.

Okay. I think it's dead. It should be. Right? I need to get out of here and call the police. And go to the hospital. Damn, it hurts... Glenn winced as he prepared to check his injuries until a strange, soothing sensation calmed the agony. *Wait, is it... getting better?*

As he gawked at his open buffet of a stomach, the wound healed magically. His missing bones regrew, and tendrils of red flesh stretched over ruptured viscera. It didn't take long to resolve the being-eaten-alive problem, but unfortunately for Glenn, his torture wasn't over yet.

Since, well, he also had a spear skewering straight through his heart or lung. Truthfully, he had trouble remembering where the important organs were in his chest. The unrelenting pangs of pain and the lack of fresh air rendered it impossible for him to think about anything properly.

How do I even pull it out? Shouldn't I just wait for help?

Glenn's mind raced as he searched around for aid. It was only then that he came to the critical realization that help wouldn't be coming anytime soon. The ground was damp, cold, and sticky—made of mud and gore, unlike his warm, cozy bed.

Glenn glanced up, weakly raising his hands. They shivered, dripping a mixture of unidentified liquids. He looked beyond them, his eyes widening. Two colossal moons—the larger one scarlet and the other pristine white— bathed a dark field in crimson.

Two moons? What? Glenn blinked.

Corpses floating in pools of blood littered the plains. Vultures circled above, wondering whether Glenn was another body to feast on. He turned, only to discover the literal death stare of a soldier—his fractured head revealing his brain. Glenn shuddered.

There were a dozen flesh-eating fiends, similar to the one he had killed, devouring their share of corpses. They were too focused on their feast to care about him, occasionally sniffing at the sky, as if trying to sense their surroundings. The sound of teeth and claws tearing meat was... not particularly pleasant, to say the least.

Traumatizing was the best term to describe it.

A flying organ crashed just a few meters from Glenn, spraying a mixture of blood, guts, and badly digested vegetables. No need to say that it smelled horrible. His eyes widened, watching as a small bit of... *unspeakably vile things* landed on his shoulders.

Glenn's first reflex was to gag, but the spear pierced the muscles involved—causing intense pain and ultimately stopping the retching process. One monster skulked towards the sound, making him freeze in fear. But the creature wasn't going to abandon its current meal, a very well-fed specimen that might have been named Francis or Jack. Who knew?

Glenn winced as he wiped the gore off his shoulder, holding his breath with repugnance.

Argh! Oh my god! Okay, okay. Pull yourself together. And while you're there, pull that damn spear out!

On those wise thoughts, Glenn grabbed the shaft and tried to pull it out, gritting his teeth through the pain. Sadly, it had been embedded firmly into the ground. His hands slipped on the splintered wood, weakness washing over him.

I... I need to break it!

Blood continued to flow from the hole in his chest. Death was looming, and he couldn't afford to wait.

Glenn glanced at the monster he had killed, wanting to retrieve the sword. But just the sight of *it* discouraged him from picking up the weapon.

Coughing more bile, he tried to break the spear, pushing himself forwards for leverage, only to fail miserably and make him feel as if someone was wringing his guts.

Luckily, Glenn was more afraid of death than the creature who was once feasting on him. He steadied himself and inched closer to the beast's toothy abyss, his fingers wrapping around the hilt. A strange sucking noise filled the air as the blade slid through flesh, but Glenn focused on the task at hand.

As he finally drew out the sword, the corpse crashed onto the ground, a puddle of blood growing under it. Glenn used it to saw through the handle, determination shining through his eyes while each back-and-forth slice inflicted unbearable suffering. After severing the pole, he dropped his weapon. The movements were painful, and he almost screamed. But he held back, so the other monsters would not notice him.

Glenn didn't need to test his skills against another horrible creature. Even more so considering he didn't have any skills to test. He held back his shriek by biting his lips, causing them to bleed—which gifted him the appearance of a complete lunatic. As if the guts and gore already drenching him weren't enough.

He slipped off the spear skewering him and fell face first, coating himself in more mud. Blood gushed out from his abdomen, making him wonder just how many liters were left in his body. After a short but painful minute, the wound completely healed, and Glenn could finally take a breath without having to pay for it.

Throwing his head back, his eyes fixated on the two foreign moons in the starry sky—a sky that wasn't clouded by pollution or the blinking passage of a commercial airliner.

I love... breathing. He gasped. *Should I try to look for other survivors? Nope, can't afford it. I don't want to get eaten again!*

Glenn looked around, discovering a forest at the edge of the battlefield. It appeared like an oasis in this desert of blood and flesh. Behind him was the field of corpses with the same damned monsters. Flags adorned with unknown embroideries fluttered lightly in the rustling wind, acting as a guide away from this hell.

Well, he didn't have an actual choice.

Picking up the sword again to defend himself, he knew his luck might not hold against the next monster. Not understanding how to wield it properly—or even how to fight—he planted the blade's tip on the ground, using it to push himself up. His legs wobbled, and a dull sound rang in his ears.

Glenn held his head, feeling like someone was drilling a hole inside it. After standing still for a few seconds, the aching calmed, leaving him free to escape to the woods.

He proceeded with uncertain steps. The battlefield stretched several kilometers, and there were countless bodies, making it impossible to guess how many people died there. Red, blue, and gray tunics—all colors lost beneath the crimson liquid.

Glenn shivered when he accidentally stepped on the broken thorax of a dead man, the bones yielding under his weight. He almost screamed when he caught his ankle on a hand stiff from rigor mortis.

Cadavers on cadavers, horse carcasses, monsters eating the bodies... That wasn't the worst part. No, the most disgusting was the swarms of flies laying astronomical quantities of eggs. Limbs twitched as maggots wriggled through flesh, devouring the corpses from the inside out.

That was the last straw. Glenn puked his guts. Well, what remained of them. He took a few minutes to breathe in and out, trying to calm his racing heart. After wiping the vomit off his mouth, he stood back up.

Glenn's gaze fixed on the not-so-near woods. Perhaps thanks to the grace of God or his fucking pity, there were no monsters along the way. There were still the sempiternal rows of rotting corpses but nothing that looked like it would try to take a bite out of him. He steeled himself and crouched. The closer he got to the forest, the better he felt. But he restrained himself, proceeding with hushed steps.

He didn't want to stay another minute in this literal bloody mess, but not drawing any attention towards himself was even more important than running for dear life. After all, one wrong step and he might lose said life.

He *had* to get out of here.

Chapter 2

THE DAMN FOREST

The closer Glenn got to the forest, the fewer the bodies. The scent of rotting flesh lessened, replaced by fresh mud and resin. His heartbeat calmed as the risk of disturbing one of the corpse-eating monsters disappeared.

It wasn't exactly *zero* risk, but he would probably be okay as long as he didn't yell. Probably.

Glenn couldn't wrap his head around the craziness of his situation. Adrenaline pumped into his veins, although less than when he woke up in that macabre mess.

He fell to his knees, his insides churning. He held his mouth with both hands, grimacing as he swallowed whatever threatened to leave his body.

I shouldn't even have anything in my belly, thanks to that monster. Ugh—

Glenn's train of thought halted as the need to puke intensified. He breathed in and out calmly for a few minutes, kneeling at the woodland edge. After catching his breath, he pushed himself up and threw a look behind at the bloody battlefield.

Terrible mistake.

That scene was enough to force Glenn's primal instincts to claw up his throat. He barfed for the second time, getting rid of gastric acid and blood.

The blood was not too worrying, considering he had his stomach carved open.

Glenn heaved heavily as he forced himself to stumble further into the forest. Suddenly, as he walked with only thoughts of survival, reality struck him like a direct meeting with Truck-kun.

"Wait." He stopped dead in his tracks. "Did I transmigrate or something?"

Glenn grabbed his chest, finding the hole in his tunic where the spear had impaled him. *No, no, this isn't at all what I imagined back when I read those isekai novels!*

"I... I need to see my face," he mumbled, glancing around with panic. The sound of water flowing was unmistakable, and it didn't take long to discover a river.

He almost ran right away to the riverbank, but he remembered that predators usually stalked water sources. H hid behind a bush, but he couldn't find anything in the darkness of the night—despite the bright crimson light of the massive moon. It outshone its smaller, white sister. Glenn wanted to bawl his eyes out just at the sight of the twin moons.

How the hell does that even work gravity-wise? This certainly isn't Earth if there are two damned moons!

Glenn breathed in deeply, shaking these thoughts out of his head and approaching the river. He tried to be as stealthy, but between the twigs breaking under his feet and his ragged breathing, that was likely a failure.

When he reached the water, he fell to his knees, looking at his reflection. His chestnut hair was messy—covered in dirt and dried blood. His face was no better, his brown eyes bloodshot. He looked like a lunatic. But he was still himself.

"Thank god..." Glenn sighed in relief, recognizing the man staring back at him.

That, at least, was excellent news. After all, he considered himself to be quite handsome, and another body would simply *not feel right.*

"What do I do now?" he whispered as his eyes shot around the dark oak forest.

His circumstance was dire, but it could have been worse. One thing he questioned was *why* his isekai fantasy—or whatever it was called—had gone so wrong. *Where's the cute priestess? The king in need of a hero to slay the demon lord?*

"This sucks!" he swore softly, not daring to speak too loud. Instead of some cozy castle, he landed in a half-dead state right in the middle of—

"*Ugh...*" He nearly barfed again, but he held himself back successfully. That had been enough vomiting for his whole life, and there was nothing left to puke in his stomach anyway.

Alright, now isn't the time to complain. I need to get the hell out of here, but first...

He drew a deep breath and called out to the sky in a strained whisper.

"Status!"

"System!"

"Inventory? No? Nothing?"

"Fuck!"

Glenn kicked a rock. The stone didn't move, but his foot felt quite the shock. He swore as he cradled his toes.

No golden finger then. Alright, this... He sighed. *This really makes me want to spit on whoever brought me here. I'm sure it's some hidden god fuckery, like in all good stories, right? Right?*

Only silence responded, shutting him up. Yeah, it certainly wasn't helpful to get angry. Maybe his energy was better spent finding someplace far—very far away—from the battlefield.

Deep in thought, he crouched by the river, using the water to clean his face and his hands. Blood covered his body, as well as many other unidentified substances. And before he began worrying about an infection—

"Ah!"

He fell on his ass, his eyes wide open in fear as a bloated corpse floated in front of him. A trail of red and a metallic scent followed. That smell was now familiar to Glenn's nose.

Glenn clenched his teeth and stood. He winced as he noticed that the body was missing an arm, somehow ripped away. That was no sword wound for sure. *Way too messy...* But perhaps he was wrong. He was no professional on the matter.

What he could see, though, was the corpse's clothes were similar to his own: a ragged tunic, brown leggings, and a hood. It had a belt with an empty sheath hanging at its waist and leather boots. Glenn examined the torn soles of his own shoes. He wondered whether he should trade footwear with the corpse but decided against it.

It was only a minor improvement. Like replacing a 5% durability item with an 8% one. There was also the smell to consider.

Glenn fixed the corpse's sheath to his belt and peered through the dark oaks as he walked from the river. He'd rather be a long way from something that would attract predators to the area. More corpse-eating monsters? He buried the thought.

Diving back into the forest, Glenn fought against sharp sticks and thorny bushes as he followed no particular path. His aim was only to escape the battlefield—and the now-tainted river—so the direction didn't matter.

And who knows? He'd possibly stumble upon a trace of civilization. Right?

"Well, fuck my life. Oh, never mind. It's already been shafted!" Glenn angrily spat as he stared at a stump he had passed three times. He sat on it, trying his best to calm himself. He couldn't continue to run aimlessly.

Glenn sniffled before wiping the tears off his face. Now wasn't the time for self-pity. He needed to find civilization, because he was certainly not living in this creepy-ass forest—nor dying in it! He had a family back home. A sister who'd miss him.

He had to survive this hell. Because this *was* hell, no doubt. Where else would there be a bloodstained moon and corpse-eating monsters?

His resolution steeled, Glenn pushed himself up, revitalized.

Civilization, where might you be? He glanced at the sky, but the canopy made it impossible to see anything. He'd have to climb a tree.

Glenn sneered. *Well, isn't that a nice idea.*

He approached the widest, tallest tree he could find and evaluated the ascent. The many branches would make it relatively simple, and climbing had been a habit of his ever since he took those recreational classes. Fun times.

But climbing with something hanging from his waist seemed like a bad idea. Abandoning the sword on the forest floor wasn't a good choice either. After untying his belt, Glenn wrapped his sheath around his back.

"Witcher style, baby." He chuckled and rubbed his hands together.

Glenn jumped and grabbed the lowest branch, grunting as he pulled himself up. His climbing skills weren't too rusty, but his stamina was. With a lot of effort, he reached the top of the tree.

Gasping with difficulty, Glenn wiped the sweat off his eyebrows as he gazed at the forest in front of him. The corner of his lips curved upwards as he took in the phenomenal view. Crimson painted the treetops, a gift from the blood moon. The sky was clear and empty of pollution, with way too many stars for him to count.

He enjoyed the moment of peace silently, listening to the wind whistling gently as owls hooted in the night. There were also a few howls far away—likely wolves. But that seemed too distant to worry about. Glenn caught his breath and concentrated on the matter at hand. On his left, unmistakable, black smoke clouds carried burning flesh. That was the bloody battlefield he woke up on—now ablaze.

People, hopefully non-monstrous ones, had probably lit those fires. But he couldn't risk going back to check. He didn't know what factions had stakes in that battle. And more importantly, he didn't know what said factions would think of *him*. What guarantee did he have he wouldn't be pierced by another spear the second he showed up?

He turned, and his face lit up as he found a gray mountain. The peak was strange—barren of vegetation and completely flat—but it was a better vantage point compared to this tree.

And he didn't have other options.

Having made up his mind, Glenn carefully began his descent. It would be ridiculous to fall and die when he had miraculously survived having his guts torn out.

Can I still count on that healing ability that patched up my wounds? Ideally, I'd test it out, but not like this...

He placed one foot after another on the thickest branches until he suddenly heard a low growl. Instinctively, he crouched and pressed close against the tree. Quickly glancing down, he bit his lip when he saw a majestic, black wolf; its hackles raised and its pelt as dark as night. It could probably eat ten Glenns for breakfast, so he fortunately wasn't there to become a chew toy.

The wolf's fangs dripped saliva, and it snarled softly as it took one step back. Despite its powerful muscles, it looked... scared, somehow? It backed up further, shivering.

Glenn followed its gaze, trying to find what was intimidating the beast, but—

Thump!

The wolf whined as a red vine shot out of the bushes and wrapped itself around the canine's torso.

A second later, the wolf was gone.

Adrenaline pumped through Glenn's veins, preparing him for whatever lurked in the brush. Glenn muffled his mouth, struggling to regulate his shaky breathing while holding onto the branch. Sweaty palms weren't helping, making him fear a slip and fall.

He cursed mentally at his trembling limbs before glancing at the canopy.

Should I just spend the night up here? That might be the better option...

Glenn almost wanted to swear at the creature wandering in the woods.

I walked in this godforsaken forest for hours and didn't see anything. The second I leave the ground, something terrifying happens!

Perhaps he should consider himself lucky. No, if he was, he wouldn't be in these damned woods in the first place.

At least I'm not dead, he thought, trying to rationalize the situation.

Even if the branches were easy to climb, he didn't trust himself not to doze off and fall like an idiot. He had no rope to fasten himself to the tree, and his belt certainly wasn't long enough. Unless four walls magically sprouted from the trunk to protect him, he was out of luck.

"That'd be great..." Glenn whispered as he looked at the sky, but nothing happened. Why would it?

He also had no guarantee that whatever prowled the forest floor couldn't snatch him from the trees. What if it could climb?

Yeah, no sleeping up here, he concluded as he threw a tense look around, failing to find the creature that had pulled the wolf into the darkness.

As he did, a plan formed in his head. Noticing a particularly thick branch, he wondered if it was possible to hop across the canopy to a safer part of the woods.

No, that's a stupid idea.

Or was it?

Glenn wasn't confident in his acrobatic abilities, but he was running out of options.

He knew his safety in this tree was relative. And a broken leg seemed a lot easier to heal than whatever that monster could do to him.

He stood back up, getting rid of the stiffness in his legs. He drew a deep breath and repositioned himself to jump, cursing his plan.

His goal was the thick, sturdy-looking branch of the neighboring tree. It was what, three meters away? Easy. If he jumped from tree to tree until he reached the mountain, maybe he'd be able to survive until dawn—assuming the high ground was safer than the forest.

A hopeful thought indeed.

Come on... Glenn gritted his teeth. *One... Two... Three!*

He huffed and pushed off with all his strength. Suddenly, the branch broke under his feet, and he tumbled towards a certain death.

Only one word came to mind.

"Shit!"

Chapter 3

RUN, FOREST! UHH, NO. RUN FROM THE FOREST!

Creak... creak...

Alright. Breathe in, breathe out. That could have gone much worse... Glenn thought as he hung dangerously above the ground, his body swaying as he struggled to hold the buckling wood.

Heaving silently, he extended a foot towards the nearest branch. He sighed in relief, having steadied himself once again.

Glenn wiped the sweat off his forehead.

I have no idea of how I managed to pull that off. Survival instincts, perhaps?

He glanced a few meters down, failing to see anything capable of capturing a huge ass wolf. It could just be lingering in the darkness, waiting for prey to drop.

Creak...

That's quite the predicament, isn't it? Glenn thought sarcastically before dropping.

He would've landed graciously if it wasn't for a nasty, slippery rock that found its way under his foot. He grumbled as he pushed himself up, freezing when his hand touched something strange—something stiff yet soft. Like a pelt...

Glenn slowly turned his head, paling as he discovered the remains of the wolf's bleeding ear. The gnawed tip made him recall an important fact: no, he wasn't safe right now. He recoiled from the severed organ and stood. His clothes stuck to his skin with either blood or sweat; it was more or less the same by that point.

Stealthily, Glenn stepped. His heartbeat accelerated with each passing second. The more steps he took, the faster he moved. Soon enough, he was running.

His sword bounced on his back, forcing him to tighten the belt.

Thump!

Suddenly, he heard the dull noise along with breaking branches and ruffled leaves. As if something *large* had landed nearby.

Glenn gulped and hurried away. Beads of sweat pearled down his forehead, but he didn't care. With any luck, it was a territorial monster that would give up once he arrived at the base of the mountain. Hopefully. He couldn't see himself fighting a damn wolf, let alone something that snatched up an apex beast as a snack.

Glenn cursed repeatedly as he jumped over roots and ducked under branches.

The tall trees draped over him, shrouding him in darkness. The crimson moonlight clothed the forest under a bloody veil, in a manner that was both ominous and beautiful.

Thick vegetation oppressed him, as if nature itself tried to prevent his escape—catch him in a trap for that horrible predator to feast on.

Glenn huffed and puffed, struggling to breathe. His poor stamina wasn't doing him any favors, but he kept running. Stopping would mean dying. Probably. He'd rather not risk it.

"Where's the mountain?" he mumbled desperately as he threw a terrified glance backwards.

Branches snapped, and the rustling in the brush only grew louder. All the while, the distance between Glenn and the high ground hadn't decreased. He knew he was traveling in the right direction, but how long until he reached his destination?

He hid behind a tree and took a deep, ragged breath. Leaning on his knees, he realized the muddy soil was becoming much rockier.

Glenn's eyes lit up; he wasn't running in circles. He couldn't confirm it, but he had to believe he was getting closer to the mountain. That realization pumped hope into his heart, and he darted forwards, ignoring his burning lungs.

Breathing was overrated anyway.

He dove into a bush, gritting his teeth as the thorns and the branches scratched his face and ripped his clothes. A snake-like hiss echoed behind him, making him accelerate to a speed he never knew possible.

Glenn's desperate thoughts were interrupted when he failed to notice a massive root protruding out of the ground.

His foot tangled in the fibers, and Glenn flew headfirst. His body bounced off a few stumps and trees like a pinball before finally stopping.

He was about to curse the evil root's whole lineage when his eyes caught a red flash shooting right where he had previously stood. He grunted painfully and pushed himself up.

Holy shit. Holy Root, thank you! I swear I'll build a shrine in your, uh, name... Glenn quickly thanked his savior, his eyes widening as the red lightning flashed again, landing at his feet.

It planted in the stone and missed Glenn's ankle by a few centimeters. Glenn paled and jumped back, struggling to pull his sword out of his sheath.

Fuck! Of course it looks way easier in the damn game, he cursed, watching what looked like a rotten tongue retract. It smelled of putrid meat, but he doubted 'eau de pourriture' was its fragrance of choice.

He finally unsheathed his blade and clenched it firmly. Fleeing was no longer an option—that much was clear. He had to fight. But how could he? Before tonight, he never held a weapon in his hands!

A rumbling sound intensified through the trees. Glenn gulped, holding his sword dead straight.

He could approximate where the fiend was coming from thanks to the many branches it broke along the way. Whatever it was, it was *huge*. Glenn did his best not to faint, his wobbly legs threatening to collapse at any moment.

His throat was dry, and he was a hair away from puking again in fear. Luckily for him, his bladder was empty, saving him the embarrassment of dying soiled in his own piss.

It's kill or die, he thought as he drew a deep breath, forcing his hands to stop shaking. *I already killed that ghoul on the battlefield. Another larger one is no problem!*

He tried to calm himself, but his face paled chalk white. A tree collapsed, and the bushes opened, revealing the hunter.

It wore a black, unusually large clergy robe and hunched over as it approached. The creature was the size of a compact car, and each step shook its surroundings. Glenn peeked under the habit. But he noticed no recognizable body parts or anything remotely similar to a face. Only shifting darkness that fueled his fear as the monster walked with agonizingly slow movements.

Its garments billowed. Something *squirmed* under the dark fabric like a massive worm. The scarlet moonlight shone brightly for a second, letting Glenn see a black, oozing tentacle.

His heart stopped as the monster muttered in a raspy, inhuman voice. The closer it got to Glenn, the louder it spoke. At first, he couldn't recognize the phrases, but the more he listened to it, the more he deciphered bits and pieces.

It wasn't English, nor any language from Earth he had ever heard. And yet, *strangely*, he could still understand it. The foreign words magically translated into his mind. Glenn wasn't going to complain; it sure was convenient, after all.

"Ilif im... My son... I... Ettimrep em... Let me... Let me... Ni enimon suie... In His name..." the being hissed, and a scrawny arm extended out of its clergy robe.

Glenn stepped back, his lips sealed. He gulped with difficulty and strengthened his grip on the hilt.

Wanting to do something—*anything*—was futile while frozen in fear. Be it fleeing, attacking, or even screaming, his body betrayed him.

As the fiend spat more nonsense, Glenn realized he would have actually preferred not to understand its language. Because now, it was clear that this horrid creature was once human, or something close.

Glenn finally gazed upon what lurked beneath the robe. It was an abomination that, for his sanity, should have remained hidden.

The shifting darkness was a mass of black tentacles, each moving by their own volition. Short and long feelers swayed lazily, oozing with a purple substance. Barely concealed under the appendages was deformed skin riddled with scars and holes, revealing bones and rotten flesh.

Noticing Glenn's horrified gaze, the monster suddenly stopped and stood on two skeletal legs. Thousands of worms ate through the little tissue that remained.

The creature opened three arms wide, as if to hug him—each covered in that disgusting, dark ooze. Each arm bore two hands with far more than six fingers. The creature's belly had a massive mouth gaping in a most illogical placement. Tentacles acted as the beard for said mouth. It salivated at the sight of Glenn.

"My son... Maediv et suiporp... Let me see... see you closer... Oge, retap... I, Father Albenas... I... I must..." the figure spoke, raising its arms towards the sky.

Father Albenas continued its slow yet pressuring advance. For each of the being's steps, Glenn took two back. In his retreat, his heels touched something. A thick oak blocked his way out, towering over him.

There was no escape.

It suddenly stopped and fell on all fours, blowing the dust and leaves away with a small gust. Then it waited silently for a few seconds, unmoving and unbreathing. The silence suffocated Glenn.

Finally, it spoke with a raspy but lucid voice.

"I shall give thou, my son, His blessing! Come, so that thou can be freed too!"

As soon as Father Albenas finished speaking, its rotten tongue flashed from its belly and wrapped around Glenn's waist. Glenn screamed, cursing every god he knew. He violently expelled the air from his lungs as the appendage tightly clenched his chest, squeezing and burning his skin.

With his arms restrained, he held his sword pointed at the creature. Glenn *had* to do something, but it was too late.

In an instant, Glenn flew into Father Albenas' tentacles. A mix of sulfur and blood assaulted his nose, making him retch.

Glenn closed his eyes, refusing to watch the painful, horrible death that was sure to come. But his desire to live was stronger than his fear. And in a last, desperate attempt, he stabbed forwards with all his might.

His blade dug through the fiend's skin like a hot knife through butter, but Glenn knew it wasn't enough. For such a terrifying monster, that injury was probably a mosquito bite.

Yet, one second...

Two seconds...

Nothing happened. Nothing that spelled *death* anyway. The area where the tongue grabbed him hurt like hell, but what was pain if not proof of life? He was still restrained, but the creature's ragged breathing had gone silent. It wasn't moving either.

Glenn hesitantly opened an eye, then another. He flinched when he saw the massive maw filled with sharp, shark-rotten teeth. Glenn tensed, expecting the mouth to chomp down on him, but it remained still.

Still terrified, Glenn nudged the creature, only to discover that his last, desperate measure had been successful.

His sword had stabbed deeply into the being's disgusting belly. Purple, sticky blood gushed out of the wound like a macabre fountain.

The fiend's jaw suddenly clenched, the sharp teeth closing menacingly. Glenn yelped and hurriedly used his hilt like a lever to push the creature back. Father Albenas' body fell, bringing Glenn with it.

A short moment passed, but the corpse didn't move. Glenn blinked, unable to contain nervous laughter as he realized what had just happened.

Thanks to a mix of luck, skill, and circumstances, Glenn's blade perfectly pierced through the monster's vital point, killing it in a single stab.

Somehow, Glenn defeated that monstrous beast, Father Albenas.

Chapter 4

IT'S TALENT, NOT LUCK (MAYBE THE OTHER WAY AROUND?)

"Hah... hah... hah..." Glenn heaved, undecided whether he should be happy or terrified. Father Albenas, the nightmarish eldritch entity that almost ate him, died. Or so it seemed.

"Fuck..." he blurted out as he tried to extricate himself out of the late Father's embrace.

The disgusting, sticky tentacles adhered to his clothes, making it difficult for him to escape. Saliva, blood, and... *whatever that liquid was* didn't make the task any easier. Nonetheless, Glenn managed to break free, not without much effort.

"Ugh... So it's dead... For sure, right?" Glenn mumbled, wincing while worms ate through the monster's corrupted flesh.

He turned away to save himself from puking his guts out *again*. Sitting down, he drew a deep breath, checking his shaking hands. He clenched them, shivering, before quickly examining himself for any injuries.

The area where the tongue grabbed him burned with vivid pain. His shirt sizzled with a growing hole, revealing bleeding blisters beneath. Glenn hurriedly took off his tunic, gritting his teeth tightly and almost screaming. He watched in horror as his body struggled to fight off the skirmish's lasting effects. Small wounds closed with extreme difficulty.

This... magical healing... Why isn't it working as well as before? Glenn worriedly examined himself for more battle scars. His remaining scratches and abrasions refused to patch themselves.

"Those powers were only temporary?" Glenn questioned. "Damn it!"

"In what hell did I land?" he muttered before pushing himself up and turning back towards the dead creature. Braving his disgust and the scent of rotting meat, he reached for the sword.

"Can't give up the only thing I have to defend myself, can I?" Glenn snickered.

The hilt was covered in dark blood and stuck to his hand. He pulled, trying his best to ignore the questionable squishy noise.

Gush!

He gasped and took a step back as he retrieved his weapon, shielding his eyes from the black blood... He hurriedly retreated, keeping a safe distance between him and the oozing corpse.

"Man... This isn't getting any better, is it?" Grimacing, he flicked sludge and flesh from himself. *Oh, and there's even a feeler!*

A bath would do him a great favor, be it to boost morale or so he wouldn't smell like the tastiest treat in the whole forest. He examined his sword, frowning when he realized the steel was now stained purple and slightly corroded.

"Did the blood somehow?"

The weapon didn't look capable of cutting anything, the edges dull due to the corrosion. *Perhaps it's only cosmetic damage, and it still cuts well?*

Glenn hacked a nearby vine, but the blade slipped harmlessly against the fibers. Glenn groaned.

It didn't matter. It was all he had to defend himself. He couldn't afford to be picky.

"A dull edge is still better than a stick... But I'd rather have a sharp one, man..." Glenn shook his head, saddened.

Hopefully, the blade wouldn't break in two the next time he used it. No, if he hoped for anything, it was to not get into any more fights. *That* would be nice.

After sheathing the sword in the scabbard on his back, he glanced around the forest.

"I need to clean this shit up..." Glenn said, listening attentively for the sound of flowing water. The fact that he had just slayed some kind of hellish—probably once human—monster was still disturbing him, but he couldn't spare the time thinking about ethics and whatnot, could he?

Glenn was about to leave when he suddenly remembered.

The Holy Root!

He quickly searched through the darkness, smiling when he found the root that unexpectedly saved his life. While building a little cairn next to it, he tried his best to ignore the awkwardness. Once he was done, he whispered a quick "thank you" and stepped away. He wasn't going to begin his adventure in this new world by not upholding his promises!

With steady steps, Glenn resumed his pace towards what he hoped was the mountain, concentrating on the sounds of the forest. A rat squeaked, a bat flew past him, a wolf howled in the distance... And finally, he heard flowing water. He barely accelerated before remembering that there was a very *large* probability of something else being out there trying to eat him.

"Yeah, let's stay calm and composed for now. Calm and composed..." he mumbled through his teeth as he pushed through thorns.

Once at the river, he paused by a bush in search of any apparent predators. The coast seemed clear, and he stealthily walked up to the water, gathering a handful to splash on his face. It was freezing but refreshing—like the wind on a cool autumn night.

Glenn gazed into the stream, finding it translucent but not pristine enough to ease his worries. It would have to do. He absolutely needed to clean himself of all the blood, mud, and slime. His clothes were probably the perfect bait to attract every predator in the woods.

First and foremost, fire was crucial. If he was going to jump in the frigid river, he'd rather do it with a heat source nearby. So, Glenn gathered moss and wood to build a campfire. He made a circle with large stones and placed the sticks upwards. Once he finished, Glenn squinted at his unremarkable wooden pyramid.

Not my finest handiwork, but it'll get the job done.

The blood moon cast the river's surroundings in a crimson hue. Thanks to it, Glenn could barely see the difference between normal stones, other normal stones, and... Flint!

Glenn knelt in front of the unkindled bundle as he drew his dull sword from his sheath. He sighed.

This is going to take a long time, isn't it?

On those wise thoughts, he struck the flint against the corroded edge, creating a few sparks. He directed them towards the dry moss, but it simply wouldn't light. After half an hour of effort, he stopped and wondered whether he should just give up and throw the little piece of shit far away.

He smashed the damned rock against the sword once more. Sparks flew and landed on the kindling, igniting a tiny ember. Glenn's eyes widened, and he blew carefully on the tinder to grow it into a larger flame. The night's breeze sent a shiver down his neck, but he ignored it. After a few minutes of concentration, he managed to start the fire.

"Phew..." Glenn sighed in relief as he fed a few more branches to the campfire. He then glanced back at the stream and released a slow, shaky breath.

"Here we go then..." He took his clothes off and rolled them under his arm before jumping into the river, gasping from the cold.

Glenn's teeth clattered as he scrubbed his garments and body of filth. "Ooohhh, sh-sh-shit. It's colder than I thought!"

He almost let out a chuckle, feeling slightly more human now that he wasn't so damned dirty. But the glacial water stopped him from doing so.

Instead, he shook like a leaf.

After a thorough but much-needed bath, Glenn jumped out of the river, completely naked and shivering. He snuggled next to the blaze, cursing at the night's freezing wind. His clothes would probably dry faster if they were on him rather than rolled up in a ball.

He slipped the rags back on and rubbed his arms to warm himself up.

"T-The b-bathing did feel good..." Glenn muttered. "N-Not t-the b-best t-temperature, though..."

His heavy eyelids closed by themselves. Before he nodded off, he jolted awake.

No. Shit! I can't sleep now! Fuck hypothermia. Glenn bit his cheek, using the pain to wake himself up.

If there was one place he couldn't fall asleep, it was by a water source—barely hidden. The next monster he'd meet would likely be the last.

Glenn held his hands above the fire, warming them. His stomach grumbled, reminding him that *food* was also a problem he needed to solve. Alongside many others, of course.

He forced himself up.

"I'll dry if I keep moving," he whispered.

Pushing away the urge to lie next to the campfire and sleep, he searched through the forest. He scavenged for anything that looked edible, pulling roots, wild vegetables, and a few mushrooms. Meat would have been nice, but...

Perhaps I could hunt?

He shook his head. Theoretically, he knew how to make traps, but he wasn't planning on staying around too long. Once his clothes dried, he'd move towards the mountain to find civilization.

Glenn brought the products of his scavenging back to camp. He used the light from the flames to give them a closer look.

Hmm... This mushroom has a red cap with white spots covering it. Not that one then maybe these brown ones are okay to eat? That root looks like... a root. And that thing... is it a cucumber? But it's blue...

"I'll just throw away the obviously poisonous mushroom and cook the rest," Glenn decided.

He sharpened twigs and skewered the vegetables and fungi before placing them over the fire. While waiting patiently, he hugged himself. His wet hair stuck to the back of his neck, causing him an occasional shiver.

Suddenly, a nearby bush stirred. Glenn stopped breathing, hoping he might have hallucinated. But then the leaves shook harder. He slowly unsheathed his sword as silently as he could and drew a deep breath. Fighting yet another nightmarish creature wasn't his first choice, but if he had to, he would.

Survival before all else.

A small, white form jumped out of the brush. Glenn lunged forwards; his weapon hit something hard like bone. His eyes opened wide, and he blinked a few times, wondering if he was dreaming.

Impaled on his corroded blade was a rabbit. A fat bunny that was only asking to be eaten.

"Is that my reward? Hah," he chuckled in disbelief.

The tension in his shoulders released. How did he even stab the rabbit? He never used a sword before tonight, and yet... his arm instinctively knew where to swing.

"Well, whatever." Glenn dismissed those thoughts. *That'll do for some meat.*

A few minutes later, a poorly skinned rabbit cooked atop the fire. Glenn washed the fresh blood off his hands in the river, salivating at the smell of grilled meat. Although he had little to no experience in butchering, he admired his accomplishment.

"I could feel sad about the bunny..." Glenn muttered when his stomach grumbled. He nodded, agreeing with his hunger.

"Or I could eat meat. I'd rather eat meat."

He wondered whether he should drink the water. In the end, he decided against it. Once he climbed the mountain, he'd be able to quench his thirst closer to the source.

A crackle caught Glenn's attention as fat drizzled and fell into the flames.

It had been what, an hour? Two? He couldn't tell.

And yet, he already slayed a ghoul, a tentacle fiend, and a rabbit.

Quite the bloody adventure, isn't it?

Chapter 5

CALM BEFORE THE...

"So... Let's try to review what happened to me," Glenn spoke aloud, arranging his memories.

"First." He frowned while adding a few sticks to the fire. "Why did I get transported to this world? Did I die?"

That's weird. I was in good health and in my bed until I woke up on that battlefield, so that excludes the Truck-kun cliché. Unless a truck crashed into my house? Glenn laughed, shaking his head.

"*Tsk.* What if the tacos and tequila did kill me..."

Maybe my sister already found my body, dead from alcohol poisoning. What would she even write on my grave?

Glenn chuckled a bit more before returning to silence. Laughing made him feel a little better.

Only a little though.

He rubbed his forehead, recalling any noteworthy events among his last actions on Earth. From what he remembered, it was quite a normal day.

"Let's see... I got up late in the morning due to the party the night before. I ate breakfast, then lunch about an hour later... After that, I went to uni where nothing happened like usual and came straight back home."

Inspecting one of the grilled mushrooms, his eyebrows creased. He hesitated for a second until he shrugged and bit into it.

It was disgusting. No... It just tasted like dirt. Rubber dirt.

Glenn forced himself to swallow. He was going to need all the nutrients he could get if he wanted to stay alive.

But he'd prefer something tastier.

"Back home, I played around, ordered that taco... which that bastard took an hour and a half to deliver..." Glenn winced, realizing he couldn't order food at his place ever again. Another loss he'd never recover from.

"I ate the tacos, which tasted... okay, I guess? Miles better than this shit anyway." He gagged.

"My night ended with that party and that last shot of tequila. Shit, maybe someone poisoned it?"

Glenn seriously considered that option, but he remembered he somehow safely returned home to his comfortable mattress. And he was still alive well into the evening.

Looking at the sky pensively, he thought about everything he'd miss. Graduation wasn't far away, even though he didn't work hard for it. His sister was going to participate in that national fencing competition... He'd never get to watch her compete.

Damn, and I even got that girl's number... I'll never see her again either. Glenn peered into the flames.

She was really pretty. What was her name? Ania, Onea... Uh, Olga? Whatever. It doesn't matter anymore...

Glenn sighed, throwing away a wet branch that couldn't feed the fire. He truly was at a loss for how to feel. He wanted to cry, but yet, he was unable to.

And now he was here, with cannibal ghouls, tentacle monsters—or whatever Father Albenas was—coexisting. There were *two* moons, and one of those was a blood moon. As if this world wasn't ominous enough.

"God damn it... I should have taken those sparring lessons..." Glenn regretted, thinking back to his sister's insistence.

Well, what's done is done. There's no use dwelling on the past.

At least he got the thrills he wanted so much. A very, very gory journey so far, but an adventure still.

He grabbed the rabbit skewer, pinching his nose before forcefully biting through the flesh. It didn't taste good. Worse than the mushroom, actually. *Is that because there's no salt?*

The meat was tough and dry with stringy fibers and not a drop of juice. The cherry on top was the gamey taste, which was probably made worse by Glenn's cooking. And let's not talk about the charred bits.

Glenn still ate every single scrap, pushing through his disgust. Nothing stopped him from grimacing badly at each bite, though.

The sun wouldn't rise anytime soon, so Glenn gave up his very small hope of seeing it. He'd have to traverse the mountain under the crimson moonlight.

He stored the untouched grilled vegetables in his pocket to eat later. That'd make a snack just in case; he was taught to never waste anything.

Glenn held his hands above the fire for a moment, enjoying the warmth as he tried to motivate himself to stand. He was going to need it. The higher he climbed, the colder it would get, after all.

"Hopefully I'll be able to find some settlement once I'm up there..." He sighed before shaking his head.

Glenn watched the blood moon and its little, white sister, thinking.

Is it always this bright? Living in red every night must be strange. Unless everyone is used to it. Then, I'm the strange one. Glenn chuckled.

If there were moons, there had to be a central star, right? There wouldn't be any moonlight without a sun, after all. Or *suns*.

Unless the rules of reality were broken in this world? Then Glenn could not expect anything. Full unknown ahead.

"How exciting," he muttered in a deadpan tone, searching through the shadows of the forest for any threat before he departed. He picked a large branch and lit it on fire, waving it around to test the safety of the torch.

"It probably won't last that long... Alright, let's go then—"

Howl!

Glenn froze. The wind had died down at some point. But the wolves kept howling. And that howl was quite close.

Too close.

He hurriedly kicked the campfire into the river, extinguishing it before leaving. He was almost entirely dried by now, so that was one issue off the list.

Howl! Howl!

A bead of sweat dripped down Glenn's back, sending a shiver through his whole body. There were many howls, which meant many wolves. A pack.

Uh oh.

He picked up his pace, checking his surroundings worriedly.

When he finally spotted the mountain through the foliage, it was still a fifteen-minute jog away. Or a ten-minute run. Both worked, but the latter seemed more appropriate.

A growl emerged from the bushes, giving the last push Glenn needed to bolt without looking back. *Something* panted and charged behind him. But he couldn't pay it any mind.

The growls intensified. That *something* became two then three *somethings*. Glenn clenched the torch tightly, aware that it might be his only lifeline against the fiends.

"Fuck, fuck, fuck!" Glenn heaved, dodging trees and roots. The ground shifted rockier, and vegetation scarcer, signaling his destination was near.

A flash of amber irises leered ahead, and Glenn suddenly stopped. He turned, finding yet another pair of eyes to the left and right. They were everywhere.

The wolves stepped out of the shadows like embodiments of darkness, their pelts as black as the night.

Five, six, seven... Oh, and that must be the Alpha. That makes eight. Eight fucking wolves.

Glenn clutched his sword and torch tightly. He swung the flame, pushing the beasts back, except for the one that was particularly massive.

It had a mean, white scar on its eye and gave him the scariest stare. This was his opponent. Well, every predator posed a threat, but the only one unafraid of fire was the Alpha.

"Come on, fuck off!" Glenn spat as he lunged with the flame. The wolf jumped to safety, slowly circling him.

Glenn glanced at the mountain. It wasn't that far. He could make a run for it.

He just needed a distraction. Glenn waved the torch as he carefully stepped towards the foothills. The rest of the beasts backed off as soon as the embers approached them, but the Alpha remained undeterred. It beat its tail against the soil and prepared to attack. Its incredibly large fangs were yellow and sharp enough to chew through any armor.

The Alpha clacked his fangs. It lunged forwards with its maw wide open, trying to rip off his arm. Thankfully, he was prepared for such an eventuality. With precision that could defy the best baseball player, he threw the torch straight down the beast's throat. The wolf whined as the flames singed its esophagus. The rest of the pack clamored around their wounded leader before concentrating back on Glenn.

Sadly for them, he was already a dozen meters away, running as fast as he could.

"Fuck, I can't believe it worked!" He grunted and jumped over a collapsed tree.

The wolves finally came to their senses, abandoning the burning Alpha and racing after Glenn.

His eyes gleamed in relief as he arrived at the mountain's foot. A dark purple mist rose from cracks in the soil, sending a shiver down his spine. That was nothing, however, compared to the sharp fangs of hungry predators.

Without wasting a second, he dashed through the haze. There were natural stairs carved into the ridge, which Glenn used to climb.

It seemed unlikely that stones would naturally carve themselves, so he accepted it as a man-made path. And man-made paths meant humans! If that wasn't good news, he didn't know what was.

Once the wolves reached the mist, they abruptly stopped in front of it. Glenn turned back, heaving raggedly as he watched them. The canines glared at him and growled before returning to the forest. Breathing in and out, he was unable to emote. Then...

"Fuck yeah! Haha!" Glenn laughed, collapsing on the stairs. That was a risky bet, and he won.

"*Phew*, haha... That was crazy." He wiped the sweat off his forehead.

Now, he felt safer. On the clear, rocky slope, he could see more of his surroundings—as much as the red moonlight allowed anyway. He'd see any threats coming.

Glenn gave himself a few minutes of rest before sheathing his sword and looking up at the mountain peak. It was high, but not *that* high. There were no trees or bushes—just moss alongside the river. A colossal chunk of gray stone blocked his view.

"Alright, then. Let's get this over with already."

* * *

The wind whistled gently as Glenn slept in a hammock, an open book resting on his face. His body rocked in the breeze.

"Glenn! Miller!" an older woman's voice roared.

The young man didn't react, far too deep in sleep. Angry steps trotted towards him, and a pale hand grabbed the book away, letting rays of light assault his face. Glenn grimaced, lazily shielding his eyes. Who dared to wake him from such a nice dream?

"I can't believe it. Your exam is in three weeks. And here you are, lazing around!" The lady yelled, clearly animated by evil intentions. Glenn simply plugged his ears to continue his comfortable sleep.

Doing this angered the assailant, and the hammock suddenly inverted. He crashed to the ground, stirring awake. After grunting painfully, he yawned and then stretched as if nothing had happened.

"What are you worried about, ma'? It's just a test. I don't understand what you're getting on my case about." He asked, half with confusion and half with mockery.

His mother sighed loudly. She was in her mid-forties but still very beautiful. Her hair arrived at her shoulders, the same brown shade as Glenn's. She looked at him with a mix of anger and worry. Hands on her waist, she seemed helpless to decide whether she should beat some sense into her son or give up the fight.

Glenn preferred the second option, of course.

"I leave for five minutes, hoping you'd focus on your lessons, and yet..." She shook her head. "Here you are, sleeping. What am I going to do with you?"

Glenn shrugged and took the book from his mother's hand.

"I don't know, but I'm pretty sure that..." He glanced at the author's name. "That reading Jankélévitch isn't helping me, ma."

He chuckled, smiling brightly at his mom. She gazed at the horizon before gesturing at the house behind her.

"Come on, let's get inside."

* * *

Glenn stopped and leaned on the rock wall, one hand calming his chest. His heart beat madly. He had to admit, his stamina wasn't the best. Thankfully, the climbing classes were showing their worth as the mountain's stairs grew increasingly steeper.

On a positive note, there was no hint of wind on the higher slopes, not even a breeze. Glenn had expected it to be much colder, but no. As a matter of fact, it was *warmer*.

What kind of fuckery is going on? He had no idea, but that certainly made the ascension more pleasant.

Gasp... Gasp... His calves burned, and his lungs desperately asked for a break.

With one last ditch effort, he pushed forwards and arrived at the peak. The top was flat, as if a giant had cut it with a knife to create a plateau.

"*Gasp...* Fuck... *Phew...*" Glenn wiped the sweat off his eyebrows and leaned against the smooth stone.

"*Phew...* I'm exhausted..." he mumbled before pushing himself up and examining his surroundings.

The peak had to be man-made. It was completely level—as if he had climbed onto a pedestal. *Who bulldozed this, and for what purpose?*

Glenn had no idea.

Chapter 6

WAIT... WHAT THE MOON DOING?

The blood moon and its pale little sister hung in the sky, covering the land in a crimson, mystical hue. Glenn smiled softly, exhausted.

"At least the view is nice..." he muttered. He glanced down at the slope, tensing when he realized how high he was.

"There should be some kind of settlement around, right?" Glenn wondered hopefully, squinting as he peered into the distance. It didn't take long for him to find an absurdly large metropolis, a community built for titans.

It was a majestic, circular city enclosed in gigantic walls. At the center, a tall tower—the main source of blinding light—reached for the stars. Glenn rubbed his eyes in awe.

"Wow..." He chuckled. "I want that as my destination, but is there someplace closer?"

Back the way he came, past the battlefield's black smoke, stood two smaller settlements. Two cities—one on each side of the plain. They were... not exactly nearer.

Either way, he was much more interested in that titanic city—without even counting the fact that it would take him far away from the bloody battlefield. That was the last place he wanted to return.

"Bigville it is then..." Glenn stretched as he determined his next goal.

He was glad he chose to climb the mountain, even though some elements still struck him as strange. No wind, warm air, a purple mist that warded off predators... And a leveled peak where nothing awaited him...

Wait, is that true?

Glenn examined the flat stone curiously. There had to be a reason for someone to carve stairs into the mountain, right? There were no monuments, so that only left...

He crouched, grinning as he pressed his hand on the ground.

"Found it."

Barely illuminated by the bloody moonlight, Glenn discovered engravings. He also realized that the stone was not as... cold, as it should be. No, it was *warm*, as if it had been bathing in the sun.

That's weird.

Glenn ignored he had been walking over some... *probably* important cultural engravings and studied them closer. After blowing on a thick layer of dust, he stood back for a wider view.

A large circle with a vertical slit at the center—separating it into two halves—drew his attention. Two dozen hooded figures prayed under it, raising their arms towards a falling orb. Runes outlined the artful engraving, in a language he couldn't decipher despite the strange power that allowed him to understand Father Albenas' words. They looked primitive but had a mystical feeling about them... almost *alien*. Well, he was in another world, wasn't he?

"Wait..." Glenn frowned. *That... That looks awfully like a cult, doesn't it?*

"Shit, did I really stumble on a sacred ritual ground?" He paled and glanced around with worry.

Of course, there was no one else on top of the mountain. Glenn sighed, both at his foolishness and in relief. Perhaps it was just the stress of narrowly avoiding *death*, but he felt very, very much in danger.

What's that big circle the cultists are venerating? After pondering for a few more minutes, he gave up and sat on the warm rocks, tired.

"I'll take a breather, then head for the giant city..." he decided, his eyelids drooping. He lay down and clasped his hands behind his neck, looking at the starry sky and the crimson moon dominating it all. It was almost stupid how large it was.

There were quite a few games back on Earth that featured blood moons, like that one Zelda game, or Castlevania. He remembered when, in World of Playcraft, twice or thrice a year, the moon glowed red for seasonal events. Granted, the rewards were cool weapons or mounts—not a nagging reminder of death.

The more he thought of it, the more probable this event was just that: an event. A rare one, maybe, and that meant the satellite would revert to its regular form.

And if this was a *special* occurrence, it could've been the reason he suddenly woke up in this world. Special things happened during special times, and a blood moon did seem like a special moment. That didn't explain a lot, but at least the dots were starting to blurrily line up.

He still had no idea as to why he was in this world, what fuckery brought him here, *who* did it, and all that... But there was a good chance it was linked to the omen in the sky.

For now, though, survival was his top priority.

"Hmm?" Glenn frowned. He could have sworn he saw the crimson moonlight darken like a used light bulb. He rubbed the corner of his eyes, but he saw it again.

"The fuck? Am I... imagining things, or?" He questioned aloud, his eyebrows creased.

The white moon, little by little, disappeared behind the larger one.

And as more of the miniature satellite faded, lines appeared at the center of the blood moon. It stretched vertically, separating the celestial object in two. Maybe separating wasn't the right word? No, it seemed like it was... blooming like a flower.

"W-What is this?" Glenn gasped, standing slowly.

The rift stretched, forming a black spiral at its core. His jaw hung, and his eyes grew wide.

This was impossible. Simply impossible. A ghoul, a tentacle monster, and a weird cult he could tolerate. But a *moon* opening?

"Hah... Haha?" Glenn could only laugh. What was he even supposed to do?

Suddenly, he checked the engravings.

His heart raced. "The engraving depicts the rift, doesn't it? Doesn't that mean?"

As soon as he uttered those words, the crimson moonlight disappeared, replaced by unnatural darkness. Glenn shivered and hugged himself, feeling as if he was completely naked and monitored by some untold existence. He kept staring at the rift even though it felt like he was watching something... Forbidden.

A gigantic object extracted itself from the center. Exactly as depicted in the engravings, the object fell, roaring as it approached. A powerful shockwave threw Glenn off his feet, the mountain shaking terribly.

He failed to maintain his balance and collapsed on all fours, struggling to calculate the object's trajectory. He didn't have to search for long; a thundering explosion illuminated the entire region with a bright flash of orange flames. Glenn winced, dizzy. He squinted through the blinding effects and found a section of the forest burning, prey to a voracious fire. The flames propagated quickly, surrounding a small village.

"This is insane..." Glenn gasped, realizing he had held his breath since the explosion.

He clenched his chest, his heart beating madly as if trying to escape from his body. Glenn breathed slowly, trying to calm himself. But it was impossible.

The *void* spit one projectile after another—some landing with thundering explosions and some disappearing into the distance.

After what felt like an eternity, the rift collapsed, melding into the darkness. As if everything had been a hallucination, two beautiful white moons hung in its place.

"Phew..." Glenn wiped the cold sweat off his forehead.

"So, that confirms my theory of the blood moon being a temporary event. That means it shouldn't happen again any time soon, right?" he questioned as he looked at the sky fearfully.

This world was way too eventful. How could he tell that something wouldn't just fall from the sky and kill him?

Hiss...

He froze, listening carefully. The hissing sound was growing increasingly closer...

"Wait, no!" Glenn's head snapped back as a white projectile flew through the air.

It headed directly for him.

"Oh. Oh! Oh, shit!" Glenn blurted out, realizing he needed to flee. He looked around, horrified, but there was nowhere to hide. He was on a flat mountain peak; the only escape was down.

What should I do? Jump?

"Fuck me!" Glenn screamed as he ran to the ledge.

The projectile crashed right in the middle of the engravings, making the ground tremble. Glenn rolled, straining his tired muscles to push himself up. He looked back, bewildered, as a large, glimmering crystal sank into the ground with a humming sound.

Glenn grimaced and waited for an explosion, but nothing happened. He hesitantly stepped towards the gem, watching as it sank deeper and deeper into the stone. Soon enough, the white crystal disappeared entirely.

"Okay, so that was weird? Where did it even go?" Glenn asked aloud, knowing he wouldn't get an answer. The engraving was still in perfect condition, and there was no gaping hole.

Strange, very strange...

Cough!

Glenn struggled to breathe. He shivered, frowning as a cold wind blew around him, threatening to push him off the ledge. He gritted his teeth and crouched, resisting the winds.

"Damn it, what's happening now?" He hissed, using the cracks in the ground to maintain his position. The wind's strength increased, piercing through his skin and chilling him to the bone.

The stone tremored, and a mechanical sound echoed beneath him. Glenn froze, squinting to understand what was happening. A few clicks and clunks later, the ground shifted under his feet, letting him fall through the void.

Glenn didn't even have the chance to swear; it was already too late.

Chapter 7

JUNIOR ARCHEOLOGIST MAKES BIG DISCOVERY (CLICK FOR MORE)

"Ahhh!" Glenn screamed as he fell blindly into the darkness, certain that he'd end up as a meat crêpe. Suddenly, he hit the ground and sprung back up.

"Eh?"

He bounced up and down a few times before finally coming to a stop. A large cloud of dust rose, forcing him to cough out his lungs.

He coughed. 'What?" And again… then again." Glenn chased away the particles by waving his hand. He was lying on a tightly stretched piece of fabric, which had absorbed the momentum.

If it wasn't for this cloth, he'd probably be dead. Or paraplegic. Which was more or less the same in his situation.

After the powder settled, he hesitantly pushed himself up, only to slip and fall back on the musky textile. After struggling for a few more minutes, Glenn rolled to the edge of the trap. He disgracefully tumbled on the dirt, bruising his knees. Nonetheless, the small pain was a worthy sacrifice if it meant salvation.

This dust might be deadlier than those monsters, I swear!" Glenn spat angrily, taking a moment to catch his breath.

A mechanical sound churned above. The opening he fell through started to close, and with it, the moonlight dimmed. Glenn's eyes widened, and he hurriedly looked around for a solution—a light source, anything. He quickly found an unlit torch nearby and frowned as he realized cultists had likely left it there.

The ceiling would soon close entirely, and the darkness would swallow him. He wasn't particularly scared of the dark, but he'd sure feel more comfortable with something to guide his way.

"The flint!" Glenn suddenly remembered as he rummaged through his meager belongings. He unsheathed his sword, striking it against the flint to produce sparks.

Once the ceiling sealed shut, there was nothing left to illuminate the room. But Glenn didn't despair. He continued to strike blindly, aiming at the torch with questionable precision.

Finally, a spark landed on the torch's oily basin and the fire started, startling Glenn. He jumped back like a caveman.

"Just in time..." Glenn said.

"Good call keeping this flint, but a lighter would've been way less stress," he muttered as he looked around the room.

It was a large chamber with engraved walls, where torch-holders hung from towering pillars. A tent stood at the center.

So that's the dusty piece of fabric that saved me. Not at all out of place in this ancient, immemorial structure.

If there was a campsite, that meant there was someone around, right? Glenn raised his torch, failing to find any figures lurking in the shadows.

"Hello?" Only his echoing voice replied to him.

Glenn gulped. "Is anyone here?"

Still nothing. He shook his head and sighed.

"I might as well treat this as good news. Free shelter for me, ain't that right?" He chuckled.

He quickly checked the chamber, finding only a single exit: a dark and very deep hallway that he had no desire to explore.

Glenn carefully approached the tent. He lifted the flap, peering inside for any hidden individuals or... corpses.

Better safe than sorry.

The tent's interior welcomed the warm hue of the flames, revealing a few objects of interest. The first was a camp bed. That sight put a wide smile on Glenn's face.

"Excellent. No sleeping on the ground." He sighed with relief.

In the center, there was a small metal trashcan filled with ashes. Glenn placed the torch in the bin before turning to the last object that truly interested him. There was a desk and a chair alongside a notebook, but most importantly, there was a chest.

And a chest meant loot!

Without a hint of hesitation, Glenn kneeled in front of it, grinning with excitement. What was he going to find? Rare, magical weapons? A large pile of glittering gold?

Glenn opened the chest and frowned. No riches, nor ornate blades. Just clothing.

I'm disappointed, but... He looked at the rags he wore and grimaced. He could certainly use something clean. Pulling the clothes out one by one, he held them to the light.

"They look pretty nice..." He whistled, finding several copies of black cotton pants alongside white, airy shirts. A black trench coat that reached his knees completed the outfit.

Anything was better than Glenn's tattered garments. He examined the clothes further and chuckled when he realized they were a perfect fit.

Glenn noted the absence of underwear but decided it was a minor concern. He quickly took off his attire, wincing at the numerous scratches and bruises on his body. Shaking his head dejectedly, he threw his old clothes into the bin, letting them burn like the trash they were.

"Bye, bye, rags..." Glenn cackled.

This wasn't efficient, but getting rid of a reminder of that battlefield was a good way to work out his frustration, fear, and everything he felt since he arrived in this world.

The only thing he kept was his belt, sword, and scabbard, for obvious reasons. Oh, and the snacks and lifesaving flint, of course.

He didn't waste another second and quickly changed, groaning in satisfaction as he caressed the soft fabric.

"I love it already," Glenn said as he checked himself out.

Sadly for him, there wasn't a bathtub anywhere in the tent, which wasn't surprising. He patted himself a few times before sighing. This style of clothing didn't seem common, almost a little luxurious as he guessed from the quality of the weave. Was this tent's owner a noble or something? A rich explorer?

He then turned his attention back to the desk. An open book lay on the stern wood, as well as a pen and a bottle of ink. A half-consumed candle spilled its wax across the surface.

Glenn lit the candle, grabbed the notebook, and put his feet on the desk. He opened the book and coughed slightly as dust fell from it.

He used the candle to shower the dusty pages in light. There, waiting for him, was an entirely new alphabet made of convoluted characters. After struggling to understand it, Glenn decrypted it, little by little.

"How-ard, Jeff... Jefferson?" Glenn read out loud. That must have been the name of the author.

"The Adventures of the See—Seeker!" Glenn rubbed his eyes, trying to figure out his translation ability. He kept concentrating on the very long title.

"Seeker of New and Old... Jefferson Howard. Huh, it's getting easier," Glenn remarked.

He moistened his lips and turned the next page, wincing at the cryptic document. His head ached painfully, and he only wanted one thing: sleep. Glenn yawned and put the book back on the desk. That would have to wait until tomorrow morning. He snuffed out the candle's flames and plopped on the camp bed.

"Hah..." Glenn sighed, already thinking about what he was going to do once he had woken up. He'd have to decrypt the notebook. There might be some important information in there, and alongside that, he wanted to test the limits of his new power.

Glenn closed his eyes and fell peacefully asleep, finally getting a well-deserved rest.

* * *

"Hey, hey, come on. Come on, we're going to miss it!"

A small, pale hand tugged Glenn away as he followed reluctantly. As the two of them approached a vast crowd, Glenn took the lead. He pulled his little sister, Lina, close to him, so the creeps couldn't try something weird.

The music was beating loudly, surrounding them from all sides as many people danced to the rhythm. Even Lina bobbed her head with each beat.

"Enjoying yourself?" he shouted over the bass.

Lina nodded with a soft smile, the most Glenn had managed to get from her since...

It felt good to see her happy and not with those dull, lifeless eyes she usually bore. Glenn couldn't blame her, though. He also felt a little guilty each time he enjoyed himself.

Still, it was good news that the little one got those events out of her head. As long as she was happy, he was happy.

A drunken man suddenly bumped into Glenn, spilling two full cups of beer all over his clothes. Glenn bounced back in surprise.

"Shit, for real? That was my best shirt, asshole!" Glenn cursed, grabbing the barfly's collar.

The man gazed at him with hazy, rolled-back eyes. Glenn winced and let him go; the drunkard crashed on the ground like a squid. His complaints were useless if the guy was already asleep. He wiped his hands on a random passerby's jacket and looked at them in wonder.

Hands?

Where was Lina? Glenn's heart stopped. His vision blurring as fear took over. He shoved through the crowd, looking for that cute, tiny head of pink hair.

"Lina? Lina!" Glenn yelled desperately, but she was nowhere in sight.

He hopped on a table, disregarding the cups. He'd apologize later; his sister was more important than anything. Ignoring the protest of the partygoers, he surveyed the scene nervously.

"Damn it. Where the hell is that pink-headed idiot?" Glenn hissed, his worry growing with each passing second.

He was about to yell his sister's name once more, only to be interrupted by a chilling cry from within the crowd.

"He's got a syringe!"

The partygoers reacted instantly, some with cries of panic and others with hot-blooded anger. It had become a trend for scum to drug people at festivals. Most folks were careful not to get their drinks spiked, so creeps had to resort to other methods.

"I see him! Fuck him up!"

Glenn jumped off the table, his teeth clenched. "Where... Where..."

"There's the victim! We need a doctor!" someone shouted.

Glenn felt his blood freeze in his veins.

It couldn't be, right?

He dashed through the mob, almost collapsing when he saw the pink-headed girl lying on the floor, surrounded by a worried public.

"Shit! Lina!" He roared as he pushed the poor bystanders out of the way. His heart beat loudly in his ears as he helplessly watched his sister's droopy eyes close.

"No. No! Stay with me! Hey, can you hear me? Shit. Shit!" Glenn panicked as the light in Lina's eye faded, her happy smile from the festivities frozen in time.

Chapter 8

INDIANA JONES IS A LIAR

"Shit," Glenn whispered.

He grunted and wiped the sleep off his eyes. The restful slumber did its job, filling Glenn with energy. But it didn't help with the pain and aches from the previous day's activities. And that was without counting the bad trip down memory lane.

Glenn stood and stretched, hearing a few cracks. He was still in Jefferson Howard's tent, the *Seeker of New and Old*—whatever that meant.

Sadly, it meant that this whole horrible adventure was no nightmare. It was reality. *His* reality, now.

It had been more than a day since he arrived in this world, and he was parched. Glenn picked up Jefferson Howard's journal and left the tent. He took a torch from a nearby pillar, ignited it, and opened the book.

"Let's see if that guy's final words are worth anything..." he said aloud as his steps echoed in the wide, stone chamber. He assumed they were his last words. If Jefferson was alive, Glenn would have met him by now, right?

Yeah, he's probably dead.

Glenn prepared to strain his eyes once more in order to understand the foreign language, only to be pleasantly surprised. Where it took multiple tries to read a single word previously, it was now as easy as reading English.

That, and understanding the rantings of that tentacle monster yesterday... Glenn rubbed his temples.

Something is helping me get acclimated to this world. Something... Or someone. I could put my hand to the fire that it's the result of the same higher power who brought me here... He shook his head, sifting through the notebook as he explored the chamber.

24.11.30—I found them! The ruins of the Moon Cult! I knew it existed! Mark my words, this day will signify the birth of the legendary Seeker, Jefferson Howard!
The only issue is that there doesn't appear to be an exit. The entry hall seems to have been connected to other hallways, but the structure must have collapsed in the past. There's only one way to go, but I have a bad feeling... For now, I'll try to decipher these engravings. They should tell me more about this place...

Glenn frowned and looked up from the notebook, raising his torch to examine the walls.

He indeed found writing on the walls in a foreign and incomprehensible language. When concentrating on them, he learned his translation ability was limited.

"That's too bad..." He sighed before resuming his reading.

25.11.30—Hmm... I'll need more time to decipher the engravings. Discovering what lies down that unexplored tunnel might take my priority. I only have a month's worth of supplies, after all.
Glenn waved his torch around, soon finding the mentioned pathway. Engravings covered the stone floor and even ceiling, filling every available space. He tried to peer through the darkness, but his eyes couldn't pierce it. It seemed like this hallway went much deeper than he expected.

26.11.30—This place is clearly connected to the Moon Rift. The few words I managed to decipher all spoke of the same thing—the moons grant their 'gifts.' It's referencing the wonders that fell from the blood moon—the Fallen Pieces and the Fallen Ones. Either this cult was created around some mysterious item, a Fallen Piece of great power. Or a living being. A Fallen One. Hoho, imagine that. I would love to meet one of those guys, even if they're practically myths at this point. What with all the weird stories surrounding their apparition.

I'm almost certain that this crystal is a Fallen Piece, though I have yet to confirm it. Still no exit in sight, so I'll keep researching for now. Not like I can do anything else.

"The Moon Rift? That's the strange void that nearly killed me." Glenn paused. "Fallen Pieces and Fallen Ones... Could I be a Fallen One? I did wake up during a blood moon."

He sighed and glanced at the dark hallway. His heart tightened as he slowly came to terms with Jefferson Howard's words.

Still no exit in sight.

"Fuck no..." he mumbled as he steeled himself and entered the hall, stepping over the engravings covering the floor.

30.11.30—The water was safe, thankfully. Testing it on myself was dangerous, but considering I haven't managed to dig my way out, knowing I have a good water supply is nice. I couldn't repeat that interaction with the pedestal, and I'm still hesitant to touch that crystal.

Glenn's eyes lit up. Water? He gave up on reading and ran, his dry throat giving him more than enough motivation to reach the prophesied fountain. It took well over half an hour of running until he eventually found a white, faint glow coming from the end of the corridor.

His heart filled with excitement, and he quickened his pace. Eager to quench his thirst, Glenn stepped inside the chamber, and he wasn't disappointed.

A massive crystal—as tall as a multi-story home—shone like moonlight above a pristine pool. The shimmering reflection glimmered across the water's surface, casting strange but relaxing shapes on the walls.

Glenn dropped his torch. It rolled into the water, but he didn't care. The torch's light was nothing compared to the crystal's.

There was a pulse coming off it, pumping through the ground quite similar to bass at a concert. A rocky pathway reached across the pond all the way to the prism with a stone pedestal at its end. All of it echoed the notebook's contents.

This crystal... It's the same kind as the smaller gem that almost rained on top of me... Was it drawn to this larger one?

"Does it attract Fallen Pieces like a magnet?" he questioned aloud, his voice echoing through the room.

Approaching the crystal carefully, he observed the sanctum's layout. There were two more hallways—left and right—but both had collapsed long ago. Glenn drew closer to see whether digging a way out was possible.

He couldn't feel any wind passing through, nor hear a hissing breeze, so it was highly unlikely he'd find an exit. The opposite passageway was in the same condition. Glenn frowned.

"How the hell am I supposed to get out of here, then?" He wondered, a tinge of nascent worry poisoning his mind. He turned back to the pool with a grimace.

"Jefferson said it was safe to drink. Now, should I trust a *probably* dead stranger's words? That's the question..." Glenn muttered as he crouched in front of the pond.

There wasn't dirt or even a hint of moss growing along the pool's edge. It was the cleanest water he had ever seen. He reached with a hesitant hand, sensing its chilling touch.

Despite his reservations, Glenn brought the water to his mouth. The human body couldn't survive more than seventy-two hours without drinking. Time was ticking, and he was already experiencing symptoms of dehydration. Dry throat, headaches, sluggish thoughts... All things considered, he didn't have a choice.

"Here goes nothing." He closed his eyes, pressing his lips against cold water. It was revitalizing, as if he had just eaten ice cream on the hottest day of summer.

The feeling was so purifying, all the aches he suffered from washed away. Glenn didn't move for a few seconds, reflecting, before drinking more.

After the second gulp, all of his pain disappeared. That uncomfortable sting in his lower back? Gone. That cramp in his neck? Gone too.

"What kind of weird fuckery is this?" Glenn said, unable to believe his senses.

Using the crystal's light, he continued reading the notebook.

00.00.00—I no longer know the date. And my sleep schedule provides no clues.

"Only a Fallen One shall harness the power of the sky..." Fallen One my ass! I made groundbreaking discoveries. I can't die here! Just the news that Still Peak is a Fallen Piece is enough to get the Seekers to support my efforts!

Glenn paused, rubbed his eyes, and reread the passage. But the words didn't change. The mountain he was standing inside currently was... a Fallen Piece?

As in, *a mountain* fell from the sky?

"What the fuck?" he blurted out in disbelief. *Does gravity not work the same in this world? Wouldn't such a fall be enough to level the entire region, or worse?*

I don't know anymore...

At first, Jefferson's penmanship had been clean and easy to understand, but now, it was written with a trembling hand.

00.00.00—I haven't eaten in... at least a week. But I'll risk my life to return to King's Rise. I'll prove that my dad is a monster, get rid of his bitch, and lead the Howard Barony back to become a County!

Glenn whistled, impressed. So the author was from a noble family. That was good news. Jefferson also hated his father, which Glenn could understand all too well. The one thing that did worry him slightly was the Seeker's lack of food.

"If I understood correctly, Jefferson struggled for weeks to find an exit and failed. Where did he end up then?" he whispered as he glanced around the room.

It didn't matter how hard he tried to look away, his eyes kept returning to the massive, white crystal pulsing rhythmically. He flipped through the notebook's pages, but beyond that last paragraph, there were only copies of the engravings on the walls—and notes questioning their meaning.

Glenn stashed the journal into his coat. He walked on the stone pathway, approaching the prism. His heart skipped a beat when he found a pile of clothes beside the pedestal.

Those garments were eerily similar to the ones he was currently wearing.

"No way..." He heaved as he crouched in front of the pile, picking up a shirt with a trembling hand.

A handful of soot fell from the fabric with a silent, yet ominous rustle. Glenn tumbled back with dread, his hands still covered in the only remains of Jefferson Howard.

Dark, thick, and sticky ashes.

"Fuck!" he blurted out as he used the pedestal to pull himself up and away from the ash. His fingers slid against a large run etched into it, and a thundering voice rang in his head.

"Only a Fallen One shall harness the power of the sky. To dust you shall go back if you're not the promised one."

Glenn jumped away in fright, his hand on the hilt of his sword. He looked around the chamber in fear, ready to draw his weapon, but there was no one else with him. Sweat pearled down his forehead as his chest tightened.

A talking pedestal?

Chuckling nervously, Glenn suddenly understood what had happened.

"'To dust you shall return,' huh?" He glanced at the pile of ashes and his stomach churned. "Shit."

He shook his head and retrieved the notebook, giving it another read, but he couldn't find anything new.

"This..." Glenn sat on the floor and rubbed his temples. The pedestal said that only a Fallen One shall harness the power of the sky.

That 'power of the sky' is probably the crystal. And a Fallen One should be a living being that has fallen from the Moon Rift. Jefferson came to the same conclusion, yet he still tried to touch the damned gem because he was trapped for weeks without food. And he died. Fuck.

Glenn yanked on his hair in despair. What the hell was he supposed to do?

"*Phew...*" He drew in a deep breath. Panicking and losing his mind wouldn't help him avoid Jefferson's mistakes. First, he glanced at the pile of clothes and steeled himself. He took it away from the crystal, refusing to stay close to something that had the capability to reduce him to ashes.

He ignored his disgust and sifted through the threads.

"The same as in the chest... He wasn't exactly an original gentleman," Glenn said, noticing it before finding a small pouch.

Opening it up half-heartedly, he noted it was completely empty. He sighed and tied the pouch to his belt.

"If I survive, I'll be sure to make better use of this than you ever did, Jefferson," Glenn muttered with a deep sigh.

Would it be far-fetched to consider himself a Fallen One? After all, he wasn't from this world, woke up under the blood—no, the Moon Rift—and something special was helping him endure with the temporary healing and language comprehension ability.

He looked at the white mineral dreadfully. Glenn wasn't a gambler, but between touching a potentially deadly prism or spending weeks dying of hunger, one sadly sounded better than the other.

"All or nothing, eh?" Glenn chewed on his lower lip. "That's why I don't like gambling."

He walked up to the pulsing gem, his heartbeat accelerating. He stopped right before it, and he closed his eyes.

It took him a few seconds before he could open them again, his gaze resolute. He clenched his teeth tightly and pressed his left hand against the crystal.

Either it worked or it didn't. Jefferson had been abundantly clear in his journal.

Glenn's fingers brushed against the surface of the crystal, sending an icy chill through his veins. The experience was inexplicable, indescribable, and simply otherworldly. Somehow, it felt like he had been *purified*. Was that how it felt to die? Pure?

Energy surged through his body, leaving him simultaneously exhilarated and drained.

"Wow..." He gasped.

His mouth felt like cotton, and his tongue went stiff. Suddenly, his legs gave out, and his consciousness faded. His strength waned as he lost the fight and collapsed. With a desperate hope that he wouldn't share the same fate as Jefferson Howard—the Seeker—he succumbed to the darkness.

Chapter 9

A HANDY TALK

Glenn's senses spiraled into a blissful void. He felt comfortable, as if he had just woken up from a really good night of sleep.

His vision was hazy, the world around him a complete blur. A hand extended towards him, urging him to grasp it. Glenn tried to shake the appendage, but he was impossibly slow. His body felt ethereal, completely disconnected. The hand's insistence grew more pronounced, its urgency palpable.

Glenn forced his eyes open.

The hand hung from strips of flesh, each thread fidgeting of its own volition like the tentacles of the late Father Albenas.

Oh, shit. I'm not shaking that! His eyes widened madly as the hand retracted swiftly, as if acknowledging his unspoken refusal. The palm opened, and a mouth appeared within, smiling wickedly. 'It' moistened its red lips with a fleshy tongue before smacking them.

"What the fuck?" Glenn blurted out.

The wicked mouth spoke in a dry tone. **"Huh. What are you?"**

Glenn's heart raced. No, he didn't hear wrong. The thing *talked* with a human voice that had a slight echo. It had an otherworldly feeling—as if it shouldn't belong to this world.

And *it* spoke to him.

"Hey? You got hearing issues or something?" the mouth said mockingly, startling Glenn once again.

He shook his head. "Uh, yeah. Yeah, I heard you. Wow."

The mouth faded, and the hand made a fist, thrusting it into the air victoriously. Glenn would have probably found the movement humorous had it not been for the bloody sinew holding it like strings of a puppet.

His heartbeat was loud, but it wasn't louder than the syrupy sounds coming from his surroundings. The thick stench of iron and rotten meat made him want to puke, but he was certain doing so would sign his death sentence.

He followed the sinew's trail but could only spy a squirming mess of crimson and darkness. *It* moved like slithering snakes, worming their way through—

"Ugh!" Glenn coughed as a sudden pang of pain shot through his head. Sweat drenched his back as he averted his eyes away from the swirling void.

The headache calmed gradually, but the threat of another battle loomed in Glenn's mind. If there was one positive thing about that pain, it was that it woke Glenn up. Fully alert, he took in the strangeness of his surroundings.

He was trapped in a scarlet chamber composed of oozing flesh and coagulated blood. The dungeon pulsated rhythmically, mirroring the cadence of the white crystal—like a *heart*.

A metallic tang in the air made his stomach churn. Glancing down, he realized he was sitting on the beating tendons. He instinctively jumped away but fell into a gore-slicked wall.

"Am I... in the crystal?" he slowly inquired.

"*Sigh*... Yes, well observed." The mouth reappeared, grimacing distastefully.

Shit, I spoke out loud. That hand is certainly not a normal being. But then, nothing is normal in this world.

"**In this world?**" the hand echoed, sending a chill down his spine. "**Oh, and yeah. Don't bother *thinking* since I can hear *all of you.***"

The mouth grinned wickedly and moistened its lips as it hovered closer to Glenn's face.

"**Be it your racing heart or thoughts, they are all mine to read. So, rid yourself of your pitiful escape plans, and let's converse normally—like *normal beings.***" The hand emphasized the last word.

"What the fuck?"

The hand froze for a second before exploding in laughter. "**Hahaha, yes. That's the *very question* I wanted to pose. Maybe you can read minds too. An interesting coincidence, don't you say?**"

He shook his head. *Reading minds? What? Of course I can't! This is fucked.*

"**I agree,**" the hand said with an honest tone. "**But hey, at least you're not dead!**"

"I'm not?"

The hand made a thumbs down gesture, earning a sneer out of Glenn. This situation was so unbelievable—so illogical he could only laugh.

"**Anyway, did your parents not teach you manners?**"

"What?"

"**Shouldn't you ask my name? Or at least knock before barging in my... room?**" the tongue hissed with a veneer of authority. Glenn gulped.

"Who are you?" he asked, obeying the underlying order of the entity. He'd rather play the game than die.

"**Good choice. But who's asking? I did not invite you in, so I believe presenting yourself would be the proper thing, right?**"

"My name is Glenn, and..." He hesitated. "My last name is no longer of importance, I suppose." Anger took over Glenn as he asked sarcastically, "May I know your name?"

The hand's grin grew from thumb to pinkie, its peerless white teeth gleaming.

"Finally some *manners*." It laughed before moistening its lips again. **"You can address me as Diamanes. Not exactly my real name, but it'd be unfortunate if your brain imploded by hearing it, right?"**

Glenn disregarded the latter part of the sentence and rubbed the bridge of his nose. "It's a... pleasure to meet you, Diamanes. Uhm... What are you?"

"I'm a hand," Diamanes replied simply, unperturbed.

Glenn blinked, momentarily dumbfounded. "Okay? Care to elaborate on *whose* hand?"

"Don't feel like it," retorted the hand, positioning itself inches from Glenn's face. He held his breath, wondering what he was supposed to do. The hand's fleshy tongue passed over its teeth, its grin growing maliciously.

"Enough. I have a few questions of my own," Diamanes declared, his words ringing with an ominous weight.

Glenn opened his mouth, but his jaws clenched shut as a sudden pressure bore down on his shoulders, nailing him to the blood-drenched floor. The headache returned with greater intensity, like an ancient being raging in his mind. A forbidden horror that threatened the base of his sanity, pushing him to the very brink of madness.

Glenn gasped, his hands reaching helplessly for his throat in a desperate attempt to clear it. He gritted his teeth, feeling his consciousness mere inches from slipping away. The lack of oxygen made his sight blurry, but Glenn still fought. He knew death was worse than whatever *this was*. This was painful, more painful than that damned spear or ghoul from earlier, but he couldn't give up.

"Impressive. See, that's why I have to ask— what the hell are you? You can't be human, or else you'd already be groveling to my feet. Metaphorical ones, you know." Diamanes' voice washed over him with a sudden relief, the pressure disappearing like a mirage.

Glenn coughed, wheezing with each breath of rancid air. Rancid air was better than no air after all.

Diamanes seemed satisfied to have proved his point, as evidenced by the dirty, crooked finger he pointed at Glenn. The entity almost appeared like an excited child showing a frightened frog to its parents. Only, there were no parents, and the frog was Glenn.

"Now, humor me and explain yourself. What kind of abomination are you?" Diamanes hovered away, leaving Glenn some space to breathe.

He rubbed his throat with furrowed brows, tears welling up in his eyes. "The hell do you mean?"

Annoyed, Diamanes smacked its lips. **"I mean it very literally. Are you a Fallen One? Or... Perhaps something different altogether—a sort of aberration?"**

Glenn squinted at the floating hand. What even were those choices? Where was the 'human' box to tick?

An aberration... Maybe coming from Earth or another world counts? Wait. Shit! Glenn barely finished his thought when Diamanes groaned in puzzlement.

It cracked its fingers in a disturbing motion before caressing an imaginary chin. **"Uh. Interesting. See, last time I checked, humans shouldn't be able to touch the crystal, or they'll die. And you're from another world..."**

Glenn clenched his eyes shut, trying to empty his mind.

"Don't bother. The harder you try to hide it, the easier it'll be for me. Earth, you say? Hmm... So you *are* a Fallen One then?"

"Maybe?" Glenn suspected as much when he read Jefferson's diary, but... Something didn't add up. He arrived before the Moon Rift, and the journal said nothing about mysterious powers.

"For now, you are. I'm too lazy to understand the specifics." Diamanes decided, before adding, **"Only Fallen Ones can enter this place, after all."**

Glenn rubbed his chin. Perhaps it was wise to mirror the entity and accept the simplest answer. Until he encountered a *very old* and *very powerful* being, he wasn't going to get a satisfactory explanation.

What mattered was learning why he ended up in this world. If *someone* was the cause, he needed to talk to them. A violent talk, if possible. *That culprit better have had a very, very good reason for ruining my peaceful life.*

"*Sigh*... What should I do with you then? I feel like killing you would be a waste, as you certainly are a unique kind of being..." Diamanes wondered aloud, successfully drawing Glenn's attention.

"Perhaps... it could work, since... Hehe, yeah. Technically, he could..." The hand hung at eye level with Glenn. The palm opened towards his face, and the mouth formed a contemptuous rictus.

"I have a proposition for you, Glenn." The hand spoke in a suave tone.

He got the distinct impression that something was wrapping itself around his body, slowly slithering like a snake. He wanted to fight back, but how? What could he even do? He looked at the demon, hoping he wouldn't have to wager his soul.

"As you guessed, I'm not a *normal* being..." Diamanes trailed off, grinning. **"Shake my hand, and I'll give you power beyond your imagination—"**

Glenn sneered, interrupting the entity. Diamanes froze in shock, unable to believe his victim. Glenn knew it was over for him, but he simply couldn't contain himself. It was possibly the fatigue or the screws that were loosened from his multiple encounters with death that freed his inhibitions.

"Power? Why the hell would I want power?" Before the entity replied, he added, "Can you bring me back to Earth? To my world, away from this nightmare?"

Diamanes shut its mouth, pondering silently. Glenn gritted his teeth and resigned himself.

Whatever I said about living earlier? Bullshit. Why should I even struggle in this hell if there's no hope of escape? Am I supposed to abandon my sister? How? And what guarantee is there that dying won't take me home?

"I'm... not sure how to deliver you to your world. But..." Diamanes' grin grew wide again. **"What I do know is that *death* won't free you. This land will take your soul and never give it back. And you'll lose all chances of seeing your kin."**

Glenn held his breath, staring haggardly at the inhumane entity.

"What's certain, though, is that if you accept my proposal, I'll be an invaluable ally. Even if I don't know the way out personally, I can guarantee it exists. Otherwise, I wouldn't be here," Diamanes swore with a wild, diabolical laugh.

Glenn felt the knot tighten around his neck, and yet... Now he could see it. Passage out of this hell—the path to return to his sister and his peaceful life. But... Did he really want to shake hands with a shady entity?

Was he selling his soul to the devil?

Diamanes sighed impatiently. **"Why do you even bother contemplating the question?"**

Glenn's headache returned like a tidal wave. He yelped in pain as his mind filled with countless screams of horror.

"There are two choices available to you, Glenn."

Holding his head in his hands, Glenn could barely hear the demon. A drum beat in the background at the same tempo as his heart. Only, the sound grew louder and faster with each pulse.

"The first choice I can give you is death. A dirty, painful death that will pursue you even in whatever lies beyond."

The screeches intensified, and Glenn's eardrums exploded. His right eye burst, and blood flowed from every orifice. As his end drew closer, Glenn thought about Lina— his friends, his past... and that damned bastard.

What did I do to deserve this? Could I have done anything differently?

"**The second choice, you agree to my proposition. And I become a part of you.**"

Diamanes' voice distorted like a skipping vinyl record. Glenn coughed out the blood accumulating in his throat, the screams in his ears becoming his own.

"**You have… five full seconds to make your decision. How generous of me, right?**"

Glenn watched in horror with his remaining eye as the demon's mouth grew wider and wider, encompassing Glenn's whole body. Saliva dripped into large pools, flowing onto the fleshy floor like a fountain. Even in this ridiculous state, Diamanes maintained his greedy, voracious grin.

The pain made Glenn lose his grasp on reality.

"**Three seconds,**" Diamanes chuckled. "**Tick tock.**"

The seconds passed, as long as days, and the last thing Glenn heard was that thumping sound, the damned demon counting to zero.

"**One. Make your choice!**" Diamanes shouted hysterically.

Glenn hissed one last breath. Diamanes' laugh accompanied him down the hatch to the abyss of his mind.

"**It's a deal!**"

Chapter 10

MOIST EYES

"Wakey, wakey..."

"Ugh..." Glenn startled awake, his head searing with an annoying pain, almost as irritating as the sarcastic voice that woke him.

He opened his eyes slowly and jolted when he noticed he was underwater. The feeling quickly snapped him out of his passive state, and he hurriedly pushed himself out of the chilling pool.

He must have slept a long time, and yet, he hadn't gotten a wink of rest. His whole body ached like he had been steamrolled by a truck or two—maybe more.

Glenn sat at the pond's end under the previously floating crystal. 'Previously floating' because it was now submerged in the water, its magical glow gone. The gem wasn't brilliant white, nor was it pulsing in a rhythmic beat. It was just an old rock with moss growing on its sides.

It looks very dead.

Glenn spat out the rancid water, coughing as he did. What was once the best-tasting reservoir he had ever drank from in his life now tasted like sewage. And that only made sense where there were lichens and decaying insects floating atop the surface.

"Quite the delightful soup. Fuck me," Glenn grumbled.

He stumbled a few steps, his surroundings spinning uncontrollably. Collapsing on the ground, he rubbed his temples in deep confusion. *What the hell was that thing calling itself Diamanes and proposing a deal?*

Glenn stared at the pond, sighing because he couldn't drink to make himself feel better.

"What a mess."

A sneer echoed through the room, startling him. He jumped to his feet and reached for his sword. He scanned the chamber but saw nothing apart from scattered sunlight. The ceiling had collapsed, opening an escape path.

"Am I imagining things?" Glenn said.

"Ha!"

A mocking voice echoed once again, this time coming... from his hand. Glenn examined his left hand, only to find that his skin had turned dark purple. He slowly unclenched fist, revealing a grinning mouth with red lips and pristine, white teeth in his palm.

"Diamanes?!" he asked in disbelief. The mouth opened, and a fleshy tongue moistened its lips.

"Yours truly! Here to give you a hand! Haha!" Diamanes burst out laughing while Glenn groaned, the pun bouncing off him ineffectively.

"Do... Do I have a talking hand now?" Glenn's face turned blank as he pronounced the words, making this nightmare too real for his taste.

"Absolutely!" Diamanes exclaimed.

Glenn sighed. *What am I supposed to do? Just go around with a talking hand? What the fuck?*

"You can't even *fathom* how long it's been since I've tasted freedom. Ahh, the outside world..." Diamanes chortled before shouting, **"It's *great* to be alive!"**

Glenn clenched his fist, muffling Diamanes' laughter. "How do I get rid of you?"

"You don't. Better get used to me, unless you want to cut your hand off!" The entity mocked.

That mockery slowly changed to horror when Glenn unsheathed his sword.

"What if I hack you off?" Glenn hissed through his teeth.

He didn't like this situation one bit. But could he lob his own hand off? Diamanes waited in anticipation before chuckling. Glenn relaxed his arm, giving up.

"What? You don't have the strength to do it? I can cheer you on if you want!"

Glenn shook his head. He couldn't willingly hurt himself. Already, he suffered greatly; he didn't need to add a layer of self-mutilation.

"Good choice. I would have grown back *anyway*!"

When Glenn heard that, he realized how hellish his life was going to be. *I'll never have a second to myself, always watched by this parasite…*

"Wait, what? Parasite? You called me a *parasite*?" Diamanes screamed in outrage.

"You have a talking hand, and you're thinking of privacy? Isn't it an insignificant sacrifice to be in my presence?" Diamanes asked in disbelief.

"Get out of my mind! Damn it!" Glenn yelled, even though he knew nothing would come of it.

Observing his cursed appendage, he noticed a demarcation between the purple and white skin located exactly at the start of his wrist. Small spots sprouted along the edge, and it was more than probable that they'd continue to grow.

"I know I'm handsome, so you can stare all you want!" Diamanes exclaimed shamelessly.

"Just… shut up."

Diamanes chuckled. **"Hey, look on the bright side!"**

"There's a bright side?" Glenn questioned, less than amused.

"You'll never feel lonely again!" Diamanes' annoying grin almost made Glenn take out his sword and stab himself, but no.

"I did enjoy having some privacy, though."

"**Whatever. Stop being such a killjoy. Let's get out of here first.**" Diamanes proposed, putting an end to their banter.

Glenn looked up at the collapsed ceiling. With his blade hanging off his waist and Jefferson's pouch on the other side of his belt, he climbed out of the ruins. Once he reached the surface, he squinted and covered his eyes from the blinding sun.

Holding his hand as a visor, he checked his surroundings. The mountain was far away. It was a stupidly long walk from the tent to the crystal, after all. Instead of a flat summit, its peak had been blown to bits, leaving a collection of smaller ridges. The gray stone had blackened like soot, and ash fell like snow.

Glenn searched for the massive city and found it a reasonable distance away. *Maybe I can get there before nightfall?*

"**That's some wishful thinking. Are we going hiking, then?**" Diamanes snickered.

A vein popped in Glenn's forehead, but he forced himself to ignore it. If what he saw was correct, there were a few hours of forest to traverse before reaching the metropolis.

Diamanes' smile faded. "**So, uhm. Where the hell are we? I'm a bit of an alien. So I'd be glad if you could give me a small explanation.**"

Glenn froze in his steps. "Alien? What do you think I am? Can't you use whatever magic put you in my hand to figure that out yourself?"

"**I'd rather see what you know so we can get to know each other properly—mano a mano!**"

Glenn shoved his hand into his pocket, muffling Diamanes' laughter. *Mano a mano? Do I have to endure these puns for the rest of my life?*

"**I can hear you, you know?**"

I'll be back in civilization soon, so why don't you go hide? Nothing good will happen if I'm suspected of being possessed. Imagine being burned at the stake for something so dumb.

"Are you ashamed of me, Glenn? Don't you like me being your hand?" Diamanes frowned, not that Glenn cared whatsoever.

"You'll warm up to me eventually. Mark my words."

Glenn rolled his eyes; no way in hell would he ever trust this maddening piece of evil shit. He grabbed the small pouch hanging from his belt.

"How about you live here until I find a proper pair of gloves to—"

"Isn't that a dimensional pouch? Lucky you! It's a reasonably spacious one at that!" Diamanes exclaimed in appreciation.

Glenn paused and raised an eyebrow. "A dimensional pouch. Like in Dungeons and Dragons?"

"Uhh, maybe? A dimensional pouch is a compressed dimension tucked inside a smaller container for storage purposes. Furthermore, it only weighs as much as the sack itself; the items inside don't contribute to its weight. And as a bonus, only the first person who opens it can use it. Until said user dies, of course."

Glenn's eyes glimmered. *I hit the jackpot! But how does it work?*

He reached inside the pouch, but there was nothing.

"If you want to know the content, ask the pouch in your mind."

He shrugged. Why not? This world was already insane.

Inventory, please!

A dark void opened in his mind. Among the assortment of knickknacks, a map, a finely adorned sword, and a signet ring bearing what was probably House Howard's crest stood out.

Under the ring was a drawing of a man with a handwritten note on the back.

Wanted, a hundred gold—Unknown

"It seems like your friend was quite popular in the wrong way," Diamanes remarked.

"I'm not sure if it's Jefferson since his body was reduced to literal *ashes* when I found this. And I didn't exactly know him."

There were also medical supplies. He wouldn't risk trying the herbs, although bandages were certainly the solution he was looking for if he needed to hide Diamanes.

Digging deeper, he discovered what appeared to be this world's currency: gold, silver, and copper coins. If this was a classic fantasy world, it would probably be a hundred copper for one silver and a hundred silver for one gold. That sounded like a hell of a bother. *What would happen if I bought something worth a copper with one silver? Would I get ninety-something copper back?*

"Oh, poor you. How *ever* will you manage carrying too much money around?" Diamanes mocked.

Glenn shook his head and stopped his tangent. It wasn't worth his time thinking about. He would soon know anyway once he stepped into the city.

He retrieved the map from the dimensional pouch. The paper crackled as he unraveled it. The mountain he came from was called Still Peak, and his destination, King's Rise.

The map was limited to the kingdom, which bore the lovely name of Munirp. The two cities on each side of the battlefield—Retni's Plains—were named Satidipug and Eari. There were more villages a fair distance out, but Glenn chose to reserve that for later. Right now, his objective was to get to King's Rise.

Glenn adjusted his black trench coat and breathed out chilly air. It was quite a trek. He'd have to cross Morsquida's Stream, which flowed from the mountain and forked a few kilometers away from the city. If he understood the map correctly, there should be a bridge along the way.

"Well, here we go."

"Lead on, partner!"

"For the love of god... Shut up."

Chapter 11

HELLO, CIVILIZATION!

Glenn strode through the forest on route to King's Rise, engaged in a conversation with the uninvited guest in his left hand—a conversation mainly centered around his memories of Earth.

"So, you had these *superhero* guys, but they weren't real? Like this Spiderguy or Great Man?"

"Exactly. It was all the product of someone's imagination—put on paper or filmed in a movie," explained Glenn.

"Entertainment... It's hard to imagine a world without death lurking around every corner. It certainly differs from this land or the one I came from," Diamanes said bemusedly.

Glenn's eyebrows rose with curiosity. "What was your world like?"

Diamanes' grin grew wide. **"It was... different, for sure. And it's also wishful thinking to believe I would tell you straight away!"**

Glenn sighed, unsurprised. What was he expecting from an evil entity that could read his mind and memories?

"Anyway, what's this phenomenon, Tok Tik? Is it a time spell or something?"

Glenn smirked and shook his head. "Sort of. But let's not dive into that topic. I've been wondering... When you access my memories, how does it work? Is it like watching a movie?"

Diamanes cleared his throat.

"To put it in terms you'd understand, watching your past is akin to browsing an entire Netflix catalog. I can select which part of your life I want to 'watch', and I experience your memories as if I were the one living them, without any control. A spectator of sorts."

The corner of Glenn's lips curved upwards.

Diamanes asked, **"Did I say something funny?"**

Glenn smirked at his left hand. Anyone watching him would probably think he was insane. Then again, maybe he was. Perhaps Diamanes was just a construct of his imagination helping him endure the horrors of this world.

"If you want to know, why don't you peer into my thoughts and find out?"

"I know you don't like me mind-reading you, so I'm holding back. I'm trying to be thoughtful, alright?"

Glenn sneered. "Thoughtful... Hah."

He couldn't help but find the word 'thoughtful' a little absurd given the short yet painful time he spent in Diamanes' fleshy lair.

"Well, have fun flipping through every cringe-worthy moment, hours of boredom, and all the terrible memories I have," Glenn replied.

"Who do you take me for? I've lived centuries in a room made of meat and blood, and you think watching you jerk off will bother me? Hell, that's going to be entertaining!"

Glenn's smile cracked as he clenched his left hand, muffling the mocking laugh.

* * *

For the first time since the beginning of their journey, the duo walked in silence—an enjoyable rest from Diamanes' constant jeers. Glenn enjoyed the relative peace, barely disturbed by birdsong or rustling leaves.

There was a certain comfort in the simplicity of nature. But the singing birds suddenly fell silent, flying off in a great swarm. Glenn glanced at the sky, only for his face to twist in fear.

The 'birds' were anything but common pigeons. They were devoid of flesh and feathers. Hundreds of them clouded the sky like a bad omen.

Their beaks and claws gleamed under the sunlight in a pale, disgusting yellow.

"Oh, looks like you encountered a necromancer! Hey, why don't we go kick his ass?" proposed Diamanes.

Glenn held his breath as he crouched under the cover of a large bush.

The skeletal avians circled the vicinity, cawing and shrieking before eventually flying away, probably recalled by whatever bastard summoned them. Glenn waited a while longer, just to make sure he didn't get ambushed.

"Fuck..." He let out a heavy breath before emerging from his hiding place.

"Coward."

"Sorry I'm not suicidal, Diamanes!" Glenn hissed.

A considerable amount of time passed as he strolled carefully through the forest, following Morsquida's Stream. By nightfall, the duo finally found a bridge. It was a solid structure of thick stone bricks, wide enough for two carts to travel side by side with space left over for pedestrians. Grooves had been dug in the mud by the multiple passages of wheeled vehicles.

"Yeah, it's a bridge. Stop marveling over every little thing, damn it!" Diamanes complained.

Glenn stepped on the bridge and exhaled out with anxiety.

It would be a lie to say he wasn't worried about what he'd discover in King's Rise. Would it be a place with civilized individuals, or was he going to fight for his life?

"I just need to take it slow," Glenn muttered to himself.

"Maybe you should try to hang around the outskirts and get some intel," Diamanes proposed.

"And maybe I'll find someone who knows more about what happened to me since you're too lazy to provide a plausible explanation."

"I already found an explanation—not my fault you're unsatisfied with it!" Diamanes retorted.

Glenn pulled the bandages out of his dimensional pouch. The entity's grin faded, replaced by a scowl.

"Hey, hey. You're not muffling me, are you? You know I don't need a mouth to talk, right?" Diamanes hurriedly tried to dissuade him to no avail.

"Please don't do that! I hate being constricted—" Glenn tightened the bandage around his left hand and made a small knot.

Even though the entity appeared to be relatively friendly, Glenn couldn't forget that he was the same demon that almost killed him. The memories of the pain he felt in that fleshy lair were more than enough to make him doubt the unwanted being's pleasantries.

Tch, why are you forcing me to speak directly into your mind? It feels like putting my tongue somewhere I shouldn't. Diamanes' annoyed voice rang in Glenn's thoughts.

"Ugh, disgusting." Glenn pressed his lips together. *Anyway, it means we can communicate in private, without anyone listening. And I think you know better than I do how dangerous your presence can be for me. I don't want to be burned at the stake, remember?*

Diamanes grunted in disagreement but didn't add anything else. Glenn's words did hold some weight, after all.

The sound of creaking wheels interrupted their conversation. Looking back, Glenn noticed a cart pulled by nothing. The wagon slowed until it reached him, revealing an old man clutching a glowing, blue stone. It was the definition of simple—four wheels with a driver's seat and a small storage space.

The driver's gray beard matched his surprisingly finely groomed hair that couldn't be concealed under his straw hat. Probably well in his sixties, the old man's green eyes were sharp and darted around Glenn to evaluate him. He wore a plain tunic, as well as brown pants held up with a string. Both were sewn of the same material, likely cheap flax.

A golden monocle hung from his right eye, an expensive item that clashed with the rest of the outfit. Additionally, the old man's free hand rested on a sword sheathed at his hip.

"Want a ride? I ain't stopping until the Frozen Gate," said the old man with a creaky yet powerful voice.

Shrugging, Glenn said, "Sure, why not?"

He reached for the carriage, but the old man halted him with an outstretched hand.

"What?"

"Two coppers."

Glenn placed one copper coin in the old man's hand.

"I might be old, but I ain't blind. That ain't two coppers, lad. Pay the rest, or ya won't be riding in me cart."

Glenn produced another coin. "You'll get the rest once we arrive."

The old man's gaze lingered, but he relented and let Glenn climb inside. With the transaction settled, the wagon resumed its journey.

Enjoyable scenery distracted Glenn from the bumpy road, until a familiar shriek suddenly echoed in the distance. It sounded like a bird's cawing, but... unnaturally distorted.

Ah-ha! Sseems like the necromancer spotted you! Hehe... This is going to be a good show!

Diamanes' uncaring laughter rang like a death bell. The cart slowly came to a stop as the old driver glanced back, his sharp, green eyes searching the skies.

"Hmph... 'nother pest," he muttered as he rubbed his sword's pommel.

"O-Old man, I recognize that sound. I met undead birds on the road and—" Glenn tried to warn the driver, but the latter simply spat.

"I know, I know. Tsk... Ya better keep yar mouth shut, ay?" The old man jumped off the carriage with surprising vigor and unsheathed his sword.

Shit, of course the sole human I meet is a lunatic. Do I run? Fuck, fuck!

Glenn's eyes shot to the sky, unable to see anything. He could only hear them, snapping their chipped beaks in anticipation of a meal that was hopefully not him.

Hmm... Running away again? Coward, coward...

"Damn it!" Glenn cursed as he unsheathed his corroded sword. The old man glanced to the side and scoffed.

"What are ya gonna do with yar rusty toothpick? Club 'em to death?" he mocked as he rested his blade against his shoulder.

Glenn gritted his teeth, not sparing the old man a glance. Strangely, his politeness seemed to disappear with stress. "Try not to break your back, geezer!"

The old man laughed as he stepped back to the cart casually. Glenn's eyebrows creased when he noticed the white steam his mouth produced. *When did it get so cold?*

Oh yeah, that's the stuff. Haha! Diamanes laughed.

Glenn was about to ask him what was so funny when the moonlight suddenly shone on countless raining crystals. It was beautiful, a mystical array of pale light.

As if pulled from a dream, skeletal birds encased in a prison of ice fell from the sky. Glenn's jaw dropped as he watched the frozen monsters shatter into a million pieces.

"What're ya doin'? Climb back in, 'still have some road to do," nudged the old driver, unbothered.

Glenn silently obeyed, his eyes glued to the undead flock's remains. The wagon wandered until the corpses were no more than a blip on the trail.

That guy is pretty exceptional for a human. Diamanes' voice interrupted Glenn's thoughts, startling him.

The driver glanced back at him with a strange expression but said nothing.

Shit, I almost forgot about you.

Yep. Still here. Still very much alive.

What the hell was that? H-How did he just freeze all of those birds?

Glenn could almost *feel* Diamanes' smirk as he asked his question.

That old timer is quite the rare find. He's skilled in both Aura and Mana, both at the Fourth level.

Aura, Mana... So that was magic... Is there anything else you'd like to share? Maybe how I can copy what this respectable senior did, or? Glenn asked with hope.

Diamanes sneered. **You don't even have Mana, and yet you already want to copy a high-ranked spell. Fool... And why should I teach my jailer? The one who muffled me? Hm?**

Glenn sighed heavily.

I'm going to need to stop by a library at some point... They should have those in the city, right?

With Diamanes' unwillingness to divulge more information, Glenn didn't have another choice. He could ask the old man, but he didn't want to end up as a surprisingly realistic ice sculpture.

The cart journeyed onwards beneath the twin moon's watchful gazes. A gust of wind blew Glenn's coat tail as he wordlessly marveled at a metropolis that was likely one of this land's Seven Wonders of the World.

Gigantic wasn't enough to describe King's Rise. Even from a distance, he still couldn't see the entire city. Buildings were woven like tapestries, the massive circling wall acting as an impassable obstacle.

What's that tower? Glenn thought.

A gray spire stood like a silent watcher at the city's center, its crown hidden in the clouds. Diamond-shaped stones circled it, trading flashes of blue and red energy. Even Sauron's Barad-dûr wasn't as impressive as this, despite the evil eye.

Intricate stairs led up the tower, the surrounding buildings increasing in height. Glenn smirked. The name 'King's Rise' was starting to make sense. What was even more interesting was the difference between the areas closest to the tower and the ones furthest from it. The region around the spire was cleaner and well-designed while the places far from it were rough, dark, and dirty.

Glenn sighed as he rubbed the back of his sore neck. *It's quite shocking how you can see the divide between luxury and hardship. Some things never change, do they...*

Diamanes whistled in amazement. ***This place is brimming with magic—enhanced stability, flight restriction, and more that I can't distinguish behind the already thick magic barriers. This is a light show. They must have a lot of talented Mages and an excellent supply of Mana to hold this whole thing together. It's an incredible piece of work.***

Glimmering in the moonlight like a crystal—a little taller than the ramparts—was a gate built entirely of ice.

Is this a city for frost giants or something? Glenn thought in wonder.

On each side of the gate stood two equally massive ice statues. One was a swordsman holding a Zweihänder in both hands, the blade pointed to the ground. He was protected by plate armor but had no helmet. The swordsman's face had faded away with time, not that Glenn would recognize it anyway.

The second sculpture was a typical role-playing game barbarian—muscular and wearing a leather loincloth. His hands rested on the head of a double-bladed axe, and his face hid under a horned helmet.

That's an impressive door.

Glenn nodded. *You don't say... I can't even imagine how humans built this.*

Diamanes snickered. ***I certainly can. The gate's architecture isn't that awe-inspiring compared to whatever horrible power it holds.***

Glenn raised an eyebrow at his bandaged hand. Despite his insistence, Diamanes refused to elaborate.

A horrible power, you say... Glenn shook his head. He wouldn't get an answer, so why bother?

Abruptly, the cart came to a halt, startling Glenn. He stood and glanced around. They were still a short ride from the city walls, so why stop here?

Glenn's face paled, and he clenched his sword, ready to draw it at any signs of danger.

Chapter 12

A FAMILIAR SMELL

The old driver scrubbed his beard before turning back to Glenn. "Ay, I need to respond to nature's call, heh. Don't move from the wagon."

He safely stashed away the magical, blue stone in his pocket and left with measured steps to the nearest tree.

Glenn sighed in relief.

Paranoid much? Diamanes inquired.

Yes, very paranoid. But can you blame me?

Diamanes didn't retort. Glenn's earlier experiences, even though they were few, were rich in weirdness and horror—and probably left him with slight mental trauma. Being hunted as prey wasn't the most enjoyable situation. Meeting an eldritch parasite was even less fun.

The night was dark, and the sun wouldn't rise for at least a few more hours. In the relative comfort of the cart, Glenn slowly but surely lost grip on reality, sinking into a well-deserved rest.

"Glenn?" someone asked in a feminine voice, a strangely familiar one.

"Shit!" Glenn startled awake, his heart racing as he reached for his blade. He couldn't allow himself to fall asleep. What if the old man was bringing him somewhere weird? Or try to steal—maybe even kill him?

Wait... Whose voice was that? He frantically rubbed his eyes, blinking a few times at the night's strange hue.

Why is it so... so red?

A shiver ran down Glenn's spine as he found the blood moon of nightmares, its smaller white sister barely visible behind it.

"What the... Again? That can't—"

The green plains and forest were gone, along with the sight of the city. It had been replaced by a long, infinite stretch of black sand. A gentle gust lifted ashen clouds. He could only hear the whistle of the wind rustling against the grains of sand, his heartbeat louder than anything in the desert.

Glenn shivered in the cold. He wrapped his hands around his chest, trying to warm himself.

Something in the sky suddenly shifted.

His eyes widened in terror as the Moon Rift opened once again. The last time it did, he almost died. And then he was forced to live with some shitty parasitic, evil entity in his hand.

Glenn stood, squinting to learn the Fallen Pieces' trajectories. Maybe he could run away?

He searched around the desert, but there was nowhere to hide. Instead, there was someone standing in the distance on top of the tallest dune, watching the shower of glowing fragments.

"Hey!" Glenn shouted. Her back was turned to him, her brown hair reaching to her shoulders.

The noise of the incoming Fallen Piece was like a mortar shot, hissing in the sky. The sound of it falling was quite weird, almost like a voice, but Glenn couldn't spare a moment to listen.

"Shit! Hey, get the hell out of here!" he screamed.

The girl finally noticed, and she turned towards him. Glenn felt his blood turn to ice as he recognized the oh-so familiar face.

Lina. What's my sister doing here? Glenn's mind scrambled for an explanation. But now was not the time. The Fallen Piece was approaching, and there was doubting its impact point.

Lina looked up at the projectile, her mouth slightly open.

Glenn suddenly shot forwards with all his strength, running up the black sand dune desperately. He reached for his sister, but it was too late.

"Oh my."

"Lina!" Glenn screamed as he brusquely sat upright.

He looked around the cart in a panic, his chest rising sharply with each breath. It took a few seconds for him to realize that it was just a nightmare. An eerily realistic nightmare, but a nightmare nonetheless. He grabbed the edge of the wagon to calm himself while trying to avoid the old driver's questioning gaze.

I can't believe that was a dream... He heaved a heavy sigh.

The old man had resumed his route while he was sleeping, driving them closer to King's Rise. Glenn straightened himself, staring at the massive, frozen gate—*the* Frozen Gate. It wouldn't be long before they arrived at their destination.

After coming to his senses, Glenn tightened the bandages around his left arm.

Was that you? Don't play with memories of my sister, he asked with a bit of annoyance.

If Diamanes could mess with his sleep, that meant this forced coexistence was going to be even worse than he initially thought.

Was what me? I'm not responsible for your already poor mental health, alright? Diamanes replied.

Still suspicious, Glenn addressed the driver. "Do you know this part of town, sir?"

The old driver nodded without turning back. "Absolutely. I've been workin' in the Sewers for ages now. Got myself a few friends there, heh. Can't help it with the type of services I provide."

Glenn frowned. *The Sewers? People live there? I'm afraid to ask about those 'services.'*

Diamanes was strangely silent, leaving Glenn alone with his thoughts. Time passed relatively quickly, and the cart finally arrived in front of the

Frozen Gate. A cold wind blew on Glenn's face, the two statues and the towering doors releasing an otherworldly chill.

The structure was already impressive from afar, but it was overwhelming standing beneath it. An edifice that couldn't possibly have been built by humans.

The old driver turned back with his hand held out. Glenn fished out a copper from his dimensional pouch, already enjoying the magical item's usefulness. He gave the coin to the old man, as promised. The driver looked at the copper for a short while before gesturing at Glenn to disembark, mumbling unintelligibly.

Glenn quickly obliged, and the carriage departed the moment he left. Something made him feel like that wasn't the last time he would see that mysteriously powerful old man. He stretched, jumping up and down to get the blood flowing through his sore legs.

I have no idea how long I spent on Mr. Mystery's Magic Ride, but from what my body is telling me, it had to be quite a while.

A little less than six hours, Diamanes replied before snickering. ***You were out cold. I hope it was a pleasant dream.***

Dismissing the entity's ribbing, Glenn glanced at King's Rise's entrance. A dozen knights inspected passersby, funneling them towards an impossibly long queue.

What are they checking for? Identity papers? Maybe a little too modern for this world...

The area surrounding the gate was quite clean, and quite crowded. Many individuals seemed to be in the same situation as him, traveling with fingers gripped on the hilts of their weapons. The majority were on foot, but some led wagons drawn by horses or donkeys. Several carts moved by themselves—probably thanks to the same magic the old driver used. Glenn noticed one luxurious carriage, its windows obscured, hinting at the presence of nobles.

The diversity of travelers impressed Glenn. Old and young, men and women, mercenaries and peasants... With each passing second, King's Rise appeared more and more *the* place to be, reassuring him of his choice.

There weren't many structures outside the Frozen Gate. An inn called the Iced Beer had a worn stable built beside it. Across the road was a flat building with a line nearly as long as the main gate. A large sign hanging above the door read 'Magic Identification Bureau.'

Adjacent to the Bureau was a run-down church that would have appeared abandoned if it wasn't for the robed figures creeping inside. A shiver crawled down his spine as he looked at the decrepit monument. The front door was of rotten wood that had washed out to a dark red shade. Carved in the center was a circle wrapped in thorny vines with a cross at its core.

Just looking at it made Glenn uncomfortable, as if something was breathing down his neck. He averted his gaze, realizing he wasn't the only one who found the church off-putting. Most folks avoided it like the plague, some spitting in its direction with mixed disgust and fear.

Let's avoid that. And those robed people. I know appearances can be deceiving, but that's too many red flags for me. Glenn jeered as he turned away. *Where are all the shops? The blacksmith? The... whatever else they have in medieval cities...*

You're not really in the city proper, are you? Diamanes sneered.

Glenn sighed and gazed at the Frozen Gate, his eyes stopping on the guard post limiting entry into King's Rise.

Perhaps he could try to enter without having to suffer through the unending queue? Maybe he could try to bluff the guards with the Howard family ring and the ornate sword? Glenn considered that option before deciding against it. What if they suspected him of killing and robbing Jefferson? He would be imprisoned and likely executed. This was a medieval world, so it did feel more probable to be put to the blade.

On the other hand, it wouldn't stop him from shamelessly visiting the guard post. Glenn approached the halberds-wielding knights patting down passersby. They crossed their weapons in front of him, casting scornful glances at Glenn as if he were a bag of spoiled milk.

"Halt! State your purpose and identity!"

Glenn smiled as innocently as he could. *I wonder if I should tell them my purpose is to find a way back to my world and to get rid of the parasite in my left hand.*

Fuck you, Glenn.

Glenn ignored Diamanes' irritated voice and concentrated on the guards.

"Good evening, sirs. I came from Eari to visit a friend. My name is Glenn. No last name."

One guard frowned. "I heard there's war brewing between Eari and Satidipug. How are things there? I have a cousin living in Eari."

A bead of sweat pearled down Glenn's forehead. He shook his head, earning a few seconds to think.

"The war..." Glenn mumbled while recalling the horrid battlefield. "There was a skirmish on Retni's Plains. Countless deaths..."

The knight cursed under his breath.

Glenn continued. "To tell you the truth, I wanted to get away from there while I still could. I'm sure I can find work in King's Rise, and my friend should be able to give me a place to live."

The knights nodded. The elder of the two rubbed the back of his neck with a steel-clad hand. "We hope King's Rise will be to your liking. Nonetheless, you'll need to show identification at the Frozen Gate. We had an influx of survivors from Palancar who barely arrived with the shirts on their backs. I'd allow them swift refuge if I could, but we do have orders to follow."

"Right, of course." Glenn held back a groan. "And presuming someone came without the proper paperwork. What... would the process be?"

"Head to the Bureau." The younger knight pointed down the road. "I'd be glad to lead you past the wall when you return."

Glenn cursed mentally while bowing politely at the guards.

"Thank you for the information, sirs…" He glanced at the queue and grimaced. "I won't say see you later, haha…"

The guards laughed, and Glenn walked towards the back of the line, his arms crossed and his thoughts deepening.

That's a little disappointing, but still… I probably made a good choice lying that I fled Eari. Thank the gods I looked at that map yesterday…

Diamanes sighed. ***Whatever. Isn't it funny how they were expecting a war between Satidipug and Eari? And what about that Palancar place he mentioned? Did you see that one on your map?***

Glenn shrugged, the color draining from his face the moment he stepped in front of the Magic Identification Bureau.

The queue stretched a dozen meters, so long it spilled onto the other side of the road and disrupted the flow of traffic.

Do I really have to wait the whole night in order to get an ID? Fuck, it's like going to the DMV all over again.

Glenn's eyes were drawn back to the Iced Beer inn. He could spend the evening there—relax and enjoy the comfort of a warm bed. Inns were nests of information, too. He would probably be able to fill in a few holes just by eavesdropping.

I have to admit that a drink or two wouldn't hurt.

With the lingering scent of blood on him, he also needed a bath. He'd handle the woes of bureaucracy after that.

Glenn pushed open the saloon doors beneath the Iced Beer sign, stopping at the potent scents of alcohol, tobacco, and marijuana.

People of all ages drank and smoked—partying or crying around circular tables. Glenn drew a short breath and walked to the counter, pulling up a free chair. The bald bartender approached him while cleaning a glass.

"What can I get for you?" he asked with a friendly expression.

Glenn examined the rows of bottles behind the bartender. "Do you have something strong? Enough to forget death?"

The bartender smirked. "Hmm, something strong enough to erase death itself... Ah!"

He poured a shot of deep red liquor and extended his palm.

"We only accept upfront payments here. No tabs." He pointed at a sign hanging on the counter reading exactly that.

Glenn sneered and fished a few copper coins from his pocket.

"How much?"

"Two coppers."

Glenn pushed the coins on the table and picked up the shot glass, downing it instantly.

The first of many mistakes. Always drink in moderation.

For a few seconds, he felt nothing. But once the grace period passed, flames roared. Lava. Pure boiling magma ignited his insides like a dragon's breath—a napalm cocktail. Glenn felt the booze reaching his bowels like searing coal. And coal only wished for one thing: to burn.

Glenn coughed and slammed the shot glass onto the counter.

"Wow, this—He coughed—This is strong," he bellowed to the bartender's joy.

He read the tag on the bottle, 'Fiery Spirit Fire Mana, Southern variety.'

Glenn thought back to his partying days, trying to find something equivalent. It had the strength of rhum and a similar taste to tequila.

"Quite the fiery drink indeed." Glenn shook his head. The bartender nodded approvingly.

"You're an impressive kid, aren't ya!" He turned to another customer. "Hey, John! This kid downed a shot of Fiery Spirit like a champ! Can you believe that?"

A mercenary playing cards turned, his eyebrows creased.

"Of course not. I can't believe it! Hey, stop trying to fool me, Winston! I know you want my money, but that's too much!"

Glenn smiled at the exchange, the tension in his shoulders softening.

Is it party time? Haha, excellent! Diamanes celebrated.

Ignoring the entity, Glenn asked the bartender, "Why the surprise? It's only a shot. Who would be knocked out by that?"

Winston paused before conspicuously eyeing a sleeping mercenary.

"That's Marina," he whispered. "And she asked the same thing as you. Only, the result was a little different, hahaha!"

Glenn laughed with the bartender, the horror of the previous day's fading. He looked at his glass—wondering whether he should get another but decided against it.

"Do you have any rooms left over?" he inquired.

Shaking his head, Winston replied, "We're completely full. There are a lot of people trying to get into King's Rise these days. And the Iced Beer is way too small to accommodate them all. Even our stable is filled to the brim!"

"At least you're enjoying the profits," Glenn joked.

He leaned on the counter, deciding on his next move. There probably wouldn't be a free room for a few nights, and the boredom of waiting in the Magic Identification Bureau's queue would send him to sleep.

Guess I can just hang out here until the line clears up.

Glenn thanked the bartender and headed for the table of the mercenary, John. He was playing cards with a few other patrons.

"Mind if I join the game?" Glenn asked as he pulled in a chair. John made a wry smile and drank some ale from a wooden tankard.

"Only if you got the funds for the buy-in!"

The other players cackled as they gestured at the copper coins on the table—around a dozen each. Glenn moistened his lips and threw in a dozen copper.

"That enough?"

John patted Glenn's shoulder before dealing the cards. It was a standard fifty-two-card deck—only the Jack, Queen, and King were replaced by a

Wyvern, Phoenix, and Dragon. It looked like they were playing this world's version of Texas Hold'em.

"I'm telling you in advance, kid. We ain't pulling punches here!" John warned with a chuckle.

Another mercenary laughed and slapped John on the thigh. "You ain't pulling shit! Did you already forget you lost five games in a row?"

John grimaced and looked at his hand. "You'll see. I'll get it all back, Roland. I'll get it all back..."

Glenn smiled at his own cards, a pair of Dragons. "Don't worry, old man. I'll try not to ruin you too much."

The other players exploded in laughter while John's face darkened. Roland yelled to the bartender, "Another pint for our friend!"

Glenn grinned widely, happy to finally have one normal moment after all those horrors.

The last thing he remembered was winning the round and Diamanes' laugh echoing in his mind mockingly. After that...

Blackout.

Chapter 13

HANGOVER

The door to Glenn's bedroom slammed open, waking him slightly. But it wasn't until the absolutely god-awful K-Pop song started blasting in his ears that he woke up.

"You have an interesting lifestyle, you know? How the hell can you still get good grades?" his sister yelled above the tune, pulling Glenn out of a profound coma.

He blinked, his eyelids glued together and his tongue pasty.

"You're one to talk," he replied in a raspy voice. "Couldn't you wake me up in a gentler manner?"

Glenn held his ringing head. Last night was incredible—the craziest party since he started university. They'd just passed their midterms. If that wasn't the time to celebrate, when was it?

Propping himself up, Glenn tried to recall the events. Drinks, dancing, girls—none that he could bring home—and a bit of drugs. He was more of an alcohol guy, though, ever since that incident. He could still feel the music beating through his chest and the smell of vodka and tobacco.

"I lost my pouch. You know, the pink one?" Lina exclaimed as Glenn dragged himself out of his bed and switched off the hell-sent speaker, finally escaping the K-Pop.

"Why the hell would it be in my room?" Glenn asked.

Lina grunted as she pilfered through his shelves. She stormed out, leaving him with a painful headache and a half-filled water bottle. Glenn quenched his thirst before turning towards the door.

"Yo, Lina. You should look in the top-left drawer in your room!" Glenn shouted. He waited for a few minutes.

"Thanks!" his sister replied.

Glenn smiled, but it quickly faded away when he tried to get out of bed. *Oh yeah, I could probably use another hour of sleep. Maybe two.*

* * *

The mud in Glenn's mouth almost tasted good. He couldn't remember what happened last night, thanks to one too many drinks he had defeating the mercenaries at Eari's Hold'em. His brain felt like it became a punching bag, and the rest of his body didn't fare any better. Thinking was a challenge on its own, which wasn't helped by the constant laughter of the *parasite* living in his left hand.

Hahahaha, that was fun! Well, that's a good lesson for you at least! Always drink in moderation!

"Shu' up, you..." Glenn's eyes rolled back as he emptied his stomach, his consciousness threatening to slip away like a salmon.

After making sure he wouldn't puke *again*, Glenn propped himself up, carefully standing on wobbly legs. With sluggish movements, he wiped off the muck and vomit, his sleeve already well-tainted with blood and other fluids.

Glenn's dizziness cleared as his gaze fixed on the bloodstains.

"W-What the hell happened?" His head throbbed while he checked his surroundings. "Fuuuuck..."

It was dark, and there were other people lying in the mud—some he could recognize, such as John and Roland. Most had bloodied faces or burned hair and clothes, but none seemed too injured.

"Heh..." Glenn smirked, enjoying the small victory of being the first one awake.

He sighed in relief when he reached for the dimensional pouch. His corroded sword was gone. A pity, but that piece of scrap wasn't that big of a loss. There was still the ornate one in the pouch, after all.

Glenn looked up, finding the sky to be particularly cloudy. *Still not morning yet.*

I'd say in a few hours it will be, Diamanes commented, his voice retaining a hint of mirth.

Glenn's eyes eventually adjusted to the darkness, and he realized he was behind the inn, likely thrown out after unspeakable shenanigans.

He grimaced and walked with unsteady steps towards John, kneeling next to him. When shaking him gently failed, he slapped the mercenary's cheek. His efforts were in vain; the man refused to wake up—still in deep sleep with a face battered and body bruised.

"He got hit more than once." Glenn winced. He lifted his shirt, revealing similar bruises on his waist. "And so did I, apparently."

At least he was alive. No one appeared to be dead, just roughed up. Glenn wasn't too worried about the other unconscious customers; they were big boys and girls who knew how to handle themselves.

"What the hell happened here?"

I could tell you, but it would ruin the fun, hehe, Diamanes taunted.

Ignoring the entity, he walked to the inn's entrance. One door hung off its hinges while the other slowly swung in the breeze, creaking slightly.

Glenn dusted off his shoulders and stepped inside, dodging a collapsing plank of wood. The entire inn had been transformed into a battlefield overnight.

Of the dozen tables, only four remained, covered in broken glass and blood. The rest were wrecked in various, creative ways. A chair even dangled from the ceiling, its feet nailed to the beams.

Grimacing, Glenn walked around the mess, heading for the bartender, Winston. He was sweeping the debris with a disheartened expression. When he raised his eyes to meet Glenn's, his countenance darkened, and he rushed behind the bar without a word.

"What exactly went down last night?" Glenn asked curiously, gagging when he found a full set of teeth on the counter. "I can't remember a thing, not even the very obvious fight that happened. And from what I can see, it should be hard to forget."

"Ah!" Winston stood a second later while holding a staff crowned with a large, red crystal. He aimed it at Glenn.

Maybe it was luck or his paranoia; Glenn couldn't tell what made him dodge the bolt of fire.

He rolled away, narrowly avoiding the blast that burned a smoldering hole in a nearby table.

Glenn hurriedly jumped behind the rubble. The bartender aimed at him once again, his eyes bloodshot and his expression twisted in hatred.

"You cursed bastard! How dare you show your face here?!"

The cursed bastard in question dashed for the door, only for a projectile to fly right by his nose, burning the tips of his hair. He fell back to his hiding place, his heart racing as he reached for the sword in his dimensional pouch.

A second strike hit a table, and it exploded. Wood splinters shot out like shrapnel and pierced through Glenn's arms. He winced and crouched close to the floorboards.

"You piece of shit! First, you drained my entire cellar! You're a monster! How can you drink so much?!" the bartender screamed, shooting a few more fiery blasts at Glenn, who sprinted from one table to another. Sadly, there was only one remaining by the time Winston paused to catch his breath.

I'd love some help unless you're as useless as I thought, Diamanes, Glenn pleaded. The table's legs crackled, threatening to break at any second. The next blast would be the last.

I can try, but I'd need you to catch that fire bolt, Diamanes instructed.

"Catch it? Are you insane?"

That was the proof he required. Diamanes was batshit crazy. The next shot shattered the table, covering Glenn in splinters and exposing him to the shooter.

He hurriedly stood and raised his hands.

"And to top it all off, you set *their* Moongrass stash on fire!" Winston shouted hysterically, the red crystal burning with a threatening light.

Glenn suddenly bowed at a perfect ninety-degree angle, a bead of sweat pearling down his nose. "I apologize wholeheartedly for this mess, sir. I'll cover the damages, so let's stop it here, alright?"

The bartender froze, his staff trembling until he relaxed his arm. His anger faded, leaving space for sadness and resignation. A single tear fell down his cheek and splattered against the counter.

"You..." He collapsed on a chair, his voice shattered. "Do you even realize whose stash you destroyed?"

Glenn shuddered when he saw the bartender's face covered in tears. The latter wiped his eyes and took a bottle off the shelf. He tried to pour himself a drink, but not a single drop was left. Winston stared at the bottle like it had committed treason and chucked it away. The sound of shattering glass startled Glenn, and he sunk his hand into his dimensional pouch. He was ready to pull the ornate sword out at any moment.

"Haha... Even this one is empty." Winston laughed dejectedly, his face pale.

Glenn fished out half of his gold coins. If he was right, that sum would be enough to pay for the damages.

"We're all screwed... all screwed..." The bartender was lamenting his misfortune when his eyes caught the glitter of gold.

His despair faded, replaced by a wide, welcoming smile. Even traces of his tears disappeared. He wiped the snot and saliva off his face and straightened his posture before rubbing his hands together. Unable to blink, his gaze glued to the golden coins like a thirsty man finding water in the desert. Suddenly, he realized how he was behaving and cleared his throat.

"Hmm. I... I suppose I can overlook it this one time, young master. So long as the damages are repaid."

Young master. Glenn wanted to smirk but didn't. Money spoke the same language everywhere. He tossed the coins into the bartender's hands and glanced at the fire staff.

"How much for that staff?"

Winston, startled, swiftly hid the coins. He extended both hands to offer his staff, kneeling.

"For you, young master, my fire staff comes free of charge! You must be a Mage! Please. Remember my name, Winston, when you climb King's Rise!"

Glenn chuckled nervously, taking the staff and swinging it around. It was surprisingly heavy, the red crystal making up most of its weight.

Too bad I have no idea of how to use magic... And it's not like I can ask the bartender, can I? Well, whatever, it probably isn't that difficult. And it looks much more powerful than a sword anyway.

Glenn smiled as he pushed the staff inside his dimensional pouch. "Thanks, Winston. I won't forget you."

After almost getting incinerated alive, forgetting about him would prove difficult. Winston nodded frantically, smiling with all his teeth. Well, the ones that were left, which wasn't many.

With a new weapon and promises of magic, Glenn stepped out of the inn. His guilt from provoking a fight and ruining a business faded. *That could have gone much worse.*

* * *

Winston marveled at the gold coins in his grasp. He bit one, just to make sure. And yes, it was real. Genuine, pristine gold, glimmering in the light like fallen stars. He had never even *seen* gold before, but he knew that this was the real stuff.

He let out a happy sigh, sending a thankful prayer to Plutus, the God of his cherished Golden Church. Although he was no priest, he was faithfully devoted to his deity, and now his devotion had yielded rewards far beyond his imagination.

Winston came from a land far away, in the Southern Continent. He had nothing aside from his expertise running taverns. He picked an old, crumbling building in front of King's Rise, hoping to earn enough to secure a place within the city for his family. Never had he thought he would amass a sum that could elevate him to mercantile rank. He would have set the Iced Beer ablaze twice over for a *single* gold coin.

With renewed zeal, he resolved to donate ten percent of his earnings to the Church. He gratefully stowed the coins away in a secret compartment before pondering about *them*. Everyone knew of *them*. After all, they didn't make themselves discreet with their recruiting tactics. *They* owned the stash of Moongrass and probably already heard of the scorched supply.

Winston knew he couldn't escape their notice. Thankfully, the spotlight wouldn't be on him. It'd be on that young master.

"Best of luck, young master." Winston prayed, his eyes closed with a resigned expression. "I'll be there for your funeral."

Chapter 14

GETTING AN ID (LEGALLY)

Glenn stood outside the Iced Beer, staring at the dark sky while holding his bruised waist.

"I swear I won't ever touch any Fiery Spirit again…" he muttered while shaking his head.

That night had been anything but productive. He lost money, gained no valuable information, and to top it off, the line to the Magic Identification Bureau hadn't decreased.

What's wrong with releasing stress, even if it's by breaking a few tables and ribs? Diamanes asked in a candid tone.

Alright, Diamanes, Glenn sighed as he joined the queue. *Don't you have anything interesting to share? Some funny stories? Jokes? I don't know?*

Diamanes snickered. ***I do, but sorry. I'm too busy watching your high school years. Pure comedy gold, by the way. Most entertaining.***

"Good for you, Diamanes. Good for you," Glenn hissed through his teeth.

Bored out of his mind, he entertained himself by checking out the other people in the queue. There were mostly traveling mercenaries, recognizable from their gear and hard-boiled expressions. He noticed a few families too, their eyes darting anxiously. Glenn listened to the discussions, curious.

"No, no! We're not going back!" wheezed the husband to his wife. "I refuse to have our kids live in a feeding ground for monsters."

His wife reeled, trembling. "B-But you heard the rumors, didn't you?"

The husband stared ahead, hugging his two children tightly. "Rumors are nothing compared to what's out there. We will be safe behind the walls..."

He patted his older boy's head and smiled weakly. "And who knows? King's Rise is the land of opportunity. Perhaps one of you two warriors will make us rich!"

His kids laughed while his wife chewed her fingernails. "We could have helped rebuild Palancar..."

The husband scoffed. "And stay with those mad bastards? You can go and worship a stone by yourself. Our children's future is in King's Rise!"

Glenn scratched the back of his head. *Shit, between the Moon Rift and that necromancer running around, these people can't catch a break. I'm starting to understand the size of that queue...*

* * *

After dozing off more than once, Glenn reached the entrance of the Magic Identification Bureau. Uncertain, he waited for an invitation.

Several minutes passed, and a monotonous voice spoke from behind the door. "Neeeext."

Glenn flinched and happily obliged. Stepping inside first revealed a yawning guard. Then an odd mechanical contraption built from brass gears, occasionally hissing steam. The machine had a white crystal for a heart. From time to time, its light intensified, an event followed by the release of searing mist.

"Please come to the counter," the monotonous voice called out.

He turned his head to find a desk with a tired woman sitting at it, her hair disheveled and her skin pale. She looked at Glenn with empty eyes and indescribable weariness.

"Identification costs one silver. The full package costs double."

Glenn's eyebrows rose in puzzlement. *The full package? Can I get some bonus out of this? A starting kit for my life in King's Rise?*

Opting for more than less, he produced two silver coins and an empathetic smile. "The full package, please."

The woman moved sluggishly, pushing the coins into a jar. She retrieved a document from under the desk and glanced up at Glenn.

"I take it you can read and write?" she asked while judging his clothes.

He nodded without hesitation. The clerk handed him the paper and a pen.

"Please fill out this form first. Afterwards, we'll proceed with the Convergence."

Glenn complied and gave the document a quick read. He almost sneered due to its absurdity.

Am I a terrorist? What? Do they expect terrorists to answer yes? thought Glenn before replying negatively.

There were mainly common questions, such as name, place of residence, and date of birth. He couldn't put his birthday on Earth, could he? Luckily, the date was printed in the top right corner of the page—17/05/3032. It struck him as peculiar that this world used the Gregorian calendar, but he wasn't going to question good luck.

The form also inquired about his purpose for coming to King's Rise. Glenn settled on his fabricated excuse of visiting a friend and avoiding the war between Satidipug and Eari. Once completed, he signed and handed the document back to the clerk. She slid the paper into the machine. Soon after, a hand-shaped container emerged from the contraption, shrouded in steam.

The clerk gestured at the container and bowed, her hair falling messily over her tired face. "Please press your hand inside to begin the Convergence."

Glenn complied cautiously. The metal mold was surprisingly soft and warm to the touch, almost like a living thing. The clerk triggered various mechanisms under the silent guard's watch, and the contraption emitted a mechanical voice reminiscent of a human's.

"Please swear you have no intention of opposing His Majesty, the royal family, or their relatives."

Glenn nodded instinctively, completely fascinated by the enigmatic machine.

Claws suddenly shot out and restrained him. "Have a safe Convergence, sir."

A flash of light blinded Glenn. His limbs jolted uncontrollably, as if they were being electrocuted. Only his left hand remained untouched. Perhaps Diamanes' presence deterred whatever shenanigans were taking place.

Wow. What is that? Diamanes blurted out in an alarmed tone. ***They're putting a seal on you. Huh, maybe... Yeah, I can just get rid of it. They won't notice.***

Glenn grimaced as pain rang through his entire body.

Argh... What? A seal? Fu— Argh, damn it! Glenn's eyes widened as he tried his hardest to escape the machine's hold.

Get this over with first. We'll talk later. Diamanes tsked.

After a few minutes that felt like days, the pain finally stopped, and the mechanical voice spoke again.

"Glenn, 21 years old. Human, Beginner Initiate. Purpose for coming to King's Rise: refugee. Length of residence: one year. Please renew your license before the end of the specified period or upgrade it. The Magi Brotherhood thanks you for your sponsorship and welcomes you to the path."

The metal claws finally released Glenn, freeing him from the torture machine. He gasped and fell to his knees. His heart throbbed with a strange sensation, something he never felt before—something *bizarre*.

The guard helped him up while the clerk bowed not so graciously, struggling not to collapse from exhaustion.

"Thank you, sir. The Convergence is complete. Have a pleasant stay in King's Rise."

Glenn peered at her as if she was crazy and left the Bureau by a backdoor, avoiding the unending queue. He sat nearby and looked at his right hand, watching as a tattoo gleaming with white, mystical light slowly melded into his skin. It was a rune, similar to a trident, enclosed in a simple circle. He could have understood *something* had he been able to study the rune closer, but the tattoo faded, leaving no trace of its existence.

"So now I have strange shit on both my hands... Fuck..." Glenn sighed as he rubbed his tired eyes.

He searched for a more secluded place—a small grove along the outskirts that would provide peace and quiet. He took off the bandages covering his left hand, revealing the purple skin and the grinning mouth.

"Ahhh, the air still tastes delicious. I know you might have some weird unrealized kinks, but could you not muffle me next time? I'm not into breath play." Diamanes jeered as Glenn tried to clear his mind. He found a fallen tree to use as a seat.

"Alright, then..." He drew a deep breath and concentrated. "In order, what did they do to me? I thought I'd obtain an ID card. A document, or something like that."

Diamanes moistened his plump lips, still grinning as wickedly as ever. **"The *identification* you speak of is in your right hand. This is a magical ID, printed on your soul."**

Glenn frowned. Printed on his soul? That didn't sound too good. How could something be printed on a soul? Was a soul an actual, tangible thing?

"What about that seal you said you got rid of? And what the fuck was that torture machine?"

"I'm guessing that's a security measure to make sure you won't kill the King and his family, which is reasonable. Well, I still got rid of it, *just in case*. Although, I imagine the consequences of breaking the seal would be quite bad."

"Like what?"

Diamanes smirked. **"Remember Father Albenas?"**

"Oh."

"Oh, indeed. As for the machine, it used a Convergence function. It created the First Circle around your Mana Heart, an organ only some humans naturally possess. Others are suited to Aura. But, let's skip that and go straight to the congratulations! You officially became what is universally known as a Mage, a being that can harness mystical powers. No idea how they rank it in this world, though."

The influx of information short-circuited Glenn's brain. He looked at his hands as if they weren't his own. "So, I'm... a magician now?"

Diamanes sighed. "Yes, you are. A level one Mage, if you wish. You'll have to learn new spells and rank up as many Circles as you can. But seeing how tough it is for you to even *understand* my words, I feel like you're going to stay at the lowest level for a while. Who trapped me with this loser, I swear..."

Glenn smiled fakely with his teeth clenched. "You're the one who trapped *yourself* in my hand, remember?"

Diamanes blew raspberries. "Whatever. Can't we go kill something? That'd be fun."

Glenn drew a deep breath, digging into the dimensional pouch and pulling out the ornate sword.

"Maybe I really should cut off my hand. Perhaps it'll at least shut you up?" Glenn suggested with cold eyes, unsheathing the sword and contemplating the gleaming metal.

Diamanes laughed mockingly. "You've already threatened me once with that. Sorry, as I said before, I'll just grow back!"

Glenn stabbed the sword into the ground and hid his face in his hands.

"Now you have to admit I'm useful. I got rid of that seal, meaning you'll be able to oppose the King and the royal family of King's Rise as much as you'd like!" Diamanes happily exclaimed, earning another sigh out of its host.

"Why would I want to oppose anyone though?"

"Use your imagination," Diamanes grunted. **"Anyway, there's still a power I couldn't tell you how to command. We didn't have the occasion, after all. It's very simple. First, you need to—"**

Thwip!

Something shot through the air, whistling past Glenn's head. Instinctively, he protected his face with his hand, just in time for an arrow to lodge itself into Diamanes' mouth and shut him up. The tip was mere inches away from Glenn's eye, threatening to blind him.

"Argh! Fuck!" Glenn rolled on the ground, holding his hand in pain. Blood flowed out of the gash, tainting the mud red.

Glenn hurriedly reached for his sword. Each movement he took made the wound throb, the arrow shaft twisting his muscles and flesh.

A group in black, hooded robes approached. One of them held a bow.

"Fuck! Who are you fuckers?!" Glenn shouted at them, struggling to hold his blade.

"You fool... How dare you mess with our plans and believe you can continue to live?"

They lunged at Glenn. Thorny vines shot out of the ground and wrapped around him, sending Glenn's sword flying away. The thorns pierced his skin and fed on his blood.

Glenn desperately tried to free himself, but the more he thrashed, the more the vines tightened around his chest and limbs. He opened his mouth to scream for help, but no sound came out.

"May you see our God's light and repent in agony, maggot," the hooded man spat before swinging his pommel into Glenn's head with brutal force. Glenn blinked. Stars and echoing laughter danced in front of him.

Without a chance to fight back, Glenn's consciousness faded, and he slumped to the ground, his forehead bleeding profusely.

Chapter 15

ABYSS

Pain.

Glenn felt that more than anything else.

A searing hole pierced through his left hand, and his head throbbed with increasing intensity with each passing second. Thinking was a challenge. So was waking up.

He shifted aside, wincing when he realized there was something wrapped around his wrists and ankles, weighing them down. Something heavy and cold, like steel.

H-How??

Glenn coughed and pushed through the exhaustion, opening his eyelids only to find pure darkness. His heart skipped a beat as he wondered if he had his eyes gouged out.

Another second of consciousness reassured him that no, he wasn't blind.

How did I end up here? Glenn questioned.

He was starting to get numb to the itchy, burning discomfort from the arrow that pierced his hand. *Right, an arrow. Those suspicious, robed guys attacked and knocked me out... Did they put me in a cell? Why?*

Glenn grunted as the pain suddenly intensified, shooting through his body like a tidal wave. He leaned against the moist, cold stone behind him, shivering as a few drops of water fell on his face.

His seat was damp, with a mixed scent of dirt, blood, and piss. There was no wind and no sound, aside from the occasional clanking of chains in the distance and the scurrying of rats.

Glenn opened his mouth to call out to whoever imprisoned him, but no sound came. He tried again. Despite his best effort, his attempt was futile. The air passed through his throat, but once it reached his tongue, it disappeared.

Magic... Glenn gritted his teeth. Yes, that was probably it. His attackers had restrained him with thorny vines, which were also likely magic. He pulled on his chains, but the steel bit through his flesh.

Fuck... Tears welled up in his eyes as he heaved for air.

Why? Why is this happening to me? What... What did I do to deserve this?

Glenn cried silently. He never asked to come to this world. And now, he was mute, he'd been shot, and he was probably waiting either for more torture or death. Where was Diamanes when he needed him?

Diamanes?

Shit! Glenn called out to the entity a few more times, but only the eerie silence of his cell replied to him. His heart froze as he considered one option that might relieve him from this *hellish* world. His teeth chattered as he pushed his tongue through them.

Faint footsteps in the distance halted him. The sound grew louder with each step until it stopped before the cell. He held his breath.

A key entering the lock echoed, followed by the creaking of heavy steel. A crack of light appeared in the darkness, growing wider as the door opened. Someone entered with a candle—a robed man with pale hands and a face hidden under a black hood.

The individual pulled back his hood, revealing a mysterious pattern of scars. His cheeks were gaunt and his sclera dark, with even darker circles underneath. His eyes popped open, unblinking in a crazed expression. He shoved the candle into Glenn's face, who winced at the heat. A drop of wax sizzled as it touched his skin.

Glenn opened his mouth to scream, but no sound came. The scarred-face man didn't seem too bothered by his victim's suffering. He waved the light in front of Glenn's eyes, trying to find something within.

Suddenly, he drew an ice pick and slammed it into Glenn's right knee, pinning it to the floor. Unbearable pain tormented Glenn as he screamed silently for help, his cursed throat unable to transmit his cries.

The jailer's smile stretched, and he slowly pulled out a thick syringe. He forced Glenn's mouth open, shoving the needle down his pharynx and administering its contents.

Tears flowed down Glenn's cheeks as he was forced to swallow the substance. He gasped for air, his throat dry and sticky. He tried to puke, but nothing came out. The dark liquid traveled down his esophagus of its own volition.

It was thick and tasted like metal, a viscous mixture that was similar to… Glenn reeled in disgust. The jailer's grin grew when his prisoner understood what he had been fed. Satisfied, he ripped the ice pick from Glenn's knee and kicked him in the stomach.

Gasping for air, the last thing Glenn saw was the jailer's fist. He almost lost consciousness, but a throbbing sensation pulsed through his stomach, beating strangely. It rose to his head and then to the rest of his limbs— digging through his veins and carving a path for itself. Glenn foamed at the mouth.

Not long after, darkness dragged his mind away, freeing him temporarily from his suffering.

* * *

It wasn't his grumbling stomach that woke Glenn, nor the rats running over him to check if he was dead. It wasn't the incessant dripping of rotten water, nor the scent of piss and shit either. This time, it was the growing anxiety that clenched his chest.

Why did I wake up? Can't I spend more time asleep?

The rusty iron door swung open, and his jailer appeared, bearing a candle and a wicked grin. Glenn cried while he pulled on his chains. Out of despair, he bit his tongue, aiming to sever it, but his jailer hurriedly stopped him. He pried Glenn's jaws open and shoved a dirty, piss-stained rag inside.

Glenn's eyes rolled back as the hope of freedom disappeared like a candle's flame in a typhoon. The jailer grabbed his left hand and checked the wound; he shrugged and turned to the other. He proceeded to break each of Glenn's fingers—enjoying an evil pleasure with each snap.

Once he finished all five, he pulled out a new syringe and shoved it down Glenn's throat once again. Glenn didn't try to fight back, his mind broken and his body weak. The pain returned, twisting through his frail form like a vicious snake.

He foamed at the mouth, trembling, as the jailer laughed and kicked him. Once he left again, Glenn lost consciousness in the comfortable darkness.

He didn't dream when he slept. He never truly slept at all. He was so tired. Yet, so hungry, thirsty, and in pain that he couldn't even *think* of escaping. There was no way out. No exit. No miraculous plan that could save him. He knew that. Diamanes was gone.

Perhaps he had hallucinated from the start. There were no buckets to relieve himself, and Glenn couldn't move anyway. So he defecated on himself.

Days, nights, and weeks passed. He couldn't tell. A second could have been an hour, and a day could have been a minute. Everything was the same in this shithole. Even his jailer struggled to find new ways to torture him.

More often than not, Glenn succumbed to fever, dreaming of things that didn't exist. Or maybe they did. He so desperately needed illusions of hope.

Pain. Wake. Suffer. Drink the blood. Suffer. Collapse.

That was his life now. How long had it been? He had no idea. His voice had still not come back, nor had Diamanes'. Glenn gave up on them like he gave up on life. He was just a bag of meat enduring one punch after another. One positive was that his left hand wasn't hurting him much anymore. Glenn probably had to be thankful for the pain tolerance he gained from this.

Mr. Scarred-Face was the only jailer in this prison, it seemed. Glenn had given him a nickname, in hopes that, if he found the bastard in hell, he could kill him.

And yet.

Glenn remembered something from a book he had been forced to read: "Man is a creature that can get accustomed to anything, and I think that is the best definition of him." That quote stuck with him.

It wasn't hard to believe the author's words before. It was a classic story. The hero rises through pain and adversity to become, well, a hero.

Heh.

Now that he was experiencing hell itself, Glenn could say with certainty that the book was some bullshit.

What doesn't kill you only makes you stronger? I'd rather be dead than strong right now. But... Even taking my own life is impossible.

Glenn considered he was going crazy. He was starting to imagine foliage growing in the gaps between each stone brick and in the pool of blood, shit, and piss laying under him. He could almost see it, no matter if his eyes were open or not. He swore heard faint whispers, mocking and tempting him with promises of freedom. But what was the use of listening to whispers of something that didn't exist? Could they kill him? He couldn't kill himself. What guaranteed that they could?

The shadows danced to the rhythm of the whispers, warping and twisting...

"Accept us, Glenn..."

"Only say the word..."

"We'll do anything for you..."

Shut up.

"Death is right over the corner, Glenn. Just say the word... Make a deal with us..."

Shut up. Shut up. Shut up!

"Accept us and become more than you are, you weak wimp..."

"You wretched failure..."

"We can become your strength and make you more than a piece of garbage..."

Glenn gritted his teeth and roared silently with hatred, shutting down the voices. He couldn't speak, but he could still scream in his mind.

Shut the fuck up! I don't even want to die anymore! Shit! You — ...non-existing illusion pieces of shit! Fuck off!

The whispers reeled back in shock, apparently surprised he could reply to them in such a vindictive manner. Glenn had enough of all this bullshit. Maybe he would try one last suicide attempt, just so that he could rip the skin off the Scarred-Face bastard. He would do it with his teeth if he had to. The pain of his restraints was nothing compared to the growing hatred in his chest, burning with a fire that could consume everything. Fear and despair... All melted away in front of Glenn's fiery rage.

"Wow, isn't this a pleasure for the eyes. They really fucked you up, Glenn." another voice said, earning Glenn's sneer.

Yeah, whatever, you hallucination. Go back to the hole you crawled out. Fuck this shit.

Diamanes laughed, startling Glenn. *Wait. Diamanes? Or... Or was it not?*

"No, no, please. Keep on believing I'm an illusion. Hey, who knows? Maybe this is all a simulation? Blue pill or red pill, Glenn?"

Glenn gasped for air as tears fell. He silently sighed in relief and leaned back against the stone.

Which pill allows me to get out of here and bash Scarred-Face's skull in? he asked without hope.

Despite the darkness, Glenn still saw Diamanes' wicked grin. **"Fuck pills. Let's rip apart some bastards."**

Glenn agreed. Nonetheless, he couldn't help but frown at the entity.

Where the hell were you while I was getting... He grimaced.

"Remember when I said I would grow back if you cut me off? Well, I did exactly that. I grew back up and fixed the damage that damned arrow inflicted."

After a pause, Glenn realized the pain in his left hand had faded. He believed he had only grown numb, but...

"Anyway, you smell. How much time have we spent down here?" Diamanes asked in disgust.

Too long.

"I certainly believe that. I can taste the filth in my sacred mouth. Ugh."

Glenn shook his head. *I need to escape.*

Diamanes laughed mockingly. **"Well, just leave then?"**

Slowly biting on his lip, Glenn found it hard to deal with the entity without his usual patience.

"*Sigh*. Don't worry. I have the means to get rid of that Silence curse."

Do whatever it takes, Glenn ordered coldly.

Diamanes invited Glenn to press his left hand on his neck. Glenn complied as he pulled on the chains. The second his palm touched his flesh, he heard a suction noise. It was like something stuck in his throat finally disappeared.

"Tastes like shit, but a meal is a meal. I guess it's still better than an arrow in the teeth, heh," Diamanes jeered.

Glenn heaved, terrified at the idea of even *trying* to speak. He coughed and forced out a sound, his eyes watering when he succeeded.

"Ahhhh!" Glenn's voice was hoarse. It had been so long... He felt like he needed to learn how to speak all over again.

Diamanes grinned, his white teeth gleaming in the darkness. That sight was strangely comforting. The only happy thing to happen to him in this damned place was an evil demon's awakening.

"You're welcome, dear obligee. Now, should we get out of here?"

Glenn's lips twisted in a predatory manner, his eyes were resolute and a little insane. Whatever type of demon Diamanes was, he would shake his hand ten times over if it meant he could leave this place.

"Let's... *Cough*... Let's make that jailer bastard pay."

Chapter 16

CELL 3333, OR MR. SCARRED-FACE *WILL* GET HIS DOSE OF VIOLENCE

Diamanes let out a low whistle as he appraised the condition of Glenn's body. There were various creative wounds covering his feet, hands, torso, and face. He had a dozen lacerations across his chest and more than a dozen broken bones. It was an absolute miracle Glenn was still alive. Most of his teeth were gone, and the rest were cracked. His nose had been bashed in, and his eyebrows had been burned off too. Before, he had a relatively handsome face. But now, he'd frighten anyone who dared glance at him.

"Damn, there's a lot of work to be done. How many liters of that *filth* did they force you to drink?"

Glenn responded with a feeble shake of his head, his memories clouded. It could have been a hundred syringes. Maybe more.

"*Cough*... What... What is it?" he asked in a raspy voice.

"Beast Blood. It is supposed to kill those who ingest it, but... it seems like they added something to it. I'm not sure what. Something..." Diamanes paused. **"divine? This is some weird shit."**

Glenn drew one swift breath after the other. So that was indeed blood he had been drinking. He didn't want to believe it at first. At least it wasn't human blood... His thoughts raced. What effects would Beast Blood have on him? He shivered as he thought back to Father Albenas. Was that the same as sipping from *its* veins—that thick, black blood? Glenn retched in disgust, dismissing the image.

"Ugh... Why would my jailer feed me monster blood?" he mumbled. "It doesn't make sense. Why lock a random guy up—"

"It wasn't random. You burned their stash of Moongrass, remember?"

Fuck. That's the 'they' Winston was yapping about.

"Sure, then... *Cough*... Why bother feeding me this shit when they could just kill me?" he pondered, his mind recovering thanks to Diamanes' presence. Being able to talk to someone again was doing him a world of good, soothing the loneliness he had felt ever since he'd been locked up.

Glenn paled. "Is... Is death the sole outcome of consuming Beast Blood?"

Diamanes remained silent for a few seconds before replying, **"Hmm... the best outcome is indeed dying. But it might be possible to create monsters by feeding humans Beast Blood. Not a precise transformation, but the result would be incredible strength—with little to no mental capacity to use it. Be grateful you didn't end up like that."**

Why spend so much time creating a monster... Unless... it's not one monster but many. This is a prison, after all. Maybe... No, there certainly are other victims who've been fed Beast Blood in this place. How many? A hundred? Two hundred? More than that?

Glenn wouldn't know until he escaped from his cell. One question remained: why would an organization want to create an army of monsters?

He paused before chuckling dejectedly. The answer was *in* the question. *Then, what would they want to do with this army? Destroy the world? Did my unluckiness place me straight into the main villain's goal?*

"That would be ironically funny," Diamanes commented.

Glenn shook his head. *I'll have to unravel this later. Right now, my priority is to get the hell out of here.*

"Let's do this!" He stuck his tongue out in concentration. **"Give me a minute... Clench your teeth. It's not going to feel good..."**

Glenn raised a barren brow but hurriedly complied as he began to feel very, very hot—and not in a handsome way. His forehead dripped with sweat as the heat increased to the point Glenn felt like his blood was boiling. It was very different from the burn when he ingested Beast Blood. He felt something *leaving* his body instead of settling within.

Something viscous oozed from his orifices. It was painfully hot, but Glenn enjoyed the sensation; it was as if he was cleansing himself. His bones began to realign, breaking and reforming themselves suitably with a disgusting crackling noise. Glenn almost lost consciousness more than once, but the promise of revenge was more than enough to help him push through the torture.

Flesh regrew as wounds healed for over an hour—a very, very painful hour. It was like his whole body had been rebuilt from top to bottom. All the ooze, probably the Beast Blood, pooled from his left hand, mixing with the filth and disappearing.

Finally, the last drop fell, and every ache subsided. Glenn sighed loudly in relief. Not accounting for the restraints still biting into his flesh, he never felt better.

The torpor that had taken over faded, leaving him with crystal clear senses. He slowly clenched his fists, enjoying moving his muscles without the pain of broken bones.

He sat up, effortlessly pulling on the heavy metal restraints. His body felt light—so light he was pretty sure he could fly if he wished. Glenn yanked the chain restraining his arm, feeling it almost breaking off the wall. He stood to the limit of the chains' reach, stretching as best he could.

"Alright, we should be all done. I've purified the Beast Blood and used its energy to fix your body. You got all the benefits, and none of the filth!" Diamanes cackled. **"Wow, I really did an excellent job with the reconstruction! You look even better than before! Hey, maybe it was a fortunate turn of events in the end?"**

Glenn threw a deathly stare at his left hand. Not even the promise of the most handsome face in the universe would force him back into this hole.

"Is—*cough*... Is that reconstruction the reason I feel so much stronger?"

He opened and closed his fists, feeling an incredible surge of energy. Everything felt foreign, and it took a while for him to get used to his new capabilities. He could pinpoint the precise position of the rats running outside his cell, and he had improved vision in total darkness.

"Superhuman physique and senses. Excellent! I wasn't joking when I said that you should be grateful for the torture! You will have a real hard time dying in your new body!" Diamanes laughed without an ounce of consideration for his host.

If Glenn had to guess the entity's thoughts, it would probably be something along the lines of, "Ah-ha! My host finally has a body worth transporting my sacred presence!"

Now, what remained was to wait. Wait for the bastard that tortured him to... Shit, he really needed to know how much time passed.

It'd be nice if I could get out of these restraints without alerting everyone in this damned prison...

"I have a solution for that. I am a *hand*. I can *take* things and *use* things once acquired," Diamanes said, laced with smugness.

Glenn glanced at his hand, perplexed.

Diamanes sighed. **"Just... Just place me on the chain."**

Glenn grabbed the chain, waiting for the next step. He suddenly felt something drain out of his body, leaving for somewhere unknown. It cost him stamina and... something else he couldn't pinpoint. Once the draining stopped, he could feel—no, he could *hear* a change.

The chain was silent, despite how hard he tugged on it. Without another second of hesitation, Glenn tore the metal off the wall, ignoring the blood flowing from his wrists. He grinned widely, enjoying this newfound power before creasing his eyebrows.

"Why did you never tell me about that?" he whispered angrily.

"Because you never asked?" the hand replied in a matter-of-fact tone.

Glenn closed his eyes and drew a deep breath, suppressing the rising annoyance in his chest. He was probably going to escape this hell thanks to Diamanes. So he couldn't insult the entity.

He reached for the next chain, waiting for Diamanes to use his magic once again. An awkward second of silence passed.

"Why aren't you doing your thing again?"

Diamanes made a wry smile, a hint of shame on his lips.

"Well, because I can't. You know, I *take* something and then *give it back*. I can't just make a thousand spells out of a single one. If you want to reuse the Silence curse, you'll have to *take* it again."

Glenn rubbed the corner of his eyes. "So you're a one-trick pony?"

Diamanes scoffed. **"Right now, I'm limited in what I can do because you have shit Mana. Get a little stronger, and you'll see what I'll be able to do then."**

Glenn sat on the cold, damp ground. What could he do with only one free hand? He didn't have the opportunity to think about that as the jailer approached, his steps echoing outside the cell. Glenn hurriedly lay down on the broken chain so that Mr. Scarred-Face wouldn't notice.

The door opened, and soft candlelight invaded the cell. Scarred-Face frowned, his nose creased. It probably smelled horrible. Glenn squinted, his eyes hidden behind his long hair—able to perfectly see the jailer's expression under his hood. *Seems like Scarred-Face hasn't shaved his chin in a while, huh?*

He tried his best to try to appear as weak as before, shivering as his captor approached. Scarred-Face placed the candle next to Glenn before rubbing his hands together and picking out a new tool of torture. It looked like a corkscrew, but bigger and with a bloodied wooden handle. He reached for Glenn's head, determined to show off the exciting toy.

Glenn's grin suddenly grew wide, surprising the jailer, who reeled back in shock. The corkscrew fell from his hand into the filth.

A second later, Glenn swung the chain at the jailer's face, ripping away his jaw and digging a bloody path through his cheek. Scarred-Face dropped to the ground without time to react. Blood flowed from his mouth and mixed with the dirty floor.

Glenn gave the chain an approving gaze before pilfering through Scarred-Face's pockets. He found a single key, old and rusted, and tried to locate the keyhole on his restraints.

Only, there were no keyholes.

"What the fuck?" he blurted out.

"Seems like they're welded around your limbs. Well, that's magic for you. Better get used to it."

The jailer's body moved slightly, startling Glenn. He hurriedly punched him to make sure he wouldn't wake up. Even though he tried to strike lightly, his fist opened a wound on Scarred-Face's bald head.

These scars... They form a pattern... A circle wrapped in thorny vines with a cross in its center... Glenn paled as he realized it was the same emblem carved on that creepy church door.

"Shit... Have I been captured by some kind of sick cult? Holy shit..." He swore, shaking his head.

Diamanes laughed. **"At least that adds some spiciness to your new life, doesn't it?"**

Glenn hissed, "I certainly could have done without it..."

He glanced down at the jailer and grimaced at the growing pool of fresh blood. "I hope I didn't kill him..."

"Chances are, he's not going to wake up. But it's not like he didn't deserve it, right?"

"If I could avoid thoughtless murder, that'd be great... And..." He crouched next to the body while pressing the piss-rag on the wound.

"If that's how you want to play it..." Diamanes said dismissively.

Glenn rubbed his chin. "What if..."

He began undressing Scarred-Face—a rather complicated operation with only one free hand. The jailer only wore a black, dirty robe and no underwear underneath, but Glenn couldn't care less.

"Alright, I totally get the revenge thing. But what are you going to do? Even for me, that's too much. I never thought you were that kind of individual. You disgust me, and I am deeply ashamed of being associated with you."

"Shut it. I'm getting myself out of here."

Ignoring the naked man, he rolled the robe around the chain, muffling it as best he could. He pulled a few times, checking if his plan was viable, before ripping the metal out of the wall.

"That's another down. Two left..." he muttered before attempting the operation on his ankles.

Those chains were still too strong for him, so he had to be satisfied dragging them. They did make killer weapons, though, so that was one positive. Glenn wrapped the makeshift manrikigusari around his legs so they wouldn't rattle against the ground.

"Alright. All ready to go..." Glenn said while dusting off his hands.

He turned towards the unconscious jailer, contemplating for a few seconds what to do with the body. He pilfered through the robe's pockets, finding a corkscrew and the damned syringe. The corner of his lips curved upwards.

"Let's start by waking him up... Oh! And let's not forget to muffle him..." he whispered with a wicked voice.

He gagged his captor with the bloody, piss-infused cloth. Then he grabbed the corkscrew and twisted it up the jailer's ass. It took a good five minutes until Scarred-Face woke up terrified, destabilized, and with a bottle screw piercing his colon.

Glenn hurriedly broke both his arms and legs with swift movements, making it look as easy as breaking twigs. The jailer tried to cry out in pain, but the rag prevented him from doing so.

"Shh... shh, if you talk, I'll only make it worse. So shut the fuck up," Glenn threatened.

Scarred-Face froze in fear as Glenn gently removed the gag from his mouth. With a calm smile, he showed him the syringe.

"You know where this is going, don't you?"

The jailer's eyes widened as Glenn shoved the needle into his throat and administered the Beast Blood. His skin turned black as coal and his veins became green as he clawed desperately at his neck. Glenn gave him one last smile before knocking him out.

"There. That's probably worse than death and a fraction of what you deserve," Glenn spat before picking up the key and the still-lit candle. Without a second of hesitation, he left the cell and closed it behind him, imprisoning the jailer to die forgotten.

Glenn stretched, the heavy weight on his chest lifting. People said revenge wasn't a solution. Well, that was a lie. Revenge had never been so sweet.

"I'm impressed. That show of violence exceeded my expectations, given what I saw in your memories." Diamanes whistled approvingly.

Glenn shrugged as the relief faded, replaced by a determination to escape.

Looking at his bloodied hands in contemplation, he realized that he was probably not merely human anymore. After all, he was strong enough to rip chains off the wall. If that wasn't some monster-level type of strength, he didn't know what was. And this was only the beginning.

"You said I'm a Mage now, right? During the Convergence, my rank was listed as a Beginner Initiate. I just have to understand how to use magic to start having fun with it."

"**What did I tell you? You will gain power beyond your wildest imagination and stand above the ones watching from the skies. That's what I, Diamanes, promised you,**" the entity proudly gloated, earning a sneer from his host.

"Well, that's a nice dream, but maybe I'd like to get out of this hole before defying Gods," Glenn said as he glanced at his cell number on the wall. "3333. Huh. Anyway, time to break out of this place."

Chapter 17

IT'S PROTEIN!

Glenn shivered in the coldness of the prison. A freezing breeze pierced through the rags he wore. Everywhere he searched was dark—be it in front of him, behind, or above. The meager candle he held was simply not enough to light the way.

Suddenly, his foot missed a step, and he tumbled face-first. His fingers grasped around the closest thing they could, a narrow ledge. He looked down, only to discover he was hanging above a bottomless pit.

Sweat pooled in Glenn's palm, and his candle fell into the abyss. The flame extinguished long before he ever heard the sound of it hitting the ground.

Wow, we almost died! Maybe be careful not to jump into the first hole you find! Diamanes exclaimed.

Glenn pulled himself up, doing so effortlessly despite the chains weighing him down. His new body was a blessing.

"*Phew...* So there's a crater in the center of the prison. Right. That's good to know," Glenn whispered.

Clenching his teeth tightly, Glenn backed against the wall and followed it. Once he reached another cell, he squinted, but it appeared that his enhanced eyesight didn't double as night vision.

His hand passed against the iron door, finding another number. This time, it was 3332. Glenn paused, suddenly realizing something terrible.

There were at least 3333 people imprisoned here, *at a minimum*. And seeing how deep that hole was, perhaps—No, there certainly were more than 3333 people suffering a similar fate.

Diamanes scoffed, ***Well? Put your ear to the door.***

Glenn complied. At first, he heard nothing. But as time went on, he heard something that sounded like a slab of *meat* being dragged on a wooden board. It wasn't very loud, but it was enough to chill the blood in Glenn's veins. A mass moved slowly behind the reinforced iron door. Glenn carefully took a step away.

Whatever was inside that cell could have been him had he not resisted the Beast Blood's corruption.

With measured steps, Glenn continued wrapping around the abyss in silence, his naked feet sticking to the damp floor. The occasional rattling of chains or scurrying of rats often startled him, but he kept moving, motivated by a desire to see the sun again.

We are lucky that you're not afraid of the dark, Diamanes said.

Glenn nodded slowly. Well, he wasn't afraid, but he wasn't comfortable *either*. He was starting to miss that candle... The silence was heavy, and each step felt like wading through water. He was walking endlessly through darkness—a chilling draft acting as his own guide as he ascended.

One constant was the scent of blood.

Glenn didn't know if the stench came from him or if the entire jail reeked of death, but the thick, metallic scent of blood followed him like a curse.

"One step after the other. One step after the other..." he repeated to himself, a feeling of dread washing over him.

The numbers on the doors decreased as he passed them. Soon, he reached the three-thousand mark, feeling relief until he realized there was still a long, long way to go.

2940... 2450... 1984... 1423... 1120...

"Bah!"

Glenn jumped in surprise. He searched his surroundings with panicked eyes until he understood it was only Diamanes teasing him.

Haha, come on. It was getting boring! the entity rebutted. *How long have we been walking? An hour?*

Glenn clenched his left hand, trying his best to shut Diamanes up. He was already anxious; he didn't need some idiot salting his wounds.

Interestingly, there were no jailers on patrol—no watchmen or guard posts. Simply the cells, the hole, and the darkness.

946... 751... 542... 342... 123... 99...

Finally! Glenn's heart raced once again as he approached what he hoped was the exit. But a doubt stopped him in his tracks. What if he went the wrong way? He assumed that the lowest number would lead outside, but what if he was wrong?

No, no. This is the right way. I'm heading to the surface. There's no sense in worrying about it now anyway. And if it isn't...

With trembling steps and a hopeful expression, Glenn accelerated. After a few more minutes, he spotted a light at the end of the tunnel. Well, no. More like a glow floating a dozen meters above, across the bottomless pit. Glenn rubbed his eyes distrustfully, but the warm radiance was still there, drawing him in like a bug.

It felt like a terrible idea to trust his sight after spending so much time in the darkness. Mirage or not, it was his only sign of salvation.

Glenn finally arrived in front of a different door, illuminated by the torch's warm hue. He smiled widely. That smile faded when he found the circular symbol wrapped in thorny vines with a cross at its core.

He almost punched the damned thing, but he calmed himself. First, he had to escape. Then... Then he might as well do his best to destroy whoever built this place. That'd do for a nice side quest while he figured out a way back home.

Glenn reached for the knob when Diamanes suddenly jolted awake.

Oh, hello. That's an Alarm spell.

Glenn froze. He listened for any blaring siren, but Diamanes' mocking chuckle reassured him.

Don't worry. You didn't push the door open, so it didn't activate yet. Just give me a few seconds, and I'll take the Alarm away.

Glenn nodded, waiting as the entity sucked the magic into his hand. The Alarm spell would certainly come in handy. The more tools on his belt, the better.

What would it take to be able to use more than one spell at a time?

If you end up having talent in magic, you'll probably be able to replicate these spells. But for now, it's only a one-time trick for you, Diamanes explained. *Oh, but mind you, it would be a completely different story if you were to reach the True Initiate level.*

Glenn's focus, first and foremost, was whatever hid behind those doors. He pushed them open, and the smell of old books welcomed him. He entered a poorly lit library with rows upon rows of dusty, wooden shelves. Above him, dim crystals with barely enough power to shine acted as a light source.

The floorboards creaked sinisterly as Glenn carefully peeked between each row. Thankfully, he was alone in this library.

While tightened the chains around his leg so they wouldn't rattle, he approached a lone desk at the center of the room. Tattered books hung lazily off it, waiting to be picked up. What stood out to him was a smaller journal with something written in the bottom-right corner. It was in dark red ink, a number: 3333.

Glenn slowly picked up the book.

"That's... That's my cell, isn't it?" Glenn muttered.

With a bit of apprehension, he opened it. There was only a date written on the first page.

17/05/3032. The same date from the Magic Identification Bureau form.

"The day of my capture..." His eyes glazed over, but he turned the page, nonetheless.

Name: Glenn

Surname: Unknown

Age (estimated): 21

Profession: Unknown (estimated to be a soldier or mercenary due to the wounds on his body. A low ranking one.)

Glenn grimaced when reading that line and Diamanes laughed.

Health status: Alive. Strange condition in left hand. Skin is purple and seems to heal faster than the rest of his body.

1st Day: Fed No. 7, Black Rose. Fell unconscious and didn't turn. Shows promising results.

2nd Day: Fed No. 34, Corpse Eater. Fell unconscious and didn't turn.

3rd Day: Fed No. 12, Flesh Hive. Fell unconscious, didn't turn.

31st Day: Fed No. 28, Ghoul. Fell unconscious, didn't turn. This is a new record. This might be the One.

54th Day: Fed No. 42, Crescent Kar-Gal and No. 1, Abyss Stalker. Showed signs of turning. Finally...

Notes: The most resilient specimen yet and probably the best of them all. His sanity is on the brink of breaking. I believe he is indeed the One we are looking for. Thank God for his benevolence; the subject will show exceptional results once trained.

NB: We still need to determine what is wrong with his left hand in case it impedes our goals. The time Abbot Hank allotted us should be more than enough for more tests.

Glenn heaved and stumbled a few steps back.

"So that's what you meant when you said I should be dead, huh?" he questioned.

Diamanes' grinning lips were enough of an answer. He shoved the notebook into his ragged clothes before clenching his fists.

"What do you think... will happen to me, then?"

"I honestly don't know what to expect. You're probably the only being in this world that survived drinking that much Beast Blood without turning. An absolute anomaly," mocked Diamanes.

As long as there's life, there's hope, right? I might as well take all the benefits and ignore the horror I had to go through to get them.

Glenn's nose creased as he tried to find the exit, eventually discovering two doors. A sign hung above each: Storage and Accumulator. He pushed the first door open after checking with Diamanes for any spells.

Entering Storage, he found... Well, a storage room. There were a great number of shelves with an equally great number of items stored on them—weapons, garments, jewelry, documents, books, and bags.

He searched around, and his eyes lit up with joy when he found the clothes he'd worn before his abduction. He was about to put them on, but frowning at... whatever he was covered in, he decided to do so after a nice, hot shower.

My clothes are here, so that must mean...

Not even a minute later, he located the dimensional pouch. It stood out among the raggedy bags with its nice quality leather. He attached it to his waist and stashed his fine attire away.

Sifting through the weapon shelves, he didn't manage to find his ornate sword. Perhaps it was so valuable that they kept it for themselves. Not that he cared. He picked up a sturdy sword from the racks and sheathed it in a random scabbard. Even if he had no idea of how to use it, having a blade did make him feel safer.

Since he didn't have the time to learn how to wield the fire staff, he decided not to take it out. He geared up while throwing a curious look at the jewelry section. There was no gold, silver, or jewels. The 'jewelry' consisted of wooden bracelets, cheap rings, and rosaries.

"They probably targeted the poor since a few of them disappearing would not make much noise." Glenn understood with a darkening expression.

Diamanes scoffed, **"They can't attack anyone but the lowest of the low. Disgusting."**

Glenn drew a deep breath. He couldn't just leave. He had to do *something*—something to get back at the *assholes* who forced him to endure unending torture for *fifty-four* days.

He had no illusion about saving the other prisoners; he was already having a hard time saving himself, after all. And they likely had transformed into nightmarish monsters.

"What's this newfound strength good for if I can't use it?" Glenn muttered.

"Why not just blow the place up?" Diamanes proposed in a matter-of-fact tone.

Glenn blinked at his left hand. "What?"

His eyes widened as Diamanes' grin grew from thumb to pinkie.

Chapter 18

PURGING THE GUNK

"What do you mean, 'blow the place up'? Do you see explosives anywhere? Maybe some C4 I missed?" Glenn asked in a mocking tone.

Before the entity could reply, Glenn shook his head. "No, even if I could, I wouldn't do it. That's too much. What if we're under King's Rise? I don't want to kill thousands of innocents for some meaningless revenge."

Although, as he said that, Glenn found the option strangely alluring.

"Listen." Diamanes sighed heavily. **"You can't even imagine the number of spells protecting King's Rise. That magic lights up like a fucking Christmas Tree. So, if this place collapses—which isn't what I had in mind—the wards should take care of it. Now, if you're okay with all that, let's get to that Accumulator room you saw earlier and bring some chaos."**

Glenn didn't need much to be convinced. He retraced his steps through the library. The second door, labeled Accumulator, yielded to his touch. There was another Alarm spell, which Glenn took away, grateful for Diamanes' help.

A vortex of verdant smoke twirling at the center of the room. Runes were inscribed into the floor, encircling it while shimmering with an eerie, green hue and pulsing softly.

Glenn took a hesitant step closer. "So that's your plan? Throwing me into some suspicious void? Are you sure you don't want to kill me?"

"Don't be a fool," Diamanes snorted with condescension. **"This green stuff is the monsters' life force, sucked away by the formation you're seeing on the floor. Yeah, these runes."**

Glenn pressed his hand against a rune. He then unsheathed his sword and pointed it at one of the inscriptions.

"Wait, what are you doing?" Diamanes asked.

"I thought you wanted me to break this formation so it would free the monsters?"

Diamanes clicked his tongue. **"Yeah, well, there are better ways to break it besides stabbing the floor and hoping the runes don't explode in your face. There should be a main component storing the life force. Find that, and take it away. That'll be enough to unleash hell on the bastards who imprisoned you."**

The corner of Glenn's lips curved upwards as he tried to find the 'main component.' He soon paused and frowned.

"Wait, do you think they'll be able to cull the monsters once they're all out of their cells?"

"I sure hope not! It would be quite disappointing considering the number of monstrosities down here."

Glenn intensified his search. The harder he looked, the more pointless it appeared. There was nothing besides the vortex. What did the main component look like anyway?

Glenn turned slowly towards the ominous spiral. He squinted, trying to peer through the flowing energy. A small glint at the whirlwind's base caught his gaze. It looked like a black pearl.

"That's it! That's the main component!" Diamanes exclaimed excitedly. **"Come on, take it away, and let's watch all hell break loose!"**

Glenn groaned at the almost childish excitement of his left hand. There was one thing he didn't understand in this whole mess—the Accumulator.

"Wait, it's called the Accumulator because it accumulates life force," he muttered in realization. "But why the hell would they need the life force of thousands of creatures? I know we talked about the possibility of them creating an army... Is this gathered life force just a side benefit?"

"Does it matter?!" Diamanes' impatience burst forth. **"Put an end to this place, and let's escape. This body's survival is paramount for fuck's sake!"**

Glenn tensed before diving through the fumes and grabbing the pearl. He held his breath as he did so. The circle of runes surrounding the vortex didn't affect him, thankfully, and he managed to escape without harm.

He sighed in relief while examining the main component, the black pearl. Something swirled inside, but he couldn't tell what it was.

A distant noise caught his attention. He slipped the item into his dimensional pouch while clenching his sword.

"Where the hell did that come from?" Glenn whispered, cracking the door open to listen.

Far away, the sound of flesh hitting iron began to echo with irregularity until an absolute cacophony of roars, screams, and screeches overtook everything. Glenn paled, rushing back to the library.

"The monsters have woken up, haha! I think that's your cue to leave, Glenn," Diamanes suggested while laughing in satisfaction.

Glenn hurriedly returned to the Storage room, knocking over boxes of baubles until he found a door. That was probably the way out.

Before he grabbed the knob, he watched in horror as it turned by itself. The door opened violently, and Glenn hid among the crates.

A dozen robed figures armed with swords, axes, and torches ran inside. Their ragged breathing and restless movements betrayed some panic. Glenn held his breath.

"Damn us! Who was on this watch?" one man asked in terror.

Another replied, "It was Val, I believe! For the Accumulator to stop working... Damn it!"

"Alright, at least everyone is here besides Val. Gane, you go to the Accumulator. I'll take the others to stop the fiends. Abbot Hank is going to kill us if we let a single one of the offerings escape!" The voice paused for a moment, before spitting, "Sacrifice your life if needed! Come on!"

Their panicked reaction was music to Glenn's ears.

Diamanes snickered. ***Looks like we've stirred the hornet's nest.***

The second the robed figures left the Storage room, Glenn dashed out of his hiding place and snuck behind them. Now that they were busy taking care of the chaos he caused, he would be able to hopefully escape and—at the same time—fuck those guys over. Two birds with one pearl!

Glenn entered a hallway with dozens of doors on each side, barely illuminated by dim, magical lights hanging from the ceiling. He tip-toed through the corridor, arriving at a door with a familiar symbol—a circle wrapped in thorny vines with a cross carved at its core.

He gritted his teeth and pushed the door open. A robed figure pacing back and forth suddenly turned with hope towards him.

"Was it a false alarm? I knew it had to be one—"

Glenn swung his sword without hesitation, messily hacking through the man's throat. Due to his lack of technique, he didn't cut all the way through, but it was more than enough to kill the cultist.

Behind the corpse was a sturdy steel gate flanked by empty chairs. Glenn was relieved to find the damned exit, but that relief turned to horror when he realized what he had done.

Don't stop now, Glenn! Diamanes screamed.

He ran to the gate, but it was stuck. Taking a few steps back, he desperately charged into the steel, but it only bent.

Glenn raised his sword above his head. With one clean, precise strike, he broke the lock *and* his weapon. The blade whizzed past him and stabbed into the ceiling, leaving a small cut on his cheek. But Glenn couldn't care less about that.

"Yes!" he shouted while kicking the gate open and throwing the broken hilt aside.

Surprisingly, it wasn't the sun that assaulted his senses, nor an overbearing feeling of freedom. It was the smell. It smelled of rot, piss, dirt, and shit. Yet... Glenn couldn't help but find it a hundred times better than what he was used to in his cell.

He dashed out of the prison in a panic, chuckling in disbelief as he looked at the sky.

"Free at last..." Glenn muttered emotionally before realizing that as free as he was, he wasn't exactly *safe*. He took a few seconds to observe his surroundings, frowning as he did.

He was in some sort of shanty town built of rotten planks and rusty nails. The torrential sound of a nearby river failed to drown the groans of pain and pleasure.

Glenn hid behind a run-down fence, hugging his chains closely.

Two bald men dragged their feet as they walked, their eyes empty and a disturbing smile on their lips. They were so malnourished they looked like living skeletons. One of them was missing an arm while the other had an amputated leg.

"What the..." Glenn couldn't help but mutter in disbelief as he noticed a symbol carved in their flesh—a symbol he was strangely growing familiar with. A circle wrapped in thorny vines with a cross at its core.

Fuck, are they everywhere? Might as well kill them all. Diamanes suggested in an all too serious tone.

Glenn grimaced and watched the two stumble away. *I'd rather avoid fighting if I can...*

He gulped and stealthily ran out of his hiding spot, heading for the sound of flowing water.

Glenn almost stopped along the way when he inadvertently glanced inside one of the shacks and found a couple of old men maiming themselves with ecstatic smiles. Their backs were bleeding with the ominous mark he kept on finding ever since his fate got intertwined with the cult.

"This is a nightmare..." Glenn whispered in awe, his back drenched in sweat.

When he arrived at the presumed source of water, he only found more masochistic cultists, their fingers cradling cheap cigarettes. There were so many of the druggies that a yellow smog had appeared around the river. Just the smell of it made him want to puke.

Glenn hid his mouth in his arm and walked up to the river, only to find a torrent of literal filth. Bloated corpses floated on the surface, their mouths filled with maggots and their flesh half devoured by carrion feeders.

He stepped back in horror, just in time to see someone jump on a passing corpse and bite a huge chunk out of it. Glenn's eyes widened, and without hesitating for another second, he ran.

When he finally managed to escape from the yellow smog, he allowed himself a deep breath of relatively fresh air. His eyes followed the source of the filth, finding a giant steel grate pouring with greenish goo.

"This must be King's Rise's sewer system... Shit, are you telling me they didn't solve sewage with magic?" Glenn muttered in disgust.

Strangely, it didn't seem like he was in danger of being attacked—the sickos were too busy harming themselves or smoking whatever those cigarettes contained.

"Did I trade one hell for another?" Glenn groaned as he rubbed his forehead. He was still dragging his chains, probably the perfect cosplay of a masochistic madman. At least he didn't look too out of place.

Now that you're free, how about you get a bath or something? And not in that river of shit.

Glenn sighed. "I'd love that too, Diamanes"

He walked away carefully, searching for a way out of the labyrinth of shacks. He kept his dimensional pouch hidden in his rags and gave up on hiding his left hand. Maybe it would actually serve as a deterrent in case he met bandits.

At some point—perhaps it was a change of district or something—the people seemed to grow slightly more well-fed and better taken care of. They all had dark skin with white marks on their forehead. Every time he passed one of them, they would look at him like a piece of shit, avoiding him.

Glenn understood that. He would avoid himself right now.

Why does it feel I'm just getting lost even further? Glenn wondered, looking at a poor imitation of a house on the side of the road. *Didn't I already see that place before?*

"The hell is this?" an old voice mumbled from behind.

Glenn glanced back without thinking and suddenly did a double take. That straw hat, the well-kept white beard, and that golden monocle!

Didn't that old driver who brought me to the Frozen Gate say he had some business in the Sewers?

"Wait, I know you! You're that old man!" Glenn realized.

"What the?" the old man exclaimed in surprise.

* * *

A man in a black hooded robe lay on the ground submissively as blood oozed from his wounds. Beside him, five other black-robed individuals knelt in a similar condition.

A wide, tall man towered over them, adorned in the white vestments of a cleric. He pressed his massive foot on the nearest man's head, pushing it against the stone floor. His face contorted with anger, almost purple from the hatred. Unidentifiable scars marked every part of his skin. He held an ancient tome tightly in his hand. His bald head was hidden under a black, round hat with a flat brim.

"W-We did... all we could, Abbot Hank!" The man trembled uncontrollably under the pressure of the Abbot's foot.

He continued to plead for mercy as the anger suddenly faded from Abbot Hank's face, replaced by a strangely sweet smile.

"Do not worry, my child. You will meet our Lord shortly," he whispered in an eerily gentle and soft voice. "How blessed you are!"

He chuckled with a warm smile. A second later, he crushed the man's head under his foot like a watermelon, his face unchanging. Bits of bones, flesh, and brains exploded onto the other cultists.

The Abbot slowly took his foot from the pulverized mass and turned towards the other kneeling individuals. He questioned the first cultist he saw, his voice cold and dry.

"What was his name?"

"G-Gane, Abbot Hank!" a terrified voice exclaimed.

Abbot Hank hummed in acceptance before opening his book and revealing the old, yellow pages within. He crouched next to Gane's corpse and dipped his finger in the mixture of blood, brain, and bones.

"Gane... I see..."

With a passionate smile, he slowly wrote the name in the book, substituting the blood for ink. Dozens and dozens of names had been similarly written in a dark, faded red color. He quickly made the pages flutter, sighing in satisfaction.

"May he enjoy eternal pain in the arms of our Lord," said Abbot Hank solemnly.

"May he be blessed," the other cultists said.

The Abbot inquired, "What subject's file disappeared?"

"3333, Abbot Hank."

The Abbot paused for a second, and his sweet smile grew wider.

"So it is *him*. Find him at all costs. He is the *One*."

He left the entryway, each step trembling the stone. Once he was gone, the cultists looked through the door to the prison. Behind it, on the slope leading to the library, were hundreds of monster corpses—smashed to a bloody pulp. They never stood any chance against *him*. Their escape had always been against their Lord's will.

As was 3333's escape.

Chapter 19

A FORTUITOUS ENCOUNTER?

The old man pinched his nose, his expression twisted in disgust. He wore the same simple tunic and pants as the day they first met. And his gray hair and beard were still as well-kept as ever, barely hidden under his straw hat.

"Ugh. Did ya dive into that darn sewage river, kid?" The driver winced, taking a few noticeable steps away from Glenn. He looked him up and down with a critical eye, his expression gradually worsening.

Glenn grimaced as he glanced down at himself. He could only agree with the senior. He was still covered in filth: dry and fresh blood as well as... Whatever those unspeakable liquids were.

Shaking his head, Glenn stared back at the old man. Diamanes had already told him he was an incredibly powerful guy. And he was going to need all the allies he could get if he had a vengeful cult on his trail.

Maybe he could help? Having a strong ally would certainly ease some of my worries. Lost in his contemplation, Glenn failed to notice the geezer giving him a one-shoulder shrug and turning, unconcerned.

Your lifeline is running away. Diamanes nudged him, successfully pulling him out of his trance.

Glenn abruptly snapped back to reality and hid his purple hand. No need to scare the grandpa off with some mysterious curse.

"Wait! Sir, can you help me?" Glenn ran desperately behind the elder. He didn't stop, unbothered to entertain some weird, disgusting kid.

The distance between them only grew. Glenn almost lost sight of him and had to pick a random shortcut through the derelict streets, pausing only as he stepped on the corpse of a half-eaten rat. *Yuck.*

He managed to catch up, but the senior quickened his pace.

"I can pay!" he yelled in one last hopeful attempt.

Multiple gazes turned towards him, but once the old man paused, they all glanced away. The geezer muttered something under his beard and pivoted around swiftly to size Glenn up and down.

He grinned mockingly. "I ain't into young'uns, nor that sort of business." He shook his head while pointing at the chains wrapped around Glenn's limbs. "And ya're a man, so it's a definite no."

"Even if ya have some stashed coins somewhere, lemme tell ya that I ain't interested in your smelly ol' copper!" The elder scoffed as he waved his hand dismissively.

His sarcastic smile quickly vanished when a gold tint appeared in Glenn's dirty hands. The coin disappeared a moment later. Glenn certainly wasn't going to flaunt his wealth in this kind of place. It was already extremely risky to show he had any money at all, but he didn't have a choice. No risk, no rewards. And he hoped that his reward would be a war machine for his troubles.

The old man blinked before suddenly vanishing. Glenn opened his mouth to gasp, but a gust of wind forced his eyelids closed. He felt something clasp around his arm, and before he could react, the ground crumbled under his feet. When he reopened his eyes, he was being held above one of the dilapidated cabins, high above the streets.

This isn't going how I pictured it, Glenn thought with an uneasy feeling.

He was hanging in the air, threatening to be thrown a dozen meters.

Glenn squinted at snowflakes delicately landing on the geezer's straw hat. The wind had suddenly become freezing cold. Even now, a thick layer of ice grew over grandpa's body, and his eyes emitted a silver glow.

"I see ya're improving yar disguises every day!" the senior sneered.

"So come on, ya maggot. What's the target? What more dirty work I have to do, ya cursed trash?" he hissed through his clenched teeth in an icy and irate voice.

His grip on Glenn's wrist tightened, threatening to crush it at any second. Glenn tried to free himself, but the driver was too strong.

Was this what you meant when you said he could kill me with the snap of his fingers?

That's not exactly what I said, but yeah, I did warn you.

"This little shit is just a Beginner Initiate. What games are they playing, damn it? Do they think I'm that easy now?" spat the old man hatefully before violently tossing Glenn onto the roof, breaking a few makeshift tiles.

Glenn landed on his back, gasping as the air escaped his lungs.

Thank the weird cultists' guys for giving you a reinforced spine. Diamanes laughed mockingly, earning a grimace from his host.

Glenn coughed and pushed himself up, staring at the Mage with a renewed look of fear and respect. This... This formidable strength was incomprehensible. What was worse was that he *knew* the elder had barely used any force. Crushing Glenn would be as easy as breathing for him.

The thought of having such power crossed his mind—enough strength to crush any monsters that tried to kill him. With stumbling steps, he steadied himself and raised his hands in appeasement.

"Wait! *Cough...* This is all a misunderstanding," Glenn pleaded before narrowly dodging a thick spike of ice.

Grandpa's face had hardened, and swirls of mystical blue light appeared around his right hand, conjuring an ice spear. The same ice covered his entire body like a knight's armor.

"Who d'ya think ya're addressing, boy? Ya dare accuse me of *misunderstanding* when ya're very existence is a mistake and a shame to life itself?" the senior roared with bloodshot eyes, his teeth grinding so hard they could shatter at any moment.

A tongue as sharp as his spear, remarked Diamanes.

Maybe I shouldn't have involved myself with an incredibly powerful psychopath, Glenn suddenly realized.

"*Hah*!" The geezer drew a deep breath, and a wave of pressure fell over him. He shuddered, feeling as if he was surrounded by wolves ready to pounce. It was nothing like the ability Diamanes had used on him inside the crystal, but it was still enough to make his knees buckle.

He cast a defiant glance at the driver, whose gaze suddenly changed to one of interest.

Glenn hissed, "I mean no offense, you crazy fogey! You drove me to the Frozen Gate some time ago, and I—*argh*—I simply recognized your face in the street!"

The old man brushed his beard while his spear spun gracefully in his other hand. A gust of icy air accompanied each of his movements.

"Hmm... Oh, that kid who used my cart..." The Mage frowned before doing a double-take. "Wait, what?"

The hardness on his face melted like snow in the sun—as did the ice spear. A large cloud of white steam evaporated into the air.

"Didn't I leave ya to the Frozen Gate? Why the chains and the shit? Ya..." He frowned and took a disgusted step back. "Ya're not part of the ones that enjoy these weird games, are ya?"

"I... I would love to explain what happened to me, but I'd prefer a more *grounded* location, if possible," he articulated slowly, imagining what his skull would look like cracked against the pavement.

"My ol' knees could certainly use someplace to sit. Ya know the Iced Beer, right? I'm sure ya kiddo will forgive me for my antics if I offer a mug of ale, ay?" He laughed warmly while patting Glenn's back.

Glenn restrained a grimace as he realized that all his problems stemmed from that place and those barely stashed drugs he burned. With a bit of luck, the owner would be glad to welcome a couple of high rollers with open arms. And the prospect of enjoying a shower and a warm meal was more than appealing. His stomach grumbled loudly as if to echo his thoughts.

Everything will be fine as long as I don't touch a drop of Fiery Spirit... Probably.

Yeah, keep telling yourself that. Diamanes snorted.

Shut it, Glenn replied with the mental equivalent of clenched teeth.

He turned to the old man and rubbed the back of his head, a wry smile on his face. "Do you mind leading the way? I... I have no idea where we are."

"Don't be shy, kiddo. Despite my age, I still have yet to explore every nook and cranny of the Sewers!"

Glenn returned his smile awkwardly as he tried to get a read on the enigmatic geezer. One moment he appeared like a sweet grandfather, the next a formidable and chilling fighter who could kill him with a sneeze. The sudden apparition of an ice platform under their feet interrupted his thoughts and startled him. The senior crossed his arms as the platform gently brought them to the ground, hovering silently.

Holy... This is so cool. Hey, Diamanes, can I take this... spell or whatever?

Diamanes laughed derisively. **Feel free to try if you're keen on meeting an early demise. You're nowhere near Sir Geezer's level. Attempting to use his power would be like asking a newborn to wield a greatsword to cook some fine cuisine.**

Glenn rubbed his forehead. *Where do those crappy metaphors you use even come from?*

In the meantime, the old man had already stepped down from the ice platform, looking expectantly at Glenn.

"It ain't a bit of ice that's going to scare ya, is it?"

He jumped down and joined the Mage, glancing back at the platform as it disappeared into a cloud of steam.

Magic is really cool. One moment it's there, and the next it's gone. Fascinating.

"I'm Glenn, sir. Can I ask for your name?"

The senior displayed a toothy smile and chuckled. "It's been eons since anyone asked for my name. Back in the day, they called me Redan."

Glenn nodded slowly while Redan's eyes drifted away, heavy with memories. When one of Glenn's chains clattered against a rock, the elder frowned. A sharp ice sword emerged from his hand. A second later, the shackles crashed on the ground, severed like they were nothing but paper.

"T-Thanks," Glenn muttered, rubbing his wounded wrists.

"Ya're welcome. Let's get out of Giselle's territory for a bit, aye?"

Chapter 20

COMING OUT

Redan led Glenn out of the Sewers with assured steps, not expanding on who Giselle could be. Less than an hour later, they sat in the Iced Beer back by the Frozen Gate, both nursing pints of ale. Glenn had felt a little expectant at the idea of encountering the owner, Winston, but he was absent; someone else took over for him. According to a staff, he had left the inn over a month ago.

The aroma of roasted potatoes and chicken stirred Glenn's stomach. And it was delivered by an angelic waitress to boot. He didn't know if it was the food that made him hallucinate or if the woman had some sort of divinity to her, but to him, she was absolutely the savior he needed. He wolfed down his meal with insatiable hunger and ordered a new plate.

Despite the lack of salt and pepper, dry chicken, and mushy potatoes, this was the best dinner he had eaten in his entire life.

"Hunger truly is the greatest seasoning, aye?" Redan muttered as he sipped on his ale.

Once Glenn was finally satisfied, he leaned back in his chair and wiped his face with a towel. He gawked at it, seeing that he somehow managed to change the color of the fabric from white to black with a single wipe.

"What?" he asked nervously while looking at the old man. Redan's lips curved in a smirk, and he crossed his hands on the table.

"So, shall I listen to that tale now? How did ya end up like this, kiddo?"

"It's not that long of a story when I think back on it," Glenn realized while peering at the ale in his mug.

Actually... You're right! Diamanes feigned a gasp. *Your whole misadventure can be summarized in a few words: 'Idiot sabotages local cult after drinking too much and is tortured for two months but escapes by stealing their valuables!'*

Glenn's eyelids twitched but remained concentrated on Redan's curious gaze.

"Let's just skip to the good part," he sighed before pulling out the notebook titled '3333', which contained all the atrocities he endured—and all the blood he was forcefully fed.

Redan squinted at the sight of the book. Giving away the document would reveal that Glenn was abnormal, but he would at least gain some insight. It was a gamble. Either he gained the help of a mysterious and powerful old man or... Glenn didn't want to know what the other option was. One thing was certain, he wouldn't get drunk anytime soon.

"You heard of a cult kidnapping people around town? Because that's what happened to me, and I ended up in the worst prison imaginable and received some lovely, very enjoyable"—Glenn shivered—"Torture. Lots of it. Every day. Or more like every time I was awake. Until I escaped, of course."

Redan raised his hand in a calming gesture as he slowly opened the book. "Give this ol' man a second to read, alright? Y'all tell me the rest of it after that..."

After carefully moistening his finger, Redan flipped a page before frowning in displeasure. His brusque movement startled Glenn, but it was only to adjust his golden monocle.

"S-So, what do you think of it, sir?" Glenn said, his voice trembling with apprehension.

The Mage arched an eyebrow before rubbing his forehead with an annoyed expression. "Don't rush this ol' man, boy. I can read, but I can't read fast, alrigh'?"

Glenn pressed his lips tightly, using everything he had to hold a heavy sigh. He still had a plan B if Redan refused to help.

Maybe I'll just travel out of King's Rise and find someplace hidden to raise magical sheep.

That might be more dangerous than staying here. Do you know anything about magic sheep? Diamanes asked in a genuinely concerned tone.

Glenn wordlessly shook his head.

Me neither. And that terrifies me, Diamanes said fearfully before exploding in mocking laughter.

This time, Glenn couldn't restrain his sigh.

Instead of wasting his energy trying to reply to the snarky entity, Glenn decided to examine his current capabilities. Right now, he had a superhuman body and the potential to use magic. Too bad he had no idea how to make use of either.

I would trade my left hand to have taken sword fighting classes instead of climbing...

Go to hell, Diamanes groaned. **You're a pretty tough meat bag— expendable fodder with powers you don't know how to use and half the brain to go with it.**

Glenn clacked his tongue, earning a glance of distaste from Redan.

Is it my fault if my country didn't have military service?

Diamanes seriously considered the question before replying, **Hmm... Yes.**

There was no reasoning with the entity.

Redan finally stirred. Glenn held his breath in anticipation, only for the geezer to flip a page in an excruciatingly slow manner.

How is it possible to spend so much time reading a bunch of... nothing? There are names and dates, and yet it's going to take him half an hour a page? Glenn complained, staring at the ceiling in frustration. He had spent so long looking at it, he knew that the magical light at the north-west side of the inn flickered *exactly* every seven seconds.

Don't be a dick! Diamanes interjected. ***Not everyone possesses the gift of speed-reading. Being able to read is an incredible skill in and of itself when you consider it, even more so in this world.***

Glenn finally gave up and stood to stretch his legs. "I'm going to wash up. I'll be back."

"Hmm..." Redan's eyes remained glued to the writings, completely uninterested in Glenn's comments. The latter made his way to the counter where a vaguely familiar face greeted him. He tried not to stare as the woman flashed him a flirtatious smile and leaned forwards to put her ample bosom on display.

"Hmm. How much for a room with a bath?" Glenn inquired, coughing awkwardly as he struggled to avoid ogling. He chose to stare at the ceiling again. *Ooh, is that mold? Fun!*

The waitress pressed her chest against his arm while moistening her plump lips. "For you, handsome, I can give you my room for free."

A mix of confusion and desire blossomed in Glenn's chest. *A very attractive woman going out of her way to share a bed with me? This has to be a trap. A very exciting one, sure. But too good to be true.*

Uh, yeah? Don't you remember her from last time? She was at the counter when you were drunkenly destroying everything. I remember because I thought she would almost pull some popcorn out of nowhere when you began setting those drugs on fire, Diamanes said in a matter-of-fact tone.

Wait, what? Glenn blinked.

And give her cleavage a glance. It's worth it, trust me, Diamanes added cheekily.

Glenn clacked his tongue. *Who do you take me for? No, I'm not going to—*

Shut it, you imbecile. Just look. You might recognize something, Diamanes insisted.

Wait, don't tell me...

A not-so-discreet glance confirmed Glenn's suspicions. A circle with thorny vines wrapped around it and a cross at its core. Of course, she had to be a part of those damned cultists.

She's probably the reason you ended up in that cell for so long. Don't you think it'd be a great idea to... take revenge on her?

Glenn clenched his fists, staring darkly at the waitress.

Should I kill her? Glenn seriously considered for an instant before realizing what he was thinking.

"No, I... I can't," he muttered under his breath as he took a step back.

The woman caught his hand and pressed it against her chest seductively.

"What? You don't think I'll be worth your time, handsome? Trust me, I know my way around cleaning a man's body," she purred.

"Somehow, I don't doubt that." He smiled wryly and tried to pull his wrist away, but the lady held on. His mind raced at maximum speed, scrambling for an excuse.

"I'm sorry, but I prefer men."

Wow, that's... Wow. Diamanes whistled with sarcastic admiration.

The inn—previously quite rowdy—suddenly fell very, very silent. Even Redan, who seemed immune to surprises, raised an eyebrow. Most of the inn's customers shot him weirded-out stares, and others looked... interested.

Oh, God.

Well, I can never show my face here again. Was it worth it? Glenn pondered as the woman's expression shifted from sultry to repulsed.

You know, according to Earth's standards, your preferences are completely acceptable. I just think it's very brave of you to be so open about it. Diamanes laughed mockingly.

Glenn tried his utmost to suppress the parasite's voice and offered an apologetic smile to the fake waitress. He swiftly snatched the key from her flabbergasted grasp.

"Pleasure doing business with you," he blurted out before dashing to his room.

It was plain: four barren walls with a desk beside a bed. There was some sunlight coming through a dusty French window looking out to the street below.

"It's no luxury suite, but it'll suffice," Glenn muttered.

He was about to relax but remembered he had a spell he could use. He grabbed the knob with his left hand.

Mind if I put an Alarm on this? Glenn asked.

Glenn felt Diamanes' energy race through his left hand and settle in the knob. And it wasn't long until he had a chance to experience the magic in action. His senses flared, and he promptly hid his palm as someone knocked on the door.

"It's bath time!" A female voice announced from outside.

Glenn opened the door, discovering a different waitress. Her cheeks were as red as the blood moon. An empty wooden barrel stood beside her.

"You... You know how to use a Shard, right?" she asked shyly.

Glenn lied with a smile and took the chestnut-sized, blue crystal she held.

"Yes, thank you."

He dragged the barrel into his room and dusted off his hands. The waitress was still waiting outside, fiddling her thumbs.

Glenn preemptively said, "No, I won't be answering any questions about my sexuality. Goodbye."

He hurriedly closed the door and sighed heavily. He looked at the barrel and the blue crystal—the Shard—trying to distract himself from Diamanes' laughter.

"Oh, Diamanes?"

"Honestly, joining forces with you was the best decision I've made. Even though you're completely *worthless* right now!"

"Thanks a lot for that. Doesn't hurt at all. Could you enlighten me about Shards, please?"

Diamanes cleared his throat. **"Alright, about this Shard. Essentially, it's condensed elemental Mana. Take your fire staff for example. It contains a fire Shard that allows it to launch fiery projectiles."**

"Right. So this Shard must be water-based since it's blue?" Glenn quickly understood.

"Exactly. You can either infuse it with your Mana, which Beginner Initiates like you can do, or you can apply blood to fuel it. Mundane folks tend to use that technique."

"Welp, I'd rather not cut myself. I think I've suffered enough in that hole," he stated, wincing as blurry memories of torture instruments appeared in his mind.

"It's the same as when you used my power on the doorknob. You have to picture the energy in your heart and redirect it to the place where you want it. That would be the water Shard in this situation."

Glenn clenched the water Shard tightly.

I have to imagine the energy in my heart, and... Move it around...

He closed his eyes to concentrate, searching for that mysterious energy in his chest. At first, he could only find darkness. But after focusing further, he managed to find... something. Something strange and mystical that he was pretty sure had never been there before. Or maybe it had been, but he could have never found it if he didn't know it existed.

He followed Diamanes' instructions and willed the energy to flow from his chest to the crystal. Water suddenly cascaded out of the Shard like a high-powered washer, filling the barrel. Glenn gasped in awe and released the Shard. The stream of water cut off as soon as the crystal left his hand.

"Wow! This is revolutionary!" Glenn exclaimed. "But where is the water coming from? Is it materializing out of thin air, or is stored within the Shard and I'm simply draining it out? Or perhaps—"

If the only resources required are a Shard and manpower, then theoretically you can create infinite quantities of water! No need to rely on natural rain or aqueducts. And hey, does that mean—

"Stop!" Diamanes blurted out. **"Stop it. I have no damn idea, and even if I did, why would I bother to explain all that? What use would it serve?"**

Glenn shook his head with disappointment. "Well, understanding something is the first step to coming up with new ways to use it. It's normal to seek answers to unanswered questions."

"And since the Shard uses my energy—or blood for the common people—to create water, that means there is an exchange taking place. Am I paying a price to something or... someone?" He shivered, wondering who or what was the recipient of the trade.

Diamanes grunted, his presence fading away from Glenn's mind.

"Oh, so the best way to shut you up is to ask you questions you don't know the answer to, then?" Glenn mocked, finally gaining the upper hand.

Diamanes didn't bother to reply, so Glenn concentrated on the Shard, pouring water into the barrel again. He couldn't tell if it was consuming much of his Mana, but it appeared negligible.

"That's darn convenient..." he muttered before taking off his tattered clothes and putting his precious dimensional pouch on the desk.

Without wasting another second, he jumped into the barrel and hummed in satisfaction. He sank under the water's surface, ridding himself of all the filth that had embedded in his skin after weeks of living in a cell.

The water was cold, bitterly so, but being able to clean himself felt great. In a matter of minutes, the water darkened, forcing him to toss the grime out the window. It wasn't the most efficient way to do it, but, well, he didn't want to risk another awkward exchange to get a new tub. *Hopefully, there's no one in that alley.*

He refilled the bath, thoroughly scrubbing himself until all the dried blood and dirt was off his body. Once putting a toe in the water wouldn't taint the whole container, he finally allowed himself to relax and simply lay in the barrel with his eyes closed.

"Is this paradise?" he said, a slight smile on his lips.

"Maybe. Or maybe the place that geezer is going to send you will be." Diamanes' reminder startled him.

"Oh. Oh, damn." Glenn suddenly stood, spraying water into the room.

He had completely forgotten about the old man. He grabbed his clothes from the dimensional pouch and hurriedly dressed himself—taking a short second to enjoy the touch of the soft fabric on his skin. Those disgusting rags he wore couldn't compare to Jefferson Howard's luxurious attire.

"I am cleansed, be it physically or mentally!" Glenn exclaimed happily.

He opted to empty the barrel one last time, only to see his reflection in the water. He stared at himself for a moment, speechless. His hair had grown significantly, now reaching the base of his chin. He would have to tie it up if he didn't want it impeding his sight.

That was the first time he had his hair so long, and he didn't dislike it. The color had deepened. Once chestnut strands now boasted a darker shade—almost jet black at the roots. He grabbed a string and pulled his hair back, discovering that his ears had grown longer and slightly pointed. Even his jawline appeared more chiseled. He had lost all body fat, replaced by lean muscle. He still looked a little emaciated, but he did not doubt that problem would solve itself.

Huh. I was already handsome before, but now I'm striking. No reason to complain.

"Your ego is... *Sigh*..." If Diamanes had a head to shake, he would have undoubtedly done so.

"The world would have lost a valuable asset had I died down that shitty hole..." Glenn said, reflecting on everything that had happened. He had to break out of prison, flee from masochistic cultists, and kill a man...

Glenn suddenly froze and looked at his hands, realizing that one important point.

That's right. He *killed a man*. He killed him. He cleaved through the guard's throat like it was nothing. He could have knocked him out, but no. He killed him.

Glenn fell to his knees and puked in the barrel, trembling from head to toe. Even now, he seriously considered killing that waitress. No matter what she did to him, she was still a human being, so why? Why did it feel like the natural course of things should be to *kill her*?

He suddenly drew a deep breath and came to his senses, his fingers tightly grabbing the edge of the barrel.

"I am a murderer..." Glenn whispered at his reflection. There was no going back now.

"Feeling guilty won't help you survive," Diamanes commented with a snarky tone.

Glenn nodded slowly as he pushed down on his guilt. *That guy deserved it, just like my jailer did. And that waitress probably deserves that same fate. But I won't be dirtying my hands any further. I refuse to become like them.*

Diamanes laughed. **"I wonder how long that vow will stand!"**

Glenn wrapped the damned hand in bandages and steeled himself. "Time to seek answers, then. Redan should have finished reading the document by now, right?"

Chapter 21

ANSWERS

Glenn left his room, smelling a hell of a lot better compared to when he entered. Thanks to the thorough cleaning, he was practically unrecognizable. That, he was thankful for. No one glanced at him, apart from a few interested women, which wasn't too embarrassing, on the contrary. He sat at Redan's table, leaning back in his chair and crossing his arms.

Redan stared at him for a moment, the emotion in his green eyes indecipherable.

"Kiddo, ya're a brave one. I'll let ya know I don't discriminate—"

"So!" Glenn interrupted him, "Did you read the document?"

Redan grinned a toothy smile as he took off his golden monocle and cleaned it with a silk handkerchief.

"If what I read in yar crappy notebook is half-true, ya should be dead right now. Or a monstrosity, some kind of Corrupted. But ya're neither." The old man leaned forwards and rubbed his chin. "Or so it appears."

Redan's eyes gleamed with curiosity, alongside a dose of wariness. The elder suddenly produced an ice knife and held it towards Glenn, hilt first. The soft lights of the inn refracted off the blade.

"Do ya still bleed red? 'Cause if ya don't, I might have to, well, put an early end to ya. No hard feelings, 'aight?" Redan stated simply, sending a shiver down Glenn's spine.

He wanted to run away, but the old man's gaze was too strong. Whatever magical fuckery was going on, it was efficient at restraining him. Glenn watched helplessly as his right hand moved by itself and took the knife. It cut a small slit on his left, purple hand. Horror seized his racing heart; he couldn't help but question whether he would indeed bleed red or... something else.

For the other parts of his body, sure, he had no doubt his blood would be as crimson as it always had been. But the blood where Diamanes resided might have been different.

The panic faded as quickly as it came. A scarlet droplet fell from the wound and onto the table. The magic that restrained Glenn faded.

Glenn gasped, clenching his heart. "*Huff*... Why couldn't you ask, you damned..."

I won't gain anything from insulting this annoying geezer, but still... What a dick!

"Darn, there's that much filth in yar blood, and yet ya remain human. That ain't normal. Heh, an anomaly, ay?" Redan snorted.

Glenn exhaled a heavy sigh. He wasn't that sure he was still human, but at least he bled like one. He took solace in that.

"Respectfully," Glenn hissed in a dry tone, "I think I could have done that without you forcing me, had you simply asked."

The old man raised his eyebrows as Glenn stole the expensive handkerchief from his hands. "I ain't forcing no one. Ya did it yourself, right? I ain't the one who held the knife, that's certain."

I like this guy, Diamanes commented with a chuckle.

Of course you do... Glenn shook his head before attempting to steer the conversation back on track.

"So, can you help me against the people who..." He gestured at the document. "Fed me this bullshit cocktail?"

He averted his gaze from Glenn's hopeful eyes. "I don't even know who these *people* ya speak of are, and I'm just an ol' man. I'm not sure as to why ya thought I could help ya, but I'm honored."

Is he for real?

Glenn clenched his teeth as he watched Redan not-so-discreetly draw a circle in his hand.

The shameless geezer is asking for money!

He sighed and pulled the gold coins out of his dimensional pouch. "I'm certain the creeps who did this to me are from that church with the vine symbol. Secondly, how expensive are you—?"

A bit of ice stuck his lips together, muting him. Redan slowly stood, clenching his hands on the edges of the table. He glanced at the waitress at the counter and understanding flashed on his face.

Redan flicked his fingers and the ice sealing Glenn's lips melted away.

"What was that for—?"

Redan's expression hardened, and he threw the notebook at Glenn, who caught it reflexively. "We don't have much time. Follow me. I need you to meet someone."

Glenn took a step back, dumbfounded.

"Wait, why would I come with you? Can't I just... hire you? You go and ice all of those cultists while I stay here in the safety of my room?"

Redan rolled his eyes and sighed with disappointment.

"Did ya lose yar guts somewhere along the way, kid? Perhaps ya want to go back into the hole ya crawled out of? 'Cause that's what will happen if ya stay here. Or worse. How could little ol' me know?"

Glenn discreetly glanced at the fake waitress at the bar. She was staring directly at him, grinning widely as she leaned forwards to reveal her bosom as much as she could. But Glenn now knew it wasn't her prominent 'assets' she wanted to show. No, it was the cult's mark.

He gulped, refusing to even think of returning to that cursed prison. Hurriedly, he left the inn, following Redan's lead. After glaring at the ominous church standing on the opposite side of the street, he swore to himself that he would find a way to burn that place to the ground someday.

He shook his head. "So, uh, who are we going to meet? And, seeing how you reacted, you must know those cultists guys, right?"

Redan raised an eyebrow. "Cult? They ain't no cult. That's one of the main religions of Munirp, ya whacko. How can ya not know that?"

The concerned whacko rubbed the back of his head, embarrassed. *I can't just tell him I'm from another world, can I?*

"I'm... I'm not from here. So, I'm unfamiliar with many things," Glenn admitted. That wasn't technically lying, so it worked too.

Muttering something along the lines of 'damn'd bumpkin', the old man explained, "They're the infamous Thorns Church. All insane, masochistic fanatics who trade pain for their divine powers."

"Among the poorest, they're also known for providing addictive *substances* to their followers, alongside their damn *repentance*," he spat the last word in disgust.

Glenn grimaced, failing to picture a group of people drugging and whipping themselves to harness some mysterious power. Was that the spell that summoned thorny vines from the ground to restrain him, or was it the Silence curse that kept him mute almost two months? Probably. Not that he cared. Right now, he just wanted to be far away from those sick bastards.

Redan continued, "They recruit actively 'cause many of their followers die within the first few months from self-mutilation. Those who survive the initiation period become unhinged madmen that nobody wants to encounter. They spend their days hoping to die under their spell, Repentir. Quite the sickening fellows."

The old man paused for a moment and picked his nose. "Ya might be right in calling those wackos 'cultists' when I think about it. Huh."

Glenn nodded. "I know, right?" No other word seemed appropriate to describe them.

Redan shook his head. "They act in the northwest of the Sewers, between the Frozen Gate and the Twilight Gate. They ain't supposed to go into the other districts because they're ruled by other groups."

"I found ya on the edge of the northeast district. If whatcha saying is true, there are thousands of monsters waiting to be unleashed there, which means war is coming. A war which will involve everyone from the Thorns Church to the Black Heirs. Maybe even King's Rise's military. Although, I doubt that."

Glenn, already overwhelmed, grew even more perplexed. Black Heirs? The military? He just managed to get the name of the cult who tortured him, the Thorns Church, and now he had new factions to learn about. *Black Heirs... At least their name sounds intriguing. Hopefully, they aren't sick bastards like those cultists.*

Redan grumbled and quickened his pace, leaving Glenn to catch up to him.

"How did Giselle miss this? Is she still worried about that damn brat? Darn it..."

Glenn held his tongue, even though he wanted to know who Giselle was. It didn't seem like the right time to inquire about a mysterious friend of Redan.

A group of dangerous-looking beggars cut in front of them, blocking their path. They had rusted knives, wooden clubs, and looked ravenously at the both of them. The largest of the party—a man with a fat belly and probably three or less hair on his head—aimed his weapon at them.

"Pay up, folks, or we'll slice you up and eat you for breakfast. It's been a while since we had fresh meat!"

Sinister chuckles echoed from the ruffians as they closed in on the duo. Glenn's eyes opened wide in shock. One of the bandits noticed and pointed a finger at him, laughing madly.

"Haha! Look at this fellow! He's going to piss his pants from fright!"

These were the kinds of third-rate villains used as comic relief in webcomics, only lasting a panel or two. He couldn't believe he met some!

Redan simply sighed before waving his hand. A wave of cold air rushed over the thieves, who shivered and took a step back. Well, they tried to do so before realizing their feet were encased in solid ice. Screams of panic resounded among the group as they struggled to free themselves.

Redan shook his head dejectedly. "I don't have time for those idiots. Let's get going."

Glenn followed behind him silently. *If I had that power... perhaps I could take on those cultist bastards by myself.*

Well, let me tell you that you won't reach Redan's level. Diamanes warned. **You'll never be able to handle both Aura and Mana, no matter what you do. That old man does it effortlessly. But... with my help... you could sail beyond the geezer's power.**

Glenn scoffed. *Sure, if you say so.*

"Where are we going?" Glenn asked Redan worriedly.

"We're goin' back to the Black Heirs' territory. Mean, dark-skinned fellows with white runes on their foreheads. Don't pick a fight with them. They're not like the fools livin' around that prison of yours."

Glenn gulped. *Let's do as the old man recommends...*

* * *

After navigating through the slums for a good half hour, Glenn realized they were back where Redan had found him.

Well-maintained tents stood among dilapidated houses. He noticed the people were quite well-fed here, and also, *they* noticed him back. They stared silently at the duo, making Glenn slightly uncomfortable. As Redan explained, they had dark skin and white marks on their foreheads. The white marks were varied—a complicated set of runes mashed together.

"Why are they looking at us?" Glenn whispered to Redan.

Redan chuckled. "They ain't lookin' at us. They're starin' at *ya*, kiddo."

Glenn frowned. *So they are the so-called Black Heirs...*

Groups emerged from their homes and tents to scrutinize Glenn, not uttering a word. Judgmental gazes. Full of hate, spite, and distrust.

"The hell? Do they hold some grudge against me?"

Redan nodded vigorously. "Oh, yes, they do. Ya're a white boy dressed in noble attire. To them, ya represent the very class that forced them into this wretched existence."

Glenn glanced back, noticing the group trailing behind them and blocking their retreat. Their faces contorted in resentment, jaws clenched. It seemed like the only thing restraining them was the old man's presence, a sufficient deterrent in the face of their overwhelming numbers.

Welp, I better shut my trap. Glenn gulped.

Yep. Do you see those white marks on their foreheads? They all possess power to a certain extent, commented Diamanes.

Glenn frowned. *What kind of power? Magic again?*

Yeah, kind of. As far as I can see, the intricacy of the mark correlates with the strength of their Aura, Diamanes explained.

Glenn's lips curved upwards. *Can I get one?*

Diamanes took on an outraged tone, **First, that would be cultural appropriation. Second, you weren't born for it. And finally...** The entity chuckled. **I am pretty sure they wouldn't give that mark to you no matter what.**

Glenn disregarded two-thirds of the sentence and instead concentrated on the interesting part. *What do you mean I wasn't born for it?*

Diamanes sighed. **Usually, the human body can't accommodate multiple sources of power without erupting like a watermelon under a hydraulic press. Well, that's what's supposed to happen, but somehow that white mark makes it possible. You still can't get it though. I think it's something to do with their blood.**

You're going through deep, dark parts of my brain to get references like that press.

And since you're already a Mage, you can't use Aura. Well, maybe you could, if you were born with a unique lineage like Redan.

Wait, did you say Redan has a special bloodline? Is he like part dragon or something?

Diamanes' silence threw a shiver down Glenn's spine as he realized that his joke might have landed a little too close to the truth.

After a few twists and turns, Glenn and Redan arrived in front of an expansive tent reminiscent of a Mongolian yurt. Black Heirs congregated nearby, consuming meals by campfires or honing their weapons—exotic curved sabers.

The Black Heirs surrounded Glenn and Redan as they approached the yurt, the cold glints of their blades incomparable to their intense hatred. They stared at Glenn with animosity, ignoring Redan entirely.

"Man, isn't it too much to hate me for the clothes I wear?" Glenn muttered through his teeth.

Suddenly, as if to break the tension, a rough, female voice exploded from within the tent in an unfamiliar language. The Black Heirs parted to create a path for the duo.

The yurt flap lifted, drawn back by a hand as dark as the night. A formidable and extremely muscular woman emerged. She stood with a powerful presence, appearing to be in her sixties. She donned tight leather pants and a sleeveless vest of the same material that could barely hold her imposing bosom. Intimidating scars intersected her face, one tracing down her left eye and the other running horizontally.

A distinct white mark adorned her forehead, much more pronounced and intricate than any other mark Glenn had seen before. She had black-red hair cut short and fiery eyes that burned like hell's flames. She held something similar to a smoldering cigarette between her lips, inhaling slowly.

Her expression traversed multiple stages: initial surprise followed by perplexity that ultimately settled on pure fury. Redan bowed and removed his straw hat.

"Giselle."

Oh, so she's Giselle. Damn.

Formidable. Another Fourth Circle Mage. This country must boast considerable strength to harbor so many high-ranking Magi, commented Diamanes with an impressed tone.

Glenn almost couldn't restrain himself from gasping out loud. *What?!*

Giselle took a deep breath before pointing at Redan with a shaking finger. "You..."

The surrounding temperature suddenly climbed. *Why do I feel like I can predict what's about to unfold?*

Her eyes blazed with intense, fiery anger as she roared at the old man, "Redan, ya old fogey! How dare ya try to cheat on me?!"

Surprisingly, when a massive fire sword hurtled mere meters from his face, Glenn found himself a little less taken aback than he should have been. *Am I... getting used to this? Already? Still. Damn it.*

Chapter 22

THE BLACK HEIRS

Glenn glanced suspiciously at the bubbling cup of... *something* that Giselle had given him. He slowly brought it to his lips, half-curious and half-worried. He winced at the smell. Whatever was in that mixture was probably not supposed to be ingested by humans.

Is that really a problem for you? You're a superhuman now! Diamanes exclaimed.

The latter's eyelids twitched as he placed the cup down. He peeked into the Black Heir's leader's office where Redan and Giselle competed in an intense staring contest.

Glenn rubbed the back of his head, recalling what happened moments ago. When that fiery sword almost sliced both the old man and him, an ice wall rose out of the ground. The resulting shockwave managed to knock him down but not harm him in the slightest.

After the ice disappeared in a cloud of hissing steam, he remembered finding Redan completely unperturbed, as if attempted murder had been a perfectly normal event. The Black Heirs burst into laughter and dejected sighs as they exchanged pouches of coins. Apparently, they were betting on how their boss, Giselle, would react to the sight of the old Mage.

This really is an insane world, isn't it? Glenn pondered before shaking his head.

Diamanes scoffed mockingly. *What's wrong with enjoying an entertaining spectacle? Pity there was no popcorn!*

What's wrong with that? Aren't they playing with people's lives a bit too much? I almost became a casualty!

Glenn sighed and turned to the old couple arguing, their words too distant for him to hear. He was occupying a corner of the yurt, resembling a waiting room, while Giselle's office lay on the opposite side. Steam spilled from the doorway as Giselle and Redan traded spells once again.

Glenn stood and dusted off his shoulders. The yurt's entrance let in some gentle light, creating a cozy ambiance. A table in the center of the room held various objects: an obsidian dagger, shimmering crystals of different colors—probably Shards—and the skull of a mysterious creature. Its bone structure lacked familiar features—no teeth, jaws, or eye sockets. Only a gaping hole that gave some hint of its function.

It was surprisingly flat, being half a meter wide and a dozen centimeters tall. If it weren't for the fact that it was made out of bone, Glenn would never have guessed that it was a skull. *It is a skull, right?*

"Never seen an Ossiva skull before?" a mocking voice chimed in from behind him.

It's a skull! That's one question solved, remarked Diamanes as Glenn turned to face his interlocutor—a young man in his twenties, dressed in an outfit more suited to a desert than a shantytown.

His bright green eyes were full of energy, an affable smile floated on his lips, and yet, he seemed a little haughty. His skin was tanned, and he had an athletic build. He had a mark on his forehead, but it wasn't as detailed as Giselle's. Chestnut-gold strands escaped the constraints of his white shemagh.

"I'm Sahro. Sahro Sand," said the newcomer as he approached the table, his gaze fixed on the skull. "It's not surprising you've never seen one. It's a rare creature that only appears during moonless nights. See that hole?"

Sahro pointed to the rounded opening Glenn had previously noticed. "The Ossiva's tongue shoots out of there and pierces through skin and steel alike to suck the bones from its victims."

Glenn scoffed at the description. *Thanks to whoever shoved me onto that battlefield instead of the damned desert. I wouldn't have survived the first night.*

It would make for a pretty good pet, commented Diamanes.

Glenn blinked. *What?*

"This was the Alpha of the Ossiva herd, and Giselle hunted it by herself back when we were still living in the Ink Dunes."

"Not surprising," Glenn remarked. "Your boss is scary—and I mean that as a compliment."

Sahro scoffed, "Anyway, who are you? Why did Sir Redan bring a human noble here?"

Glenn frowned. "Glenn, pleasure to meet you. But... Human noble? What do you mean?"

The Black Heir looked him up and down. "Such good quality fabric doesn't come easily. The only ones wearing those types of clothes are living deep within King's Rise walls, you damned nobles!" he spat the last word with hatred.

Glenn took a step back, momentarily stunned by his interlocutor's hostile attitude.

"Wait, isn't it a bit too much to assume my identity based on my clothes?" he tried to calm the hot-blooded Black Heir.

Sahro clicked his tongue. "You can say what you want, but you won't fool me. I've seen enough of your kind to recognize you at the first glance!"

"Believe what you wish." He waved his hand dismissively and changed the subject. "I've actually been wondering about something. Why do you call yourselves Black Heirs?"

"Why would I tell you?"

"Because..." Glenn restrained himself from rolling his eyes. "I'm just a very curious, not noble man who would like to understand more about this world. And the Black Heirs appear to be a *very powerful* group of individuals, so of course I'd like to know more."

Sahro rubbed his nose with a satisfied smile. "Haha, yes, we are indeed very powerful! You have a good eye, at least for that, noble scum."

They're also very gullible. Or is it just him? Diamanes remarked.

Sahro pressed his thumb to his forehead, pointing at the white runes. "This is an Inheritance Sigil. It makes us able to use both Aura and Mana. And only us Black Heirs can receive that sigil."

Glenn whistled in awe. "Wow, aren't you supposed to explode when using both at the same time? And... Let's say I somehow got that sigil. What would happen?"

Sahro grunted with irritation. "I doubt an Alsaahir would ever want to do the ritual for a human..."

Glenn sighed, "If you say so."

Diamanes suddenly interjected, ***Why don't you ask him about his parents? Because as far as I can see, he has some human blood too.***

Oh, is that right? Glenn happily obliged.

"Can a half-human, half-Black Heir have that mark?"

Sahro looked at him in sudden disgust. "What are you even thinking about, you fiend?"

Glenn shook his head. "No, no, I mean, let's be honest, one of your parents isn't a Black Heir, right?"

Sahro froze, and his demeanor suddenly hardened. He clenched his fists tightly, a sharp, crimson light covering them threateningly.

"Don't even speak of my parents, bastard!" the Black Heir hissed as he stepped in Glenn's direction.

The latter hurriedly jumped back and almost pulled the fire staff out of his pouch, just in time for Redan to suddenly enter the room. The Black Heir's anger melted away like snow in the sun, and he bowed at a perfect forty-five-degree angle.

"S-Sir Redan!" Sahro stuttered.

The old man grumbled in his beard, "Tsk... I already told ya not to do that, ya fool."

Glenn almost whistled in awe but restrained himself. *That was a swift change in attitude. Who the hell is Redan exactly if his presence is enough to make a prideful prick like Sahro bow down?*

The elder tapped on Sahro's shoulder, but the young man didn't move an inch. With an exasperated sigh, Redan turned towards Glenn and nodded in the direction of Giselle's office. Glenn grinned widely and waved at the Black Heir.

"Well, see you around." He tried to keep as friendly of a face as he could, but Redan eyed him suspiciously.

Why did you fuck with him? Diamanes asked curiously.

Glenn shrugged with a smirk. *Oh, mostly because I was bored. But also because he was trying to assert some kind of dominance. I couldn't just let him bully me like that.*

Diamanes grunted hesitantly.

What? Glenn finally asked.

Well, you know that red light around his fist when he was about to punch you? That was Aura.

Oh.

Even with your strengthened body, you might have suffered from a couple of broken bones, or worse.

Glenn winced. *Why didn't you tell me that before I made the idiot angry?*

You were so busy disparaging him that I simply couldn't interrupt such an entertaining show! Diamanes laughed wickedly.

Glenn brushed aside his thoughts as he entered the office, glancing at Giselle's muscular back. She paced angrily. The temperature in the room was increasing at the same speed as her fury until she finally turned towards him. She rubbed the Inheritance Sigil on her forehead—pondering—before slouching in the comfortable leather armchair behind her desk.

"So ya're the guy. The ol' bastard told me all about ya."

Now that Glenn had the opportunity to talk to the leader of a powerful force, he certainly was going to take advantage of it. After all, the Black Heirs sounded more than strong enough to fight those Thorns Church bastards. Glenn explained exactly what happened to him, spare for how he escaped or anything concerning Diamanes. He didn't hesitate to curse the cult multiple times, unable to restrain his hatred.

After he finished, Giselle sighed and pulled a drawer open, taking out a cigar.

"Wan' one?" She held one towards Glenn, but he politely refused.

She shrugged and bit on the cigar, conjuring a blue flame at the tip of her pinky and using it as a lighter. She took a few puffs, creating a small cloud of smoke that she blew in Glenn's face. It smelled of rich tobacco and spices.

Giselle leaned back and stared at the ceiling, her red, fiery eyes lost in thought.

"My people came from a place that was worse than this damn shithole," she suddenly said with nostalgia.

"From the Land Beyond the Dark Wall. From the Ink Dunes."

Sahro mentioned that place before but... Come to think of it...

"Wait, the Ink Dunes, as in a black sand desert?" interrupted Glenn as he thought back to the strange dream he had on Redan's cart.

It's a little too far-fetched to believe it's the same desert as the one I dreamed of. I really need a map that spans further than this kingdom. Maybe it'd be worth checking out those Ink Dunes if that's the only location with black sand.

Giselle looked at him strangely and then nodded in confirmation.

"We had a single rule. Stick together and survive to fight and see another day. Everything worked well. It was a tough life, but we were tough people," she said, shaking her head in reminiscence.

"Until the arrival of the Gods." Her tone shifted, dripping with spite.

Glenn also detected another emotion, something he didn't expect to find in the badass lady.

Fear.

Chapter 23

GISELLE'S TALE

"Gods?" Glenn's voice carried incredulity. Actual, living *Gods*? He kind of expected those to exist with the cult and whatnot, but...

Giselle's hand clenched tightly on the armrest of her seat, her gaze distant and locked in painful memories.

"They called themselves that, and they had every right to do so," she began slowly, searching for the words. "They were... overbearing. So overpowering that even someone as formidable as me couldn't think of challengin' them."

Hmm, I wonder if they were actual Gods or just really powerful entities... The latter seems more probable, Diamanes commented.

She took a measured drag from her cigar, her hand slightly shaking. Her eyes seemed to see beyond the yurt's confines, recalling souvenirs in a desert of black sand.

"We were caught in the crossfire of their battles, insignificant as ants. We had no choice but to flee—lest we wake up one day to find ourselves wiped out." Her tone carried a mix of resentment and bitterness as she replayed the events in her mind.

"My tribe... Annihilated. All the strongest... Dead. Only the children were left, alongside a few chosen ones. I was part of those. We had to leave." She sighed.

"Twenty years ago, crossing the Black Gate and the impassable Dark Wall seemed like our only option. To seek shelter in Munirp and finally be freed from the Gods' tyranny." Giselle smirked dejectedly, trailing off with a mocking tone.

Glenn sat silently. He had no intention of interrupting the powerful lady. It was evident that this story was heavy on her heart, and he was more than happy to lighten her load. *More information for me, and a better state of mind for her. Win-win.*

"We forsook our pride as the Ink Dunes striders and crawled on our knees to beg Comte Noir of the Dark Gate to let us in. We knew him; he was Munirp's hero during the War of Four Fronts, ninety years ago."

"When he told us that the King had agreed to take us in, we were overjoyed. We would finally be able to live without fear of losing our lives, or having to watch helplessly as one of those Gods slaughtered our families..." Giselle's gaze wandered in the smoke rising from her cigar.

She stood abruptly, striking the desk with a raging fist and creating a crack in the wood. The wood creaked faintly, crying out for help. A dusting of smoking ash fell on it, a large flame suddenly appearing. Giselle simply crushed the fire in her hand.

Glenn blinked, taken aback by the sight, but the Black Heiress resumed her story, unbothered.

"Then we arrived here. We thought this place would be an oasis after the storm of violence in the Ink Dunes. But it was the opposite!" Giselle flailed her arms furiously.

"We all are living in the gutter, surviving on the trash of the ones who live in the city." Her fist shook, not with fear anymore but with wrath.

"Why not enter King's Rise then? If your people are as powerful as I imagine, you could surely manage to pay for the identification process."

"Hah!" Giselle snorted.

"Even if we were as rich as Plutus, we'd still be denied entry to that damn city. You damn nobles don't want to see our dark skin—way too damn scared of it," she said as she stabbed her finger in Glenn's chest.

"My grandson..." She paused, her emotions overtaking her. She took a long breath and rubbed her eyes before returning to the offensive.

"You damn nobles took him, and ya still have the nerve to come here asking for help? I won't do your dirty work *ever again!* Unless... Unless I see my damn grandson!" she blurted before smashing the table. Splinters flew as the unfortunate desk buckled.

Glenn jumped behind his chair. This went from zero to one hundred too quickly for his taste. When he peeked out of his hiding spot, Giselle was back in her armchair, slouching in exhaustion.

I mean, look at the poor woman. She needed someone or something to vent on. You just were the unlucky one. Bad place, bad time. Diamanes relativized, laughing at him.

Glenn inhaled a deep breath, seeking the right words to assure the agitated grandmother that he was *not* aligned with whoever took her grandson.

"What the hell?!" he blurted out.

The temperature in the room increased. "What did ya just say?"

Me and my big mouth... Glenn raised his hands in a placating manner.

"No, wait. I didn't mean it like that! I don't know anything about any of this, and I'm certainly not a noble!"

He paled when a fiery longsword appeared in Giselle's hand. She took a long puff of her cigar before crushing it on the desk and pointing her flaming weapon at Glenn.

"Don't try to fool me! I know a goddamn noble when I see one! Those damn clothes, and that annoying face!" she spat.

Ha! Did you hear that? She thinks your face is annoying!

Shut it, Diamanes!

Glenn looked for a solution. He noticed that despite the fire, the tent's fabric wasn't burning. *How strange... Can she control flames? How impressive! But now isn't the time to get absorbed by how cool her magic looks!*

"I... I mean, these clothes aren't mine to begin with!" Glenn admitted. "I just picked them up in a random dead guy's chest, and they fit! And I apologize for my face, but I was born with— Damn it!"

Giselle's fury subsided, and the fiery sword vanished in a cloud of red particles, dissipating along with the heat in the room. She slumped back into her seat, sighing wearily. Meeting Glenn's gaze, her eyes seemed void of hope.

"Then what do ya want, kid? Are ya here just to make an old lady feel miserable?"

"You said earlier that you can't enter the city, is that right?"

Giselle nodded silently. "I can get one or two of my guys to enter, but only rarely. And they'd have to move in the utmost secrecy, so I can't just send a detachment. They wouldn't even be able to get to the Bourgeoisie anyway..."

That's my bargaining chip. Glenn realized.

"Why not ask Redan to find your grandson? You seem to be friends," he inquired.

Giselle looked at him as if he was crazy. Then, a second later, she exploded in laughter, slapping her thighs.

"Hehe, asking that old fogey? That's a hilarious idea. Hehehehe!"

"Is there something stopping you from asking him?" Glenn insisted.

Giselle wiped away her tears. "Not really, but that poor old man can't help me. He's in the same damn condition as us, for some other damn reason."

Her fit of laughter seemed to have made her feel better. Glenn thought about it, and indeed, he never heard Redan talk about *entering* the walls of King's Rise.

Then... this might work to my advantage. I can even hit two birds with one stone. Glenn came out from behind the chair and sat on it.

"I have an idea, but I need something from you. From the Black Heirs, more precisely," he declared.

Giselle's gaze lifted with visible curiosity. "What's yar proposal, kid?"

"You're aware that the Thorns Church is coercing and kidnapping people to join their cult, right?" he asked. "Well, it's not just to bolster the funds in their collection plates. They're building an army. And they need to be flushed out before it's too late."

If Giselle accepted, it would mean war in the Sewers and the death of countless Black Heirs. But if it was personal...

"I need you guys to stand against them. In exchange, I'll go into King's Rise and find your grandson. I'll bring him back from whoever kidnapped him," Glenn proposed.

Giselle regarded him with a mixture of amusement and skepticism. "And why in the world would I trust ya? How can I know that ya can do the job, huh? Do ya even know where to start looking?"

Glenn tapped on his chin, pondering her question.

"I have a... *peculiar* set of skills," he said while revealing the purple skin under his left arm. "I'll just need a drawing of him or a physical description. And of course, his name."

"He was taken from me and his parents twenty years ago. I can't possibly know what my sweet grandson looks like now. Callum... Callum was his name..." she said sullenly.

"But you must have some lead—some information about who took him?" Glenn pressed, eager to find any starting point.

Giselle paused, and then her eyes brightened. "I do remember somethin'. The Howard family! That's right. It was that bastard Baron Howard!"

Wait, Baron Howard? Isn't that the same family name as the guy whose pouch and journal I found? Glenn realized. *I'm wearing the clothes of the noble who kidnapped the Black Heirs' leader's grandson! Of course, they hate me!*

That's... right. Seems like everything is linked. Diamanes confirmed with a tinge of surprise in his voice.

Glenn felt a boost in confidence. "If it's the Howard family, then that's even better. I have leverage on them."

"Leverage? How? That's a Baron noble family we're talkin' 'bout." She frowned.

Glenn fished the Howard house signet ring out of his dimensional pouch.

"I have my ways. Do I need to explain more?" He queried confidently.

Giselle's eyes widened, and she slowly reached for the ring. Disbelief and astonishment flashed across her scarred face.

"That... Where did you get that?" she asked softly as hope was reborn in her eyes.

Hah! You just can't tell her you stole it from Jefferson Howard's dead body! Diamanes exclaimed mockingly. The latter's eyelids twitched, but he kept up his confident facade.

Giselle shook her head and handed him back the ring. "No matter. I don't wanna know. You want to destroy the Thorns Church, then..."

The Black Heiress stood and held her hand out for him to shake, grinning widely. "That's a fine deal we have here. My grandson for a war."

Glenn took her hand with a similarly wicked smile. "A fine deal indeed."

Chapter 24

A PROPER BEGINNING

Giselle slowly stood up from her leather armchair and turned her back to Glenn. They spent a few minutes in silence as Giselle considered how she was going to approach this new war.

"Ya know, sonny, I was gonna do this anyhow," she finally said, crossing her arms with a knowing look. "They think they can stir up a pot o' monsters right by my doorstep? Well, I reckon it's high time I remind 'em who the Black Heirs are. We've been sittin' quiet too long."

A wave of fear crept over Glenn. Whatever Giselle was planning, it felt downright terrifying.

"Getting rid of those cult weirdos is my main and only goal right now. But... you wouldn't happen to know anything about the Moon Rift, would you?" he asked, wondering if Giselle would have any information about the strange event that *probably* brought him into this world.

Giselle glanced at the ruined desk with a dejected expression. She rubbed the white mark on her forehead, the Inheritance Sigil.

"Well, child, I ain't no expert, that's for sure. I've only lived through three o' them in my whole life," she said, and Glenn was about to ask her how long that was before remembering the golden rule: never ask a lady her age. "The first time, I was a young'un. Hid in a tent, tucked away by my family. Didn't see much 'cept that Big One in the sky turning redder than a bloodied hog."

"The second time, I was fightin' with the soldiers—taking on all them horrible creatures that showed up that night. Gods, it was something awful, like the sky itself was comin' down on us. Things falling from the Big One, crashing all over. Never seen anything like it in all my years."

"The monsters were different, too. They were smart and mean—crafty as a fox. We had to team up just to take one down! Back in the day, one of us could handle a whole pack o' them beasts, no problem." She froze for a second, then pulled something from the chest. She brought the item to Glenn, who stared at it wide-eyed.

"We were lucky enough to find this little doohickey that fell near us. The ground was covered in some kinda red slime where it landed."

Slowly, Glenn reached for it, surprised at its weight.

"No one knows what it is, and we're still waitin' for someone to tell us what purpose it might have." Giselle shrugged with uncertainty.

Glenn felt his heart beat loudly in his chest. In a sleek, metallic frame, its body was divided into two distinctive sections—a ten-centimeter-long barrel and a handle grip. On the side of the cannon, engraved in small letters, was 'Smith and Wesson .38'. He flipped the gun over, finding 'Springfield, Massachusetts, 1899' written on the other side. For some reason, the trigger was missing, making the weapon as good as a piece of junk.

This is an actual item from Earth. A revolver! This... This changes everything! Glenn carefully opened the cylinder while pointing the gun downwards, discovering in utter shock that six lead bullets rested in perfect condition.

Giselle looked at him with a shocked pair of eyes. He awkwardly put the cylinder back and returned the gun to her. He never used a firearm before, but this one was pretty straightforward to handle.

"Uh, it just opened by itself."

Giselle mimicking his actions. She gazed at the firearm in awe, clicking the cylinder back into place.

"Well, bless my soul... I've had that thing for forty years and never knew it could do that!" she said, her voice tinged with wonder. "Tried everything on it—poured Mana, Aura, even a bit o' Divinity, but nothin' ever worked. Always felt like something was missing."

Glenn shrugged, trying to look as innocent as possible. *They would have probably figured it out if the trigger was still there. Maybe that's for the best.*

He wasn't sure he wanted to be the one to bring hot weapons into a medieval world. Giselle stored the beautiful Smith & Wesson away. Even if the weapon was centuries old, it still came from Earth. Which meant that the chances of him having fallen from the Moon Rift were higher than he thought.

Giselle sat back on her chair before continuing her tale. "Now, where was I? Oh yes, the third time was just a few months back. You were there, right?"

Glenn nodded, remembering that night all too well. "No wonder ya're curious about it. The first Blood Moon always shakes folks up. We were lucky here—didn't have too many monsters to deal with..." Her face darkened suddenly. "Though there were some poor souls who lost their minds. Started killin' folks left and right. Awful business. Let's not speak on it."

Glenn silently nodded in agreement, not wanting to make the old woman relive such grim memories. He had learned plenty and was more than satisfied.

Giselle clapped her hands. "Well, that's all I know. I'll try to get my kids to find out more, but right now, that's all I have."

Glenn shook his head. "That's more than enough already. Thank you very much."

"Well, I still have to verify if what ya said is true, so don't get your hopes up too quickly," she scoffed. "And I hope ya do realize that if I discover that you lied or, worse, fail to save my grandson..."

Glenn shivered. The lady didn't need to finish her sentence for him to understand the looming threat.

"I wouldn't be there if I intended to kill myself this way..." he hissed through his teeth. The pressure disappeared as Giselle sneered, dismissing him with a wave of her hand.

Glenn bowed, taking his leave. Once out of the yurt, he sighed. The meeting had been mentally exhausting, and he was glad it was over.

This is a bet I can't afford to lose... But between the Thorns Church and the Black Heirs, he had to admit that the first scared him a little more than the second. One could be reasoned with while the other was a sickening cult, after all.

I have the Black Heirs as allies. For now, that's as good as it can get.

Good job! If you succeed in finding her grandson, she'll be indebted to you! Congratulated Diamanes, before scoffing, ***Being in the good graces of powerful leaders is always fortunate! Until they betray you, that is.***

Glenn ignored the last part of his left hand's phrase. *I hadn't thought that far, but she was going to fight the Thorns Church without me asking anyway, so I'm practically saving her grandson for free. I even get a positive relationship with the Black Heirs out of it.*

Oh. You didn't plan anything. Of course. Why does it surprise me? Diamanes grumbled.

Glenn's eyelids twitched as he forced himself to ignore the entity's snarky comments.

Let's just hope I can save Callum. I don't want another powerful organization trying to skin me alive... He glanced across the camp and found Redan sitting next to a bonfire, chatting with a few other Black Heirs.

Rubbing the back of his neck, he said, "Why do I feel a sting in..."

He turned around, catching Sahro glaring at him. Glenn waved at him with a wide smile. The move seemed to surprise the Black Heir, who flipped him off in return. That made Glenn strangely happy.

Redan's gaze welcomed Glenn to the campfire as he threw a small chunk of wood into the flames. As soon as he sat down, the Black Heirs left swiftly, treating him like he carried the plague.

"I certainly didn't expect to be the victim of racism in this world…" he muttered dejectedly. Sahro sat in front of him, grinning mockingly.

"We lived in the Ink Dunes. Did you expect us to break bread with you?"

Glenn glared at him. He thought back to that dream again, the one where he found his sister in a desert of black sand. What could be the connection between these two things?

"So what? Because you lived in the desert, you refuse to trust other people? How does that make any sense?" Glenn snapped, startling Sahro.

Redan drew in the dirt with a sharp stick, watching the exchange silently.

The Black Heir quickly gathered himself. "Well, in the Ink Dunes, cooperation is a necessity for survival. We lived centuries like that, and guess what?" He proudly puffed out his chest. "We lost the ability to betray each other."

Sahro laughed at Glenn's doubtful reaction. "Every Black Heir is linked to each other, forming an intricate, indestructible web. *This* is what makes us truly powerful!"

Glenn wondered how such a thing was possible. He didn't have any distrust in humanity—well, maybe a little towards the Thorns Church— but he knew that greed was part of human nature. And most people were ready to betray their loved ones to get what they wanted.

Imagining a community free of such issues seems…

"Utopian, right?" Redan smiled when he saw Glenn's face. The latter coughed in his fist, averting his eyes.

Redan grinned knowingly. "I thought the same until I immersed myself in their culture and got a bit… close to the granny. But it's real." His expression darkened, and he turned to Sahro. "Too bad it doesn't apply to every Black Heir, right?"

Sahro's prideful expression cracked. He clenched his fists and suddenly stood, bowing in Redan's direction.

"Sorry, I need some air."

We're already outside, though? Diamanes' puzzled comment almost made Glenn laugh, but the underlying meaning of the old man's words stopped him in his tracks.

Redan shook his head and spat on the ground. "Bah! It ain't our place to intervene. Anyway."

"The reason they don't trust ya, kiddo?" Redan continued, "Ya look like a noble little shit, the same noble shit that promised them safe shelter and gave them these Sewers. The same noble kind who kidnapped their kid. The same noble trash that wants to use them as slaves."

Regaining his breath, he looked into Glenn's eyes. "And mostly, ya have the damn face of a noble. And I think that's enough for the explanation, ain't that right?"

Didn't Giselle say the same thing about your face? commented Diamanes maliciously.

Glenn groaned with annoyance, "But I'm *not* a noble! I wish I was, but I'm *not*. That's... That's just discrimination based on appearance!"

Redan nodded. "It is."

"Perhaps saving their boss' grandson will help change their minds."

Redan's gaze shook for a second, but he quickly went back to his nonchalant self. Glenn noticed the awkward reaction and cleared his throat.

"Can I ask you to teach me magic?"

Redan stared at his left, bandaged hand.

"Don't ya have a Circle already?"

Glenn explained his situation, revealing that he had only obtained his Convergence moments before his imprisonment.

Redan scratched his chin in thought. "So there ain't no one who taught ya... That means ya're pretty much a blank slate, ready to absorb knowledge..."

Glenn nodded hesitantly. The latter shrugged and gestured at Glenn to come closer, who obliged without complaint.

"Well, there ain't nothing complicated." The old man poked his finger in Glenn's chest, on his heart's side. "I'll send some Mana to your circuits, so I can figure out your affinities and also to show ya how it feels to use some good ol' magic."

Before Glenn could ask about any precautions, a feeling akin to a worm wriggling through his body surged from Redan's finger. The sensation was unsettling, as if a foreign object was trying to invade him. Glenn closed his eyes, trying to get a better feel of it.

"Ya feel that? It's Mana—the essence of spellcasting."

The old man's voice was strangely ethereal, as if he was...

"Yeah, I'm talking through the Mana link. Ya wouldn't be able to hear me if I wasn't."

Wow. This is so weird.

"Ya don't tell me. It's been a while since I've done this."

So reassuring.

"What I'm doing right now is puttin' ya into a simulated Meditation— a state one attains when they're in synchronization with their Mana flow. It's damn useful to check if there's somethin' wrong with yar body, or to recuperate yar expended Mana quicker," Redan explained as Glenn's mind settled into the strange flowing state.

It was as if his consciousness was floating *inside* his body.

The darkness soon took form, and Glenn found himself observing his own form from a surreal perspective. He saw his veins pulsing with blood and muscles contracting with each heartbeat. His heart pulsed with a dark blue mystical hue, calling to him.

"Yar perception of yar own body is remarkably realistic," Redan remarked.

Glenn could probably have watched it for hours if Redan hadn't pulled him out—or more like pulled him in, his point of view slowly approaching the pulsing heart.

"Don't worry, I'm the one drivin'. Next time, ya'll be free to do whatever ya want. But right now, since it's yar first ride, let me guide ya," Redan reassured him.

Glenn let go of his apprehension and let himself be led by the experienced old man. He felt like he was in a movie and couldn't help but marvel at this out-of-body... No, in-body experience.

What can I even call this? Introspection? Whatever. Redan said it was Meditation, so Meditation it is.

Glenn *entered* his heart, discovering a new space plunged into darkness. In that darkness—like a lighthouse illuminating the way—was a beautiful, massive ring made of gray light, revolving around a small gaseous ball emitting every color of the spectrum.

On closer inspection, he discovered that the ring consisted of strange runes, and trying to decipher them gave him a headache. *It might be wise to take a look at that later on.*

"This... This is impossible..." The ethereal voice of the old man shook.

Glenn flinched as he was abruptly pulled back to reality. He gasped, his heart racing as he clenched his chest. He had a wide grin on his face while opening and closing his hand.

"So that's magic. Palpable, visible magic." He closed his eyes before laughing out loud with pure happiness. "Hahahaha!"

He felt like a child whose dreams had been fulfilled. Magic... What made the impossible possible. And now he held it. It was real.

"I can't believe it," Glenn muttered.

Hey?! Where did you go? I've been trying to talk to you for fifteen minutes. Are you ignoring me? Diamanes' voice pulled him out of his exhilarated state.

He flinched and glared at his left hand. *I... I'm sorry. I went into some kind of... space? Redan called it Meditation. I felt like I was inside my body. It was... woah.*

Glenn lacked the words to explain what happened to Diamanes. The entity groaned in understanding before chuckling slightly. ***So that was your first Meditation. Damn, you guys were gone for ages, I swear.***

After smirking, he looked up. Redan was staring into the void, an expression of deep shock etched on his face. Glenn frowned and waved his hand in front of the old man's eyes, but he didn't react.

"Mr. Redan, are you okay?" Glenn asked hesitantly. He shook the old man gently, but his eyes were wide—unblinking, and unmoving.

Glenn checked the old man's pulse.

He didn't find one.

Holy shit! I killed Redan?!

Chapter 25

YOU'RE A WIZARD, GLENN

In this situation, Glenn had two choices: either bring Redan back from the dead himself or risk death by calling the Black Heirs for help.

Evidently, he only had one true option.

His hand shot out instinctively, connecting with Redan's cheek in a masterfully executed slap. The old man's head snapped to the side, and he fell from his seat, kicked the hell out of his trance. Redan blinked as he rubbed the spot where Glenn struck him.

Wow, did you just slap around a helpless old man? That's low, even for you, exclaimed Diamanes.

"No, I didn't!" Glenn said aloud, his relief palpable. The geezer wasn't dead; that was one crisis averted.

Redan, still disoriented, looked around in confusion. "What... You didn't what?"

Glenn's brain raced as he quickly improvised. "Oh, I was just wondering why we didn't continue." He awkwardly cleared his throat.

The senior rubbed his sore jaw, his cheek red with the trace of Glenn's hand. He pulled himself up, shaking his head in puzzlement.

"Lad, I tell ya somethin'. I think me heart near stopped when I saw what was inside yar Mana Heart..."

Glenn almost scoffed. *No shit, Sherlock! Is he speaking metaphorically, or does he actually know he was technically dead for a second there?*

"What I saw in there shouldn't exist. Ya're not meant to be..."

A troubled expression settled on Redan's face as he locked eyes with Glenn. "Ya... Who are ya?"

Glenn hesitated for a moment, considering whether to reveal his true identity. Eventually, he decided against it—not due to a lack of trust but because he doubted Redan would believe him. *Who would? Hey, I'm actually from another world, have an evil entity in my hand, and probably fell from the Moon Rift, which makes me a Fallen One.*

Yeah, no, he'd rather keep that to himself. He wasn't nearly strong enough to handle the potential consequences of revealing that. Maybe later, once he reached the old man's level.

Glenn shrugged. "I'm Glenn. And I'm pretty sure I'm human. If that ever was in question."

Redan squinted at him. "Hmph. And yar parents? Ya o' some fancy royal blood, perhaps?"

Glenn scoffed, his eyelids twitching. He dismissed the unpleasant memories that surged. *Royal blood? That seems particularly strange to ask...*

"Then... Never mind. The Mana Heart is the core of yar magic. It stores yar Mana and serves as the source of yar spells. The higher level yar Mana Heart is, the stronger ya are," Redan explained.

"The shape and color of yar Mana Heart defines yar magical affinities. I, for instance, have a Mana Heart shaped like a spear made o' white ice." He held out his hand, the image of a white spear appeared. Four ice rings hovered around it.

"Due to some unusual circumstances, I can wield both Mana and Aura—a trait shared with the Black Heirs. But that's not feasible for ordinary people." A crimson hue appeared, enveloping his body in a much more menacing way than Sahro.

"I suppose there's a difference between Aura and Mana, then?" Glenn asked.

"Well, Aura is destructive energy while Mana is creative. Of course, that's an oversimplification, but it should suffice for now." He leaned forwards and began drawing in the dirt, gesturing at Glenn to look.

"A Mage uses Mana Circles to gather and store Mana in their Mana Hearts. The more Circles a Mage has, the stronger they are. Logical, right?" Redan chuckled while pointing at something vaguely in the shape of a human before adding a circle within it.

"But makin' a new Circle? Well, that's tricky business. Takes understandin', skill, and most of all, luck. For some, they just gather enough Mana and rank up. But others, well... Like me, I had to stare death in the face more than once to break through." He chuckled, but there was a somber edge to it.

Glenn nodded slowly. "I'll have to explore that by myself, then. There's no sure way of doing this?"

Redan shook his head with a smirk. "There probably are, for nobles' bastards. But for us, we do it the hard way."

His expression darkened, and he pointed back at the drawing with his stick. "But, keep in mind that there is always a risk of dying. If you fail to converge a new Circle..." Redan smashed the twig in the center of the drawing. Glenn gulped.

"But there's no reason for that to happen, so don't worry, kiddo. Of course, it goes without saying, more Mana Circles means more Mana capacity and more powerful spells," he continued, as if what he just said wasn't *terrifying*.

"Magic uses Mana as fuel. Ya weave spells by envisioning what ya want and by manipulating Mana accordingly. Of course, depending on yar attributes, that might change. I have a tough time using fire magic, for example. I can do it, but it needs me to use magic words, and that sucks..."

Redan trailed off. He shook his head and gestured towards Sahro, who was observing them from a distance. Glenn suddenly realized that the Black Heir had probably seen him slap the hell out of Redan.

That might be a problem... Oh well.

Redan picked up another stick and drew a humanoid figure. This time, he added arrows inside the body that circulated through every limb.

"Aura, on the other hand, is fueled by one's life force. At a certain level with Mana, ya have a reserve of it in yar Mana Heart, making it so that it doesn't strain ya when ya use spells. Of course, in the beginning, it does—as all things do when ya start learning 'em. But that's the difference with Aura."

"It also gets measured differently. Instead of being stored in a central organ like yar Mana Heart, Aura is stored in yar whole body, transforming it into an Aura Core. Much tougher than a Mana Heart, but a death sentence if it breaks. When yar understandin' of Aura or its capacity becomes too grand for ya body... Well, it gets upgraded. I think ya can guess what happens if ya fail to go up a rank."

Glenn gulped. The phrase 'Everything had a price' seemed very fitting. If he wanted great power, he needed to get ready to pay a great price.

Redan grinned at Sahro. "Ya see, Aura draws from your life force... Aura requires constant energy but also strengthens your body over time. Black Heirs like Sahro possess bear-like strength. And that strength can grow massively. I, or Giselle, for example, can crush steel with our bare hands."

Glenn looked at Sahro, having a hard time believing the old man's words. He thought this guy was just a random dumbass, but he was strong enough to kill him if he wanted. Well, Glenn still had his abnormal body to rely on, but he doubted that would be enough against Aura.

I really needed to stop making enemies, don't I?

Redan snorted and threw his twig into the campfire. "This division between Mana and Aura is clear on the battlefield. Aura users on the frontline, and Mages in the backline. Well, I'm not that kind of Mage, though. And ya won't be either. Dumb Mages never train their bodies and always die from a knight's sword. Yar body gets reinforced by Mana eventually, just not at the level Aura does it."

Redan toyed with his canteen and poured a bit of water into the air. It transformed into ice, which he fashioned into a makeshift compress for his jaw.

"Damn, that hurts. How did I manage to hurt me self?" he muttered.

Glenn cleared his throat, pulling Redan's attention back to a subject he preferred. No need for the old man to realize he had been slapped by his newfound apprentice.

"So, what's wrong with my Mana Heart?" he asked.

Redan studied Glenn before answering. "Ya lack affinities. Or rather, ya don't have a common specialization."

Glenn's face lit up hesitantly. "Isn't that a good thing?"

Redan shrugged. "It might have been if yar Mana Heart had taken a shape. Unique doesn't mean good."

"It hasn't?" Glenn recalled the rainbow-hued gas sphere from his Meditation.

"No, it's formless. Well, not in a form that I can recognize," he said, a perplexed gesture accompanying his words.

"Yar First Circle settled smoothly, but your Mana Heart remains shapeless. The shape should determine yar preferred spells and the color of the element. But yars is of every damn color—formless to top it off! And yet, it doesn't feel like ya can use every damn element!"

He sighed deeply, returning his straw hat back to his head. "Just my rotten luck. Fallin' in with the only one who don't fit the rules..."

Am I supposed to be disappointed, excited, or worried? Isn't being irregular a sign of great potential?

I agree with the irregular part, Diamanes chimed in, to no surprise.

With a wicked grin, Redan clapped his hands. "Enough o' that. Scrap the standard trainin'. I'll teach ya the way I learned."

"Okay, I can live with that." Glenn smiled.

Receiving the same education as Redan meant he could probably become as strong as the old man, right? Which meant a hell lot stronger than he was currently, either way.

The old man clicked his tongue and muttered in a worried tone, "Ya'll just have to work on findin' your specialty, but that's a problem for later..."

Redan positioned himself a dozen meters away and conjured an ice ball above his palm. The sunlight made the spell gleam like a diamond. The spell hovered away from the old man and stood above the ground, waiting silently.

"Recall the feeling when I led ya into Meditation? Try to recreate it, and when ya do, envision yourself projecting something at this ice ball."

The ball hovered at Glenn's eye level. "Any projectile?"

"Yeah, lad, whatever tickles yar fancy. A rock, an arrow, a sword... I don't really care." The old man took a sip of his water.

"'Kay..." Glenn said before closing his eyes.

He sought the presence of Mana once more, attempting to reconnect with it. But the only thing he connected with was Redan's finger flick on his forehead.

The young man yelped, "What was that for?!"

Redan chuckled. "Think an enemy would wait while ya close yar eyes to cast?"

He's got a point, Diamanes added.

Glenn sighed and tried to feel Mana once again, his eyes wide open this time. He held his palm out in front of him, envisioning the only projectile that came to mind, a bullet from that Smith & Wesson revolver. After a minute of full focus, a ball of dark blue Mana started to take shape.

The intense concentration made him hyper-aware of his body. The pulse of his heartbeat, the droplets of sweat falling down his back, the fluttering of his clothes in the wind. His senses felt exacerbated, and that's when he realized it. For the first time, he was doing something truly magical—summoning water with a Shard back at the inn was a mere parlor trick in comparison.

Just pure, innocent magic fueled by Mana. Not like making a contract with an evil, demonic entity.

Fuck you, man.

Glenn ignored him and concentrated. The image of the bullet imprinted in his mind, and Glenn moved the Mana in his body, much like Redan did it. Mana shaped under his will, taking on a simple, piercing form. He flicked his finger and the bullet flew, speeding through the air with a whistling sound.

The ball of ice tinged as it emitted a crystalline ringing sound. A crack cut through the ice ball, ruining its previously perfect geometry. Redan clapped slowly.

"Well done, kid. Ya won't be a spellblade by tomorrow, but ya do seem like ya have some talent. Was that some kind of invisible arrow? It was shaped strangely."

Glenn looked at him, a hand covering half his face. This was the moment he waited for all his life, a fantasy his youngest self had always wanted to fulfill.

"I call it... the Bullet of Death..."

An awkward silence welcomed his declaration until Sahro's distant snort disrupted it.

I don't even need to say anything. Big L, Glenn, mocked Diamanes.

Damnit, just leave me to have my fun! the young man despaired, his excitement ruined.

Redan shook his head. "I have me work cut out for me, don't I?" He sighed and restored the ice ball. "That's great and all, but now ya have to do this same thing in a second."

Glenn froze. *What about celebrating the creation of my first spell? Isn't there some kind of... ceremonial thing? One where I'm appointed as an official Mage?*

"Until then, ya don't eat, ya don't go nowhere, and ya don't sleep," Redan ordered with a wicked grin.

Glenn gulped. *What?*

Chapter 26

TRAINING MONTAGE

Glenn lay on the ground, contemplating his life and all that came with it. It had been two months since he arrived into this world. During those two months, he got eaten alive, attacked by an eldritch priest, chased by wolves, struck a deal with an evil entity now living in his left hand, and—of course—was kidnapped and tortured by a cult of masochists.

And now, here he was, wondering if living was even worth the struggle. He had started learning magic with Redan three days ago. The idea of being the artisan behind the creation of a spell was still something he had a hard time grasping. He was a magician. A real one. How cool was that?

The first spell he managed to cast—the Bullet of Death, which he renamed Magic Bullet out of shame—was still extremely weak. It was comparable to an arrow shot. That was why he was now forced to work his ass off and practice throwing spells beyond the limits of his Mana.

Lazy bastard. Diamanes laughed loudly in his host's mind.

Glenn's eyelids twitched, groaning as he pushed himself up. These past three days had been hellish, to say the least. Each time he recovered enough Mana to practice his spells, Redan would force him to train again, and again, and again.

First, he had to reduce the casting time, which took an hour or so. That was simple. Next was hitting a moving target, which was incomparably harder. Following that, he had to run while casting his spell, which he eventually succeeded in doing. After all, Redan had refused to let him rest until he cast his spells ten times in a row successfully while running as fast as he could.

In the last hour, he had managed to accomplish all of those tasks perfectly—finally earning himself a short rest. And Glenn had no doubt it would soon come to an end, hence why he was enjoying it as much as he could.

Each time Glenn managed to fulfill Redan's expectation, the difficulty increased, plunging him into an endless cycle of pain, sweat, and struggle. Bottoming out on Mana was quite annoying. Fever, aches, loss of consciousness... having no Mana meant spending *everything* he had.

Glenn gritted his teeth, a vein popping out on his forehead as he recalled the old man's words: "It's for yar own good, kiddo!"

Sure, yeah. That geezer just wants me to suffer because he knows I slapped him. Which... isn't wrong. But this is still annoying!

Perhaps he would have been able to endure the training better had he been able to explore other spells, but Redan insisted that Glenn needed to learn the basics first. Learning to crawl before he could walk. He was thinking about how to cast that damned Magic Bullet every second of the day, wondering how to improve it quickly so he could move on from the lesson. The sooner he mastered it, the better he would be.

His physical condition was also not the best. He could only eat when his Mana had completely bottomed out, and sleep only when Redan was done torturing him. 'Sleep', in this scenario, actually meant Meditation. Apparently, reaching a high level of Meditation would allow him to recover energy more quickly than through traditional sleep. Almost like a cheat.

Glenn stretched with a heavy, tired sigh. His back was drenched in sweat from the intensive training. That was one thing that left him puzzled. Why did casting spells only leave him physically strained? According to Redan, it should have been worse—five times worse if he trusted the old man's words. But his abnormal body spared him much of the struggle untrained Mages usually faced.

Magic had always seemed mystical and refined—made for the pale guy with a pointy hat and a scrawny body. Something that was *not* supposed to be physically demanding.

Or perhaps it was just Redan's training methods that strained the body so much? Glenn shook his head. He had no way to know. He gritted his teeth and mentally cursed the old man who was subjecting him to this torture. He also cursed Diamanes for finding amusement in his every mistake.

Glenn watched the sun go down, absentmindedly rubbing the back of his neck. He smiled when he remembered that he got a free meal every evening, motivating him to move. He stood, determined to fill his belly, only to find a familiar face. He expected it to be Redan, but to his surprise, he recognized the young Black Heir he had a beef with a few days ago. *What was his name? Sandro? Zoro?*

"Tired?" Sahro inquired mockingly, his arms crossed.

He wasn't wearing his shemagh, letting his golden-chestnut hair flow freely. Glenn was persuaded that any girl back on Earth would have been jealous of the Black Heir's hair. But he wasn't persuaded that Sahro was there to do anything but chide him.

I do not have the patience nor the energy to deal with his bullshit, Glenn thought.

Glenn brushed the dust off his body and tied his ponytail tight. He was wearing the plain clothes that Giselle had graciously lent to him from the Black Heirs' stash. With any hope, that'd help dispel the illusion that he was a noble.

He walked away without uttering a word, ignoring Sahro's groan of displeasure However, the Black Heir quickly intercepted him.

"Do you have something to say to me?" Glenn asked with a frown.

Sahro opened his mouth before shaking his head in frustration. Glenn sighed and walked past the Black Heir, heading for his quarters—a small tent hosting an equally tiny bunk bed close to Giselle and Redan's tents.

The old couple seemed hellbent on training him personally and keeping him at hand's reach.

Why are you complaining? You have a teacher, a place to sleep, and training—all for free! Diamanes exclaimed.

I know, but I feel like it's a lot of investment for someone they don't know that well. They seem to be in a hurry for some reason, even though the war with the Thorns Church hasn't started yet.

What I meant was that you should hasten your progress to become stronger. Reaching the Third Circle should suffice. At that point, I'll be able to reveal my purpose, stated Diamanes mysteriously.

Glenn scoffed. *Hah, so you do have a purpose. You're not just a magic hand?*

Diamanes laughed heartily. *Hey, you're no longer calling me an evil hand. I sense progress!*

Shut up, sighed Glenn, tired of always losing in these mental jousts.

"Glenn, right?" A voice called him from behind.

Glenn groaned and turned back to Sahro, who had followed him all the way there.

"Listen," Glenn began in a tired and annoyed voice, "If you're here to bother me, please, don't. I'm exhausted, annoyed, and most of all, hungry."

Sahro shook his head, appearing somewhat ashamed. "No, I'm… I'm not trying to bother you. Giselle spoke to me."

Glenn blinked. "And?"

The Black Heir rubbed the back of his head, "She told me you're no noble. So, I've come to apologize for trying to provoke you last time. Sorry." He smiled awkwardly.

Glenn paused for a moment and smiled back weakly. "Thank you. I also take back what I said about your parents, if that means anything."

Sahro held his hand out peacefully. "It does. We're good?"

Glenn shook the extended hand. "We're good."

Sahro nodded and left Glenn, who was finally able to go back to his tent and collapse on his bunk bed.

"Well, it seems like he just had a problem with nobles, not me. Great!" Glenn said with a laugh.

Well, well, well, isn't that an opportunity to make a good friend? Diamanes mocked.

Glenn's eyelids twitched. *That might be pushing it a little too much. He still almost punched me out of rage. I'm fine with us not hating each other, but...*

But what? Diamanes replied in contempt. *I'm pretty sure he wanted to make amends. And don't you think it'd be time to find people of a similar age? I know you're fond of older folks, but...* Diamanes trailed off with wicked laughter. Glenn rolled in his bunk bed while plugging his ears.

Why do you even care? he grumbled, trying to find the best position to sleep. *Ah, no. I can only use Meditation... That's right.*

He forced himself to sit up and concentrate, his consciousness slowly but surely pulling away from Diamanes' pitiful arguments. He would have loved to sleep traditionally for once, but he was sure that if he did so, Redan would fall from the ceiling to violently wake him with buckets of ice. That wasn't even a metaphor. The damned geezer actually did that the first night he slept for real instead of Meditating.

Nonetheless, Glenn had no choice but to admit this form of 'sleep' was more advantageous; he could recuperate his energy more efficiently while using the time to contemplate his Mana Heart and deepen his comprehension of Mana. In addition, every time he emerged from a long Meditation session, all the aches and pains in his body disappeared.

It was, undoubtedly, one of the best discoveries he had made in this world. The ability to have a pain-free body, even after a grueling workout, was a welcome relief. Too bad he was training it under such a sadistic teacher...

A chill against his forehead pulled Glenn straight out of his Meditation. He sat up brusquely as ice cubes ran down his cheeks. Glenn rubbed his eyes tiredly and got up from the bunk bed under the watchful green eyes of the old man.

"Come on, time's ticking. Ya can't be lacking in yar training! I hope ya Meditated last night as well!"

Glenn hid a yawn with the back of his hand as he nodded with difficulty. It felt like he had spent barely a few seconds with his eyes closed.

"Yeah, I did. Remind me why you're training me again. Oh right, because I asked you to." Glenn shook his head, adding under his breath, "Why did I ever think this would be like Hogwarts classes?"

The old man glanced at him. "This ain't gonna cut it."

Glenn paused, his tiredness fading away. "What isn't?"

Redan crossed his arms and leaned against the tent's entry. "Kid, why do you want to learn magic?"

Glenn took a second to think. Right now, the priority was to survive against the Thorns Church and grow strong enough so they wouldn't capture him again.

"To defend myself," he replied confidently.

Redan sneered, "In that case, go learn swordsmanship or somethin'. Don't bother with magic if it's just for 'defending yourself.'"

"What? But—"

"No buts," Redan cut him off dryly. "I ain't teaching someone who considers magic a martial art."

He left the tent, spitting on the side of the road with disappointment.

Glenn rubbed his eyes in disbelief. "What just happened? Did I just lose my teacher? Why?"

Diamanes whistled. ***Great job! You somehow managed to drive away your teacher in just three days! That's a real talent!***

Your sarcasm isn't helping, Diamanes.

He sat back on the bunk bed and mulled over the question Redan had posed. Why *did* he want to learn magic?

Well, survival was the most evident answer. But it wasn't the right one, or Redan wouldn't have reacted that way. The old man was right; why bother with magic if he only wanted a way to protect himself? Why not train in swordsmanship?

"What even is magic?" Glenn questioned.

It was an art—an art that made the impossible *possible*. That was the simplest, and yet most precise explanation he could come up with. A realm of boundless potential, limited only by one's Mana reserves, imagination, and effort.

And apparently, Circles too, but that was another issue entirely. That probably counted under the effort square anyway.

Let's assume I learn magic and become strong enough to easily defeat the cultists. What then? Glenn wondered, his hands clasped together.

Getting revenge and destroying the Thorns Church was only a side goal, not an end in itself. No, what he really wanted... Glenn's expression darkened, his fingers trembling slightly.

To be free.

Free to do whatever he wanted, free of the fear that shoved him down ever since he arrived in this world.

Free to go back to his home and family—to Earth... To find who or what brought him here and kick their asses for good measure. He was greedy for magic, not because he wanted to destroy, but because he wanted to create a way back. Create new things, new spells, and climb the stairs to power so no one would ever be able to torture or look down on him again. Strong enough so that he could stand up to *anyone*, even... Glenn's fists tightly clenched.

He wanted magic to be strong enough to pursue his goals. Because if he gave up, what would happen to his sister?

Glenn's eyes focused with cold determination. No, he needed to go back. He needed to survive and search this world for an answer—be it by asking Gods or demons. *Oh, and if I could get rid of Diamanes the same way, that'd be perfect.*

Hey, I thought you were finally warming up to me! Diamanes protested.

Glenn chuckled and clenched his bandaged hand. "I'm just joking. Alright, it felt great to have this little introspection."

He stood and stretched before suddenly pausing. He remembered Giselle's revolver, the Smith & Wesson. It was ancient, two hundred centuries old. *What if time is passing at a different rate between here and Earth?*

Then you'll have to learn time magic or something. Whatever, man, you have no way to go back right now anyway. Diamanes sighed in annoyance.

Glenn's worries disappeared with the entity's words. He slapped himself on the cheek and pulled the tent's flap. He headed straight for Redan, who was sitting nearby with an unreadable expression. The old man did not even give a glance at his approaching apprentice. Glenn took a seat in front of him and clasped his hands together.

"I know why I want to be a Mage," he began as he drew a deep breath. "Magic is the only way I'll be able to understand this world and its mysteries."

The corner of Redan's lips twitched, but he kept his gaze on the floor.

Glenn gritted his teeth. "And I also want to be strong. Strong enough to survive and to forge a path forwards."

"And finally." He closed his eyes and tried to keep his emotions in control. "Magic is the only option that will allow me to find my family again."

He stared into Redan's eyes resolutely. The old man looked before shaking his head.

He sighed loudly, a smirk hidden underneath his beard. "Damn clueless kid..."

Chapter 27

PUGILAT

"**A**lright, boy. Let's take things up a notch, shall we?" Redan grinned. He opened his palm, and a small, toothpick-sized spear appeared above it. Four rings of snowflakes circled around it, pulsing with power.

"This is Projection," the old man explained. "Consider it a trainin' tool to sharpen yar concentration while also helping ya understand the attributes of yar Mana Heart."

"To conjure it, ya need to will yar Mana Heart to show outwardly. If ya maintain yar concentration and don't waver, it should be simple enough."

Glenn nodded slowly and followed Redan's instructions. Similar to when he created his first spell, he concentrated on his Mana, channeling it carefully. A trembling image of his Mana Heart appeared, a gaseous sphere displaying a spectrum of rainbow hues. A delicate arrangement of ethereal gray runes formed a ring—no, a *Circle* spun around it. The whole Projection was barely the size of an apple.

"Good," Redan acknowledged. "Now, consider it this way. The first three Circles for any Mage are relatively simple to obtain. It's what comes after that's really challengin'."

Glenn wiped the sweat off his forehead and nodded. "Okay. And what do I need to do to get to that Second and Third Circle?"

Redan pointed at Glenn's Projection. "Ya need to find a way to put yar Mana Heart's essence *in yar spells.* When ya succeed, ya'll automatically purify the surrounding Mana in a much more efficient way and rank up a Circle. And ya'll also be able to create more powerful spells—not like that *unsavory* Mana Bullet ya first conjured."

Glenn gritted his teeth and endured the critique.

"What about those gray runes?" he inquired. "Mine aren't the same as yours. And I can't seem to focus on them."

Redan shrugged. "These runes are unique to everyone. Once ya understand them... Well, ya'll just see what happens then. But it's a good thing. Now, back on infusing yar essence, kiddo!"

Glenn exhaled heavily. *Alright. Infusing the essence of my Mana Heart in my spell... That shouldn't be too hard.*

He attempted to accomplish Redan's task in a rather hopeful manner, only for his Mana to suddenly disperse.

"What?" Glenn exclaimed. "I thought that was it!"

Redan chuckled and patted his shoulder. "That'll be yar homework. I'll be headin' off for some time. Ya better be done before I'm back. Don't forget to do yar Meditation to recuperate."

"Yeah, yeah, sure." Glenn barely listened to him as he tried again to conjure a spell with his attribute.

"And don't ya think yar leavin' camp till ya unlock yar Second Circle. I've got eyes and ears posted—ready to whack ya back in gear if ya even think of cuttin' class early." Redan smirked and left to attend his unspecified business.

Great. And if I asked, would he tell me where he's going? He's probably just taking a shit and wants to be all mystical about it.

* * *

The next ten hours were filled with frustration for the newly-minted Mage, complimented with the disappointment of failed attempts and Mana exhaustion.

Glenn sighed heavily as he lay on the floor, annoyed.

"How am I even supposed to do this when I don't have a clue what that gaseous mess is supposed to be?" he questioned aloud.

Are you enjoying banging your head against a wall? Diamanes questioned in a falsely innocent tone.

Glenn grunted and rose, refusing to give up.

"Perhaps I should try again to combine my Mana Bullet with the ball?" he contemplated.

Diamanes groaned, ***Didn't you try a hundred times already? Did I ever tell you what the definition of insanity is?***

Glenn blinked before scoffing in disbelief, *Are you seriously quoting Far Cry?*

Diamanes, unperturbed, kept on going, ***Insanity is doing the exact same thing over and over again, expecting it to change.***

You're aware that I'm the one who played the game, right? Glenn said with an amused look.

Admit that it was a good imitation, at least! Diamanes demanded proudly.

Glenn stared at the gaseous sphere hovering above his palm. A bead of sweat pearled down his forehead as he concentrated, willing his Mana to create a Magic Bullet. He tried his hardest, but his spell dissipated in deep blue particles, failing to come to life.

Glenn sighed and rubbed his temples slowly. *What am I doing wrong?*

"I can't even ask Redan for help, the geezer abandoned..." he muttered as he leaned against a collapsed wall on the edge of the camp's training area.

He watched as the Black Heirs sparring nearby exchanged whispers. They grabbed their weapons and left for the sinuous streets of the Sewers. It wasn't the first time Glenn saw that happen today.

More and more Black Heirs are heading off camp... He rubbed his chin.

An air of change enveloped the area, like the calm before a storm. *Too bad that change doesn't apply to the accursed smell of the Sewers...*

Perhaps the gears of war between the Black Heirs and the Thorns Church have started to turn! How exciting! Diamanes exclaimed with a wicked laugh.

Maybe that's the case, maybe it isn't. No one deems me important enough for basic information!

Glenn looked up at the sound of approaching footsteps. Sahro steadily strode towards him, a scroll clenched in his hand. Other Black Heirs spat behind him, cursing him with deathly glares.

Glenn crossed his arms and raised an eyebrow. *What's up with them?*

"Experiencing some difficulties?" the Black Heir inquired, a curved saber hanging off his waist.

Glenn shrugged dismissively, suppressing his frustration. "Nothing of concern to you. What do you want?"

Sahro handed him the rolled-up scroll. "From Dame Giselle."

"Giselle?" He scoffed, his frustration with his training poisoning his words." So you're the delivery boy, Sahro?"

Sahro's expression darkened as Glenn's fingers unrolled the parchment. Glenn cleared his throat and read aloud:

To facilitate your training, Sahro shall accompany you as a sparring partner. Although possessing tremendous potential, he clings to stubborn notions and refuses to learn magic.

I trust this experience will enlighten you both, and that Sahro will be of tremendous help when he joins you on your mission. His entry into the city has been arranged. Enjoy yourselves.

P.S: Find my grandson, or you'll return to the damned hole you came from.

Glenn exhaled in dismay before vocalizing his sentiments, "Fantastic. Just perfect."

Glenn observed Sahro, discovering a similar incredulity on his face. It seemed the Black Heir was unaware of the new obligations thrust upon him. A mischievous idea suddenly popped into Glenn's mind. He leaned back on the scroll, exclaiming in surprise.

"Oh wait, there's another postscript!" He squinted as if trying to decrypt some ancient text. "No way, Sahro, it's written there that you have to do a hundred backflips to prove yourself. Wow, that's crazy!" Glenn exclaimed with an exaggeratedly shocked expression.

The Black Heir paled, and without taking a look at the scroll, he started doing backflips as fast as he could.

Glenn paused, watching with a bemused look. He hadn't expected Sahro to blindly follow such a nonsensical order. He just did it. And wow, he was doing it *perfectly*. Glenn had never seen such perfect flips in his life. It almost made him feel bad. He crumpled the letter and threw it into the nearby campfire.

Glenn watched the Black Heir doing backflips for half an hour, grinning without restraint at the enjoyable show. Eventually, Sahro was done with his task and stared at Glenn, barely out of breath.

"So, I'm supposed to babysit you?" Sahro's tone oscillated between disbelief and annoyance. It almost made Glenn angry that he was as fine as before the hundred backflips.

Life is unfair sometimes. Wait, could I try to do backflips now? I do have an abnormally strong body after all...

He dismissed that thought and smiled wryly, retorting, "Excuse me, isn't it the other way around? Who's keeping watch over whom? Didn't you listen to the letter's content? Wasn't *stubborn* the word Giselle used to describe you?"

Sahro bit on his lower lip. "They forced me to apologize to you, then designate me your guardian? What's so exceptional about you, anyway?"

Glenn raised a pleasantly surprised eyebrow." Oh, so they were *forced excuses* then. Well, to answer your question, maybe I'm not exceptional at all and you're simply *that useless?*"

The Black Heir clenched his fists. "Do you wish to see if I am?"

Glenn snorted and opened his arms in a challenging manner. "Come on. Do you think I'd be scared of a prejudiced idiot? I'll make you apologize for real this time!"

A good ol' battle is the perfect start for the best bromances! Go, go, Glenn! Diamanes cheered happily. Glenn ignored him, his eyes glued to Sahro's fists, which were shivering with crimson Aura.

"Enough talk! Let's settle this with our fists!" Sahro yelled, pointing his Aura-covered finger at Glenn.

"You know what? No Mana, no Aura. Deal?" Glenn answered confidently.

Adrenaline coursed through his veins, fueled by the past hour's frustration. He needed to think about something else, and Redan wasn't here to stop him. Getting into a brawl probably wasn't the way to solve his issues, but whatever.

"Don't come whimpering afterwards, bastard!" Sahro roared as his Aura disappeared.

He dashed at Glenn, swiftly crouching to deliver a punch. In a heartbeat, a kinetically charged fist collided with Glenn's chin. The world seemed to ripple in slow motion as the impact reverberated, and saliva mixed with blood expelled from his mouth. Sahro's hand recoiled, a self-satisfied grin adorning his features.

"I've been craving this since I first laid eyes on you and your arrogant face. There is more where that came from," Sahro proclaimed, a triumphant gleam in his eyes.

"Very well, then. Let's begin," Glenn muttered, clutching his throbbing cheek.

He charged the Black Heir, only for his fist to be effortlessly parried. Glenn's back hit the dirt once more. He pushed himself up and spat out blood. This was nothing. Compared to the pain he had been subjected to in prison, Sahro's punches were as painful as mosquito bites. Annoying, but ultimately useless.

Sahro bounced side to side, grinning widely. He suddenly disappeared from Glenn's sight. Instinctively, the latter squatted and blocked, barely intercepting a powerful kick aimed at his chest. He rolled back, only to be forced to dodge once more.

Glenn drew a short breath and steeled himself. Sahro dashed forwards, his fist hitting Glenn perfectly in the waist. Glenn coughed but clenched Sahro's arm, grinning wickedly, his gums bleeding from the beating. Sahro frowned and tried to get away, but Glenn's abnormal strength held him into place.

"No running away, now!" Glenn warned with a vicious smile as he grabbed Sahro's other hand and headbutted him powerfully.

Sahro recoiled back, dizzy, but Glenn wasn't done. He headbutted him again, and again until Sahro finally managed to kick him away.

"Shit!" Sahro held his bloody nose and spat, looking at Glenn with renewed wariness.

Glenn took a deep breath and mimicked Sahro's previous relaxed appearance.

"Well, not what you expected?" He laughed madly.

Sahro's expression darkened and suddenly, he disappeared. Glenn tensed, only to be swept off his feet. The world turned over as Sahro threw him above his shoulders before punching dead center into his chest. Glenn's lungs were emptied of air, forcing him to kneel and catch his breath.

You're taking quite a beating, Glenn. Want some help?

How could you help? You're a talking ha—fuck! Glenn cursed as Sahro's foot made contact with his chin, kicking him a few meters away.

His vision blurred and his ears rang. A trickle of blood escaped from his mouth as he stumbled on wobbly legs and landed in a half-collapsed cabin—rotten planks falling on him. The second the Black Heir had gotten serious, it had been impossible for him to follow his movements.

Listen, Diamanes' suave voice dispelled the haze that was slowly taking over Glenn's mind, *just do what I tell you when I tell you to. If you do, you can strike back.*

"Shit." Glenn coughed as he pushed away the planks and made his way out of the collapsed cabin. *Should I thank the Thorns Church for giving me a reinforced spine, or curse them? Probably a question for a later time.*

"Want more? Come and take it, you filthy human!" Sahro taunted, his eyes bloodshot. Glenn wiped the blood off his mouth as he stared at the damned Black Heir.

"I'll make sure you get a taste of that filthy fist then!" Glenn roared as he dashed forwards.

Step to the right, Diamanes commanded.

Glenn sidestepped, watching in surprise as Sahro's vertical kick missed him. Confusion flickered in Sahro's eyes.

"How?" he muttered before resuming his attacks. Diamanes issued new orders, guiding Glenn's actions like a marionette.

Crouch. Evade left. Step forwards. Jump. Straight hook now!

Diamanes' instructions reshaped the fight's dynamic, creating a more balanced exchange. While Diamanes consistently ordered a straight hook aimed at Sahro's right chin, Sahro deftly evaded every attempt.

It's not working; any other ideas? Glenn gritted his teeth, barely blocking an uppercut with both of his hands.

Don't worry, trust me. Persistence is your greatest asset against someone like him, Diamanes assured confidently.

Slowly but surely, the tide of the fight began to shift against Sahro, with Glenn taking most of the opportunities and improving at a visible rate.

"Can't you see the right hook isn't working? You've tried it so many times," Sahro attempted to taunt, his confidence wavering.

Glenn remained focused, his attention on Diamanes' guidance.

Alright, now that he's doubting, feint a right hook and trip him.

Glenn nodded in agreement, evading another of Sahro's attacks before executing the maneuver. A fake right hook set Sahro off balance, and Glenn's true blow landed, a powerful kick in his legs. His opponent was swept off his feet, falling to the ground. The Black Heir gasped as he brought both his arms together to block the incoming punch.

Now, the real right hook! Glenn's fist clenched with determination.

"Dodge this!" he roared as his fist connected with Sahro's jaw, projecting him onto the ground.

Dirt rose from the small shockwave; the Black Heir was completely knocked out. Glenn heaved with difficulty, closing his eyes in satisfaction. *Oh yeah, that felt great.*

Hands on his knees, Glenn looked proudly at the outcome of the fight. Collapsing backwards, he caught his breath as sweat dripped from his hair and back.

A chill suddenly crawled down his spine, abruptly gripping him. He urgently sat up, focusing back on his opponent. Sahro rose slowly, his hand pressed against his chin. A predatory gleam flickered in his eyes, worsened by the trickle of blood flowing from his mouth.

"Time for round two, bastard."

Chapter 28

STAR RIZZ

Man... Why did I provoke that idiot? Glenn winced painfully. Diamanes snorted, ***I don't know. It's a natural talent of yours, haha!***

Glenn rubbed his sore spots, practically giving himself a full body massage. It felt like he had been driven over by two or three trucks. Sahro had utterly demolished him after Glenn managed to get in one knockdown. Once he understood that Glenn could actually pose a threat, he went at him full throttle.

After the fight, Glenn was forced to crawl back to his tent. His face was swollen, his bones were aching, and his ego was shattered. When he finally reached his bed, he Meditated, taking the moment to examine his battered body from within.

It appeared different from when he was healthy. The hologram representation was glowing red, with every pain point highlighted. Bruises, cuts, damaged bones, internal wounds... *Perhaps it would be wise to invest time into a healing spell, or some other way to treat myself. Maybe potions exist in this world?*

Glenn allowed his body to rest, watching the red lights fade gradually while thinking about the creation of a healing spell. Strangely, he was practically persuaded that such a spell wouldn't fit with his 'specialty', the attributes his Mana Heart possessed. Even though he hadn't clearly identified such an attribute, he was certain healing magic wasn't part of it. He already recovered faster than normal individuals, to the point he wasn't too worried about the cracks in his bones.

Glenn emerged from his Meditation and sighed deeply at the sight of his hands caked with dirt and blood. A bath would be a welcomed relief. Maybe inspiration for Redan's homework would strike amid his shower thoughts. He groaned while pushing himself up.

After retreating to a secluded area, he withdrew the water Shard from his dimensional pouch. He grimaced painfully while taking off his clothes and used the blue crystal to conjure a well-deserved cold shower.

After an appeal to God for soap and a thorough cleansing, Glenn scrubbed his training clothes and put them back on, wincing at the bruises that covered him. Sahro had unleashed all his fury during their fight. The next time, Glenn swore to himself it would be Sahro on the ground nursing his wounds. Hopefully.

Glenn exhaled deeply as he headed back to the training grounds, walking with his Mana Heart Projection in his palm. Maintaining the image while moving was much more challenging. But by doing so, he hoped he'd be able to find the enlightenment he needed to create his Second Circle. That was his ultimate goal, after all.

Redan had made one thing very clear: Glenn would be stuck in the Black Heir camp until he unlocked his Second Circle. What's more, once he'd reached that stage, he'd finally be ready to learn more powerful and diverse spells.

A sudden robotic imitation interrupted Glenn's thoughts. *Careful, careful! Jerk incoming!* Diamanes playfully interjected, prompting Glenn to spin around.

"Back to gloat after your victory, Sahro?" Glenn's teeth clenched as he stared at the one who pummeled him.

Sahro raised his hands in mock surrender, a pronounced bruise marring his jaw.

"Shh... Sheems like you're healin' pretty fasht. I washn't expecting you to be on your feet for a few daysh 'fter that beating' you took," remarked Sahro.

Glenn's eyes opened wide as he struggled to suppress the rising laughter. He hurriedly turned away while hiding his mouth with his hand.

Just the way he's speaking... No, I don't need another beating. I can't... laugh... Come on, breathe in, breathe out... He steeled himself, finally recovering his seriousness.

He stared at the mark on Sahro's face, a big purple egg that seemed to grow larger every second.

"Whot? Do you 'hasve an isshue with me?" Sahro inquired.

Oh, I can't hold it!

The laughter erupted, uncontrollably.

"Hahaha!" exploded Glenn, crying tears of joy.

Perplexed, Sahro's face reddened. "Whot? What'sh funny?"

"Haha... No, no. It's nothing... Hahaha!" Glenn tried to restrain himself, but he couldn't help it.

"Are you laughin' at shme? I'm the one who won, 'member?"

"Yeah, yeah, you won. Haha... Phew..." Glenn leaned on his knees and drew one deep breath after the other.

After a few seconds, he finally calmed himself. Sahro's sense of triumph dimmed. Glenn was the one who had been knocked out, but the Black Heir was the one worse for wear.

Man, I'm feeling reinvigorated, thought Glenn.

Count yourself lucky not to have any scars on your face after you took so many hits, Diamanes remarked. **I don't even understand how your face isn't worse than his.**

I don't know, perhaps the stars wanted me to be able to mock him again, Glenn quipped.

Thump, thump!

He glanced at the Projection that he had barely managed to maintain during his fit of laughter. *The stars?*

Glenn's heart skipped a beat. The enlightenment he searched for... It was right there! Right in the damned Projection, in the stupid Mana Heart! Without wasting a second, Glenn manipulated the Projection, wishing to enlarge the colorful, gaseous orb. It swelled two meters, revealing its true nature.

It now looked like a galaxy—a swirl of cosmic dust and stars. That was no coincidence.

It *was* one.

Glenn gazed upon it, the name of the formation suddenly appearing in his mind, a whisper from his consciousness—from the Mana. Known since ancient times, the Magellanic Clouds appeared as spiraling twins. And now they were in the palm of his hand.

"Incredible..."

Glenn's concentration broke, too surprised by the truth of his Mana Heart. The Projection dissipated like a mirage. A silence installed itself between the two young men, both taken aback. They stayed still for a few minutes, not saying a word.

Sahro's voice broke the silence. "Wash that?"

Glenn replied, shaken, "Yes, that was my Mana Heart. I'm... I don't even have the words to describe it. So that's what shocked Redan..."

He didn't remember studying the Magellanic Clouds before; the knowledge just popped into his head with his enlightenment.

How I could have such a beautiful, powerful phenomenon as my Mana Heart, I have no idea. I would have honestly been satisfied with a simple fireball or something, but no. Instead, I have a damn dwarf galaxy!

Beautiful, indeed. That's really... impressive and unique, added Diamanes.

Glenn stared absent-mindedly for another minute before darting off for the training grounds.

* * *

Sahro remained still, his initial purpose forgotten. Moments passed before he ran to Giselle's tent, shock still written on his face.

Giselle looked up at the young man who entered her office, her eyes fixed on the bruise marking his jaw.

"Gishelle, Ish have a report to mashke," Sahro said.

Giselle suddenly struck the desk, her whole body shaking with tremors. Sahro was shocked but remained silent.

Finally, Giselle clenched her teeth and said, "Your... Your jaw?"

Sahro's eyes lit up, and he leaned forwards. "Yesh, that'sh that bashtard, Glenn. We fought, but I won, of courshe."

Giselle shook her head. Sahro was touched seeing how angered Giselle seemed by the news.

"You... Your report will wait. Give me some time," she muttered, her fists tightly clenched.

Sahro bowed and left the tent.

Giselle breathed in and out. A serious, concentrated look was on her face, her eyes resolute.

Do not laugh, Giselle. Do not laugh...

* * *

Glenn couldn't explain why, but he felt as if his whole world had been shaken. The sight of the Magellanic Clouds demolished and rebuilt his conception of reality.

After calming his racing heart, Glenn took a breath to finally accept it. He then made a sudden realization. *What if I infused the feelings of awe and admiration into a spell? Or, what would happen if I created a spell based on those feelings?*

He had to try and see.

Glenn stood in the center of the training grounds. He inhaled a deep breath and moved his Mana from his heart to his right hand. He imagined that feeling of awe—of liberty—and tried canalizing it into a single orb of pure power.

A rotating sphere containing something similar to a cluster of stars gradually appeared above his palm, hovering and humming with mysterious power. Glenn felt his Mana draining away, sucking all the strength he could muster. His reserves bottomed out in a matter of seconds. Glenn gritted his teeth and kept pushing, finally shooting the spell towards a ruined cabin.

The ball moved gradually, as if time itself had slowed down in front of the mighty spell. Glenn knew it was an illusion, and yet, he could hear his heart thumping madly. A single droplet of sweat slid down his chin, falling to the ground with an imperceptible *plic*. The second the ball made contact with the cabin walls, a white flash blinded Glenn. Without another sound, the light disappeared.

Glenn blinked in confusion.

Where there previously was a shabby cabin, there was nothing. The wood was gone. The ground had been plowed into a small crater. Glenn fell to his knees, feeling something expanding in his chest. His sight blurred, and his consciousness faded. With the last bit of strength that he could muster, Glenn conjured a Projection.

His Magellanic Clouds were now enveloped in two gray, mystical Circles. He was now a Second Circle Mage.

The ascent to King's Rise had never been closer.

* * *

Redan was coming back from the Black Market situated in the Military Outpost. He had been looking for ancient books on celestial formations and astrological knowledge. Books were rare outside of King's Rise and could only be obtained in the underbellies of Munirp.

Even rarer were the books on such specific knowledge. The best he managed to find were basic tomes on the movement of the sun and moons, which wasn't useful at all.

The book had been held by the expeditionary forces, so it was to be trusted. He also found a practice Shard that had been artificially created by a Forgemage. Its purpose was to help Mage who couldn't converge a second

Circle. He knew it wasn't really necessary for Glenn, but time was of the essence.

He bought it after asking for a few favors, being not very rich himself. He sighed at the thought of his pupil.

"What a waste..." he muttered, navigating the labyrinthic streets of the Sewers back to the Black Heir's camp. The lowlifes and tramps walked out of his way without saying a word, avoiding his eyes like their lives depended on it.

Glenn probably wasn't aware of it, but that kiddo was always curled up in a ball, shaking as he slept. After seeing that, Redan understood, although he didn't let on, that Glenn had been traumatized by his experience in that Thorns Church prison. And perhaps there was more beyond that. It was already impressive to see the young man's mental resilience as he faced his arduous training. Most people would have given up after the first day.

That's why he forced the kid to Meditate every night, hoping that his mind would restore. He knew that kid had immense potential, even more so after seeing the cosmic cloud in his Mana Heart. But if he was held back by his trauma, he'd never get to the Second Circle.

Giselle had mentioned that he got on well with that other youngin', Sahro. Maybe making friends was what he needed.

On those thoughts, he went to his student's tent, discovering that he wasn't there. He ran to the training grounds, and he arrived just in time to discover Glenn's new spell.

The ball of light flew off with incredible power and destroyed a whole cabin, leaving nothing but a crater behind in its wake.

The Shard slipped out of Redan's hand as shock took over his old body. The words escaped from his mouth, "Incredible. Simply... incredible."

Redan snickered before shaking his head. *What was I even worried about?*

Chapter 29

KING'S RISE

Glenn groaned, forcing his eyes open. It was as if his head was caught in a vice. He coughed and struggled to sit up, blinking as he took in his surroundings. He was lying in his bunk bed, the dim light of the evening's sun entering the small tent.

Hello, sleeping beauty... How was your day? Diamanes asked sarcastically. *For me, it went terribly. Terribly boring.*

Glenn rubbed his forehead, ignoring the entity's words to Meditate instead. He needed to make sure of something. He slipped naturally into the meditative state, finding his Mana Heart where he left it.

"I really did it..." he muttered, bewildered.

Spinning lazily around the Magellanic Clouds were two rings of gray, mystical runes. He had indeed managed to break through to the next rank.

Glenn sighed in relief and pulled out of his Meditation, returning to the entity's complaints.

You don't even bother replying now? I see, if that's how it is, I can also shut up and not say a word for the rest of my life! Diamanes hissed.

Oh, but please do! Glenn snorted.

He left his tent, finding Redan and Sahro seated at a nearby campfire. Both looked up at the same time, one with relief etched on his face, and the other with mixed apprehension.

"Kiddo!" Redan saluted with a warm smile barely hidden by his white beard. "Seems like ya did listen to my lectures, ay?"

Glenn nodded with a smirk. "It appears so. I'm a Second Circle Mage now."

Redan laughed. "Yes, I know, boy. Just like Sahro here!" He patted the Black Heir's shoulder, who tensed up at the contact. "Well, we can speed things up now! Prepare. Ya're both leaving in an hour!" he declared.

Glenn paused. "Leaving? For where?"

Redan grinned. "For King's Rise proper, of course! No need to keep ya here if ya reached the Second Circle. Go crazy in the city, kiddo!"

He nudged Sahro and added, "Your friend will be waitin' for ya in the Auberge, 'aight? He has to use some more... underhanded means to go into town, after all."

Sahro nodded slowly as he clenched the hilt of his sword. The nearby Black Heirs smirked as they shot disgusted glares in Sahro's direction.

Glenn dismissed them, though, too excited for the upcoming adventure. *So it's finally time to get the hell out of this cesspool.*

After those few words, Redan and Sahro left Glenn to prepare. The latter meticulously checked the contents of his dimensional bag, ensuring he had everything he needed. He had carefully cleaned and folded his training clothes, leaving them on his bunk bed. He grinned widely as he once again donned Jefferson Howard's black clothes, the trenchcoat fluttering pleasantly. He strapped his fire staff on his back, intending to get his money's worth out of the magical weapon. And it was way easier to use than the incredible spell he created.

Come to think of it... Diamanes interrupted his preparations with a serious tone. ***...Did you not settle on a name for the spell?***

Glenn tapped his chin for a few seconds and shrugged. *Actually, I did.*

He tightened the bandages around his left arm and grinned. "Implosion. I'm naming it Implosion."

Diamanes scoffed, *What a grandiose name for a watered-down explosion.*

Glenn ignored the entity and left the tent. He walked to the edge of the camp, finding Redan and Giselle waiting for him.

"Well, I hope ya'll find the grandson, kiddo. Don't anger the lady; she's particularly mean." Redan clenched the young man's shoulder in a supportive way.

"I can hear ya, ya old fart! Don't worry, I'll only kill ya. Nothing too painful, so ya better find my kin," Giselle said with an easy tone, making it all the more terrifying.

Both of them chuckled, but Glenn gulped. His survival depended on their good graces, after all. He did not doubt that after the mess he made in the Thorns Church prison, he was probably priority number one of those sickos. Having Redan and the Black Heirs backing him was the only way he would be protected. It wasn't the best solution, and it was only temporary.

"A few things ya need to know..." Redan's expression turned serious. "There are two religions that have a monopoly on King's Rise: the Church of Onnea and the Gold Church. They both hate the Thorns Church, so ya should be pretty safe with them around."

"The Gold Church... They believe in Plutus, the Golden Dragon—the Lord of All that Is Golden. They control the mainstream bank in Munirp, and most if not all merchants use their services."

The old man shook his head and continued, "The Church of Onnea... They're alright. Don't be evil, and ya'll be fine. I won't spoil the experience further. Go out and explore the city, will ya? That's the best way to grow."

Glenn nodded tensely as Giselle handed him a sheathed sword. "Here's a gift from me, boy. Ya'll learn to defend yourself with a weapon too, and a sword is as good as any. Also, show the pommel to any Black Heir, and they'll help ya and Sahro, 'kay?"

"Okay," Glenn muttered as he accepted the sword.

The pommel had an emblem carved into it: a black tree with crimson droplet-shaped leaves within a white circle. *That's badass.*

Glenn breathed in deeply, a little anxious. King's Rise massive walls loomed over him, adding to the pressure on his shoulders. The city was massive, and it would be a lie to say that he had no fear of entering it. He'd have to do with what he had, and—all things considered—that wasn't much.

Redan had always avoided discussions about King's Rise when Glenn wanted to find out more. Nevertheless, Glenn wasn't interested in whatever aversion Redan seemed to harbor towards the city.

Giselle's demeanor shifted into solemnity. "Alright, kid. One last thing. The Howard family are nobles. They won't be in the Fringe and will probably live in the Bourgeoisie. Ya'll have to find a way to get up there and bring Sahro with ya. So, good luck."

She patted him on the back, reinforcing his apprehension.

Great, I don't even know what the Fringe or Bourgeoisie she's talking about are, but okay, thought Glenn, despairing.

Couldn't they give me some kind of tourist booklet like 'The Top Three Places in King's Rise', or maybe 'The Most Delicious Tavern Food in the Whole City!'? That would do as well. No? Alright...

Glenn's sigh marked the commencement of his journey, and he departed from the Black Heir's camp, his mentors fading behind.

The more he thought about it, the less qualified he felt to rescue Callum. He had pretty much lied about his resume—even if he did have a blurry connection to the Howard family, thanks to finding Jefferson's dust pile in the Still Peaks' ruins. But Glenn didn't want to remain indebted if he could help it, so he was better off fulfilling his end of the bargain as fast as possible.

He made his way through the Sewers' sinuous streets, glancing at the few ragtags lying on the ground like zombies. They were the people who didn't have enough money to enter the city, nor enough skills to make that money. Drug addicts and disabled people, that was the majority of the folks living in the Sewers.

Glenn had asked Giselle about them one time, but she didn't seem to care—unable to understand why she should bother helping some tramps when she already had a hard time supporting her own. She also seemed to be a stranger to the notion of charity, but that wasn't surprising. The Black Heirs weren't exactly rich, after all.

Lost in his thoughts, Glenn failed to notice that a group of lively guys had started following him. The sound of their steps finally startled him, and he discovered a small crowd of ruffians in ragged clothes holding rusty knives and broken planks. He gasped when he recognized the same group that tried to rob Redan and him when they arrived some days ago.

Well, I would have mugged myself if I were in their positions. But don't they learn from their errors? He thought sarcastically as he took his fire staff off his back.

Their boss seemed to have changed—a skinny guy obscenely licking his knife.

"Well, look who's lost in our dear Sewers... You look like a noble." He snorted. "Smells like someone is going to die today!"

Two times I get mugged, and it's the same speech. Can they even intimidate anyone with these skills?

Cackles echoed as the brutes drew closer.

Glenn sighed and waved his fire staff towards them, infusing the bare minimum of Mana into it. A cloud of flames shot out from the crystal, lighting up the emaciated faces of the pitiful bandits. That little show of strength was enough to discourage all of them, except for a single kid trembling like a leaf. Glenn yawned and slid the staff away.

The kid held a rusty blade with both of his hands as snot dripped from his dirty nose. His rags couldn't hide his skinny body, so scrawny it was more bones than blood. The most disturbing aspect was probably his eyes, empty of any desire besides hunger.

Glenn stopped for a second. Taking out a bit of food from his dimensional pouch, he knelt beside the kid.

"Listen, if you want to rob someone, just do it instead of talking, alright? It's lame otherwise."

The kid nodded and ran away. Glenn didn't even walk a few steps when he heard the child already licking his fingers.

That's a real shame. I don't understand how the people in the walls can live knowing that a whole population is living like this outside their home. Glenn questioned, staring at the absurdly high ramparts.

Well, the truth is that human beings care mostly about themselves. So the pain of others is certainly saddening but not enough for them to care about it. It's fine as long as it doesn't happen to you, ain't that right? mocked Diamanes.

* * *

Glenn finally arrived at the Frozen Gate. He peered at the two ice sculptures guarding it. Curious, he placed Diamanes on the foot of the left statue.

Hah, nice try. But you'll have to wait for at least the Third Circle to try 'taking' magic as powerful as this, said Diamanes.

So I can 'take' it. Noted.

If he could obtain the magic guarding the Frozen Gate, Glenn was pretty sure he would be safe for quite a while.

Hey, that's another thing that should motivate you to get to the Third Circle! exclaimed Diamanes.

Yep.

Arriving in front of the guard post, he saw two knights holding halberds. They weren't the same ones from when he first arrived a few months ago.

"Identification, sir!"

Glenn held out his right hand, recalling it was the one he had used during the Magic Identification process. One of the knights scanned Glenn from head to toe using a wand with a white crystal embedded in its tip.

There is no reason it wouldn't work, right? Glenn's stomach churned.

The white crystal shone green, and the guard gestured him forwards. A small door—enough to let a single person pass—opened at the base of the gigantic gate. Glenn hid a short sigh of relief.

I mean, that makes sense. No way they're opening that giant gate every day.

Nonetheless, Glenn was still a bit disappointed. He followed in the guard's footsteps. The door led to a narrow passage where a small box in front of another door awaited him.

The guard glared at him. "Is it your first time here?" he asked, twiddling with his halberd.

Glenn nodded affirmatively, wondering what else would block his way to King's Rise.

"You need to pay the toll. It's one silver." A mocking grin appeared on the knight's face as he casually rattled his blade against the stone, creating sparks.

Hah. He's so blatantly asking for a bribe. We're off to a great start.

He took out a single silver coin and pushed it into the box.

The guard smiled even wider, but he quickly lost it when he saw the ring on Glenn's finger. That was the Howard family ring.

"I'm sorry, sir. Please execute me now!"

The previously cocky guard knelt. His forehead touched the ground, and his hands shook uncontrollably.

So that's power. It's scary to see the influence the Howards have. I'll have to be careful. Glenn realized as he stepped over the guard and opened the door.

Finally, it was time for him to enter the biggest city he had ever seen in his life—be it in the real world or fiction—King's Rise.

Chapter 30

THE FRINGE

Glenn gasped as he discovered the breathtaking sight beyond the door. Instead of the bustling cityscape he expected, he found himself amidst vast wheat fields that stretched kilometers. The cereal leaves rustled gently in the breeze, the light creating an illusion of golden waves flowing across the land.

The twilight sunlight fell on the wheat like a gentle caress, making it glow in an otherworldly manner. Beyond the fields—a fair distance away—appeared to be a village, markedly more prosperous than the Sewers. Farmers wielded scythes, meticulously reaping the harvest alongside some strange-looking scarecrows.

Glenn enjoyed the sight, a trust feast for the senses when he realized that the village he noticed was nestled against another towering wall, even grander than the one through which he entered.

They really like walls here... He silently thought before sighing in confusion.

So this is King's Rise... It's weird, it didn't look like this from up top when we were traveling from Still Peak, Glenn mused. *Maybe I hallucinated or remembered it wrong?*

I told you this place is lit up with magic like a rave, Diamanes said. *It is quite insane to have an illusion spanning hundreds of kilometers, though. King's Rise is by no means a small city.*

Glenn shook off the awe. "Well, it seems like this is where it all begins. I need to find the... Auberge, right?" Glenn murmured, glancing at a piece of paper Redan gave him. "Where the hell is it?"

A mischievous grin played on his lips. "I think I'll indulge myself in a bit of exploration. After all, it took me what... Three months to get here? I might as well savor the experience now that I've arrived," he declared, stashing the paper back in his pouch.

Well, you're free to do so, but Sahro probably won't be too happy about it, Diamanes warned.

Glenn chuckled, the aches of his fight against the Black Heir throbbing slightly. "Oh, but I'm counting on it. I'm sure Sahro will understand after I remind him I spent *three months in a hole.*"

With a wide grin, Glenn strode with measured steps, enjoying the last sun rays before nightfall. The scent of cereal grain was simply wonderful compared to the stink of the Sewers. There was a dirt road cutting through the fields with a few carriages heading for the village. Glenn paused when he noticed a farmer sitting under the shade of a tree, his scythe and straw hat beside him. He was drinking from a leather flask, water trickling down his chin.

Glenn approached him. The farmer's annoyed eyes rose to face him as wiped his mouth.

"You're too early. We've already paid the tax; there should be quite a while until the next harvest. What do you want?" he spat, eyeing Glenn's attire.

I'm going to need a change of clothes if this is the reaction I get. Being mistaken for a noble had its pros and cons, but the cons outweighed the pros, it seemed.

"Could you tell me the way to the Auberge, please?" asked Glenn politely.

The farmer blew his nose into his hand and wiped it on his tunic.

Glenn's eyelids twitched as he struggled to keep up a polite smile. He almost spat an insult but instead chose to draw a deep, measured breath. *Are nobles hated everywhere by everyone? I know this was kind of a common thing in the medieval era with the lords overtaxing their serfs and the like, but still.*

"You just have to follow the road; you'll see the signs when you arrive. Now, stop bothering me. I have work to do." The farmer picked up his scythe and hat and walked towards the fields.

He paused for a second, still showing his back to Glenn.

"Oh, and remember. Stay on the path," he said with a serious tone.

He then disappeared between the wheat stalks to reap the product of his labor. Glenn, wondering what he should do with that tip, simply shrugged. He resumed his journey.

The walk was quite pleasant; the sound of cicadas was music to his ears. Birds perched on scarecrows, cawing and singing. He was enjoying the peaceful atmosphere so much that he knew something had to be wrong.

Hey, Glenn. Diamanes' voice startled him.

"For fuck's sake," cursed Glenn, "Can't you let me enjoy my peace for a moment?"

Come on, where's the fun in that? Now, I say we go into the fields.

Glenn looked at his left, bandaged hand. "Are you dumb? The farmer clearly warned us against it—"

Diamanes groaned. ***So what? A random farmer told you to not do something, and you just obey? That's sheep mentality, Glenn. You won't rule the world with that attitude!***

Glenn swore under his breath and dove into the fields, pushing the wheat out of his way.

"There, are you happy now? Can I walk to the village without you cursing or mocking me?"

Diamanes remained silent, a chilling response to Glenn's ire. The atmosphere began to shift strangely. At first, it was just a feeling. But the closer he got to the village, the weirder Glenn felt. There were a few signs that disturbed him: the wind had stopped blowing, the birds weren't chippering, and the cicadas had stopped droning. The silence was heavy and ominous like a shadow extending over him. The only thing he could hear was the sound of his feet hitting the ground, as well as his breath and heartbeat.

No matter where he looked, he couldn't find the road. There was only more and more wheat, as still as trees.

He continued to walk, slowly scanning his surroundings. Every farmer had mysteriously disappeared at some point. The sun was descending, little by little, bringing with it a magenta shade that gave the fields an even weirder property. Glenn rubbed his eyes, wondering if he was going crazy. *Wouldn't be that much of a surprise, really.*

Glenn's gaze searched for a movement, only to find one of those grim scarecrows.

"Weird... It felt as if—"

As if something moved? Yeah. Take out your staff; you're going to need it, warned Diamanes without further explanation.

Glenn complied, turning his head to find another scarecrow standing in the wheat a distance away. It almost felt like it was staring at him. Glenn's fingers wrapped tightly around his fire staff, his heart racing as adrenaline coursed through his veins.

"What kind of weird shit am I going to..." he muttered only to shut up as more scarecrows appeared. If Diamanes warned him, that meant this was going to be some serious business.

"I hate this! Why do they need to build up the tension?"

A bead of sweat trickled down his forehead. His body was ready to act at any sign of movement. It wasn't like the first time—back when he met

Father Albenas in the forest. Now, he felt more like a soldier on the front, ready to defend himself.

His pace increased gradually, synchronized with the appearance of more scarecrows. He prepared a Magic Bullet in his hand. The sound of rustling leaves made him jump as he looked back and found yet another menace, closer than ever as it stood in the middle of the golden cereals.

Continuing in the direction he hoped was the correct one, Glenn stepped on something. It made a cracking sound.

Looking down, he found a white bone, probably a humerus. He paused and checked his surroundings, the blood draining from his face. There were more bones and skulls hidden among the wheat.

"What the hell is going on?" Glenn questioned.

Diamanes maintained his silence as an ominous feeling crept up Glenn's spine. He glanced around, noticing more scarecrows standing in the fields, surrounding him.

Glenn took a deep breath and jumped above the wheat. His eyes locked onto the village in the distance. It was probably a five kilometer run. His pace quickened, and the scarecrows seemed to follow him through the fields, approaching him.

"The farmer clearly said to stay on the path. Was this what he meant?" Glenn questioned as he ran at full speed, his knuckles white from gripping the fire staff too tightly.

Probably. Stop worrying about that and focus on your surroundings. I can count at least twenty of those creatures, Diamanes warned.

"What are they?" he questioned while looking back.

Diamanes scoffed. ***No idea, but they don't seem like they want to be friends with you.***

"No kidding," snorted Glenn.

One of the scarecrows shuddered and a polearm emerged from its hat. Glenn ducked at the last second, feeling the air rush. The weapon was a long, sharp bone. Without giving it another thought, he smashed his fist into the appendage, breaking it in two. The scarecrow reeled back silently, hiding behind its kin.

"That was a limb?" Glenn exclaimed.

He glanced at the broken bone, discovering that a few pieces of flesh were still attached to it, completely rotten and filled with maggots. That strangely didn't disturb him as much as it would have a month ago. He lived in a septic tank for a while, after all. *Well, i's still disgusting.*

Glenn pointed the fire staff towards the scarecrow and shot a fire bolt. The flames wrapped around the monster easily, burning it quickly. The bony limb vanished into ashes along with the main body. Strangely, the wheat fields remained unaffected by the fire.

The other scarecrows closed in, no longer hiding their monstrous appearances. Their heads were made of flesh and bone, giving them a grotesque look. Their arms and legs were simple branches, and under their garments, there were black, beating hearts. Glenn managed to discover that by shooting a Mana Bullet into the torso of one of them.

"Alright, they have a heart. So that's probably a weak point. And fire is very effective. Good to know," he huffed, jumping above another attack.

He charged his staff with a huge chunk of Mana—a quarter of his reserve—and shot off an impressive short-range ray of fire. A dozen scarecrows went up in flames, leaving nothing but ashes.

Glenn picked up the pace, wondering when exactly he was going to arrive at that damned village.

"Hey! Hey! Over here!" A voice called out to him from beyond the fields. Glenn sped up as he ran in the direction of the voice.

"This better not be an ambush! If these damned scarecrows can talk, I'll eat my staff!" he yelled.

His palms were sweaty as he held the fire staff and continued to push back against the fiends. His Mana was quickly bottoming out, making the situation that much more dire.

He kicked away a scarecrow a little too close for his taste and dashed under another attack.

"You're almost there! Come on, come on!" The voices kept on shouting, guiding him through the golden wheat. He suddenly emerged out of the fields, finding the road and a group of farmers holding scythes and torches, their faces grim.

The scarecrows followed him out of the fields, hunting him.

Seems like the road doesn't deter them much once they're in a rage. Diamanes commented casually.

"Hell, Diamanes, why did you put me through this shit!" Glenn cursed aloud, knocking a bone away as if it was a branch.

He didn't know who he had to thank, his abnormal body or the brittleness of the scarecrows' limbs. He clutched the fire staff tightly, infusing half of the Mana he had left into it.

Thank God I bought it from that bartender, Glenn silently thanked himself, readying to unleash the most powerful attack he could muster.

The fire Shard on top of the staff gleamed brightly with incredible power until it broke into a myriad of pieces. Glenn blinked, unable to believe what he was seeing. He cursed and threw the broken staff into the nearest scarecrow's face.

"Fuck my rotten luck!" Glenn screamed as he ran for dear life.

The fields were completely overrun by the army of monsters. Yet, he couldn't hear any sounds except for those he produced.

"I hate this!" Glenn blurted out, narrowly avoiding another attack.

He hurried towards the farmers, no longer bothering to be on the offensive. The more scarecrows he shot down with his Magic Bullets, the more appeared, swarming him. With his Mana close to bottoming out completely, Glenn jumped into the farmer group and unsheathed the sword Giselle gave him, refusing to go down without a fight.

But the scarecrows had stopped right in front of the farmers. One of them walked up to the monsters, a defiant look in his eyes. The scarecrow and the farmer exchanged a silent, intense stare-down.

"What the fuck?" Glenn muttered in disbelief.

Suddenly, the scarecrow retreated and disappeared amidst the wheat fields alongside the rest of its kind. The fields returned to their normal state, the wind rustling through the golden leaves. The sun set, leaving its place for the twin moons to take.

Glenn sighed in relief and collapsed to the ground, wiping the sweat from his forehead. The farmer he had met earlier emerged from the group, approaching him while shaking his head. He extended his hand, prompting Glenn to stand back up.

"It's been a long time since I saw someone voluntarily head into the Golden Fields. You must be suicidal or something."

Glenn blinked. "H-Huh? What? What the hell are you talking about? What the fuck was that?"

The farmers looked at each other, their faces marked with confusion.

"Well, weren't you warned about scaring the scarecrows?"

"Of course not! I didn't even know there were monsters *inside* this damned city!" shouted Glenn.

The farmers exchanged a look and sighed. "You're an unlucky one, aren't you?"

Chapter 31

THE NORTHERN TOWN

Glenn dusted off his shoulders, verifying the scarecrows didn't get in a strike without him noticing. It wasn't *that* great of a triumph since the scarecrows' attacks were easy to predict, yet Glenn still felt a little pride. He wasn't a fighter, after all.

He shook those thoughts out of his head; there were more important matters at hand.

"Could you…" Glenn faced the farmers with a frown. "Explain to me why there are *monsters* in the damned wheat fields? Hello?"

The farmer who helped him up sighed and gestured to the others, who left with worried expressions. He took his straw hat off and rubbed the back of his head. He cleared his throat and led the way to the village.

"Well, uhm, you see, entering the Golden Fields and fighting against the scarecrows is an old rite of passage," the farmer explained awkwardly. "An ancient tradition to, uh, make sure you're worthy of entering King's Rise."

He pointed at the imposing gray tower in the distance, far behind the massive wall. Diamond-shaped stones floated around it, hovering magically. The tower looked the same as when Glenn first glimpsed at it from Still Peak.

"That's something the First King put in place long ago, but no one bothers doing it anymore and everyone just uses the road."

I suppose they couldn't hide that under an illusion spell.

Or perhaps they didn't want to, added Diamanes.

The farmer clicked his tongue. "That's the Royal Tower. And at its base is the Court. It houses all the most powerful noble families and most important members of Munirp. They're the top dogs, and no one can do anything to them. Besides the King..."

He shook his head dejectedly. "Back when I came to King's Rise, I thought I would also be able to make it all the way there. But look where I am now..."

Glenn almost rolled his eyes. *Why is he telling me his life story?*

But the farmer continued with his monologue, undeterred.

"The fields weren't like this in the past. In the legend, the First King—the one who built King's Rise—defeated a mythical monster here, fighting for ten days and ten nights without respite."

"After he finally defeated the beast, its body created a fertile zone where crops grow at unprecedented speed. Cereals filled with Mana and magical properties. The Fringe became the granary of the whole city thanks to those fields."

Glenn glared at the *magical* fields with a hint of annoyance.

"But all this concentrated Mana created these... things. The scarecrows. They haunt the fields and attack any traveler who walks through them. Probably a leftover Rift if you ask me."

He paused with sudden realization and stared at Glenn. "But that's common knowledge. Even people from outside the walls know about this. Even if you didn't, the Watchers should have told you!"

Glenn's eyebrows twitched as he recalled the unpleasant encounter with the corrupted guards at the Frozen Gate.

"Besides asking for more coins than they could bear, they didn't tell me much," he explained casually.

The farmer clenched his fist and spat on the ground, his face quickly turning to a purple shade.

"These Watchers... That's why there are less and less newcomers these days... That's all his damn fault," he said through his clenched teeth before exhaling in frustration.

"About them..." Glenn pointed at the scarecrows. "Why did they stop?"

"They don't bother farmers. And, I know, you probably think we should get rid of them, but... It's impossible." He shrugged. "You saw it, right? You kill one, and ten more pop up. True pest those guys."

Glenn nodded and glanced back to the fields, wondering if he would be strong enough to deal with threats of this level one day. There probably was some sort of spawning point hidden in the wheat fields. *Well, it's not my problem to deal with, and the people seemed to have no issue living besides these creatures.*

They finally arrived at the village, the farmer smiling warmly as he crossed his arms.

"Welcome to the Northern Town. I hope your stay will be pleasant and help you forget your... unpleasant encounter with the scarecrows."

Glenn grinned, enjoying the sight. The Northern Town, nestled against the huge walls, had adopted a picturesque style. Provincial houses—with their charming thatched roofs and whitewashed walls—lined cobbled streets that wound their way through the heart of the village. Each house had flower boxes adorning their windows, bursting with vibrant colors that added to the village's rustic charm.

The village was incredibly large, reaching far beyond what Glenn could see. The 'town' title seemed a little too modest. 'City' was certainly more appropriate. There were countless shops and streets, with signs indicating the way to every point of interest: Church of Onnea, Cleaner's Workshop, Magi Brotherhood Bureau, Gold Church, Heart's Bakery, and a whole lot more.

The town was humming with activity as people went about their daily routines—mostly returning home after a hard day of labor. Glenn suddenly realized he had somehow spent the whole day in those damned fields fighting the scarecrows. Well, most of it had been spent enjoying the walk, spare for the last bit.

He sighed as he glanced at the massive wall before turning to the farmer.

"If the Court is up there, then the area we're in, what's it called?" Glenn asked.

The farmer blinked and snorted in disbelief. "You don't know anything, don't you?"

Glenn shrugged dismissively.

The farmer sighed. "We're in the Fringe. It's where people like... like *me* live. The working class, if you'd like... Still quite a pleasant place to spend one's life in. It's also one of the rare places in Munirp where you can find fertile soil worth cultivating."

Resentment briefly flashed in his eyes, but it disappeared as quickly as it came.

"Then there is the Bourgeoisie. It's intended for the most successful in our class, and it gives a taste of what nobility feels like. I've heard that the lowest-ranking nobles like the Barons live there, alongside the richest merchants and the middle-ranked officers of the army. I think. Never went there."

Glenn perked up at the mention of the Bourgeoisie and Barons.

Hmm. So that's why Giselle told me about that. Baron Howard probably lives in the Bourgeoisie, since he's only a low-ranked noble.

Glenn restrained a sigh. *The main challenge is going to be to find a way to go up there, isn't it?*

I'm sure it's nothing too demanding, Diamanes said with a sarcastic tone. **Probably only a lot of money or connections. Good thing you have plenty of both of those.**

Glenn's lips twitched but he managed to make abstention of the entity and concentrate back on the farmer's explanations.

"Well, I've told you everything I knew. Since you survived the fields, I suppose you'll be able to take care of yourself, ain't that right, kid?" He patted Glenn's shoulders before pausing. "Oh, and also, I'm Carys. Don't hesitate to come by the fields if you need anything!"

Glenn smiled and shook Carys' hand. "Pleasure is all mine. I'm Glenn."

Carys grinned and departed. Glenn took a long, deep breath, and exhaled loudly.

"That guy sure loved to talk," he said, feeling a strange feeling of satisfaction.

Glenn glanced at the nearby signs, looking for the Auberge where Sahro was supposed to be awaiting him.

On his way there, Glenn couldn't help but contrast the Northern Town with the Sewers. Relatively clean streets, no abandoned corpses, and no ruined houses. The scent of supper lingered in the air as mothers dragged their kids inside and fathers returned from work. There were also a few warriors, with swords or other weapons at their waists, headed in the same direction—probably to a mercenary office or something. There weren't any guards, and yet criminality didn't appear to be a striking problem.

You don't say, thought Glenn.

After a few twists and turns, he arrived at the Auberge, an immense inn. The Iced Beer looked more than shabby in comparison. He passed through the doors, discovering a cacophony of laughter, glasses clinking, and chairs rattling. There was even a bard playing, carried by a chorus of drunk voices.

Glenn longed to relax in this pleasant atmosphere, but memories of his last stopover at an inn weren't helping. He grimaced until he noticed a group of silver-clad paladins laughing heartily. Further along, a group of merchants emptied mug after mug, discussing the profits of their latest venture.

No fake bartenders. No cultists. No drugs.

Just a normal inn.

Thank goodness for that.

He sighed in relief and spotted a hunched figure sitting by himself at a secluded table, the fabric of his white hood easily recognizable. Glenn sat in front of him, grinning as he made himself comfortable.

"I hope I didn't make you wait," he snorted while raising his hand for a waitress to serve him.

Sahro choked and hurriedly pulled Glenn's hand down, searching around anxiously.

"Wait, what the hell is happening to you?" Glenn asked, pleasantly surprised. "Where did the brave, confident, and cocky Black Heir go? I can't recognize you!"

He laughed heartily while patting Sahro on the back. The Black Heir flinched and pushed Glenn away while adjusting his hood.

"Damn it, Glenn!" Sahro hissed in a half-whisper. "This is a secret mission given to us by Giselle and Redan themselves! Tone it down! What the hell took you so long anyway? I had to avoid spies and potential enemies all day!"

Glenn coughed, struggling to contain a mocking laugh. "Sorry, I was forced to deal with some scarecrows. They had a bone to pick with me. Long story, and not an interesting one."

Sahro shook his head in incomprehension. "Speak in Common Tongue! Now..." He glared at their surroundings. "Where do we begin?"

Glenn sighed and raised his hand once more, slapping Sahro's poor attempt at stopping him.

The Black Heir's face reddened. "Are you stupid?! They're going to notice us! Don't do anything that could get us caught!"

Glenn couldn't contain it anymore and laughed heartily. "Sahro, when you're in an *inn*, it's either to eat, drink, sleep, or fuck. Mostly drink, I believe, but I *could* be wrong."

Sahro paused, his eyebrows creasing. He slumped on the table, his forehead hitting the wood with a loud knock.

He was about to mock the Black Heir once more, but the waitress finally arrived to take his order.

"Two beers and whatever food has the most meat," Glenn ordered.

The woman smiled and nodded before scurrying back to the kitchen. Sahro slowly peeked out of his cape.

"What the hell is up with you, seriously?" Glenn asked with honest confusion.

Sahro straightened up, his mask of pride crumbling away. "Man... this place is so fucking crazy!"

He discreetly pointed at the other tables in shock. "Can you see that? They're eating *whole-ass chickens*! I ain't ever seen a damn chicken in my life!"

He buried his face in his hands. "And did you see the town? Spotless. No dead bodies, no rivers of shit or blood. Nothing like that. Bro, I can count on one hand the number of emaciated people I saw!"

Glenn paused for a moment, unresponsive. His brain slowly analyzed the Black Heir's words.

He laughed. "Okay, Sahro, this might surprise you, but this is the *normal* way of life. You... You're aware that how you live in the Sewers isn't normal, right?"

The Black Heir sighed deeply.

"I know. Trust me, I know all too well. But it's one thing to hear about how well-off people are within the walls, and another to see it directly."

Glenn's grin faded away as he thought back to how the Black Heirs were currently living. No, surviving was a better word. Sahro stared dejectedly at a full-course meal on another table, his fists clenched.

He was about to say something, but the waitress arrived with their order. Two massive wooden mugs overflowing with ale and two deep plates of creamy mashed potatoes with thick slices of sausages. The corner of Glenn's lips curved upwards as he grabbed his mug and brought his lips to the beverage.

His heartbeat suddenly raced as adrenaline coursed through his veins, and he slammed the mug back on the table. A bead of sweat pearled down his forehead. He looked at his hand—his fingers trembled.

What the fuck? He gulped as fear crept in his stomach.

As if to save him, the woman smiled at Glenn and sneakily took a peek under Sahro's hood. Her mouth formed an 'O' as she offered him the same seductive smile before hurrying back to work.

The Black Heir's face suddenly hardened, and he reached for his blade, his eyes flaring up with crimson Aura.

"Another spy... Shit, I couldn't hide my face this time. We need to get rid of her."

Glenn sighed. *This is going to take some time, isn't it?*

Chapter 32

THE CLEANERS

Glenn brushed his hair back, observing the serious Black Heir had been on the verge of darting after the waitress checked under his hood. His intentions were clear, and it wasn't a romantic goal.

Believing a waitress is a spy... I mean, considering your experiences, it does make sense. Diamanes laughed mockingly.

Glenn's lips twitched, focusing on Sahro, who was staring at the foam covering the beer as if it held the secrets of the universe. His plate of food went similarly untouched.

"You can drink it. It's not poison, see?" Glenn quipped before trying once more to down his ale, only for his lips to stop at the liquid's cold touch.

Sahro gritted his teeth and hesitantly grabbed his jug. Glenn watched silently. It was strangely entertaining to see Sahro struggle with these basic pleasures.

After a moment of contemplation, the Black Heir drew a deep breath and emptied the mug in one gulp.

Glenn choked. "Wait, that's not—"

He raised his hand tentatively. But Sahro slammed the jug on the table, exhaling an alcohol-filled groan.

Glenn couldn't help but chuckle softly. Sahro hiccupped and released a hearty belch. He jolted upright, a hand over his mouth to stifle any further outbursts.

"What did I just drink?" he asked, his voice somewhat unsteady. "I'm feeling... a little weird. Glenn—I knew it, it's poison!"

"Well, it's beer, my friend. A drink that most people—sorry, most *humans*—enjoy. But..." He paused. "It can certainly be considered a type of poison. A pleasant one to enjoy, though."

Suddenly, a flicker of concern danced across Glenn's eyes as a thought struck him.

"Wait, Sahro, how old are you?"

"Twenty-one, why?" Sahro replied, his head tilted in confusion.

Glenn shrugged. "Oh, nothing, nothing."

Sahro, his curiosity piqued by his previous degustation, decided to inquire further. "Can I get another?"

"Sure, whatever, just drink mine," Glenn acquiesced with a slight smirk. *Looks like this is getting interesting—entertaining, even.*

Is it really a good idea to get a powerful warrior drunk? Wait, of course it is! Diamanes laughed wickedly.

Glenn waved him off, too eager to see how Sahro would react to being inebriated. He would be careful, but no reason not to initiate the Black Heir to the novelty of alcohol.

"Listen Sahro, I'm pretty sure we can locate the Howards if we manage to gain access to the Bourgeoisie. You know what that is, right?"

Sahro nodded. "I've heard you need to be either a mid-ranking officer, a wealthy merchant, or at least a Baron to enter that part of King's Rise, but I could be wrong."

"We need to find a way in. Once we're there, I'll be able to negotiate with Baron Howard, thanks to this."

Glenn retrieved the family ring from his dimensional pouch and spun it on the table.

"At the same time," Glenn continued, "we might want to earn some money— quickly. I have some funds, and I assume you do too."

He eyed Sahro expectantly, who looked away, whistling awkwardly.

"What, Giselle didn't give you anything?" Glenn inquired.

Sahro shook his head, a touch of embarrassment coloring his features. In the Black Heir's camp, he had exuded pride and confidence, but now, he appeared more like a pitiful lost puppy. Glenn couldn't help but facepalm at Sahro's unpreparedness.

"Alright, that means we'll have to find some work and earn some moolah."

"What's moolah?" Sahro asked.

"Stop asking questions," Glenn dismissed without another thought. "What can you do?"

"Fight?" Sahro ventured.

"Besides that?"

Sahro coughed awkwardly.

"Damnit."

Glenn finished his sausages and leaned in his chair. Sahro had also wolfed down his meal, probably more than happy to be treated to something other than the slop he ate back in the Sewers. The waitress arrived with two beers, letting them sip peacefully. Well, as peaceful as the rowdy Auberge allowed.

"Hey, handsome," she said with a seductive smile, "We are offering new *intimate* services—if you have the coins."

Glenn and Sahro looked at her blankly, one with surprise and the other with barely veiled murderous intentions. She cleared her throat and ran back to the kitchen. The two men shrugged it off.

"Let's pass the night here and see what we do tomorrow," Glenn decided while stretching.

Sahro nodded slowly. "We must be in perfect condition for our secret operation. We don't want to enter a conflict with the locals, but we still need to be prepared."

Glenn rolled his eyes and went to pay his bill at the counter. He also reserved a cheap room with two beds, choosing to keep an eye on the Black Heir just in case. It wouldn't hurt to be careful, and he was saving money. Two birds with one stone.

* * *

The evening was uneventful, except for Glenn enjoying the comfort of a straw bed and the fact that he did not need to Meditate. Meditating every night was great to recover physical strength, but mentally, it was a little draining. This side effect was supposed to disappear the more he trained, but he did not want to bother with that for now.

Just a good sleep for once.

The next day, Glenn and Sahro left the Auberge, yawning and ready to tackle the Northern Town. The morning sun cast its gentle glow over the village as shopkeepers set up their stalls and display windows. The farmers had gone to work right before dawn to make use of the stillness of the day.

"Maybe there's a mercenary guild or something," Glenn pondered aloud.

"I think I saw a sign for a Cleaner's Workshop, but nothing about mercenaries," Sahro commented as he rubbed his forehead with a frown. "Why do I have a headache? I've never been sick since awakening Aura."

"Cleaner's Workshop? I think I saw a sign about them too..." Glenn mused as he ignored the Black Heirs' struggle with his light hangover. "Well, it won't cost us anything to see what it's all about. But before that, we need to verify something."

The pair headed towards the massive wall that cast a shadow over the village. After about half an hour following the main road, they arrived at a checkpoint with an imposing gate.

If what I'm seeing is correct, this one was probably constructed long after the outer wall. The magic used on it seems less impressive, Diamanes mentioned, intrigued.

Wait, what? The inner wall is less secure than the outer wall? Glenn couldn't fathom the logic behind that. After all, the inner wall was easily taller than the outer wall.

Well, it's like comparing a thousand tanks to nuclear bombs. Both are strong, but the difference is still like heaven and earth, Diamanes explained.

At the checkpoint, a contingent of soldiers stood guard in steel plate armor, laughing casually. One of them noticed the duo, appearing to be an officer from the golden ridges on his pauldrons. He glanced appraisingly at Glenn's outfit while scoffing at Sahro, who was wearing a balaclava and desert garb to hide his tanned skin.

The guard positioned himself squarely in front of Glenn and adopted a formal stance, locking eyes with him. "Hello, good sir. Are you here to ascend?"

Ascend? Glenn thought, caught off guard.

Thinking on his feet, Glenn responded, "Maybe not today. I'm trying to figure out what my friend here needs to do to enter the Bourgeoisie. He's from outside the walls."

The agent pursed his lips skeptically but, at Glenn's innocent expression, cleared his throat and produced a document.

"To enter the Bourgeoisie, one must either own a Baron-rank, possess a gold recommendation from the Gold Church, hold a third-tier military rank, or pay a one-time fee of a hundred gold. These are the rules established by the Court," the officer read. "Anything else, gentlemen?"

Glenn swallowed his shock and forced a smile. "No, thank you."

The officer nodded sternly and rejoined the discussion with the other soldiers. Glenn pulled Sahro away from the checkpoint. A short distance away, he turned to him with a questioning gaze.

"A hundred."

Sahro tilted his head. "Is that a lot?"

Glenn checked the contents of his dimensional bag. "I only have five gold coins. Remember the drinks we had?"

Sahro nodded.

"I can buy a mountain of drinks with only a single gold coin."

Sahro gasped.

"And we need a hundred. A hundred. We're never getting inside the Bourgeoisie," Glenn lamented.

"W-What about the other options?" Sahro asked hopefully.

Glenn shook his head in resignation. "No way we're entering the military, so no. We're not nobles, and we have no connection with the Gold Church. I could try using the ring of the Howard family, but..." He grimaced. "If they verify our identity, it's game over."

Sahro sighed deeply. "And here I was hoping I'd be able to get this mission done quickly..."

Glenn patted the Black Heir on the back. "Hey, who knows? Maybe we will be able to get everything done in a month or two. Maybe less if we put our backs to it!"

Sahro looked up with renewed determination. "Yeah, you're right! Let's not lose hope!"

With these thoughts in mind, the two left in search of the Cleaner's Workshop. Eventually, after asking passersby for directions, they finally arrived at their destination. It stood as a sturdy building with thick stone walls adorned with banners featuring a grand flame.

A central tower loomed over the structure, its pinnacle crowned with a perpetually burning torch.

"Well, it doesn't quite resemble the 'cleaners' I had in mind," Glenn remarked, a tinge of awe in his voice.

Sahro nodded with uncertainty. The entrance was unguarded, allowing them to enter without issue. Inside, stood a grand hall fixed with elaborate tapestries, giant skulls, and exotic weapons.

"I think we found our mercenary guild," muttered Glenn.

Various individuals moved about, each equipped with an array of effects and armor. Most appeared to be seasoned warriors, though some donned robes and wielded staves—hinting at more scholarly roles.

A cluster of people gathered around a central board filled with job offers. The atmosphere within the workshop exuded an aura of vigilance, punctuated by the sounds of clashing steel from what seemed to be a training hall further away.

Glenn sought the job board where a counter stood staffed by three attractive, young women. Approaching the first one, Glenn was met with a finger raised in admonition and a nasty tongue click.

"Please take a ticket and wait with the others," she instructed, pointing to a dispenser and a waiting area, where a dozen individuals sat.

The duo complied and obtained a ticket. They took seats next to each other, surveying the other patrons.

Sahro leaned in and whispered, "Now what?"

Glenn shuddered, repulsed by the sensation of Sahro's breath against his ear. "Never whisper in my ear like that again. It's dreadful. As for your question, we wait. Try to listen and gather some information."

As they surveyed the surroundings, they noticed several people with cloaks, allowing Sahro to blend in better. Tattooed barbarians, hooded hunters, scrawny priests, and even eastern swordsmen carrying katanas at their waists. These individuals hailed from different backgrounds, adding diversity to the crowd.

Among them were some 'common' humans, a population Glenn had primarily encountered in the Fringe. They possessed blond hair, blue eyes, and pale skin—the mainstream physical appearance in this world. Darker shades of hair seemed uncommon.

A hooded figure occupied the vacant seat beside Sahro, their long black locks releasing a pleasant scent of mint that filled the air.

Mint? That's... an interesting choice of perfume, Glenn remarked.

Well, whether it's perfume or not, this person seems stronger than you. So hurry and reach the Third Circle, urged Diamanes impatiently.

"Number 346!"

Glenn checked his ticket and rose with Sahro following suit.

"Time to see if being a Cleaner brings in the big checks!"

"What the hell is 'checks'?" Sahro inquired.

Glenn sighed. "Don't bother."

Chapter 33

REGISTRATION

Glenn arrived at the counter, his gaze fixed on the woman behind it. She wore a pristine white dress adorned with a red cross on each shoulder. A name tag reading 'Alisson' rested on her chest.

He looked around the hall, discovering that a few people also wore pure white with red crosses—be it on their clothes or armor. It seemed to be the Cleaners' uniform.

Alisson, the attendant, tossed her long, blond hair back and offered a sweet smile. "Welcome to the Cleaner's Workshop! Information, Cleaning contracts, and the finest mercenary service in the entire Fringe! How can I assist you?"

Glenn returned her smile and pointed at Sahro with his thumb. "My friend and I are newcomers to King's Rise, and we're in search of work. Mercenary-type."

"I see. Please give me a moment."

She crouched, looking for something under the counter. Glenn glanced away, noticing that the two other attendants—who were equally attractive as Alisson—dressed in the same white robe with the red crosses. Each attended to their clients with pure, wide smiles.

Sahro tapped lightly on Glenn's shoulder, his expression grave as he nodded towards the clerks. They tossed their hair back at the same time, mimicking Alisson's motions in a mechanical manner.

Glenn rubbed his eyes, wondering if he perhaps had seen wrong. The next second, the two clerks leaned back and stretched *in unison*, sending a shiver down his spine. He tensed and exchanged a concerned glance with Sahro.

The latter whispered discreetly, "It didn't happen only once. They seem... connected."

"What the hell?" Glenn said in awe. *Diamanes, any idea what they are?*

Hmm... Diamanes groaned hesitantly. ***I... I honestly don't know. Maybe it's because I woke up not that long ago, but I can't tell. They're neither alive nor dead, but not even magic can do that. Necromancy doesn't work that way.***

Glenn exhaled heavily, his hand tightening around the hilt of the sword Giselle gave him. This Cleaner's Workshop wasn't merely a mercenary guild. He could feel the weight of ominous secrets hiding behind the strange clerks.

Alisson eventually found what she was searching for: a stack of documents with the Cleaner's red flame logo printed on each page. She handed them to Glenn, her pleasant smile almost unsettling.

"Here are the regulations for becoming a Cleaner, as well as a Fixer. Feel free to read them and make your decision. Once you're done, complete the questionnaire on the last page and bring it to the Testing Hall."

She pointed towards a hallway. Then, slapping her forehead in a somewhat endearing manner, she said, "I nearly forgot your companion. I hope you'll become my colleague in the future!"

Glenn would have certainly found the mannerism cute if he hadn't seen the two other attendants do the exact same movement in the corner of his eyes.

With a shiver running down his spine, Glenn took Sahro's copy and bowed. "Thank you, Miss Alisson."

He and Sahro left the building and sat on a nearby bench. The Black Heir kept a wary eye on everyone that passed. Glenn sighed deeply as he perused the documents and paraphrased the key points.

"The Workshop proposes two contracts. The first makes us a main member with a basic salary of five silver, accommodations, and provided equipment. We earn the Junior Cleaner title and receive bonuses depending on our performances."

"We will receive training according to our rank, and support will be provided for our advancements. After six months, the pay increases to ten silver, along with the title Cleaner. However, as an integral Workshop member, we can't leave the Fringe unless ordered to, which means no return to the Sewers or advancement to the Bourgeoisie."

Glenn scoffed but continued reading the document, "We're also bound by an oath of secrecy. There are opportunities for advancement once we've proven our loyalty, but it means giving up our freedom, which I don't intend to do."

"I'm not about to let any human be my superior. Only Giselle can give me orders!" Sahro spat. After a moment's thought, he added, "And you, but only in human settlements. And that's a heavy exception already!"

Glenn raised an eyebrow. "Your trust will be repaid, my good sir. This humble and terrible human will surely live up to your expectations."

He went back to reading the contract while the Black Heir's face became redder than a tomato.

"The second contract makes us a Fixer, a mercenary. Our abilities—which will be assessed—will determine our rank: Copper, Bronze, or Silver. Depending on that rank, we'll gain access to bounties. We'd handle specific requests with prices determined by the requester. The Workshop, in this situation, acts as an intermediary and takes a ten percent fee."

Sahro snorted. "Silver rank is the minimum that we have to get. That one pays the most, right?"

"Copper Fixers receive no support from the Workshop, except for general combat classes. They are responsible for their equipment and do not have access to the Workshop's facilities. Yeah, that won't do us any good."

Glenn exhaled and leaned back on the bench, the choice evident in his eyes. As far as he could tell with his meager legal skills, there didn't seem to be any loopholes—not even a non-compete clause.

Sahro crossed his arms. "Let's become Fixers. We can just complete bounties one after the other and quickly gather some moo... moo..." He frowned and tried hesitantly. "Moolah?"

Glenn laughed. "Yeah, you got it. From what I've seen of the contract board, there are more than enough jobs to keep us busy. It shouldn't be too hard to earn a lot of money quickly."

The two exchanged grins. Glenn paused as he thought back to the strange clerks.

"What do you think about what we've seen? The attendants, I mean?" he asked.

Sahro rubbed his chin. "Hmm... All I can say is that the motions were very natural. They weren't forced, as if they were being controlled by someone. The three move as if they are the same entity. It's very..."

"Disturbing?" Glenn finished Sahro's sentence for him, nodding in agreement. "Let's stay careful of this 'Workshop', alright?"

Sahro snickered and focused on the form. Glenn looked down at his own and quickly filled in the required information. The questions were quite traditional: a name, age, profession, and place of residence. Glenn was relieved to discover that Sahro knew how to read and write in the Common Tongue.

The Common Tongue, huh... How do I even know that name? I guess it's like you can't know English without knowing the word 'English,' Glenn thought with a hint of sarcasm.

Since they didn't have a permanent residence, they decided to simply write 'The Auberge' as their home. *We'll probably be living here for a while anyway.*

In the section for professions, there were several multiple choice options to pick from. Glenn ticked 'Mage' and hesitated to tick 'Hand-to-hand combatant' too, but he had to admit that he hadn't mastered melee combat—especially when he remembered how badly Sahro had beaten him. Actually, he sucked ass at fighting. He could guess what Sahro's pick would be, and after a few minutes, the duo completed their forms.

They made their way inside the Workshop and to the Testing Hall, walking through the corridor while listening to the sounds of clashing steel and explosions. Glenn felt a tinge of excitement.

Soon, the two arrived in an arena with a high red and white glass ceiling and empty stands. Most of the space was occupied by a large, sandy field where mercenaries faced off against Cleaners. The distinct attire of the Cleaners shimmered in the sunlight as they engaged in combat, clearly dominating their opponents. After forcing their adversaries to admit defeat, the Cleaners handed them a piece of paper and sent them off.

A Cleaner approached Glenn and Sahro, his face devoid of emotion. His bald head was striking, and there wasn't a single hair on his body—not even eyebrows or eyelashes, giving him an eerie appearance.

"Papers, please," he stated robotically.

A name tag inscribed with 'Tak Delora' was pinned to his red-crossed white uniform. He extended a rigid hand towards them, waiting for their documents. Glenn and Sahro exchanged glances and handed their forms over simultaneously.

Tak Delora? Does he have two first names? Or is Delora his surname? Come to think of it, the only person I met so far with a surname was that Jefferson Howard guy. Do only nobles have surnames or something? Not that I assume this guy's one of them, Glenn silently wondered.

Tak Delora swiftly examined the forms and indicated separate areas of the sandy field to each of them. The duo nodded and proceeded to their designated spots.

After waiting for a few minutes, Glenn noticed a slender figure approaching him. Wearing a simple knife at her belt, the woman stood in front of Glenn. Her round face exuded an air of gentleness while her blue eyes seemed to scrutinize Glenn's posture for any weaknesses. A cascade of red hair flowed messily to her shoulders. She was dressed in the Cleaner's attire and appeared ready for action, playing with another sharp dagger.

She then executed a swift and exaggerated bow.

"Nice to meet you, Glenn. I'm Mary, and I'll be overseeing this test. Since you're a Mage, your task is to hit me with one of your spells. Of course, try not to injure me, as this is merely an assessment of your casting speed and accuracy," she explained quickly. "And if you're a power-oriented Mage, don't worry. There's another test after this one."

Glenn grinned and took a step back as Mana swirled around his hand. "It's my pleasure, Miss Mary."

Mary smiled with a wolf-like grin as she stopped playing with her knife. Glenn prepared himself as he considered his options. *Since there's another test after this one, I should go at this one with restraint to conserve Mana. That way, I'll be able to later demonstrate Implosion if needed.*

A Magic Bullet hovered above his hand, particles of deep blue light floating around him.

It was time to spar with Mary.

Chapter 34

TESTS

Glenn observed his opponent, Mary, before suddenly shooting his Mana Bullet.

The Cleaner swiftly dodged the spell, the deep blue glint of the magic reflecting off her dagger. She dashed and slipped right under Glenn's defense, striking upwards without hesitation. Glenn hurriedly jumped out of reach and shot another Magic Bullet, forcing her back.

With that short exchange, Glenn was now certain. If he were to categorize her in an RPG manner, she would undoubtedly fall under the rogue class. *Which isn't great since my own archetype is a mage. Oh well.*

Come on, liven this up a little! Diamanes chuckled wickedly.

Gritting his teeth, Glenn prepared an invisible Magic Bullet and infused more Mana into it than usual. He shot it while aiming for Mary's leg, hoping to reduce her mobility.

But the Cleaner simply deflected the attack with a swift motion, the spell dissipating in a loud, metallic clang. Glenn felt a shiver crawl down his spine. He was able to anticipate her arm's rapid movement.

Mary spun her dagger in her hands, unfazed and composed. Glenn clicked his tongue and changed his strategy. If speed didn't work, he only had quantity over quality.

He drew a deep breath before unleashing a barrage of Magic Bullets, firing them rapidly at a rate of forty-five projectiles per minute. While this barely matched Earth's semi-automatic firearms, it still felt immensely impressive. If he had this back when he met that pack of wolves, he certainly wouldn't have been as terrified.

The shots were cost-effective, and Glenn calculated that he could sustain this pace for at least five minutes, considering he didn't have to worry about his defense.

However, Mary seemed to effortlessly predict the trajectory of each bullet, dodging or blocking every one. Sometimes she just stopped in place and the bullets would shoot past her. Glenn didn't manage to hit her even once.

Try something other than brute force. Maybe it'll have better results, Diamanes suggested with a mocking tone.

Glenn suddenly stopped his bullet barrage, switching strategies. Mary shifted from one foot to another while glancing at the tinted glass ceiling. Glenn resumed his attacks with a slower firing rate, but with more power. They also demanded greater concentration, as each was precisely aimed at Mary's hand.

He circled her, a bead of sweat sliding down his forehead as each shot failed to tire his opponent.

Mary laughed, struggling to comprehend what Glenn was trying to achieve. She deflected another shot lazily before yawning from boredom. Soon enough, Glenn completed a full circle around Mary and halted in place.

Mary rolled her eyes. "Whatever you're attempting, it's not working. Care to change your tactics?"

Glenn shot another Magic Bullet in response, which Mary easily blocked. Only, hidden behind the first bullet was a second one charged with even more Mana. Mary blinked in surprise and hurriedly deflected that attack too, only to stumble and lose her footing.

In that same instant, Glenn flicked his finger and activated the thirty Magic Bullets he had set up. The sound of thirty cannon shots firing simultaneously filled the air as the Magic Bullet rushed for their target.

Mary's lips curved upwards slightly as the Magic Bullet made contact with her, creating a large cloud of dust. Glenn waved the dust away while smiling in satisfaction.

"That should have done it..." he mumbled hopefully.

You should have screamed "The Worldooo!" when you shot those bullets, Diamanes commented with a tinge of disappointment.

Glenn's eyebrows twitched, but he remained silent, squinting as he peered through the dust cloud. The sand eventually settled, only revealing an empty space where Mary had stood earlier.

A cold, sharp blade pressed against Glenn's neck from behind.

A cheerful voice chuckled, "And *that* does it. I did warn you it wasn't enough, but a very good effort nonetheless."

Glenn turned to find Mary unharmed, standing proudly with not even a speck of dust on her shoulders. She sheathed her dagger with a grin before producing a fountain pen and a sheet of paper.

"Shit." Glenn rubbed the back of his neck.

He knew that he had no chance to win, but still. It was frustrating. *What could I have done better? How could I have won? Having more spells certainly would have helped. Using Implosion was out of the question since Mary would have probably dodged that too.*

Mary scribbled one last word and handed him the sheet. Glenn took it and received a light pat on his shoulder. The document mostly contained a lot of technical gibberish.

The memo at the bottom read, "No fighting experience, lacks versatility, potential of twenty."

"Potential of twenty? What does that even mean?" he pondered.

Diamanes broke the silence with a mocking laugh. ***Well, it means you just got schooled and that you've got much to learn. But hey, they can somehow see something interesting in you!*** The entity paused. ***Maybe they got a glance at my marvelous existence?***

Glenn sighed loudly and headed off to find his non-demonic travel companion. Sahro had probably performed much better than him. It was infuriating, but it made sense. After all, Sahro was a combat specialist while Glenn never fought a single time in his life before coming to this world.

He quickly found Sahro, who was also strolling towards him. The Black Heir shook his head with a dejected smile.

"How did you do?" Glenn asked.

Sahro shrugged and showed his document.

"Recommended for Silver rank, exceptional combat skills, defeated a Junior Cleaner, high potential. Huh, you defeated your Cleaner?" Glenn exclaimed in surprise.

Sahro nodded and picked his nose. "Yeah, but the Senior Cleaner completely destroyed me. Damned human... Shit, I thought I wouldn't lose to anyone besides Redan and Giselle!"

Glenn rolled his eyes and sighed with a pang of frustration. *Why the hell is he complaining?*

Don't worry, if you start using me more, you'll soon become stronger than Sahro, whispered Diamanes.

Glenn almost laughed out loud, but held back to avoid Sahro's unwanted attention. *Well, you're honestly not very useful. Don't take it the wrong way. I'm starting to enjoy having another inner voice, but you don't add much to the power table right now.*

How about you get to the Third Circle, and we'll see what I can really do, alright? Diamanes implored eagerly.

Glenn and Sahro arrived at the next testing area, a small child in the Cleaners' garb waiting for them. A few other candidates filled inside, all wondering what the next test was going to be.

Glenn hesitated to ask the child if he had lost his parents, but given the display of the last Cleaner, it probably wasn't a good idea.

After a few more minutes, the rest of the participants joined the group. A few worried whispers from the growing crowd echoed around them, until an immense man with bulging muscles and an equally immense sword volunteered as tribute. He took a knee in front of the child.

"Are you lost, kid?" he asked with a gentle smile.

The white robe covering the child trembled, and a second later, a steel column erupted from the ground, kicking the huge man a dozen meters away.

"I'm... Tom..." The child spoke with an unusually raspy voice that sent shivers down Glenn's spine. "I'll be... the Tester."

Glenn took a step back. That was no child's voice. The Cleaner Tom was struggling to speak, having a hard time pronouncing even one word. Glenn glanced a little closer and indeed, he discovered a tag on his robe reading "Tom Delora."

So he's from the same family as that bald creep. Well, I don't see why I would be surprised... he thought.

"I'll conjure steel pillars... for you to destroy... Do your best, my cute maggots..." Tom crooned in an unnatural cadence.

An eerie laugh echoed from under the robe as the aforementioned pillars manifested, numbering the same as the candidates—including the huge man who had been sent flying.

One large steel pillar appeared under Tom's feet and took him above the challengers. He looked down, his face hidden behind the darkness of his hood.

Glenn suppressed the instinct to curse and run away but held his ground, driven by one sole goal: money. And also to not look like a coward in front of that Black Heir bastard.

He rolled up his sleeves, wondering how the hell he was supposed to break the steel column. *Magic Bullet... will probably not be enough. But it's still worth testing.*

Glenn shot a quick spell at it, only for a loud clang to resonate. The pillar remained unscathed, not even a scratch.

"I'm going to need more firepower..." Glenn muttered as he prepared an Implosion.

Diamanes sighed and interrupted him. ***Why don't you use this perfect opportunity to create new spells or enhance Magic Bullet? You already know Implosion is going to reduce this pillar to dust anyway.***

Huh. Good point. Glenn dismissed the Implosion, recovering most of the Mana.

"I need to pierce that thing... How can I achieve penetration power?" Glenn pondered.

Eventually, his thoughts drifted back to Earth. There were tools capable of breaking even the strongest materials, bending them to human will. The firearms industry created armor-piercing rounds. Nonetheless, besides *a tank round*—which he had a hard time envisioning—Glenn couldn't imagine a bullet strong enough to pierce through five meters of steel.

"Maybe I'm looking at this from the wrong angle..." Glenn took a step back and changed his focus.

Besides explosives and highly charged kinetic projectiles, there were only a few things that could cut through tough materials. Such as a drill. It was made with that purpose in mind. Of course, for a five-meter-thick steel pillar, the equipment would be considerably larger and more powerful than a handheld drill.

But this wasn't Earth. This was... whatever this world's name was, and there was magic. That meant that if he could properly envision the spell he wanted, he could probably create something strong enough to do anything.

Fusing science and magic—that was the only way he could solve this problem. The prospect of shooting out literal magic drills was strangely exciting, and he began shaping his Mana.

Meanwhile, Sahro unsheathed his curved sword, drawing a long breath. A crimson light, his Aura, covered the blade from tip to hilt. He assumed a battle stance, and without hesitation, cleaved diagonally at the steel pillar.

For a moment, nothing happened. Then the top of the pillar slid to the ground in a thundering noise, leaving a clean cut.

"That should be enough, right?" Sahro asked with a cocky smile, challenging anyone to surpass his feat.

Ignoring the gloating Black Heir, Glenn completed his spell. It wasn't perfect yet, but it was functional, and that was all he needed.

He extended his hand forwards—fingers outstretched—and traced a circular motion in the air, as if twisting the void itself. Mana flowed out of his body and gathered into a massive, spectral drill, shimmering with a deep blue, otherworldly radiance. It spun with extreme speed, invisible to the naked eye, and made contact with the pillar.

A sharp sound rang through the hall as the magical drill burrowed effortlessly through the column, rapidly creating a one-meter-wide hole in the five-meter-thick steel. Glenn chuckled hysterically at the sight, maintaining the spell without losing his concentration until it pierced the whole pillar.

"Science *and* magic, bitch. Haha, I love it!" He laughed heartily. *This is fun.*

Chapter 35

TOP OF THE CLASS

Glenn panted as he leaned on his knees, staring at the hole he bore into the pillar. An uncomfortable silence had settled as every other candidate stopped to find the source of the ear-piercing noise. Even the examiner, Tom Delora, glanced down at Glenn's work. His platform sunk into the ground and brought him with it.

The terrifying kid-sized Cleaner inspected the one-meter-wide hole. The cut was perfectly smooth, as if the structure was an abstract art piece.

Tom's robe dragged over the floor and sucked up any steel shavings left by the drilling process like a magic vacuum cleaner.

Diamanes groaned in satisfaction. *See? You just need to use your brain for, like, what, a second or two?*

Glenn ignored him and instead enjoyed the shock on Sahro's face. *Small victories, I guess.*

Tom's hood turned to Glenn, his expression still hidden under it. An object slipped out of his robe and delicately landed on a miniature pedestal he summoned. Glenn picked the item up, a small, metal plate the size of his thumb engraved with runes. On the back read, 'Magi Brotherhood.'

Are they some kind of Mage guild? I swore I heard that name before. They could be interesting... Glenn thought.

Tom Delora's chilling voice resounded, "Come... see... us... after the... damned tests..."

He then rose up on his steel pillar, watching over the remaining candidates who had yet to destroy their columns.

"Get back... at it... maggots!" he spat with evident disgust.

Sahro, who easily cut his own target in two, approached Glenn, and they both sat in the stands while they waited for the test to be over. Sahro's eyes were filled with confusion and curiosity.

"Glenn, how did you manage to do that? What was that, actually?"

Glenn shrugged casually and leaned back in his seat with a slight smirk. "Well, it's evident, no? I just created an Arcane Auger spell."

Sahro's brows furrowed. "The hell is an Auger?"

Glenn's eyes widened exaggeratedly. "Wait, you don't know what an Auger is?"

Sahro crossed his arms, an uneasy, haughty smile on his face. "Hah! Of course, I know what it is! Who do you take me for?"

"Ah, alright, I'm relieved. I almost thought of you as an uneducated person right there. *Phew*!"

Diamanes laughed, ***You're still blaming him for trashing you the other day, aren't you?***

Nope, you're completely mistaken. I'm just trying my best to make use of all that experience I have trash-talking people on the internet. It would be a waste otherwise.

The candidates who could damage the pillars were separated into different groups—those who chipped away at it with attacks or spells, and those who barely left a dent. Glenn noticed the guy from the waiting room who smelled like mint.

He pressed one hand against the steel pillar in an unassuming manner. A second later, a loud clang echoed throughout the auditorium and a dust cloud rose to hide the results.

When the dust settled, Glenn discovered that the column was bent in half at a perfect ninety-degree angle.

Minty headed for the stands as well and sat a few meters from Glenn. *What? Just like that? It looked effortless! Fuck, I had to think of a whole new spell. But that guy just bends it like it's nothing. Ridiculous.*

Diamanes chimed in, **You know, if you touch that pillar, you can 'take' the spell.**

Wait, I can use it? For real?

Yep, it's at your level. It's pretty powerful, but it works in similar ways to your Arcane Auger. It uses relatively low-level Mana for high-level results.

Glenn smiled but quickly contained it. *Wouldn't it be weird to go back on the field just to check another contestant's spell? Unless...*

Turning towards his absolute best friend ever, Glenn grinned widely. Sahro shivered as a chill went down his spine, seeing this asshole's sudden friendliness.

"Hey, wanna check that out with me?" he asked, pointing at the bent column.

Before Sahro opened his mouth, all the steel pillars—untouched or destroyed—sank to the ground, forming a gray, shimmering liquid that was once again sucked by Tom Delora's robe.

His raspy voice echoed loudly in the Testing Hall while paper sheets flew from his sleeves.

"The power... test... is over... maggots!"

Glenn stared at the sheet that landed gently on his knees, a little disappointed that he missed the opportunity to finally 'take' a cool spell. He knew he still had the Alarm spells from the Thorn's Church prison, but what was he supposed to use them on?

Besides him, Sahro, and Minty, every other contestant fought to grab their flying papers from the air. The giant with the equally giant sword seemed to have passed, as he roared with laughter after struggling to catch his results.

So this is what it feels like to be top of the class? I don't hate it, remarked Glenn.

He gazed down at his paper.

"Silver Might? Recommended to the Magi Brotherhood for a Savant position?" he read aloud, wondering what it all meant.

He could understand why he received 'Silver Might', which meant he probably had the minimum required strength for a Silver-ranked Fixer, but a recommendation for the Savant position? What the hell was that?

Minty quickly stood after receiving his sheet, leaving for who-knows-where. Glenn still took note of him, as his spell was intriguing.

Why didn't Tom Delora give that guy a recommendation to the Magi Brotherhood? Glenn wondered.

Glenn was almost certain that he earned one thanks to his Arcane Auger being a unique spell. But Minty's spell had been even more surprising.

"Well, whatever..." Glenn shook his head and pocketed the documents.

Glenn and Sahro compared their results, with the latter having simply received a 'Silver Might' mark as well. Since he only used Aura, it seemed pretty logical for Tom not to be interested.

Mary, Glenn's previous tester, came to them with a wide grin. "If you're done with the assessments, please vacate the Testing Hall. We will be contacting you directly in the coming days."

Glenn and Sahro nodded and complied. It was a little disappointing, as they had both hoped to get to work right after the tests were done, but it seemed like administrative procedures also plagued this world. The two of them decided to go back to the Auberge to rest.

I still need to learn what this Magi Brotherhood is all about.

* * *

The Auberge was filled to the brim with countless customers, most of them being Fixer candidates. Some drowned their sorrows, while others drank happily in celebration of their success, dancing and singing with hearty laughs.

The owner—a small, round man with blond hair and blue eyes—smiled while he served each of his patrons.

"Drink, drink, my friends! Let's show the might of the newly crowned Fixers!" laughed the chubby man as he filled mug after mug. Disregarding those who failed, the lively atmosphere rubbed off on the two young men.

"It seems like passing the Cleaners' test was something worth celebrating!" Glenn shouted above the noise, Sahro nodding slowly.

The Black Heir glanced at a free table and quickly took a seat, inviting Glenn to do the same. The latter chuckled and made himself comfortable.

"Looks like you're already getting used to living like a human," Glenn said mockingly.

Sahro frowned and was about to reply, but two tankards of ale landed in front of them—served by a particularly attractive waitress. Glenn squinted at the beer.

"I mean, that's just fate, right?" he said as he clinked his mug with Sahro's.

He attempted to drink from it, but once again, the fear returned, stopping him from touching the beer. Glenn shivered and tried to shrug it off, but it didn't help. He set his jug back on the table.

The Black Heir sipped on the ale, carried by the mood, before suddenly slamming it down. "Wait, no. What did you mean earlier?"

Glenn clicked his tongue and pointed at Sahro's face, which wasn't hidden under a hood. His dark skin was in plain sight, and he hadn't been half as suspicious as the previous day.

"You're not hiding anymore and starting to enjoy life a little. Isn't that a sign that you're getting accustomed to living like humans?" Glenn said casually.

Sahro paused, only to frown even harder. "Why are you insisting so much on *humans* every time? Do you have a problem with me?"

Glenn rolled his eyes. He shook his head and focused back on the Black Heir.

"There's a simple reason for that. I personally believe there is *no difference* between Black Heirs and humans, aside from skin color and cultural differences."

Sahro blinked before exploding in laughter and downing his ale. "You really are a stubborn guy. You know what? I won't even get angry!"

Two new mugs appeared in front of them, interrupting their discussions. The waitress flashed a charming smile.

"Hello again, handsome. Changed your mind from last night? Me and my girls' services are still available…" she said with desperation.

Both Glenn and Sahro paused, only to resume their arguments, ignoring her. Glenn still couldn't touch a beer, but he tried to act as if it didn't bother him. At some point, he ordered some food and paid for the night's room for the both of them—swearing internally to force Sahro to pay him back one day *with interest*. His initially considerable stash of money was dwindling quickly with him taking care of all the expenses, after all.

Tonight we rest, and tomorrow we check out that Magi Brotherhood. All while waiting on the Cleaners to get back to us… That sounds too simple. Ah, shit. Why do I have the feeling that nothing will come easily?

* * *

A caped figure swiftly climbed the stone stairs, rapidly ascending to the top of Still Peak. The magic that guarded the mountain had gone, and snow started to cover the charred remains.

The icy and violent wind alone made the peak a place where living beings weren't welcome. Yet, the figure didn't seem perturbed. He held his sword in his hand, striking the ground and breaking the scriptures that described the Moon Rift.

He ignored the tent and went directly to the room where the giant, white crystal awaited. His face hardened when he discovered that it was lying in the pool—the previously pristine water completely frozen. He tried to touch the gem but received no feedback.

The figure breathed out a cloud of hot air while his fist tightened. Finally, after a few minutes of standing still, he punched the crystal, obliterating it into a burst of shards.

He walked in the middle of the shards, picking up a black mirror that had been sealed within. A face was imprinted on it. Glenn's face. The mirror reflected the figure's face slightly.

It was purple.

Chapter 36

HANGOVER 2

Glenn groaned, his eyelids pressed together with no intention of opening. He held his head, feeling as if his Arcane Auger had drilled a huge hole inside his skull. Carefully, he turned to the side, fighting to keep the contents of his stomach where they belonged.

After struggling for a long moment, Glenn finally managed to pry his eyes open, the world spinning in front of him. To his right, something strange was affixed to the wall. Upon closer inspection, he realized that the strange *something* was Sahro sleeping in an incredible position—his feet in the air and his head dangling towards the floor, all while entirely naked.

"What the f—Actually, should I even be surprised?" Glenn muttered in disbelief.

He summoned his strength and hoisted himself up from the bed and perched on the edge. Each movement provoked a tumultuous upheaval in his belly. He remained still for several minutes, waiting for the queasiness to subside.

Sahro tumbled and landed awkwardly onto the blankets. His face turned an unhealthy shade of green, and he abruptly shot up—all color draining from his complexion. He rushed to the window, leaned on the sill, and vomited whatever had plagued his stomach. After he finished, Sahro basked in the sunlight with mouth agape and eyes droopy.

Glenn observed the scene with bewilderment, struggling to recall the events of the previous night.

I am almost certain that I've been careful not to drink too much. I don't want a repeat of the Iced Beer accident, after all... The last thing he remembered was reclining in his chair at the inn, immersed in the relaxed atmosphere while digesting a hearty meal.

Usually, he would have at least a few memories left, even if he was dead drunk. Yet, he had absolutely no recollection of what had happened.

Glenn cautiously rose, each step precarious as he moved towards the mirror. He had slept in his clothes, and aside from a parched tongue, an agonizing headache, and the lingering stench of alcohol, nothing seemed out of the ordinary. There were no injuries or signs of a brawl this time. Or if there had been one, it left no lasting marks.

"Shit... Diamanes?" Glenn called out, hoping for an explanation.

He glanced at his left hand, only for his stomach to churn violently. He hurriedly joined the unconscious Sahro, puking his insides out. Conveniently, a large bucket had been placed under the window, seemingly prepared for such an occurrence.

After relieving himself of the mix of acid and alcohol—as well as a few misplaced mashed potatoes—Glenn sat on his bed, leaving Sahro hanging on the frame.

A voice nudged at him mockingly. ***Finally done? I told you, always drink in moder—***

"Diamanes," Glenn interrupted, his tone urgent, "What happened? I couldn't even *force* myself to drink!"

The evil hand grinned. ***Well, from what I've watched, you've succumbed to the temptation of alcohol quite easily—***

"God damnit, Diamanes! I'm not joking right now!" Glenn shouted, provoking a small moan of dissatisfaction from Sahro. The Black Heir was snored heavily.

"Something is seriously wrong. Tell me." Glenn demanded.

Diamanes' grin vanished.

In short, you and Sahro drank yourselves to death. I didn't expect it to go this far. You started quite reserved, ordering water and the like. But you had a change of heart at some point.

Glenn arched an eyebrow. "When? How did it happen?"

Well, after you finished eating, you sat down in your chair, and that guy joined your group. A skinny man with a badly shaved beard and brown hair. You went on talking and celebrating, downing one beer after another when you said you could drink a whole bottle of Fiery Spirit without flinching. That's when things started to get messy since you also challenged Sahro to do the same, who, by the way, is hilarious when he is drunk, but—

Glenn shook his head, interrupting Diamanes' enthusiastic storytelling. "Did you see anyone put something in my beer or anything?"

Nope, Diamanes replied firmly.

Glenn groaned and massaged his temples. He closed his eyes and attempted to piece his fragmented memories together, only for his headache to worsen. *Perhaps Sahro could provide some insight, but...*

The blackout had occurred when Glenn reclined in his chair after eating. He had only consumed food and water, served directly by the waitress. He should have seen if something was amiss.

Could it be magic related? Wait.

Glenn hastily checked his pockets. His dimensional pouch remained, and everything seemed intact except for two things: all his coins were gone, as well as the damned plate from Tom—the recommendation for the Magi Brotherhood.

"Why didn't I secure my pouch? All of my money's been stolen! What the fuck?!"

Diamanes chimed in, *Actually, during your drunken state, you took it all out, be it the plate or the coins. You don't seem to heed my advice once you start drinking, which is rather frustrating... You know, after you went to play cards again with...*

Glenn disregarded the rest of Diamanes' remarks. He could understand the disappearance of his money, but what about the plate? If he had removed it from his pouch, it indicated someone had taken an interest in it. But why? Why would someone want his recommendation to the Magi Brotherhood? It made no sense. What use would that even have?

...after displaying the plate, several other candidates joined your table. You became the center of attention, thanks to your impressive displays of strength during the test. Maybe... Diamanes continued rambling.

Glenn rubbed the bridge of his nose in contemplation.

There were quite a few people who knew that I got the recommendation plate—every candidate at the test, in fact, he thought.

"Diamanes, did you see the one who took my shit?"

Diamanes paused. *Hmm... Nope! What I did see, though, were those three guys who were salivating at Sahro when he took his clothes off, which was really funny too...* The entity trailed off once again with his lengthy explanation.

Sahro emitted a feeble moan, his head hanging out the window, clearly disturbed by Glenn's chattering.

So Diamanes didn't see the act itself, which means I wasn't aware of it either, Glenn deduced.

There weren't many explanations for the night's previous events. Could he have been drugged? But this was a magical world. Maybe there was some kind of mystical bullshit that compelled him to consume more alcohol despite his reservations. Possibly... mind control?

"Holy shit!" Glenn gasped, interrupting the entity's nonsensical tales. "Fuck, Diamanes, can magic be used for mind control?"

Diamanes stopped abruptly, his smile fading. *Yes.*

Glenn felt his blood freeze inside his veins. *Unbelievable.*

But you can't be subjected to mind control, Diamanes added casually.

Glenn blinked. "Ah?"

"Why?" he asked before answering his own question. "You, of course."

Diamanes clicked his tongue in agreement. Glenn leaned back in his bed, his mind racing to piece the puzzle together.

"So I had to have gotten drugged somehow, right?" Glenn surmised, furrowing his brow. "I just don't see any other explanation. I know I was eager to celebrate, but after everything that happened at the Iced Beer... No way. I wouldn't have made the same mistake twice."

A wheezing sound came out of the body—no, from Sahro. He remained slumped against the frame, uttering a few unintelligible words.

"Food... Ugh..."

Glenn laughed, "Damn, he really is off the deep end—*Burp*!"

He ran back to the window, another fit of nausea seizing him. He blocked his mouth with his left hand, making Diamanes retch in horror.

"No! Don't you dare throw up on me!"

Glenn struggled against his churning stomach as Sahro eventually awoke from his alcohol-induced coma.

"Ughh... I... I can't remember anything..." Sahro wheezed, now dressed and a little more lively.

Glenn shook his head, carefully making sure he wouldn't worsen his headache by doing so.

"Me neither. If my theory is right and we got drugged, someone is out to fuck with us. So let's be careful," he said in a worried tone.

Sahro's expression hardened, and he nodded. They finally left their room with slow and unsteady steps.

Since they were both still lost a little in the fog of alcohol, they also decided to stay in the Auberge until they felt better. They sat at the same table as yesterday and tried to put their thoughts together, witnessing other customers doing the same thing as them, all with a serious hangover.

"Seems like we're not the only ones who got affected..." Glenn mumbled.

"Hey, you... Glenn, right?" A burly man called to him, a greenish tint to his face.

Glenn turned with a frown. "Yeah?"

"Fuck... Can you tell me if you remember anything from last night?" He winced while holding his head painfully.

"Wait, you too?"

The mercenary nodded heavily. "You probably forgot, but I'm John. We're not the only ones." He pointed to the other shit-faced customers.

Didn't I get drunk with this guy back at the Iced Beer too? Oh, come on.

"I had a ring I intended to gift my bride, but..." John clenched his large fists angrily. "It's gone! I guess you also lost something, right? We all did."

Glenn nodded slowly. "My memory is blank. It's not even blurry; I can't remember a single thing."

John held back a dangerous burp and excused himself, his face turning to an even deeper shade of green. "Sorry, but I—*burp*—I need to purge myself a little more."

Glenn rubbed his chin as he watched John run off. If no customer could remember what happened the previous night, that meant they had all been drugged. Of course, it could also mean someone was faking it, but...

The only way for so many people to be drugged against their will was for the substance to be planted when and where no one looked—like in the kitchen. In the damned food, the only thing he hadn't been scar—*careful* of.

"The food..." Glen said, "Whoever did this must have slipped some drug into the food."

"Shit, is that why I got hit even harder than you?" Sahro muttered when Glenn shared his theory. "I think I ate four or five plates of that stuff yesterday."

"If it were truly drugs, it's a miracle that you survived. You probably ingested enough to kill a horse."

Remember, he's an Aura user. His body is different from mundane humans, Diamanes reminded him.

Glenn rubbed his chin. "I endured relatively well too... Shit, once again I have to thank the physique the Thorns Church gifted me, huh..."

"But Glenn..." Sahro mumbled while glancing at the kitchen discreetly. "That means that the one who drugged us was..."

Glenn gritted his teeth. "Yes, they're probably members of the Auberge's personnel. The cook, or anyone with access to the kitchen..."

Sahro froze. "Wait, do you think?"

Glenn nodded gravely as he gripped the edge of the table tightly. "Yes. They're probably all in on it."

His anger flared up, but he hurriedly calmed it down.

"Let's keep a composed mind. There might be another explanation. Let's do this methodically: look for evidence, and then bash the head of the culprit. I know we're not the only ones angry at our situation..." He said while glancing at the other customers, who were getting increasingly rowdy while looking for their lost belongings.

"I swear I'll find the person who broke my vow of being responsible..." he muttered through his clenched teeth.

You never swore anything, though? Diamanes remarked.

Glenn's face suddenly paled, and he bent over to reach for a bucket conveniently placed by the owner, vomiting whatever was left in his stomach.

"Damn it..." he wheezed. *hangover.*

Chapter 37

GLENN HOLMES

Glenn rested his chin on his hands, wondering how he should go about his 'investigation'. He watched the kitchen suspiciously, Sahro imitating his posture.

I don't understand. What's stopping you from just storming in there and interrogating these cowards? Diamanes asked.

Common sense and politeness. But I'm losing my grip on both of those... Glenn replied, his anger growing with every passing second. The simple thought of falling victim to drugs *again* made his blood boil.

I do believe you've ingested more than your fill of filth, commented Diamanes with a sneer.

Glenn gritted his teeth and suddenly slammed his fist on the table, pulling in the gazes of the other patrons. He stood and, with his fists clenched, sat at the counter—staring fixedly at the barman, the Auberge's owner. He glanced up and down at the portly man, who was sweating profusely. Sahro followed suit and took a seat next to Glenn.

"Can... Can I help you?" The owner stammered tentatively as he wiped the sweat off his forehead.

Glenn looked at him coldly and pounded his hand on the counter, the resounding thud echoing through the tavern. The noise put an end to any nearby discussions and drew the attention of those who weren't already looking.

"I hope you can, or this Auberge will have to disappear from the Fringe," Glenn threatened. "You'd better explain why every one of your customers was drugged and robbed of their prized possessions!"

He poked his finger into the proprietor's fat chest, watching his reaction carefully. The owner's little blue eyes widened as he gasped. "What? D-Drugs? Theft? Impossible!"

He composed himself, clutching his round belly. "I assure you, I would never drug any of my customers or steal from them. My reputation means everything to me." The owner paused, then countered, "On what basis do you accuse me, sir?"

"On what basis? Are you kidding me?!" exclaimed John, who was back from purging his insides.

"Yeah, fuck you! You better have some good excuses!" The other customers clamored angrily.

"Call up your workers—every one of them!" Glenn ordered angrily, his blood boiling. He turned to the other customers and pointed at the door. "If anyone tries to leave this damned inn, that's the culprit, alright?"

The Auberge's owner hurriedly scrambled to halt the inn's operation and bring the staff together.

"Everyone! Stop working and get your asses here!" he shrieked, his forehead covered in greasy sweat.

Glenn turned to the twenty suspects as they arrived—one chef, two sous-chefs, five cooks, three kitchen assistants, eight waitstaff, and the owner.

He drew a short breath before jumping on a table and making sure everyone could hear him.

"Someone, or maybe *an organized group,* drugged this inn's customers and robbed all of them—including myself!" Glenn hissed angrily.

Sahro glared at the boss silently, his fingers already wrapped on the hilt of his sword.

Glenn stabbed his thumb into his chest. "And I *swear* that I will catch the culprit. Or…" He slowly turned back to the other patrons, who nodded at him with dark expressions. "We'll turn this whole inn over to find our stuff."

"Yeah!"

"We'll burn it to the ground if we need to!" The customers pumped their fists, surrounding the Auberge's staff threateningly.

Glenn crossed his arms and coldly stared down at the Auberge's owner.

"Now, please, explain to me why *nobody* remembers what happened last night? And you better reply *fast*, mister…what even is your name?" He leaned closer, exhaling a foul breath in the owner's face. The latter gulped heavily, twiddling with his thumbs as he glanced at the other angry customers.

"I'm Andres, this modest Auberge's owner. But I'm not sure I can help you with—"

Sahro scowled and suddenly grabbed the boss' collar, lifting the chubby guy against a wall.

"Speak, you *keparat*!" he spat, his red Aura flaring up threateningly.

"You can't do that!" The inn's staff exclaimed in disapproval, even though not one lifted a finger to help their boss. "How dare you!"

All bark and no bite, these fuckers. Not a shred of loyalty, remarked Diamanes with a disgusted tone.

"Alright, alright, I—I'll talk!" Andres wheezed, pushing against Sahro's arms helplessly.

The Black Heir grunted and dropped the chubby man on the floor.

"You, you, and you—guard the exits!" Glenn ordered some strong-looking customers. "John, can you look through the Auberge to see if our stuff isn't hidden somewhere?"

John grinned as he flexed his massive muscles. "I'll be more than pleased!"

A few other mercenaries followed him as he headed into the 'staff-only' areas.

"Last night... Last night was a hell of a party," the owner admitted through several coughs as he held his throat painfully. "Alcohol flowed freely, the music was loud, and a lot... All of you *ungrateful* bastards were drunk like hell!"

Glenn's face hardened as Mana swirled around him violently.

"It wouldn't have come to that if we weren't robbed of everything we owned, bastard. Now, keep going before I behead you," he threatened as Sahro happily unsheathed his sword and stabbed it into the floor.

Beheading him? Wow, Glenn, you're making progress in intimidation! Diamanes laughed mockingly.

Andres swallowed with difficulty and pushed himself up.

"At... at some point, you were all so drunk, you began fighting among yourselves! We had no choice but to close the cellar and abandon the premises! You can ask everyone in my crew—they'll testify!" the boss yelled.

"Y-Yeah, that's right!"

"You were all insane! We almost called the Church and the Cleaner's Workshop to calm things down!"

Glenn rubbed his chin, pondering. *Hmm... Of course they'd testify for him. If they're all in on it, they would gain nothing by abandoning their ringleader.*

"Shit, maybe they're telling the truth?" someone in the watching crowd muttered.

Glenn raised an eyebrow. Just like that, the seeds of doubt had been planted. The boss' eyes suddenly widened, and he pointed an accusing, stubby finger at a scrawny aide.

"I know who did it! It's that little prick!" he exclaimed, wiping the sweat from his brow. "He's some bastard I rescued from the Sewers! He probably drugged everyone while you were drunk and stole your stuff! We were all safe in our rooms, so it couldn't have been us. But this idiot sleeps in the kitchen!"

Sahro scoffed, and he pointed his curved sword at the boy. "Is that right? Did you drug us all?"

The kid paled and opened his mouth, only for the other members of the staff to slap him on the forehead and kick him.

"Yeah, it's obviously this asshole!"

"I saw him steal food the other day. I knew he was no-good! That's the case for everyone in the Sewers!"

Sahro tensed, and he clenched his sword tighter, but Glenn grabbed his shoulders in a placating manner. He coldly stared at the child, and without a second thought, made his decision.

"Alright. I'll interrogate the boy."

Sahro stabbed his sword back into the floor and crossed his arms. "I'll watch over these fools meanwhile."

The other customers exchanged glances before raising their voices.

"But what about us?"

"Yeah, we're also victims! We want to help!"

Glenn looked at them and shrugged. "Listen to my comrade here. If there's anything, he'll let you know."

He hoisted the child on his shoulder and headed into a closed-off room, locking the door behind him. He released the kid and sat on a nearby chair with a heavy sigh. The child gulped heavily, trembling, but his eyes never let go of Glenn's.

"Alright, what's your name, kid?" Glenn asked tiredly. His stomach was still churning, but his fury made it easy to push through it.

"L-Liam," replied the boy, before hurriedly adding, "Sir!"

Glenn grimaced. "Ugh, don't call me sir. I'm twenty-one. Alright Liam, this will be rather simple. Did you do it?"

The boy looked at the closed door hesitantly, his hands trembling. Glenn grabbed his shoulder firmly.

"Liam, rest assured. *I* will punish the culprit—whoever *he or they* might be."

Liam took shallow breaths, his eyes flickering with a mix of fear and rage. But also something else.

A profound desire for revenge.

"So, did you do it?" Glenn asked.

The boy shook his head and replied, "No, *sniffle*. But I know who did it."

Chapter 38

SAHRO WATSON

Sahro watched over the employees with a wrathful look in his eyes. *There's something wrong with this situation. Even if Glenn took that kid away...* The Black Heir's hand tightened around the hilt of his sword. *No, I'm sure the child is innocent and is being framed. Glenn probably also knows that, so... It must mean that he's getting the boy's story. I need to buy time and find more proof...*

"Hey, uhh, Sahro, right?" John suddenly surged out of the kitchen, a small leather pouch in hand.

He looked around confusedly. "Where did Glenn go?"

Sahro glanced at the scornful employees of the Auberge and replied, "He's interrogating a suspect. What did you find?"

John grinned and handed him the satchel. Sahro opened it up hesitantly, only to take a step back from the smell.

"Moongrass..." he mumbled in mixed hatred and disgust.

He threw it on the floor and crushed it under his foot. That shit—and he wasn't exaggerating—was an absolute cancer to society.

It was primarily distributed by the Thorns Church to their followers to numb their self-inflicted pain—conjuring 'visions of their God', which were nothing more than hallucinations.

It had infested the Sewers as many chose to surrender to its numbing embrace rather than confront their suffering head-on. Sahro had witnessed several unsuspecting Black Heirs succumb to its allure. They trusted the words of those damned cultists, believing it would make up for their hunger.

It did, but in the worst of ways. Sahro's face darkened as he thought back to his people's condition. That wasn't a way of living. And it had to change. As soon as he rescued Callum, it *would* change. Nothing would tie them to this accursed city anymore, and they'd be free to look for 'greener pastures', as humans liked to say.

He snapped back to the present and refocused on the truly perplexing matter at hand. How did Moongrass end up here? Was there a Thorns Church priest amid these idiots? Unless it was a delivery... But then, it wouldn't be such a small quantity. This was nowhere near enough to drug the whole inn—

"Hey!" Andres suddenly exclaimed, his eyes set on the bag Sahro had crushed under his boot. "I recognize that! It's Liam's pouch! I know because it was the last gift from his wench mother!"

Sahro froze.

"Wait, if it's that boy's..." the patrons whispered.

Sahro picked it back up, dusting it off. He noticed the poor embroidery and cheap material.

"Shoot..." he muttered under his breath before guiltily cleaning it off the best he could. He glared at the whispering customers and clenched his fists.

"I'm also from the Sewers, you bastards! Does it mean I'm guilty?"

A Fixer candidate gulped heavily before replying, "I—I mean, you don't look like someone who would steal. That kid on the other hand..."

"Yeah, you're a Black Heir. You're not the sort to do those things. It's known," nodded another mercenary.

Sahro breathed in deeply. He tried to shrug it off and glanced at John. "Where did you find that pouch?"

John pointed back at the kitchen. "There's an animal cage in there with dirty rags in it. I searched it and found that stuff."

"An animal cage?" Sahro repeated in confusion, only for Andres to exclaim victoriously.

"Yes! That's where Liam sleeps! He's no better than an animal—hence the cage!"

Sahro coldly glared at the gloating Auberge owner, his patience running thin.

"John, can you and the other humans look after this piece of garbage before I bury him alive?" Sahro asked through his clenched teeth.

John nodded and crossed his massive, muscular arms. "Sure, but what are you going to do?"

"I'll give a second look to that kitchen," he replied while looking at the owner and his employees. Sure enough, they all tensed.

Yeah, that's right. It's not a question of who did it anymore, but how to prove that they did. Sahro stormed into the kitchen before he inadvertently beheaded these scumbags. The owner followed him with worry, creeping at the door.

"If I was a scummy bastard, where the hell would I hide drugs?" Sahro asked himself aloud.

He began opening every drawer, cupboard, and cabinet. He ripped them off their hinges and searched for any hidden compartments. John had already looked through them, but he probably hadn't been as thorough.

There was that whole 'politeness' matter Giselle spoke about. But I think even she'd agree that humans like these don't deserve it.

"Hey, hey, you can't do that! You're damaging those! You Sewer bastard, you have to pay for that!" Andres exclaimed worriedly as he tried to stop Sahro from ripping off another drawer.

The Black Heir paused and glared down at the chubby man.

"Try stopping me. I'll be more than happy to slice off your fat, pig." His Aura flared up as he spoke, sharply erupting around his fists.

The owner fell back on his ass, his face drained of blood. Sahro didn't even spare the bastard another glance.

"Not here... Not here either," Sahro mumbled as his thorough search turned out fruitless. John, who was watching from the doorway, shrugged.

"I've already checked everything out. I'm certainly beginning to think that the boy the owner mentioned is the culprit."

"I mean, he did come from the Sewers..." another customer mumbled.

"Hey, do you think the Black Heir is also in on it?" someone else whispered.

Sahro glared at them but didn't say another word. He needed to stay calm and wait for Glenn. The latter probably knew what he was doing.

"Did I miss something?" The Black Heir whispered while looking at the ceiling.

His eyes stopped on a hanging bundle of plants. He paused as a sly grin crept up his face. While walking up to it, he slowly unsheathed his sword. The owner stood in protest, but it was already too late.

"Where do you hide a tree? In a damn forest!" Sahro spat as he sliced open the leaves with a swift stroke of his sword.

A small leather bag fell from the bundle. The employees squirmed.

Sahro opened the sack and stepped back, the acrid smell of Moongrass assailing his senses. He tossed it aside and inspected the other packages, discovering five more bags—all filled with Moongrass.

John laughed in disbelief. "Ha! Incredible! Forget about an inn. That's enough to drug the entire town's water supply!"

"Fuck. Is this Auberge richer than I thought?" another customer asked as he stared at the drugs in awe. "That's enough Moongrass to buy a few houses!"

John shook his head as he glared at the staff. "No way. They wouldn't serve us that piss-like beer if they were rich. No, that only means one thing!"

"The Thorns Church..." Sahro hissed as he unsheathed his sword. "Seems like we won't need the boy's testimony!"

The Black Heir suddenly realized that despite the threat of his blade, the personnel's eyes were glued to the leather bags. Dismissing them with a scoff, he tossed the entire collection into a massive pot in the corner of the room, sealed the lid, and guarded it. Predictably, panic washed over the employees. The boss rushed towards the pot, halted in his tracks by the tip of Sahro's sword, emanating an intimidating crimson Aura.

"Come on, tempt me," Sahro hissed as he forced the owner back. He turned to the other employees. "If anyone so much as touches this pot, I swear on my name, that I, Sahro of the Black Heirs, will carve them into a thousand pieces."

With this stern declaration, he drove his curved sword into the ground, both hands resting on the pommel.

Now, he just had to wait for Glenn.

* * *

Glenn rubbed his eyes as he observed the young child voraciously devour one of the rations he kept in his dimensional pouch.

I don't understand. Why wouldn't they feed Liam? He practically lives in the Auberge, which produces a ton of food, Glenn pondered, genuinely baffled by the mistreatment.

It simply did not make a shred of sense to him. *Additionally, why starve one of your workers? It would decrease his efficiency, and he would have a harder time completing his tasks.*

Even my dumb boss at my part-time job knew that I wouldn't work as well on an empty stomach. And it's not like this place is exactly drowning in poverty...

It's because he came from the Sewers. Racism seems quite prevalent in this city, Diamanes remarked.

"Hey, slow down," Glenn advised, attempting to calm the child who was gobbling down the food like a squirrel that had stumbled upon its first nut in ages. He took the opportunity to examine the emaciated figure beneath the oversized assistant-cook outfit, noting visible bones and bruises, some appearing quite severe.

Glenn threw Liam a leather flask of water, which the kid graciously accepted and emptied. Taking out his last ration, he presented it to the child.

Liam's hand shot out to reach for it, but Glenn halted him. Overeating after being starved was a common cause of death for vagrants. He wasn't going to kill the boy because he fed him too much too quickly.

"Don't worry, you'll get your food in due time," Glenn said as he placed the ration beside him. The kid followed his movements, his shoulders hunched in disappointment.

Sorry kiddo, but I've been drugged. I couldn't care less about getting robbed, but the drugs? That makes it personal, he thought without a shred of guilt.

"Tell me everything you know about who did what and why. If my hunch is right, this has been hurriedly planned," mused Glenn.

Liam took a deep breath, carefully licking each finger to savor the crumbs before wiping his face. "Well, uh, mister, first, thank you for stopping the boss. My dad always said to express gratitude to those who help you..."

Glenn nodded gently, aiming to put the child at ease. "Were you living with your parents in the Sewers?"

Tears gathered in Liam's eyes before he wiped them away. "MMy parents thought it was a chance for a better life when Mister Andres offered me work."

No wonder. Glenn thought back to the kid that tried to rob him in the Sewers. *Liam is probably ready to do anything to survive. That's why he's still here instead of running away from the abuse.*

The kid fiddled with his thumbs as he looked down dejectedly. "At first, it wasn't so bad. They didn't treat me as an equal, sure, but I had a roof and warm food. I still felt like a human being. It was better than the Sewers for sure." A flicker of resentment flashed in his eyes as he clenched his tiny fists. "But then some strange men visited Mister Andres. They gave him Moongrass."

Glenn rubbed his forehead, connecting the dots. *Moongrass? It was already personal before, but I might even consider it a vendetta now. Thorns Church, of course they're implicated.*

"Do you know what those strange men told your boss?"

Liam nodded gravely. "I hid in a cupboard to eat a piece of bread because Jason, one of the cooks, decided I didn't deserve any food that day. I was famished, so I couldn't help it..."

He paused for a moment, taking a sip from the leather flask Glenn had given him. "They spoke right beside me, and I dared not move. I could barely see through a gap in the cupboard. There were three robed people, and one had removed their hood."

Liam's voice trembled as he recalled his memories. "His head had these weird scars that formed a scary pattern. The same as those ominous men always muttering about Repentir. He gave something to the boss—a ring, I think. After a few minutes of silence, he collapsed on the floor. I almost gasped, but I was too terrified to even breathe."

"He had seizures, writhing on the ground with a happy smile. Then he snapped out of it. That's when they made a deal. I know because I saw the paper one of the strangers took from their satchels, and the boss hastily signed it. They then gave Mister Andres a few bags of Moongrass."

Liam sighed as he reflected on these memories. "After that day, everything changed for everyone—be it the boss, the employees... or even me."

He shuddered as he hid his bruises. "They... They started hurting me, feeding me spoiled meat and dead rats. They made me sleep in a cave, then outside like a dog. When customers were present, they acted normally, but once no one was around, they... transformed."

Liam sniffled again, wiping away any remaining tears and mucus. "It happened about a month ago... Last night, they received a message demanding payment for their Moon Grass supply. I know because I read it for them. My pa forced me to learn how to read and write…"

Glenn smiled, gently patting the child's head. His smile disappeared when he noticed all the bruises on the boy's body. His arms, as thin as twigs, were practically blue from the constant beating.

"Your father was a wise man. And a good one."

Liam smiled back weakly, his hands tightly clenching the water flask.

"So, when they saw that, they panicked. Then, a bunch of folks arrived from the Cleaner's Workshop. So they used the occasion to rob you of all of your things to make the money." Liam shook his head with a surprisingly mature coldness. "They're idiots. Fixers and Cleaners are rumored to be as rich as they are powerful. It was a foolish move."

Diamanes' laughter resounded in Glenn's head, egging him on.

"That it was, kid. That it was…" He sighed deeply, everything falling into place.

He had one more question for Liam before he descended to deal with Andres, the employees, and, especially, Jason. "Do you know where they hid all of our stuff?"

Liam pointed at Glenn's dimensional pouch.

"In a magical pouch like yours, mister."

Glenn rubbed his hands together and licked his lips. *Hmm, a batch of bad guys to beat up. What better way than that to relieve some stress?*

Suddenly, Liam propped himself upright.

"Oh, and everyone was clear about one thing: the Church of Onnea shouldn't find out what's happening here."

Glenn's grin widened as he brainstormed ideas. He placed his hands on the child's shoulders, noting the deep navy blue of Liam's eyes.

"Listen, Liam. I'm sure you want to get back at those bastards downstairs, right?"

The kid nodded eagerly.

"Well, then, I have a mission for you. While I take care of them, you're going to the nearest Church of Onnea. Tell them the Thorns bastards are in the Auberge, and they'll come running. Probably." Glenn shrugged. "If that doesn't work, just tell them your story. Okay?"

Liam's fear had disappeared, replaced by a vengeful smile. "Okay!"

He jumped out of bed, revitalized, only to stop and look at Glenn with wonder.

"Also... I didn't read it to them, but there was something about using the Auberge's crew as payment in case they couldn't reimburse their debt. I thought you might want to know." Glenn opened the door.

"I'll keep that in mind."

Glenn didn't know exactly what the Church of Onnea did or who they were, but anyone who had a bone to pick with the Thorns Church was an ally in his book. If those bastards were scared of them... That meant they had to be strong enough to scare them.

Glenn cracked his knuckles and returned to the kitchen, ready to divulge the truth to everyone and deliver rightful retribution to the culprits: the employees, Andres, and especially, Jason.

Oh yeah, Jason was going to have a delicious time meeting his fist, Glenn was sure of that.

Chapter 39

DON'T DO DRUGS

Mister Andres, as Liam called him, and his employees looked at each other restlessly—their anxiety intensifying with each passing moment. That anxiety only worsened when Glenn returned without their chosen scapegoat. Sahro stood like a sentinel beside the towering pot filled with Moongrass bundles.

"Come take a look," Sahro gestured at the container, his eyes still glued on the staff, waiting for them to give him an excuse to use his sword.

Glenn opened the pot and paused, his lips curving upwards. His smile had taken on an unusual quality, eerily similar to the sinister grin Diamanes favored.

"Keep that jar in line of sight, Sahro," Glenn commanded, his sneer fading to a dark, impassive countenance.

His gaze swept over the staff, the patrons, and the boss. He sighed and clapped his hands sharply. The sound reverberated through the kitchen, capturing everyone's attention.

Glenn had never been particularly fearful of being in the spotlight, but he wasn't enjoying it either. However, his time spent in the confines of the Thorns Church's cell had changed him. He found himself doing things he'd never imagined before, almost as if it came naturally. Or perhaps, he had shed some inhibitions. *Oh well, I'm not going to complain if I became a little bolder 'thanks' to the torture.*

"Well," he sighed, "It's time to reveal the results of my investigation."

His devilish smile returned as he gestured towards the Auberge's personnel.

"Starting with the boss, 'Mister' Andres, and his corrupt staff—all of them are affiliated with the Thorns Church."

The employees' expressions crumbled. One sobbed on the floor, another angrily shouted at the owner—shifting the blame on him—and so forth. Only Andres remained silent, his expression blank and his thoughts indecipherable.

Glenn continued, "My witness—the mistreated child from the Sewers—was able to give me confirmation that Andres struck a deal with the Thorns Church. He and his staff became addicted to Moongrass."

Sahro pulled a bundle from the giant vessel. The employees fixated on it—clinging to it as if it were their lifeline.

It was quite the opposite.

Glenn continued, unfazed, "The whole crew got hooked on it, and since they were consuming it, they needed a substantial stash to supply everyone. Which, as you might have guessed, wasn't cheap."

As Glenn paced, Mana swirled angrily around his clenched fists. He stopped between the patrons and the staff, addressing both at the same time.

"Naturally, the Thorns Church wasn't providing the grass for free. They had no choice but to obtain funds—and quickly. Taking on a loan was an option they could have considered, but perhaps there wasn't enough time to do so. They needed their drugs. And they needed them *now*."

He paused and drew a small breath. Glenn then gestured towards the patrons gathered at the door.

"Just when they grew desperate, we arrived—a group of easily distracted individuals seeking drinks and revelry. So, what did they do?"

He raised his hands as if the answer were self-evident. "They drugged us. They used their precious plant to 'enhance' our food, erasing our memories of the entire evening. They then took advantage of our inebriation to pilfer from our pockets, seizing anything of value."

Suddenly, Glenn dashed behind Andres and kicked him forwards. The plump man collapsed, trembling as his eyes remained glued to the bundle of Moongrass.

"Still, it seems strange... Where the hell could they have hidden all of our belongings? That many things couldn't be transported easily nor secured in a chest. Care to show them, boss?" Glenn pressed his foot on the owner's back, pinning him to the floor.

The boss stuttered, clutching his pudgy fists tightly. "I... I don't know what you're talking about!"

Glenn rolled his eyes and sighed exaggeratedly. "Ah, if you don't know, I suppose you serve *no purpose,* then. Since we can't get our stuff back, we'll have to be satisfied by taking our anger out on *you.*"

The moment he finished his sentence, a massive, spinning Arcane Auger appeared inches from the round man's face. Andres paled, and he hastily tossed a leather pouch similar to Glenn's.

"I-It's all in there, I swear!" Andres cried.

Glenn looked at the bag emotionlessly and pulsed the Arcane Auger towards the plump man's flesh.

"Come on, boss," he hissed. "You know no one but you can retrieve our shit from a dimensional pouch. Unless we kill you. So, your choice?"

Andres hurriedly grabbed the sack as Glenn let him stand. "O-Okay, I'll do it," he stammered as his pudgy hands sank inside the leather.

Whether by coincidence or design, the initial item revealed was Glenn's recommendation plate, evoking a satisfied smile from him.

Minutes later, Andres surrendered every stolen belonging. Each patron displayed a mix of happiness and astonishment—dimensional pouches were rare in the Fringe, after all.

Glenn grinned at Andres. "Well, that's one problem solved, wouldn't you say?"

Andres nodded hesitantly as he fiddled with his thumbs.

Glenn patted him on the back. "Don't you feel better? You're already on the path to redemption. Isn't that wonderful?"

"Are... Are we good?" he inquired.

Glenn pondered. "Hmm... I think so?"

He turned to leave the kitchen, but halted at the doorway. He approached the trembling man, placing a hand on his neck. Andres looked up and froze in fear as he stared at Glenn's devilish sneer.

"No," Glenn slowly said as his smile widened. "I almost forgot something, you see."

He clenched his fists tightly. "Personally, I believe there's a special place in hell for those who abuse children. Did you like beating Liam and starving him?"

Andres opened his mouth to answer, but Glenn didn't give him the time to. He pushed with all his strength, sending the owner back on his knees—his head colliding with the floor loudly, the tiles breaking under the might of the blow. The kitchen fell into a heavy silence. No one dared to utter a sound. Meanwhile, Sahro's eyes revealed approval.

Glenn flashed an evil grin at the quivering staff. "By the way, who's Jason?"

The employees betrayed the man with accusatory stares.

"Wait, no I—" Jason raised his hands in a pitiful defensive manner, only for Glenn to grab his arm.

"Jason..." Glenn took a deep, measured breath as his expression hardened. "Do you enjoy beating children?"

"I—*Ugh*!" Jason kneeled on the floor, his shoulder shattering within Glenn's grip.

Glenn coldly stared down at him. "Never mind, I don't want to know."

He slammed his fist into Jason's chest, breaking his ribs. Jason fell aside coughing blood, his rib cage caved in. No one said a word.

Glenn casually dusted his hands off and retrieved the Moongrass from the pot. He gave one last glance to the employees before shaking his head.

"Terrible customer service," he muttered before departing.

Sahro followed closely behind, his sword still drawn. Simultaneously, Liam flung open the main door of the Auberge—panting—as two colossal, silver-armored giants entered, forced to bow to navigate the short doorway.

A small priestess—almost an ant compared to her formidable companions—joined alongside them. She disregarded the crowd and headed straight for Glenn, who paused curiously.

"You must be Glenn?" the priestess asked with a warm smile.

Glenn nodded and shook her extended hand. "My pleasure. I take it you're from the Church of Onnea?"

The priestess bowed as the two silver-armored giants grunted in agreement. She looked at the Moongrass. "If you'd allow me?"

Glenn obliged and surrendered the bundle. Without ceremony, the holy trio threw the drugs into a white jar, sealed it, and activated a magic rune on its side. The container emitted a blast that soon ceased, signaling the destruction of the Moongrass.

Somehow, I feel like they hate those insane cultists from the Thorns Church as much as me... he thought, bewildered. *I'm certainly visiting the Church of Onnea after this.*

The priestess and her paladins then directed their attention towards Andres and his subordinates. All the while, Liam observed joyfully, witnessing the fulfillment of his vendetta. Yet, a shadow clouded his expression when Glenn tapped his shoulder.

"It's finally over. You're free from them now." Glenn smiled before taking him out the front entrance.

"Why don't you return to the Church of Onnea and wait there while we sort this out?" Glenn proposed. Liam gave one last glance to the Auberge before nodding.

"Thank you, Mister Glenn," he said with a smile before running off.

Glenn hurriedly checked the contents of his dimensional pouch, ensuring his recommendation plate was right where it belonged.

He suddenly paused, feeling as if he had forgotten something. There was one mystery left unsolved: what did the Thorn's Church gain from that venture? *What purpose did they have? Getting the Auberge's crew hooked on Moon Grass doesn't seem like it would achieve anything...*

Fascinating detective work and all. But you're forgetting one very important thing. Your money! Diamanes reminded him.

Glenn paused and instinctively rechecked his dimensional pouch.

"Oh. Oh shit, I did forget about that..." he grunted in annoyance. *But I just made my dramatic exit! Come on. I can't go back there now...*

Glenn sighed heavily. At least he had the Howard ring and the Magi Brotherhood recommendation plate. Those were the two most important items he owned, after all. But still. Before, he was a king among peasants. Now, he was a dung pile among peasants. Not exactly the transition he hoped for. It set back their original goal—paying their entry into the Bourgeoisie—even further.

Glenn sighed and turned towards the Auberge, disregarding his shame.

"Maybe I can go back and ask for my money, right?" He frowned and glanced around. "Where the hell is Sahro, by the way? Didn't he follow me out?"

Diamanes chuckled dejectedly as Glenn grabbed onto the Auberge's doors open once again. His eyebrows creased when a bloodied, silver ball of metal rammed through the wall, blowing a gust at Glenn, who froze in confusion.

He turned, discovering that the metallic mass was one of the paladins, crushed and compacted in a ball. A roar made the ground shake as every window in the district exploded—projecting glass shards in a destructive symphony.

Glenn jumped back, his heart suddenly racing. Mana swirled around him, ready to be used for destructive spells.

Glenn gritted his teeth and hissed, "Why the hell can't it ever be simple?!"

On those words, he dashed back into the inn, Giselle's shortsword in his left hand and a Magic Bullet in his right. Diamanes' mocking laughter accompanied his steps.

For some reason, Glenn felt like he had just found the Thorns Church's motive.

Chapter 40

FIGHTING THE BOSS

Glenn quickly dodged as another body hurtled in his direction. But it was too late. It landed squarely on top of him.

After pushing the lifeless form aside, he recognized one of the tavern's former patrons. The man's head hung at an unnatural angle—a good chunk of his skull was gone, and his brain trickled out.

Averting his eyes and wiping the blood off his hands, Glenn returned his gaze to the chaotic scene inside the Auberge. The inn was filled with a cacophony of screams intertwined with the sound of weapons slicing flesh. Glenn protected his face as a flurry of wooden shards exploded, his heart racing as he searched for Sahro.

"Where did that idiot go?!" Glenn muttered through his clenched teeth.

His gaze widened as the kitchen erupted in an explosion. A grotesque monstrosity ran rabid as fighters struggled against it. Glenn gasped and instinctively took a step back. At the horror's core was the once-familiar face of Andres—now lost within a fusion of limbs, torsos, and heads. The abomination oozed pus and bits of flesh, creating a chilling amalgamation of human forms.

The monster was the size of a haul truck, blood gushing between broken bones. Limbs extended from every part of its wretched body, belonging to the former members of the staff. Those arms and legs intertwined, covered in teeth and desperate, bloodshot eyes.

A dozen mouths opened to emit a horrific, otherworldly scream—a cacophony of bestial sounds mixed with the cries of human agony. The noise pierced through Glenn's eardrums and sent him to his knees. The human faces merged within the monster, releasing a steady stream of moans and pleas for mercy.

Glenn pushed himself up, shooting his Magic Bullet at the fiend. It punctured a hole through the fleshy mass effortlessly, but the wound closed. Strands of flesh restitched themselves. Dozens of eyes of different sizes—each gleaming with madness and pain—blinked independently.

"You *ungrateful* b-bastards!"

The beast unleashed a deafening sound wave that sent Glenn reeling backwards. Seizing the opportunity, a bloodied man attacked the creature with a curved sword covered in crimson light—uttering profanities in an unfamiliar tongue. His blade tore into the monster and carved off a huge chunk of flesh, a torrent of blood flooding out of the wound. The monstrosity shrieked back and threw a bloated limb in retaliation.

How the hell am I supposed to fight that?

* * *

Sahro sent his Aura into his legs, reinforcing them so he could jump above the bloated limb.

The sudden calamity felt like a fever dream. One moment, he was talking to the guys from the Church of Onnea, and the next, Andres, along with his colleagues, exploded into a black ooze of tentacles. The sludge gathered and reformed itself into that monstrous amalgam of flesh—a monster he could have never imagined, not even in his worst nightmares.

A paladin had tried to nip the threat in the bud, just to end up compressed into a ball and tossed away like a toy. Sahro wiped the blood off his forehead and dashed back into the action, his crimson Aura flaring up with every strike.

Every slice of his blade burned deep gashes into the dark flesh, preventing its supernatural healing.

A tentacle shot at him, but the Black Heir simply leaned aside, dodging the hit effortlessly. Each attack of the monster was brutally simple. Avoiding them was nothing to Sahro.

His sword was a crimson blur as it carved more tentacles that the fiend couldn't grow back. A dance of dark steel, battling off corruption.

This was an opponent worth fighting, and nothing would stop him.

* * *

Glenn rolled away as a wooden beam fell, his back drenched in cold sweat.

"Holy shit!" he cursed as he shot more Magic Bullets at the abomination.

The creature didn't seem to care, healing each wound easily. It was too concentrated on Sahro, who was cleaving huge chunks of flesh—one after the other.

Well, see you in Hell, I guess, scoffed Diamanes, his words filled with resignation.

"What the fu—!" Glenn's protest was interrupted by meat landing on his shoulder, still writhing despite its separation from the main body.

Panic surged through him as he frantically tossed the disgusting mass aside and crushed it under his boot.

That's a Corrupted One. And a fairly strong one too, for your first time, remarked Diamanes casually.

"I noticed, yeah!" blurted Glenn aloud.

Blobs of gore fell from the main body, creating wolf-like monsters that lunged at the fighters. The minions were even more disturbing; they had the face and mouth of a human juxtaposed against a canine body.

"O-Our b-beer is the coldest in t-town!" barked the human-faced beasts.

Golden light flared from a corner of the room, luring in most of the minions. The other paladin—the one who didn't end up crushed into a ball—swung a massive sword while protecting the priestess. The woman knelt, her hands clenched while she chanted a holy ritual.

Glenn averted his eyes and concentrated back on the main threat at hand—the abomination. He attempted to cast his Arcane Auger, but one of the wolves lunged at his face.

He fell to the floor, the minion gnawing on his sword savagely. The beast clawed through Glenn's clothes, tearing bloody gashes into his skin. Glenn roared and shoved with all his strength, his blade carving through the wolf's head and cleanly cleaving it off. The corpse collapsed on Glenn's chest, trembling with post-mortem tremors.

Heaving as he pushed the body away, Glenn used his sword to help himself up. He fell to a knee, his heart racing madly.

What should I do? An Arcane Auger? Will it be useless? Shit, I can't afford to touch one of my allies!

Glenn coughed out a lump of blood, ducking as someone flew past him and crashed onto the wall in a bloody explosion—his upper body missing.

While heaving with difficulty, Glenn hurriedly dragged himself behind a pillar. His heart thumped loudly in his chest.

The priestess' chant quickened, her holy aura radiating pure divinity. The Corrupted sensed her presence and intensified its attacks, the paladin's once-silver armor now stained with viscous, scarlet.

The paladin, bloodied and battered, roared in defiance as he fended off another brutal assault—his dented shield a testament to his valiant efforts. He screamed something about needing more time, but Glenn's ears failed to catch the words.

The holy knight's helmet hung askew, revealing a desperate face. Glenn suspected that arresting the accursed tavern's staff was supposed to be a mere formality for the paladin. And now, both he and his brother-in-arms had met dire fates, fighting the otherworldly monster.

Sahro joined the chorus of roars with his battle cry, covered in his crimson Aura as he relentlessly carved through the monstrous abomination. The creature screeched in pain, flinging Sahro through the air with a ferocious, bony slap.

Glenn gasped as he struggled to breathe, his hand tightly clenched around the hilt of his sword. He froze as a thought crossed his mind.

Should I run away? He considered that option for a second before dismissing it. *No, I can't abandon Sahro. I can't run from my enemies, or I'll always run...*

Glenn leaned on the pillar. He coughed and struggled to stand back up, stumbling onto his feet. Time seemed to slow as Glenn diligently sought a path to survival. If running wasn't an option, that meant he could only do one thing instead.

Kill that monster.

He took a deep breath, like a man about to drown, and dashed out of his hiding place. The ever-expanding mass of flesh shifted and a dozen pairs of eyes locked onto him—an easy target.

Glenn felt his consciousness slipping away but shook his head. The sounds of the battle and the screams of pain disappeared, replaced by the pounding of his heart. Andres' distorted visage protruded from the grotesque amalgam, painted with hatred as it looked at him.

Amidst the chaos, Glenn finally grasped his role in the unfolding mess. A celestial cloud of stars shimmered within his hand, pulsating with latent power. A robed figure ran past him, a scent of mint following. He dodged the creature's attack and managed to press his palm on its grotesque form.

"Minty?" Glenn mumbled in confusion. *What the hell is he doing here?*

In response, the creature contorted. It bent in half as a shockwave pulsed through its body, pinning it to the ground as a torrent of blood cascaded from the wound. As if by design, the monster lay before Glenn.

He slowly extended his hand and released the luminescent orb of energy fueled by incredible quantities of Mana. The sphere shot out and settled into the monster's flesh. As the spell drained his entire reserve, Glenn's whispered incantation resounded louder than any scream.

"Implosion."

A blinding flash enveloped everyone, the deafening shockwave sending them sprawling. While the monstrosity may or may have not been gravely harmed, Glenn's hope had been to at least disrupt its senses.

As the world gradually reappeared before his eyes, Glenn beheld a smoldering hole penetrating the monster's body. To Glenn's horror, however, the abomination rose, tendrils of flesh growing to fill the void.

Roar!

A seismic tremor flung every fighter off their feet, and the creature lurched towards Glenn with unbridled fury. With his Mana reserve empty, Glenn held his shortsword with uncertainty.

Perhaps Diamanes had been right all along, and this was indeed the day of his demise. As Glenn stood helplessly, he saw no salvation.

Yet, a mere second before the fleshy limb could pommel him, a brilliant light descended upon the fiend, crushing it to the ground. The monstrosity writhed in agony, its human faces contorted in horrified screams.

The priestess, her hood now down, radiated a silvery luminance as she hovered above the abomination. Her hand emitted a beam that subdued the creature, leaving it struggling to even utter a scream.

As her feet touched the smoldering mass, her very presence exerted pressure upon the loathsome entity. Uttering cryptic words in an unfamiliar language, the priestess pressed her palm down, and the Corrupted One ignited in a holy, white flame.

"J-Just one last... smoke..." Its voice faded away.

Within seconds, the colossal monstrosity, along with its minions, vanished into the inferno, leaving nothing but smoldering remains.

Exhaustion overcame Glenn as his body swayed, and his knees gave way. He collapsed into a pool of blood.

"Well, that was over quickly," he muttered.

And then, without further ceremony, he abandoned himself to the comfort of the darkness.

Chapter 41

HOMELESS

Glenn forced his eyes open, his head ringing painfully. He coughed out a thick lump of coagulated blood as a gentle hand pushed him back onto the ground.

"Don't move, I'm almost done," a soft yet commanding voice ordered.

Glenn's blurry sight focused, revealing the priestess kneeling beside him, her hands glowing with golden light as she treated him. Glenn silently obliged, leaning back as he slowly recovered his senses.

Well, it could have gone much worse, Diamanes commented, startling his host. Glenn winced as the pain in his chest intensified.

"I did warn you not to move," sighed the priestess.

Glenn forced a weak, apologetic smile. "Sorry. Couldn't help it. I'm Glenn, by the way."

The priestess wiped the sweat off her forehead and stood. "Astrid Di Forte. I'm done, but you'll have to rest for a few days to make sure it heals correctly. Don't worry too much about your loss of consciousness; it was only the Mana overload."

She paused and hardened her expression. "Remember, you need a lot of rest. So rest."

Glenn pushed himself up with a groan. "I'll do just that then."

Astrid nodded and left to treat another wounded. Glenn slowly shook off the confusion as he looked at his surroundings. At some point, the Auberge had completely collapsed, leaving him in the middle of the debris.

He stumbled for a few steps before slumping into one of the rare chairs that had survived the battle with the Corrupted monster. Glazing down at himself, he grimaced at his ripped-open shirt and nasty wounds. He took a few minutes to meticulously pick and toss away the bits of flesh that had been splattered onto him.

The remnants of that gruesome fight still lingered in his mind. Mana overload—a consequence of using more Mana that the body can handle. It was only meant as a last resort. And yet... *Holy shit. I'm still alive.*

Sahro sat nearby, nursing his arm. It hung at an awkward angle, awaiting its turn for the priestess' attention.

The silver paladin walked past Glenn and collapsed on his knees in front of his less fortunate comrade. The crumpled ball of metal had been carefully unraveled, revealing a somewhat human corpse.

"My condolences," Glenn said solemnly as he took a few hesitant steps.

The paladin nodded slowly. "Thank you. His soul will be resting in Her embrace..." He closed his eyes and sighed deeply.

After a brief prayer, he shook his head and stood.

"I'm Alabaster Di Fors. This..." His voice trembled slightly as he looked at the corpse. "This was Kerion Di Fors. My brother."

Glenn chewed on the inside of his cheek, unsure of how to respond. Alabaster wiped a tear with his steel-clad fist and extended a hand.

"Thank you for your help. It was impressive magic, sir?"

Glenn shook his hand. "Glenn. Just call me Glenn, without the sir."

Alabaster patted him on the shoulder before glancing back at the corpse of his brother. "Could I ask you to give me some time alone, Glenn?"

"Of course."

The paladin smiled sadly, looking down at the body. He clasped his hands together and closed his eyes.

"May you rest in Onnea's arms, brother..." he whispered.

Glenn averted his gaze, giving Alabaster the privacy he deserved. He stepped over a shattered wooden beam, wincing as his foot dipped into a fresh pool of blood. Dry, writhing tentacles lay around like abandoned corpses, a malevolent aura emanating off them.

"So that was a Corrupted One, huh?" Glenn mumbled as he walked the battlefield.

Creatures who lost their way and devolved into twisted entities. Corrupted by Mana, or some other force. That's what they are, Diamanes explained ominously.

Wait... Isn't that what I was supposed to become after being fed with the Thorns Church's blood back in the prison? Glenn shivered from head to toe.

Feeling lucky yet? Diamanes sneered.

Glenn's gaze wandered through the grim aftermath. Limbs that had yet to be collected lay strewn across the blood-soaked floor. Gorey trails marked where fallen fighters had been dragged outside during the chaos. Glenn lent a hand retrieving the bodies for burial; it was the right thing to do.

The dreary atmosphere made it so that few people dared to talk, giving only awkward glances and brief thanks.

Minty was there, searching through the remains. He didn't take long to leave the scene, as silent as when he attacked the abomination with his powerful bending spell.

Glenn examined his trembling hands, still shaken by the ordeal. While he understood that what they had fought was a monster, the pleas for help from the former employees of the Auberge continued to echo in his mind, refusing to be silenced.

Now that the adrenaline had settled down and the threat had disappeared, he couldn't avoid hearing those screams again, and again.

The monstrosity's body had been completely consumed by the holy flame, leaving behind a small, awe-inducing purple ring. Glenn watched from afar as the priestess carefully picked it up with a tissue and threw it in the jar that they previously used to destroy the bundle of Moongrass.

Sahro sat beside Glenn on a bloody stool that survived the battle. He had just finished receiving healing from the priestess, who was almost done taking care of the injured.

Astrid looked down at the stump of a man who had his leg ripped off. She held her head solemnly, as not even her divine powers could restore the loss of a limb.

"You alright?" The Black Heir asked as he cleaned his sword methodically.

Glenn shrugged, gesturing towards the gruesome scene of the once-thriving Auberge. "Better than them, I suppose."

Sahro let out a cynical scoff, his face etched with darkness. Glenn clenched his hands tightly, trying to hide the tremors. Had it not been for the priestess' timely intervention, he would have been crushed to death by the abomination. Even his most powerful spell, Implosion, hadn't been enough to deal with the monster—even though it used all of his Mana.

Glenn mentally replayed the battle, pondering his inexplicable reaction during the fight. It had been different from his previous encounters, particularly when he had faced the scarecrows upon arriving in the Fringe. Then, he managed to maintain his composure. But this time, panic overwhelmed him. *Was it because of the wounds I suffered, or because of all the dying men around me?*

It's because they were once human, Diamanes explained, his tone weighted with gravity. ***They were a mass of humans mutated by monster blood, or something with similar consequences. You might have killed those Thorns Church bastards before, but these were innocents. Well, they had their faults. But to deserve this?***

Diamanes sighed. ***Fighting people is vastly different from fighting monsters. When you fight monsters, you can compartmentalize them as threats to be eliminated without moral qualms. But in this case, you had interacted with them just moments before they transformed into... whatever that shit was.***

Glenn rubbed his face and rose from his seat to approach Astrid.

"What now?" he asked dryly.

The priestess sighed, her fair hands stained with blood. Despite the gore, she possessed a delicate beauty—her white hair returning to its natural blond hue, and her only divine attribute evident in her black eyes, which held a peculiar golden tint.

"Well, the Church of Onnea is going to send a specialized team to take care of this mess. All of that is way above my pay grade..." she grunted.

Glenn threw a dubious look at her, wondering what the salary for a priest might be.

"We'll also investigate the source of this catastrophe," Astrid continued, pointing towards the enigmatic jar. "*Sigh,* I can't fathom why those masochistic cultists would go to such lengths if they indeed are the catalyst for this incident."

Glenn nodded while thinking about the potential motives. If he thought about what they'd gain—besides money and followers—there weren't a lot of options. Most of the time, people came to an inn for three things: drinks, rooms, and... information.

The priestess looked back at him, a questioning gaze in her eyes. "Excuse me?"

Glenn proceeded to share his line of thought. "They wanted information. Rumors are bound to circulate through places like the Auberge. My question is why would they want intel on the Fringe when they have no foothold in it..." He paused with a frown. "And why the hell would they set up their lackeys for failure?"

The priestess paled. "Maybe they are trying to *create* a foothold. What if they've already started to distribute Moongrass? By Onnea..."

She excused herself and joined her paladin companion. They swiftly departed, the body of their dead friend on the shoulder of Alabaster di Fors.

Hey, what if the drugs the Auberge's crew consumed were laced in monster blood? Maybe that's how they ended up mutating! Diamanes suddenly made a realization, only to step back on it. *Wait, no, why wouldn't they have mutated before then? Ugh, why does corruption need to be such a nonsensical thing?*

Glenn watched the Church of Onnea's team, wondering. He felt that plans were in motion, but he couldn't place a finger on what those plans were.

Sahro joined him, grabbing his shoulder tightly. "We have to find another inn now, right, Glenn?"

The latter's gaze shook. "No, we can't go to an inn. I don't have any money left."

Sahro's eye twitched. "What do you mean you don't have any money? Didn't you have gold co—"

"It's gone," Glenn interrupted abruptly, his face filled with anguish. "We're broke, Sahro."

The Black Heir stared at him until their new, poor reality settled in. "You mean, we can't eat what we want and sleep in a bed again?"

Glenn nodded slowly, driving the wedge even deeper. Crestfallen, Sahro returned to his seat, Glenn following suit as they watched the remains of the Auberge crumble. The few walls that had survived collapsed in clouds of dust, as if to signal the end of the affair.

"Well, that is quite the sight."

It wasn't Sahro's voice that said that. Glenn swiftly turned his head, discovering someone right in between his colleague and him.

Surprised, he stood, turning towards the uninvited guest—an impeccably dressed gentleman wearing a black tuxedo that fitted him like a second skin. A neatly knotted, black bow tie adorned his collar. Atop his head rested a black top hat, making him seem like a character plucked from the pages of a classic novel. Perhaps his most distinctive feature was his meticulously groomed mustache. It was a work of art, carefully trimmed and waxed to perfection.

The gentleman stepped back courteously, tipping his top hat to the two companions. A polite smile graced his face, framed by confident brown eyes. "My apologies for the intrusion. You may call me Sir Reginald, or simply Sir. I am a Senior Cleaner at the Cleaner's Workshop, and I will be overseeing your training for the next three months," he introduced himself politely.

Glenn and Sahro exchanged confused glances. *Weren't we applying for the role of Fixers—the position that promised freedom and independence and all that?*

"I understand this may be perplexing," Sir Reginald continued, as if reading Glenn's thoughts.

"But rest assured, you retain your freedom. I am here as your contact with the Workshop, serving as your mentor. The guild has assigned me to you because of your exceptional performance during the evaluation..." He paused and glanced at the remains of the Auberge. "Which I believe might have still been a little under-evaluated."

Glenn raised an eyebrow. "So, does this mean we passed?"

Sir Reginald hesitated for a moment, seemingly puzzled.

"Well, yes. Did the messenger not inform you of this last evening?"

Glenn massaged his forehead while Sahro struggled to recall any such meeting. Unfortunately, the drug had erased any memories.

Sir Reginald clasped his hands, allowing Glenn to notice they were covered by white, silky gloves.

"In any case, welcome to the Cleaner's Workshop. You are now officially Silver Fixers. Congratulations!"

Chapter 42

GUIDE REGINALD

Glenn and Sahro exchanged a dubious look as they followed Sir Reginald through the grand entrance of the Cleaner's Workshop.

"As I've mentioned earlier, you have both received the maximum rank for the evaluation, Silver," Reginald explained as he stopped in the middle of the main hall. "That means you will receive accommodations and access to special services that non-Fixers can't have easily."

Reginald played with his mustache and smiled. "You have your high potential to thank as well. We are all truly impatient about what kind of Fixers you will become in the future..."

Glenn almost scoffed. He could understand Sahro having great potential, but him? The only thing he did was conjure a magic drill. That seemed rather strange.

I'm not going to complain about receiving better treatment, though... Glenn thought. If the guild thought him worthy, who was he to argue?

After their encounter with the Corrupted Amalgam—a term they had collectively agreed upon for the menacing creature—Glenn's mind was abuzz with questions and uncertainties. First, their financial situation was *terrible.* Second, he was way too weak to continue strolling around this world like everything was fine. He didn't exactly trust others to protect him, and a greater personal power meant that he would be able to accomplish much more.

Getting stronger. That's going to be the most important thing in my life, isn't it?

I'd place my bet on surviving, personally, Diamanes added with a mocking snort.

Glenn rolled his eyes. What he had now was the basic foundation to learn magic, which he gained thanks to Redan's tutelage. He had three spells in his arsenal—with Implosion being impressively powerful for his proficiency at using Mana—but that was it. Well, since he was touted as a 'high-potential' mage, that meant he could probably leverage that to learn more about magic and create more spells. He wasn't great right now, but later?

Something like that Corrupted Amalgam would only be a pebble on the side of the road. Hopefully.

You sure do have great hopes for someone who's still not at the Third Circle, Diamanes mocked.

Glenn continued to ignore the entity's mocking laughter and clenched his fists tightly. The reinforced body he acquired after his stay in the Thorns Church prison was a weapon he had to learn how to use. With the support of the Cleaner's Workshop, Glenn could only hope he would have the time and resources needed to test his abilities.

He also had another item on his agenda—a visit to the Magi Brotherhood. Having two powerful organizations backing him was a great boon. The Brotherhood might have held information about the Fallen Pieces, the Moon Rift, and other mysteries that Glenn encountered since coming to this world.

As for Sahro, well, he could do as he pleased. *Perhaps the idiot will finally be useful for something other than fighting and eating through all my money. Not that it would happen again anytime soon, since we don't have any coins left.*

Sahro sneezed and scanned the surroundings with a suspicious gaze. "Who's bad-mouthing me?"

Reginald guided them through a hallway branching off the lobby. Along the way, they passed a massive dining hall where members streamed in and out without stopping.

Reginald paused near the entry and straightened the fabric of his clothes before providing some insights. "This is the Dining Hall where you can enjoy hearty meals. Depending on your Fixer rank, you'll have access to different qualities of food—for a price, of course. You can also opt for a monthly subscription, guaranteeing two meals a day. I'd recommend it, especially since you both are Silver ranks."

He chuckled. "The chef is a genius at using spices."

Sahro's eyes gleamed with interest, and he tried to discreetly wipe the drool from his chin. The Black Heir couldn't resist a quick peek inside the Dining Hall where members were already satisfying their appetites. Reginald continued their tour, seemingly oblivious to Sahro's hunger.

The next stop was a room with only a few robed individuals passing through. Reginald offered a brief explanation.

"Welcome to the Library, a tranquil haven filled with ancient tomes, maps, scrolls, and more. The dust doesn't particularly appeal to me, but perhaps you'll find it to your liking."

This time, it was Glenn who couldn't contain his excitement. A library! Finally, somewhere he could fill in the gaps in his knowledge of this world.

I'll have to come back here at some point. This place is a gold mine for me, he thought.

Afterwards, Reginald led them to a serene courtyard bathed in natural light, a refreshing oasis in the heart of the fortress. The sun was setting, bathing the lush landscape in the twilight.

"This is the Nexus," Reginald explained. "It connects to every area within the Workshop complex, as you can see from these archways."

He gestured towards several stone arches, each inscribed with names such as Testing Hall, Dormitory, and Infirmary.

"Feel free to use it for relaxation. I often enjoy afternoon tea here; it's quite soothing after a challenging day."

Reginald continued the tour, unveiling the well-organized and surprisingly expansive facilities. Glenn was impressed by the guild's comprehensive offerings; it was a self-contained stronghold within the city.

Some areas were out of bounds for non-official members and could only be accessed by the Cleaners or the high-rank Fixers. The last area the Senior Cleaner led them was the Dormitory, a multi-story building divided into floors based on rank—with private rooms and access to better facilities for higher-ranked members.

Silver Fixers had private rooms on the second floor, but they were bare, austere, and possessed only a simple bed and a window. Bronze Fixers shared rooms—or more like bunks on the first floor—and were cramped together.

Fate had it that Glenn and Sahro were neighbors—probably more out of design than chance. Both of them were satisfied with the turn of events.

At least I know I'll have an ally next door. Glenn recalled the strange attendants in the main lobby as he looked at his barren room. *Housing problem solved. Just have to figure out my money situation...*

Reginald dusted his gloved hands off and smiled. "That concludes the tour of the Cleaner's Workshop, at least the areas you are allowed to use and visit."

He searched his tuxedo's pockets, struggling for a few seconds, only to come up empty-handed. He cleared his throat awkwardly. "Well, if you need any information, don't hesitate to ask the attendants. Your Silver identifications will arrive tomorrow, so you have the evening to yourselves."

With a tip of his top hat, Reginald hurriedly left with a preoccupied expression.

Glenn turned to Sahro, a hint of relief on his face. "Well, it seems we're not homeless. That's something, at least."

Sahro nodded, savoring the idea of having a room to himself. Glenn thought back to their financial state and shook his head dejectedly.

"We'll have to find a way to make some money soon. We can't rely solely on the guild. I hardly believe that they'll just accommodate two freeloaders forever."

Sahro's expression darkened. They were still broke, and their shelter in the Cleaner's Workshop was a lifeline they couldn't take for granted.

"Anyway, let's rest for now. Tomorrow will be a new day," Glenn suggested as fatigue began to wash over him.

The Black Heir nodded and entered his room silently.

The fight had been exhausting, and sleeping in a drugged state wasn't great to recuperate. Glenn couldn't wait to collapse onto his bed. He took the bandages off his left hand, leaving Diamanes free to speak aloud.

"Well, it's great and all that you're getting comfortable inside this Workshop or whatever, but it doesn't push us closer to our goal!" he exclaimed, his voice filled with annoyance.

Glenn looked at his hand strangely. "Our goal?"

Diamanes clicked his tongue. **"Well, yeah, you know. Reaching the Third Circle, so I can tell you my secrets and all?"**

Glenn felt a strange sense of urgency from the entity. "Diamanes... There's something you're not telling me, isn't there? You've been really insistent about this matter."

Diamanes remained tight-lipped, his silence speaking volumes. He sighed before finally answering, **"All I can say is that you *want* to get to the Third Circle. Once you get there, I'll tell you all you want to know."**

Glenn shook his head, understanding that pushing any further would be useless. He settled onto his comfortable bed. At least the accommodations were decent, even if there was barely any furniture. He assumed a lotus position, finding it oddly tranquil for Meditation. There was something about it that allowed him to connect more deeply with his body.

Perhaps there was a scientific or magical reason for that, but he didn't know. Yet. Because he sure as hell was going to get as much information as he could out of that Library...

"You're salivating again. Weirdo."

Glenn wiped away the drool before diving into Meditation, contemplating the mysteries of his magical abilities. He needed to refine his skills, especially Implosion, which had drained him. He couldn't rely on a spell that entirely emptied his Mana reserve.

I could find a way to reduce the Mana consumption somehow, but I have no idea how to tweak that... I can only hope that better Mana control will come the longer I use spells... Maybe that's just another benefit of getting to the Third Circle...

He also had to find new spells that implemented his specialty. More tools on his belt could never hurt. He opened his eyes, exiting his Meditation, and gazed through the window at the two moons shimmering in the night sky—momentarily obscured by a few fleeting clouds.

"*Sigh*... Whatever I want to achieve, it'll have to wait until tomorrow." He decided as he threw away his dirty, bloodied clothes and jumped into the clean bed. This time, he was opting for actual sleep instead of Meditating. His mind needed to rest too.

Tomorrow will be a new day.

Chapter 43

FIRST CONTACT

Glenn stared up at the abomination looming over him—a grotesque mass of writhing flesh, protruding limbs, and pulsating veins. He focused his Mana and concentrated, ready to unleash his Implosion spell.

The monstrous form sent shivers down his spine. Glenn's heart raced as he prepared to strike. He aimed the spell at the abomination's head. But as the energy gathered, something unexpected happened. The monstrosity's misshapen face contorted, and a human visage emerged from the mangled mass of flesh.

Andres' face.

A feeble cry for help escaped his lips just before Glenn released the ball of Mana.

"Help..."

Glenn tried to pull his energy back, but it was too late, and the spell made contact with the monster.

A bright flash of white blinded Glenn, forcing him to blink. It took him a few seconds to realize he was in his bed, and the blinding light was the sun coming from the window.

"Shit..." he muttered as he rubbed the tiredness off his eyes.

Knocks on the door drew his attention, shattering the remnants of his unsettling dream. Glenn reluctantly climbed out of bed, annoyed and disoriented. He yawned and stretched before quickly putting on the black attire he had acquired from Howard Jefferson's chest. The pants were stained with dry, pungent blood, and the shirt was ripped to shreds. He decided to just throw away the shirt and close the trench coat.

"I'm gonna need to clean this eventually…" Glenn sighed as he bandaged his left hand.

He had expected to hear some kind of complaint from Diamanes, but the latter remained silent. *I guess he's still sleeping. Do evil hands need sleep? Well, why not?*

Opening the door, Glenn was greeted by the familiar smiling faces of Sir Reginald and Sahro. The Senior Cleaner tipped his top hat, his mustache bouncing with the movement.

"Good morning, dear Fixers. I came to deliver your Silver identifications, so here they are."

From his coat, he produced two daggers—their hilts shimmering with an argentine hue. Glenn examined one closely, discovering that the blade itself was crafted from silver and etched with intricate runes. The memory of nearly losing his Magi Brotherhood recommendation resurfaced, and he couldn't help but voice his concern.

"What if we lose them?"

For a moment, Sir Reginald appeared perplexed, but then a polite chuckle escaped his lips as he covered his mouth with a gloved hand. "Oh, yes, of course. Well, you don't have to worry about that. Just infuse some Mana into it. I'm sure you're both capable."

Glenn and Sahro followed his instructions, infusing energy into their daggers. The blades glowed with a soft, blue radiance before dissipating into a cloud of white particles.

Diamanes' voice rang through Glenn's head. ***Who the hell sent a knife into my space?***

Sir Reginald cleared his throat and summoned his dagger from thin air. White particles emerged from his hand as it materialized, gradually forming the complete blade. This one had an ebony scabbard and a handgrip adorned with rubies—much more elaborate than its silver counterparts.

"The daggers provided to Silver Fixers and above have a Soulbound enchantment. They will be safely stored within your soul," Reginald explained as his dagger dematerialized.

Glenn gazed upon his hand as he willed for the weapon to manifest. The weapon appeared similarly, appearing from thin air through a mass of white particles.

"That's interesting…" he commented, lost in his thoughts.

Sir Reginald took out a sheet of paper. "Hmm. Of course, if it gets destroyed one way or another, you'll be entitled to pay the fee for the original cost of the dagger plus the cost of replacing it. So, I'd advise not to use it beyond its original purpose."

Glenn grabbed the document and gave it a quick read. His face paled as he swiftly went over the dagger's cost.

"Holy sh— Two gold coins for one little knife?!"

Sir Reginald smiled awkwardly, rubbing his chin. "Hmm, yes, it's indeed a little expensive. So, don't break it, alright?"

Glenn carefully returned the dagger to his soul, sighing in relief knowing that it was safely stored away. Suddenly, an idea struck him. He took the Magi Brotherhood recommendation out of his dimensional pouch, inviting a gasp from Sir Reginald.

He then sent some Mana into it, the plate shining with a deep blue hue before disappearing in yet another cloud of white particles.

So that's why there was no warning against losing it. Because it wasn't possible to lose it, Glenn mused.

Sir Reginald clapped his hand—his previous surprised expression gone.

"Alright, I'll be showing you how to take your first contract and present you to your instructor. After that, you'll be free to do whatever you want."

As they followed Sir Reginald through the hallways of the Dormitory, Glenn bumped into a figure in the archway, offering a quick apology.

"Sorry."

It was a robed individual, and a faint scent of mint surrounded him.

Could it be that Minty guy again? Glenn wondered, recalling the strange fighter with bending magic.

However, he decided to set aside his curiosity for later. He followed Sir Reginald and Sahro, still wondering who would be weird enough to perfume themselves with mint.

They soon arrived in the main lobby of the Cleaner's Workshop, standing before a contract board. Since it was early in the morning, there weren't many people around. Sir Reginald examined the board for a moment before plucking a contract from it.

He handed the paper to Glenn, who read it aloud for Sahro's benefit.

Silver request: Solve the Rift problem under the bakery

Reward: Twenty-five silver, ten contribution points, and the baker's gratitude

Glenn turned back to Sir Reginald, a puzzled expression on his face. "A Rift? Like the Moon Rift?"

Sir Reginald rubbed his mustache as he considered the question. "Well, hmm... Yes and no. A Rift is... an opening in King's Rise defenses. You're probably aware that zones with high concentrations of Mana have a likely chance of spawning monsters. Mutated beasts or beings of Mana—it can happen anywhere at any time."

Glenn and Sahro nodded, one because he knew, the other because he couldn't afford not to.

I can't wait to get in the Library and fill in all the blanks missing in my common knowledge, Glenn thought shamefully.

"King's Rise isn't supposed to allow fiends inside. However, sometimes a Rift can form, gradually summoning monsters until it eventually explodes, unleashing a horde of them," Reginald explained with an ominous expression.

He shook his head and rubbed his mustache. "Your task is to deal with these Rifts before they become a larger threat. Rifts are the main sources of contracts for the Cleaner's Workshop."

The gentleman then walked towards the counter, where the attendants gestured them forwards.

He continued, "Now if you'd be so kind as to show the contract to these ladies, they will mark it as accepted. And don't worry about wait times. As Fixers, you enjoy certain privileges."

Glenn grinned awkwardly at the attendant, the same who took care of his registration, Alisson. She smiled naturally, not showing any of the bizarreness that Glenn had previously found in her behavior.

"Hello, Sir Reginald, Glenn, and Sahro. Can I help you?" She tilted her head inquisitively.

Sir Reginald handed her the contract. He explained their purpose, and Alisson quickly reviewed the agreement before stamping it with approval. She noted something in a nearby document and handed the stamped paper back to Glenn.

"Here you go. You can undertake the request at your convenience. But remember, you have forty-eight hours to complete it." She smiled widely.

Glenn nodded and stored the contract in his dimensional pouch.

"Of course, rewards are split equally between the contracted Fixers. We leave to you the discretion to further solve any issues surrounding your share," Alisson added.

Glenn simply responded, "Naturally."

Sahro seemed indifferent to the reward, scoffing at the mention of it.

Sir Reginald turned towards them, a wide smile on his face. "And there you go. I'll leave you gentlemen to your business. I'm sure you'll be able to take care of a Silver request easily. Have a nice day."

The Senior Cleaner excused himself. Glenn couldn't help but wonder about the enigmatic gentleman.

This Sir Reginald is quite the elusive character.

Indeed. I can feel some power from him, but I don't understand it. It's similar to those strange attendants, but I can't say yet. If you were at the Third Circle—

Glenn groaned. *Yes, yes, I know. You will probably be able to make me the strongest man alive once I'm at the Third Circle.*

Diamanes clicked his tongue, unhappy. Not that Glenn cared. He still noted the information about Reginald in the corner of his mind. If there was one thing that his gut told him, it was that something was going on in this Cleaner's Workshop. But, whatever that was, it would have to wait for him to get a bit stronger—and mostly, wealthier.

Glenn and Sahro left the lobby, heading outside. As they walked along the main road, searching for the bakery, Glenn observed the names engraved on the ground at each corner. It was a practical method of labeling streets that he hadn't noticed before.

The place where the names were inscribed never got dirty, somehow. Glenn knew because he accidentally kicked a potted plant, only to witness the dirt being pushed away by some invisible magic.

The Cleaner's Workshop stood on Central Street, No. 13—right in the heart of the Northern Town. Their destination, the bakery, was on Rampart Street, running alongside the massive wall that separated the Fringe from the Bourgeoisie.

Glenn turned to Sahro, eager to formulate a plan. "We don't know what to expect, but being proactive wouldn't hurt. Let's aim to complete this quickly."

Sahro agreed, echoing Glenn's sentiment. "It's just a Rift. There might be a monster or two at most. Even you can handle a few goblins, right?"

Glenn shot his companion a deadpan look. "I'm pretty sure I can handle *more* than a few goblins."

The Black Heir shrugged nonchalantly. "If you say so."

Glenn let out an exasperated sigh, realizing there was no point in arguing further. They eventually arrived in front of the bakery, a modest establishment with the sign 'Hearts Bakery' displayed above the entrance.

Sahro couldn't help but voice his skepticism, "It's hard to believe they're baking bread in such a tiny place."

Glenn blinked and looked at his friend with curiosity. "Why? What did you expect?"

"I don't know, something... bigger, I guess? Isn't bread rare and precious?"

Glenn contained a laugh and patted Sahro's shoulder silently. The door bore a 'Closed' sign, as the lack of activity inside confirmed. They knocked.

After a brief wait, a high-pitched voice called out, "Give me a minute!"

The sound of jingling keys followed, and the door swung open to reveal a slightly flustered, red-faced lady. The baker was a petite woman with a round figure and face. Her rosy cheeks accentuated her warm smile. She wore practical glasses and sported a no-nonsense haircut.

"I already told you I can't pay until you— Oh?"

Her annoyance evaporated when she laid eyes on the two strangers at her doorstep.

Glenn froze. *She... She looks like my mother.*

"Who might you handsome gentlemen be?"

Chapter 44

MAKING SOME DOUGH

Glenn and Sahro stepped into the bakery, graciously welcomed by the rotund lady, who swiftly orchestrated a display of hospitality. With deft, professional movements, she set up a quaint table adorned with a checkered napkin and served them two cups filled to the brim. The duo savored their drinks before they could even inquire about the unexpected gesture.

"Milo, make sure the guests are comfortable while I go find my damn stuff!" The baker ordered as she headed to the back hallway.

A boy, probably the same age as Liam smiled as he stood beside them, holding the bottle of cider.

Sahro, visibly perplexed by this unanticipated show of generosity, hesitated as he took a cautious sip. Meanwhile, Glenn drank his fill. The surprising sweetness, dominated by the flavor of apple and tinged with a hint of carbonation, refreshed his senses. And it didn't have the same terrifying effect that beer seemed to possess on his psyche. The boy beamed proudly.

"That's Mr. Hearts' cider. He makes it with apples from a nearby communal orchard. It's pretty good, isn't it?" he inquired.

Glenn nodded, taking another sip. "I might become addicted." He slowly settled the cup on the table. "We didn't get to introduce ourselves.

I'm Glenn, and this is Sahro. We're Silver Fixers sent by the Cleaner's Workshop."

He retrieved the contract from his dimensional pouch, extending it towards the boy. He took a step back with an apologetic smile.

"Ah, I'm sorry. I'm just a servant."

The baker dashed out of the hall and grabbed the document. She gave it a glance.

"Oh, finally!" She sighed in relief. "I'm Mrs. Laurence, the owner," she added.

She wasted no time stamping the contract before shaking her head heavily. "To be honest, I was starting to lose hope... Those damned pests have made it impossible for me or Milo to access the basement where our supplies are stored. And we can't possibly work with the knowledge that they are scurrying beneath my floorboards."

Mrs. Laurence handed the paper back to Glenn, who safely stowed it in his pouch. He had a hard time keeping his eyes away from her face. The resemblance to his mother was uncanny.

Puzzled, Glenn inquired, "Pests?"

He wondered if twenty-five silver wasn't a bit much for exterminating rats. It seemed weird to even pay a mercenary guild to take care of those.

She nodded grimly, frustrated. "Yes, those damned pests. Milo managed to dispatch one of those wretched creatures, but their numbers are overwhelming. I sometimes feel they'd devour me alive if I didn't descend into the basement armed with a torch."

Mrs. Laurence patted Milo's back and grinned widely. "Who would have known this Sewers' chap would be so nice to have around?"

Milo awkwardly rubbed his head with a wry smile. Sahro raised an eyebrow.

"You're from the Sewers? What part?"

"I fled from my parents' hut and somehow ended up here," said the young boy.

Sahro's gaze softened, and he sipped on his cider silently.

Glenn shivered and instinctively clenched the hilt of his sword. "Let's get to it then. I'm not a big fan of rodents either."

Mrs. Laurence patted him on the shoulder with an encouraging smile. "Perfect. Just..." She frowned. "Remember to not damage my basement. There are important resources, and the furnace is also down there. All of it costs more money than I can afford to replace."

Even her warnings sound like my mother's.

Glenn and Sahro exchanged a glance and smiled at her as they rose from their seats. "Of course, Miss Laurence. We will be careful."

Mrs. Laurence chuckled and waved her hand dismissively. "Miss? I'm no miss. Call me m'am, that'll do nicely."

"As you wish, m'am."

The baker laughed heartily before directing them to a trapdoor, granting them access to the basement. They walked down a steep staircase that led to a well-lit room with a wooden door reinforced by sturdy beams.

Mrs. Laurence looked at them from above as she closed the hatch. "I'll let you remove the beam, okay? Good luck!"

Glenn shrugged. *How hard could it be to take care of some rats? Even if they came out of some Rift.*

And there you go. What do you call that... you jinxed it?

Disregarding his hand's snickers, Glenn motioned for Sahro to lift the wooden bar while he readied a torch and a Magic Bullet. The door creaked open, and a smell of carrion forced him to step back. He could hear the sound of scurrying in the darkness but could not see the damn creatures.

His torch shone light on something metal—a pitchfork. The tool's four blades were covered in dry, red paint up to the hilt.

"Wait, how big are those rats—"

Before Glenn could finish his sentence, a jackal-sized rat lunged at him, teeth first.

He jumped back and instinctively released his Magic Bullet, obliterating the creature's skull. The rat's lifeless, yet heavy body landed on Glenn's chest, forcing him to the ground. He hurriedly pushed the corpse away and stood, his torch raised. Hisses and scurrying intensified within the gloom.

Glenn glanced at the mass, his eyes widening slightly. It was a damned fat rat. Its razor-sharp claws were still twitching, the life slowly escaping from it, as blood flowed out of its blown off head.

A few high-pitched squeaks came from the opened door as if to warn them. Sahro readied his sword, not sparing a glance at Glenn's vanquished foe. The latter prepared another Magic Bullet as he took a step inside the room, discovering a dozen red eyes leering at him. The torch's flame wasn't strong enough to completely push the unnatural bleakness of the storeroom.

"How the hell are they so fat?" Glenn blurted out in awe.

Sahro spat and covered his sword in a crimson Aura. "I don't know, but their size won't matter once I slice them to bits!"

Glenn stopped him. "Wait, wait, no. We can't afford to break anything. No Aura, okay?"

Sahro rolled his eyes and reluctantly nodded, the red hue around his blade dissipating. He then pointed at Glenn. "What about magic?"

Glenn clenched his fist. "Yeah, you're right." He unsheathed his sword. "Let's carve our way through."

The two hesitantly took another step into the room, only for the rats to squeak even louder. Glenn and Sahro both stayed close to the exit, refusing to lose their escape path. A rat suddenly lunged forwards, just as large as the one Glenn killed. The latter gritted his teeth and prepared to defend, but Sahro's sword delivered both the sentence and the execution. The rat's head rolled across the floor, a pool of blood forming under it.

The rats hissed angrily, their sharp claws digging into the stone foundation. Glenn gulped heavily.

"Shit, they're coming!" He warned as he took a step back, his blade raised high.

Sahro retorted, "I can see that, moron!"

One of the rodents jumped at Sahro before its head got swiftly pierced by the Black Heir's curved blade. Glenn waved his torch, shining the light on more overgrown rodents.

Another pest lunged at the Black Heir, but Glenn kicked it away before stabbing its skull and pinning it to the floor. Sahro dodged a charging fiend and sliced all of its legs off—cleanly piercing through its neck.

Glenn wiped the sweat off his forehead only to jump away as two more rats charged at him. His back touched Sahro's, causing the Black Heir to startle.

"Don't get in my way!" he yelled as he cut the head off another beast.

A second jumped over its dead comrade and landed directly on Glenn. He desperately fended off the monsters, his sword being the only thing saving him from deadly, sharp teeth. Sahro kicked the rodent away and finished it off before pulling Glenn back on his feet.

"You're the one annoying me!" the Black Heir retorted as he punched a rat in the snout and drove his weapon into its throat, cleaving it upwards in a gore finisher.

Glenn heaved, searching for another pest to slaughter. Besides corpses, bloodied bags of flour, and old shelves, he couldn't see any more beasts.

You just keep on doing it, huh? Diamanes snorted mockingly.

Glenn raised a puzzled eyebrow, only to be pushed aside, a rat landing where he was a second ago. Sahro, who saved him, cleaved the rat's head off in one fell swoop.

He cleaned the blood off his blade on a dead beast's fur. "That should have been the last of them."

"You're good at this," Glenn said as he sheathed his sword.

Sahro kicked one of the bodies, making sure it was lifeless.

"I trained in the Sewers fighting bandits and even closing Rifts like this one. You know how to close it, right?" The Black Heir asked as he pointed at a... perplexing form at the back of the room.

Glenn hobbled next to Sahro, sinking to one knee as he examined the strange, enigmatic phenomenon. It defied easy description—a disturbance in existence itself. It looked like a bundle of moving shadows, slithering with ominous intentions. A hole into a *darker* place where no light shined.

Glenn and Sahro stood at the edge of it, staring into the unnatural darkness where the fabric of reality unraveled.

Sahro muttered as Aura covered his hand. "I think something moved in there..."

Diamanes interrupted Glenn's contemplation with a puzzling proposal. ***Put me in there. It'll be quite a surprise.***

Glenn hesitantly pushed his left hand into the Rift, feeling frost seize his flesh. Sahro watched, eyebrows furrowed.

As the Black Heir was about to pull out his companion's arm, the Rift disappeared—as if absorbed by Glenn's hand. The bandages came undone, and the purple stain on his skin deepened.

"***Burp*. Oh, sorry.**" Diamanes blurted out.

Glenn paused and slowly looked at his hand in horror, Sahro's eyes widening in astonishment. A mouth manifested in Glenn's palm, and a red tongue greedily licked its lips.

"**That. *That* was a good meal.**"

Glenn, his face aghast and still splattered with blood and brains, returned a horrified stare.

Diamanes' once-smug smile vanished. "**Oh. Did I just say that out loud?**"

Chapter 45

SAHRO MEETS GLENN'S HAND

"Glenn, don't move," the Black Heir said as he readied his blade. Raising his hands in a placating manner, Glenn pleaded, "Wait, wait, wait! Sahro, you don't know what you're doing!"

"I perfectly know what I'm doing. Damned *ruh sayiya*!"

"Lower your sword, Sahro!"

Diamanes signed. **"Yeah, for real. What have I done to you?"**

"Damn it, Diamanes! You're not helping!"

"Don't worry, Glenn, I'll free you from this devil! Just... let me cut this damned—"

Glenn desperately grabbed onto Sahro's wrist. The Black Heir's expression hardened.

"It's going to be painful," Sahro warned, "but you'll thank me later."

Glenn grunted as he pushed Sahro off, his superhuman strength coming in handy.

"No, I won't! Now, listen to me— Wow!" he yelped as Sahro's blade landed a hair's breadth away from his skin.

"Ah! That was way too close!" Glenn screamed as he retreated, his back against the wall.

He hid his left hand behind his back, his mind racing.

"Glenn, stop resisting..." An ominous, crimson Aura covered Sahro's sword. "Or I will be forced to take action against you!"

He lunged at Glenn, his blade cutting through the air. Glenn instinctively discharged his Mana formlessly, creating a sudden burst. The invisible force caught Sahro off guard and knocked him back. He stumbled and crashed into a stack of crates, buried in dust and flour. Glenn's heart pounded in his chest as he panted, beads of sweat trickling down his forehead.

Sahro, disheveled and slightly bruised, slowly picked himself up. His Aura flared once more, and he prepared to dash with as much strength as he could muster.

"Oh! Are you done destroying my supplies? Get the hell out of there!" Mrs. Laurence's angry voice interrupted them from above.

Sahro paused, his eyes glued to Glenn's purple hand before he reluctantly sheathed his sword. He stabbed a finger into Glenn's chest.

"You owe me an explanation!" he hissed.

Glenn nodded silently. They both looked at each other while Diamanes kept silent. Glenn quickly concealed his left hand under a piece of cloth and made his way out of the basement. As he emerged from the trapdoor, a kitchen towel slapped him on the cheek, sending him back down.

"Don't bring that filth with you! Wipe it off, damn it!" Mrs. Laurence exclaimed in fury, her anger far more terrifying than any monstrous rat.

"Yes, yes, m'am," Glenn grunted as he obediently wiped himself clean.

He finally returned upstairs where Mrs. Laurence was waiting—rolling pin in hand. She tapped it in her palm softly, ready to use it at a moment's notice.

The lady sent a distrustful gaze towards the trapdoor, but her tension eased when she saw Sahro's head pop up. She sighed in relief and tossed the rolling pin away.

"Is it done?" she asked, her voice less stern.

Glenn nodded. "There's quite a mess down there, though. There are a lot of large bodies and blood. Will you be fine with?"

Mrs. Laurence waved her hand dismissively. "Oh, if you don't want the corpses, leave them to me. I know a few people who pay upfront for monster hides. I'll take care of them."

Glenn sighed deeply as he collapsed on a chair. Sahro stood with his arms crossed, staring at Glenn distrustfully. The latter rubbed his forehead, his eyes suddenly tearing by themselves. He blinked and wiped them off, feeling as if the world was a little clearer than it was moments ago.

What is this? He wondered, only for the sensation to go away like a mirage.

Mrs. Laurence patted both Glenn and Sahro on the shoulders and chuckled. "Well, gentlemen, I have work to do and corpses to get rid of."

She clasped her hands together and graced them with a grateful smile. "Thank you so much. I'll finally be able to be back in business. Give me your contracts. I'll conclude the deal."

Glenn complied, retrieving the document from his dimensional pouch. Mrs. Laurence produced ink and a fountain pen from one of her pockets, swiftly signing the paper. She handed the contract back to the young man before grabbing a bottle of cider.

"I know you'll already get a reward, but I noticed you liked it quite a bit. You can always come and buy some more here later!" she exclaimed, handing a bottle to Glenn.

Glenn accepted it with gratitude, noting the tag on it that read, 'Hearts Bakery — Brut Cider'.

"Thank you very much, m'am... I— We appreciate it," Glenn said, genuinely touched.

He couldn't help but feel strangely attached to the baker. *Do I miss home so much that I'm starting to see my family in strangers?*

The lady scoffed, giving Glenn's shoulder a playful slap. "Aye, I'm not the one who risked my life. Have a nice day, Fixers!"

Glenn nodded, leaving the bakery with Sahro in silence. The sun hung high in the sky, and Glenn's stomach rumbled, reminding him that it was already noon.

A watch would be greatly appreciated, he thought wryly as they strolled through the Northern Town's streets.

Sahro, however, remained fixated on Glenn's left hand with a mixture of hate and disgust.

Diamanes' voice chimed in, mocking Sahro. **Damn, that guy must really like me for him to stare so much!**

Glenn fought the urge to hurl insults at the entity, his frustration simmering beneath the surface. *Goddamnit, Diamanes. I might get killed by this idiot thanks to you appearing out of the blue! I can't believe my safety is in jeopardy because of a damned burp!*

* * *

The two men arrived at the Cleaner's Workshop half an hour later, heading directly to the counter. Glenn retrieved the signed contract and held it out to Allison. She accepted it with a smile, checking the signature before making some notations.

"Good job on your first task, Glenn and Sahro. Hand me your Fixers IDs, please."

Glenn and Sahro summoned their silver daggers, handing them over to Allison. She held both for a few moments, during which numbers flashed on the handles.

"Those are your contribution points," Alisson explained. "You can use them at the Armory, at the Smithy, or save them for the rank-up tests. They're pretty handy, so spend them sparingly."

Glenn took his dagger back, noting the number ten shining gently in an argentine hue. Allison then bent behind the counter, producing silver coins—one after the other. Two piles of twelve silver coins were dwarfed by two large copper towers, each made up of fifty coins. Glenn and Sahro accepted their pay while expressing their gratitude.

Without exchanging words, they proceeded to the Dining Hall where they paid for their Silver meal, slipping ten copper coins each into the cook's hand. The meal consisted of a golden-brown roasted chicken glistening with a hint of olive oil. Surrounding the protein was a colorful array of vegetables and an herb gravy, emanating an enticing aroma.

Glenn didn't waste any time. He quickly found an empty table and eagerly devoured his meal. Sahro joined him, equally ravenous.

After ten awkward and silent minutes of eating, hostility lingered in the air. Sahro's gaze, in particular, was fixed on Glenn's left hand, which was now tightly wrapped under bandages.

The Black Heir finally spoke, his voice hesitant and wary. "Can... Can it hear us?"

Glenn sighed as a muffled voice emerged from beneath the bandages. **"Of course I can, moron! And it's him! Him! Not it! I'm not an animal!"**

Sahro sprang from his seat and instinctively clutched the hilt of his sword. Glenn calmly rose from his chair and gestured for his companion to follow. With a bit of a mental struggle to remember the way, Glenn aimed for the Dormitory but found himself in the central Nexus instead.

The park enclosed within the Workshop's wall was as lush as ever. A few Fixers sunbathed in the grass while others jogged by.

"This will work as well as any other place," he mumbled to himself.

Choosing a somewhat secluded spot behind a few trees, As Glenn unraveled the bandages, a mouth emerged in his palm.

A relieved breath escaped, and Diamanes smiled, revealing his peerless white teeth.

"Well, it's finally time for the presentation, I suppose. Nice to meet you, Sahro. I'm Diamanes, the one and only," he proudly exclaimed.

Glenn shook his head dejectedly, fighting back the urge to slap his forehead.

Sahro observed Glenn's hand from a cautious distance before inching closer.

"What is it?" the Black Heir asked.

Glenn shrugged. "Well, for now, I've decided to categorize him as an annoying, somewhat useful, talking hand."

Sahro's expression shifted from confusion to concern. "You know that demonic possessions are very serious matters, Glenn?"

The young man sighed wearily, scratching the back of his neck. "I mean, I'm pretty sure I'm still in control. And he's more like another voice than an evil entity that wishes to consume my soul."

Sahro shot one last dubious look at Diamanes, who responded with a wide, shameless grin. After a few moments of contemplation, Sahro sighed and withdrew his hand from his sword.

"Are you certain it's not dangerous?" he inquired cautiously.

Diamanes couldn't help but interject again, outraged. **"Hey, not it. I said, he! He!"**

"The most you risk with this guy is getting annoyed to death. He's basically a tool that can talk. Don't worry too much about it."

Sahro nodded hesitantly. He crossed his arms, still not entirely at ease in the presence of the talking hand.

"So, what's the plan now?" Sahro inquired.

Glenn rebandaged his hand, ignoring Diamanes' continued protests.

"I'm going to get some new clothes and then check out this Magi Brotherhood—wherever it is. And you... Well, I guess you'll do whatever you want, honestly."

Sahro raised an eyebrow, looking somewhat puzzled. "What am I supposed to do?"

"I don't know. There are plenty of activities in the Fringe, right? I'm sure you'll find something."

Glenn stepped past Sahro, leaving him behind as he headed towards the Armory.

After walking alone for a few minutes, Glenn arrived in a hall with two rooms on each side. One emitted an intense heat, while the other resembled an arsenal. Glenn pushed open the glazed door to the latter, and a bell rang, announcing his entrance.

A thundering voice emanated from behind the shop's counter, startling Glenn.

"Welcome!"

Glenn glanced around but couldn't spot the source of the sound. It appeared there was no one at the desk, so where...

"I suppose you're a newbie, aye?" the voice called out again, this time from the ground.

Glenn looked down and found a scrawny figure, about the size of a ten-year-old child, staring up at him with a big smile and an equally large ginger beard. The man was dressed in puffy, silky clothes and had a peculiar, spiky haircut that matched the color of his beard. A small tag near his breast pocket read 'Rusty Stoneheart'.

"What can I do for you?" the little shopkeeper asked with a chuckle.

Chapter 46

THE PRICE OF CURIOSITY

Glenn couldn't help but stare at the tiny man before him, dumbfounded. Rusty Stoneheart crossed his arms while sizing him up and down. He nodded, not giving Glenn a chance to recover his senses before reaching for a measuring tape. He climbed onto a stool, grunting as he did so.

"Hmpf... It's always a lot of work with tall ones..." Rusty groaned as he forced Glenn to turn around.

The latter finally shook off his confusion as he quickly stepped back. "W-Wait! I didn't ask for anything yet!"

Stoneheart paused, his eyebrows furrowed. "What, aren't you here for a new suit? Even if you prefer the tattered style, that's a bit much, hah!"

Glenn paused as he looked down at his ripped pants, bloodied coat, and missing shirt. It was indeed a little obvious that he needed clothes.

"Raise your arms for a second," Rusty prompted him, continuing with his measurements.

Glenn silently complied, assuming various positions depending on the shopkeeper's needs. Eventually, after a few nods of approval, Rusty stepped down from his stool and freed Glenn from the measuring seance.

"'Aight, I got pretty much everything I needed. Now, I see you have a sword with you. What kind of armor do you want?" Rusty asked, his arms crossed.

"I'm more of a Mage... Something fairly light so I can dodge around easily would be nice."

Rusty scoffed. "Everyone wants light armor these days..." He turned away and grumbled in his beard. "No one wants manly plate armor anymore..."

The shopkeeper disappeared into the back of the store to rummage. Glenn wandered towards the counter, observing the diverse array of items displayed on numerous tables and racks. Weapons from simple swords and bows to more exotic crafts like flamberge blades, chakrams, and war scythes.

There were also staves embedded with various Shards, even though there was a small tag beneath it that read 'Consumable'. Glenn remembered the fire staff he used against the scarecrows and grimaced.

I don't think I will use one of those again, he thought before looking at the armor section.

It was impressively stocked with breastplates crafted from various metals and even materials from otherworldly creatures. As Glenn ran his hand along a scaled armor, he withdrew when he felt a peculiar warmth emanating from it, almost as if it were... alive. *That's got to be a little... Heh, 'restraining' to wear.*

His thoughts were disrupted by the tiny man thrusting his head through the door, his voice booming. "You said you were a Mage, right?"

Glenn nodded, grimacing as the thunderous voice assailed his eardrums. He still struggled to get used to the contrast between Rusty's size and his explosive tenor. A scraping sound echoed from the back shop as Rusty hauled what appeared to be a stone-carved chest.

Gasping for breath, the shopkeeper wiped the sweat from his forehead and opened the coffer. Inside lay fabric as dark as the night, waiting to be fashioned into clothing.

A wide grin stretched across Rusty's bearded face. "How's the color? You like it?"

Glenn hesitated and rubbed his chin, trying to picture himself wearing something carved out of that cloth. Black did seem to suit him, but he didn't wish to appear as though he were attending a funeral every day. Moreover, he needed something durable for combat, and he doubted this fabric would withstand the wear and tear he'd encounter.

"I'm sorry, but I was hoping for something more resilient, and a bit less... sinister?" he said with a sheepish grin.

Rusty froze momentarily, then threw his neck back as he burst into hearty laughter. Glenn regarded him with a puzzled expression, waiting for the tiny shopkeeper to regain his composure. Wiping away tears of mirth, Rusty Stoneheart shook his head with an even wider smile.

"Fear not, dear client. This fabric—or rather, silk—is produced by the Nightweaver Spiders beyond the Black Wall. It's as sturdy as steel, remarkably flexible, and exceptionally enchantable. Of course, it won't shield you from blunt force, but it will resist cuts and tears quite impressively. And don't worry, I can dye it to make it a bit more lively if that's your concern."

The shopkeeper beamed with pride at the contents of the stone chest. "I've had this for a while but couldn't use it due to the remote chance of a Blood Moon. You see, Night Silk becomes as frail as regular fabric under the Blood Moon's light. But now that the event has passed, it's safe to use Night Silk once more."

Glenn's eyes gleamed as he gazed at the material. He then regarded the shopkeeper with feigned unconcern.

"So, how much would a suit made of this cost?"

For now, I should be fine with just that set, but I certainly should think about preparing a few more in case of another Moon Rift...

The tiny shopkeeper rubbed his hands together as greed twinkled in his eyes. "Well, if I were to craft a splendid suit befitting a prestigious Mage like yourself, it would be worth..."

He scribbled a quick calculation on a note and showed it to Glenn.

One, two, three... four? Wait! Glenn struggled to prevent his face from contorting in shock. *This... this price is exorbitant! How many zeros are there?*

A swift check of his dimensional pouch revealed that he possessed only twelve silver and forty copper coins. That was nowhere near enough to cover the cost Rusty demanded.

"Can you give me a second to think about this?" Glenn forced a polite smile, witnessing Rusty's expression break down in disappointment.

He sat on one of the benches, pondering what to do. Having a cool suit made out of that silk felt like an excellent idea—even more so if it could protect him like leather armor.

But... I don't even have one gold. How can I pay that much? Glenn thought in despair.

Diamanes sighed. ***Your armor is the last line of defense against death. You can never overspend on good steel. Well, good fabric, in this case. Even though I would recommend full plate.***

Glenn searched his dimensional pouch for alternative resources, hoping he could trade something expensive enough to pay Rusty. He found a medley of items—archaeology tools, the Howard family ring, a map, and a wanted poster—but nothing worth the cost of the suit.

Suddenly, his mental gaze froze on a small object he had completely forgotten. A pitch-black pearl sat in the dimensional storage, inspiring a strange sense of dread. It was the item that waited at the bottom of the life-force-sucking whirlwind in the Thorns Church prison.

Rusty's hopeful voice interrupted his contemplation. "You know, you can also pay with contribution points!"

Glenn hesitantly took the pearl out of his dimensional pouch, eyeing it with suspicion. He showed it to the shopkeeper, who inexplicably fell silent upon beholding the gem.

"Would... Would this be acceptable?" he asked with a sheepish grin.

The tiny man remained still, his expression devoid of emotion. He then retrieved a magnifying glass and a white crystal from the counter.

Rusty scrutinized the object from every angle before placing it beside the prism. Within seconds, the crystal assumed a deep, unnatural green hue—reminiscent of death. It unsettled Glenn as much as the pearl itself, prompting him to avert his gaze. Rusty, however, appeared unfazed, continuing to observe the item without uttering a word. After a brief pause, he returned the cursed relic to Glenn.

"Listen, honestly, this... this item is worth far more than a custom suit—no matter how expensive its material is. And I'm uncertain whether I can accept it or not."

Glenn knew the pearl was special, but he didn't know if it had monetary value. He mainly picked it up because he wanted to fuck over those cultist bastards.

"Why not? I doubt I have any use for it."

Rusty stroked his beard in silence, casting an apprehensive gaze upon the gem. "Because it's beyond my expertise to handle such relics... Tell you what, give me a moment."

Without awaiting Glenn's response, Rusty retreated to the back shop, closing the door behind him. Glenn found himself alone, bewildered, and contemplating the enigmatic pearl. He gave it a closer glance, wondering what could have shocked Rusty so much.

Glenn hadn't had the chance to examine the mysterious trinket previously, and now seemed as good a time as any. Staring into the abyss of the pearl's darkness, he noticed something stirring within.

Strangely, he felt that with a bit more effort, he could uncover whatever lay concealed within the ominous gloom. Something... something that would change his life forever.

The obscurity moved once more, slowly and insidiously—as though a sentient entity was trapped inside the gem, gradually awakening. The eerie sensation filled Glenn with dread, yet he continued to gaze intently. He just needed a little more... Just a bit more...

Alert! Your soul's on the run, Glenn! Diamanes' urgent voice snapped Glenn out of his fixation, but he couldn't bring himself to respond.

His attention remained fixed on the pearl, driven by an overwhelming compulsion to unveil its secrets. Losing his focus was not an option. *What if I missed something crucial? I need to look a bit more...*

Idiot! Idiot, idiot, idiot! The words echoed in Glenn's mind, a relentless cacophony that ultimately shattered his concentration.

Frustrated, Glenn retorted to Diamanes, *Shut up, you damned hand! I was this close to—*

To what? Diamanes interrupted, his voice seething with anger. *Whatever you were doing, it almost took your soul away!*

What?

Rusty suddenly reappeared, his face paling upon seeing Glenn's complexion. The young man's skin had taken on a gray color, dark circles had appeared under his tired eyes, and his cheeks had become slightly hollow. A lock in the middle of his hair had turned as white as chalk.

"Hey... You didn't look inside that thing, did you?" Rusty asked in disbelief as he instinctively took a step back and pressed something under the counter.

Glenn gulped. "What... What if I did?"

Rusty Stoneheart hid his face in his hands, rubbing it a few times before taking a stool to step at Glenn's height.

He grabbed the young man's shoulders and looked at him with pity. "Don't worry, you'll be fine. It's going to be a quick, painless death."

That's... not ominous at all? In what mess have I gotten myself into again?

Diamanes sighed. *You damned fool...*

Chapter 47

GAZING INTO THE ABYSS

"You think he is going to turn?"

Rusty's brows knitted with worry as he gazed at Glenn, who was seated in a dimly lit room with chains around his wrists. "He probably will. Everyone does. Who the hell is that kid anyway to get his hand on that shit?"

Kane, the experienced Cleaner by Rusty's side, shook his head. "No idea. I heard he kicked ass in the power test he took a few days ago to become a Fixer. He's a complete newbie that no one knows, and to top it off, is going around with a Black Heir."

Rusty sighed. "A Black Heir? At least that removes the possibility that it's a mole. Never would those bastards associate themselves with the Thorns Church."

"I guessed that much since he helped destroy that Corrupted One at the Auberge. How much time does he have left anyway?"

"Let me check."

He opened his pocket watch, which produced a mechanical sound.

"Around... five minutes?"

* * *

Glenn shifted uncomfortably on the wooden chair, surrounded by five imposing Cleaners—all dressed in their signature white clothes with a red cross emblazoned on them. They held weapons of various sizes and shapes:

short swords, a massive hammer, a flanged mace, and even a... book? The last Cleaner, with fists as large as Glenn's head, looked ready to use them at any time.

He was enclosed in a room completely made out of steel, with three men and two women—none of whom he could recognize—sweating and aiming their weapons at him. A small, mechanical eyeball floated beside him, probably maintained in the air with magic. It was the magical replacement of a camera, he supposed. He couldn't help but frown at it, wondering how it worked.

I kind of want to have one, Glenn thought, before scoffing wryly. *With the situation I'm in, there's no way they would give me something like that, right? It's surely worth a fortune anyway.*

Diamanes couldn't help but remark, **You are so lucky to have me. You should be so dead right now.**

Glenn responded, *Why the hell do you sound disappointed?*

Because you deserve it, you imbecile. Never heard of the saying, 'When you stare into the abyss, the abyss stares back'? Diamanes exclaimed in incredulity.

Huh, yeah, I have. After all, you found it in my memories.

Diamanes sighed. **So why did you look inside that pearl?**

Glenn paused, taking a second to consider the question. *I don't know. I just felt like... like I could find something of importance in there...*

Diamanes snorted before laughing mockingly. **Well, you were this close to learning what being dead feels like, so you're technically not wrong, hah!**

Glenn shifted his position once again, causing the anxious Cleaners around him to tense. He raised his chained hand in a peaceful gesture, looking more annoyed than distressed.

"Don't worry, my ass is just itchy."

He turned to the floating, mechanical eyeball with a scowl. "When the hell is this joke over, Mr. Stoneheart?"

The Cleaners remained silent, their attention divided between Glenn and the gadget that watched their captive closely.

"Damn it."

Glenn decided that if he had to wait forever, he would at least spend that forever on something useful. He sat in lotus position, going into Meditation, instantly feeling calmness.

* * *

Kane couldn't help but be astonished by what he saw. The projection of Glenn on the screen showed the telltale signs of the cursed item's influence. A white lock had appeared in the middle of Glenn's otherwise dark hair. His eyes now bore a mix of green and purple hues. And his skin had paled to a slightly gray tone.

Granted, he could only trust Rusty's description from before. If he ignored those changes, Glenn could have been considered handsome with his well-defined features and air of charisma. His tattered black coat and white shirt—stained with blood, brains, and bits of flesh—added a grim contrast to his otherwise appealing appearance.

His bandaged left arm was concerning, but it was probably another wound from the fight. Kane checked his watch again. The needle kept advancing, but Glenn didn't exhibit any signs of transformation. He slumped back in his chair, staring at the projection in disbelief.

Finally, he blurted out, "Where the hell did he even get a Seed of Darkness? They're not supposed to exist anymore!"

Rusty Stoneheart rubbed his ginger beard thoughtfully. "Again, I have no idea. Let's keep him there for another hour, just to be sure. Then we'll proceed to interrogate him. Try to be nice. Until now, he did nothing wrong. Alright, Kane?"

Kane sighed, saying neither yes nor no.

* * *

Another hour passed, which Glenn tried to spend entirely meditating, but the scent of his own body started to bother him. After all, he was still covered in dried blood, and he didn't want to think of the bits of brains or flesh that he might have missed.

He chuckled. *I probably look like a complete lunatic.*

Laugh all you want. Meanwhile, it is I who's bound to suffer from the smell... Diamanes grunted.

Glenn raised an inquisitive eyebrow. *Do you even have a nose?*

Diamanes snorted, not bothering to reply.

What do you think Sahro is doing? Glenn wondered.

Diamanes replied with a mocking tone, **He's probably enjoying his time not looking at things he shouldn't look at.**

Glenn sighed. All he wanted now was a bath and clean clothes. And a good night's sleep. Was that too much to ask? He tried pulling on the chains to scratch the top of his head, but they were too short to allow it.

A heavy door made out of alloy opened behind him, the creaking sound rattling his eardrums. The Cleaners turned hopeful faces towards the entry, sighing in relief when a figure signaled for them to get out. They hurried, throwing a last worried glance at Glenn.

Two men entered, standing right in front of Glenn. He recognized Rusty Stoneheart, of course, but the second one was not familiar. He was a tall man—over two meters—and wore white pants and a vest, both adorned with the classic red cross of the Cleaners. Likely, he was highly ranked, seeing the golden tint on his shoulder.

Uh, he doesn't have a tag, noticed Glenn.

The man in question had brought a stool with him and sat, crossing his fingers together in front of his face. Rusty Stoneheart stood beside him with a concerned expression.

"Glenn, is that right? I'm Kane, and I'm the Manager of the Northern Cleaner's Workshop."

Glenn nodded, carefully observing Kane. He had blond, straight hair with brown irises that showed more tiredness than annoyance. Slight black circles formed beneath his eyes, and wrinkles appeared on his forehead. He didn't have a beard, letting everyone enjoy his ass-shaped chin.

"My pleasure... I think?" Glenn looked dubiously at the duo. "Can I ask what's going on, or?"

Kane crossed his arms. "That object you gazed into... It's a Seed of Darkness."

Glenn blinked for a moment. "A Seed of Darkness? ...Sounds ominous, I suppose."

Kane's eyelids twitched, but he continued. "Right. They are the source of absolute calamity. Normally, after an hour or so, the one who peers into the Seed of Darkness becomes a Tree of Chaos."

"I would have transformed into... a tree? What?"

Rusty Stoneheart explained, "It's named like that because, after becoming a Tree, monsters start coming out of you—like a tree growing fruit. The *one who looks* becomes a monster spawner, a moving Rift with immense power."

Glenn paled, imagining his existence if Diamanes hadn't pulled him out of his trance.

Damn. Thanks, Diamanes.

It's about time you noticed, moron! spat the talking hand.

"So that's why you locked me in there with a bunch of Cleaners to... Well, clean me if I lost control?" he guessed, letting out a snicker.

"I can't believe I almost became..." He trailed off. Once again, the claws of death came closer and narrowly missed.

Kane leaned forwards, scrutinizing Glenn. "You're sure you don't want to kill anyone or start summoning monsters?"

Glenn shook his head and snorted. "I'm pretty sure I don't want to kill anyone I didn't want to kill before looking into that thing..."

He tried waving his hand dismissively, but the chains stopped him once again.

"Hmpf... Anyway, you already took it off my hands. I'm sure you'll know how to handle it better than me."

Glenn pulled on his restraints with annoyance, his memories of being chained in the prison overlapping with his current situation. A pearl of sweat beaded down his face.

"Now, can you get rid of this shit before I lose it? I got tortured in prison for God knows how long; I have a hard time with bondage."

Kane blinked. "I'll free you in an instant. I just have a few more questions. First..." He clasped his hands together and his expression hardened. "Where the hell did you get that Seed of Darkness?"

Glenn's face beamed with a wide grin. "Oh, that was in the Thorns Church prison. Yeah, I escaped that place a week ago or so." He paused and his eyes widened. "Wait, it's only been a week? Damn, it feels like it was ages ago."

Rusty sighed deeply as Kane clenched his fists. "I see. Taking care of this is above my pay grade. Right now, the priority is to send the Seed of Darkness into capable hands."

"Do you know that bringing such an item to us is an immense contribution? The Cleaner's Workshop owes you for that." Kane bowed his head gratefully.

Glenn's eyes went from Rusty to Kane before eventually settling on the door. "So... Can I leave now? I might go insane if I don't take a bath and get some new clothes soon."

Rusty chuckled nervously. "Please don't joke about that, Glenn. Insanity is way too common when cursed objects like these are involved."

Kane cleared his throat and unchained him. Glenn didn't waste a second and hurriedly stepped out, closely followed by Rusty Stoneheart. The little man turned towards Glenn, smiling under his beard.

"Listen, you'll be able to get your armor tomorrow at dawn. I'll make some expensive additions to it as well. Oh, and don't worry about the payment. You might not understand now, but later you'll probably realize how big the contribution you just made is."

Glenn hesitantly nodded, bidding his goodbye to the tiny man. He then returned to the Dormitory.

I'm in danger way more often than I should be. I'd say I have to be more careful, but—

Of course, you have to! Do you want to get yourself killed? Because if that's so, don't worry. I know 101 ways to get the job done, mocked Diamanes.

It's still cute to see you worry about my safety. Glenn's lips curved upwards as he climbed up the Dormitory's floors.

Diamanes groaned and fled in the comfort of his host's memories. Glenn eventually arrived at the Silver floor, and directly headed for the communal hot spring—one of the perks of being a Silver Fixer.

Steam clouded his vision as he unclothed and immersed himself in the purifying water. He sighed contentedly, savoring the warmth as he stood motionless for half an hour.

Ah... That is what living is... Enjoying a nice, mint-perfumed bath. Definitely not killing a flesh abomination.

Glenn paused and took another whiff of the fragrance. *Mint?*

Something suddenly brushed against him. When he turned his head, he discovered an incredibly attractive woman with long, raven-black hair and flawless fair skin. The mint scent wafted from her.

Magnificent, marine-blue eyes widened in shock when she noticed him. "Oh."

Well, those were details he only noticed afterwards, as he couldn't stop himself from staring at two huge—

Slap!

Chapter 48

AN EXILE BROTHER

Glenn rubbed the stinging handprint on his cheek. As hours passed, steam enveloped the dimly lit bathhouse, shrouding it in hazy obscurity as he lay in the warm water. A sigh escaped his lips, and he shook his head in incomprehension.

"Why did no one tell me these were shared baths?" he mumbled.

"Why would they bother separating males and females, though? That's boring," Diamanes mocked Glenn, enjoying the bath.

Glenn had taken the bandages covering his left hand off, trusting the steam to hide the annoying parasite.

Glenn's mind drifted back to the encounter with the woman, 'Minty', her presence as fleeting as always. Although the steam left a little to the imagination, he could tell she was exceptionally beautiful.

Not to mention her, um, 'consequential attributes'. He chuckled dejectedly.

He sighed as he floated in the water. The thought of a romantic adventure with a mysterious, hot woman had certainly crossed his mind, but it wasn't worth it. His main goal was still to find a way back to Earth. He couldn't afford to create that kind of relationship. *It'd be too cruel to lead her on.*

"**Falling in love and entangling one's fate with another will only invariably end up in tears and pain,**" Diamanes said in a sarcastically yet poetic tone. "**Time is much better invested trying to reach the Third Circle.**"

Glenn snorted and clenched his left hand shut.

"Right. And I'll never get to enjoy any privacy while there's a demon living in my hand." He drew a deep breath before sinking into the soothing bathwater, completely submerging his head to cleanse his hair thoroughly.

After another fifteen minutes of relaxation, he reluctantly emerged from the bath. His clothes, still tattered, were lying in a locker nearby.

Glenn grimaced and only dressed in his pants and boots. He looked at the blood-stained black coat and clicked his tongue.

"No way I'm putting this garbage on again." He decided as he brought the clothes to a trash can.

Can't I clean them with magic? Glenn thought as he suddenly paused.

"Wait." Glenn blinked. "Why don't I try that? Maybe I can fix the coat."

He tossed it onto a nearby table. Other Fixers came and went, paying little attention to his activities. With a glance, he confirmed Diamanes was well hidden under the bandages, away from prying eyes. Glenn put his hair back in place, looking at the coat with a puzzled expression.

"How the hell am I supposed to do that, though?" he muttered.

Mana was a tool that made the impossible possible. Could he just... ask the Mana to clean the clothes? How? He couldn't talk to Mana. It wasn't a living being, after all.

Or was it? Glenn shook off those thoughts. He wasn't ready to think about such perplexing, philosophical subjects.

He envisioned the spell, as Redan taught him. The first step would be to identify and separate what was considered filth and what wasn't. The second would be to make those impurities disappear.

It was harder than he expected. Creating a spell from an understandable concept was pretty easy—like his Magic Bullet or Arcane Auger. He just had to imagine each of those and manipulate the Mana accordingly. But if he willed Mana to *clean* the clothes, he had a feeling that it would work a little too well—and the garments would disappear completely.

After receiving one too many weird stares, he decided to pack up the coat and head into his dorm. Walking with only pants and boots on felt strange, but he didn't care anymore.

"And it's not like I'm ugly." Glenn chuckled as he glanced down at his chiseled abs.

Pervert, Diamanes chimed in with a disdainful tone.

Glenn ignored the entity as he entered his room and laid the damaged clothes on the floor. Those garments held sentimental value, being the first to make him feel like an actual human instead of a… Well, walking corpse. He did steal them from a dead guy, technically, but he didn't rip them directly from his bones.

May Jefferson Howard rest in peace. Glenn slapped his cheeks and concentrated back on the subject at hand.

"Whatever, I'll just take it as improving my understanding and control of Mana," he mumbled as he gave up worrying that the clothes wouldn't survive.

He deliberated the details of this new spell for nearly an hour; his room became his makeshift laboratory. Each element had to be considered carefully to avoid destructive mishaps, even though he was almost certain it wouldn't work.

Finally, with his theory in place, Glenn decided it was time to put it into practice. He looked down at the blood-stained black trench coat and gathered his focus. He conjured the spell, vividly picturing each step in his mind and directing the Mana to obey his will. At first, it seemed to work perfectly. A shadowy cloud enveloped the fabric, consuming the bloodstains and filth.

However, the moment the final impurities vanished, the coat dissolved—devoured by Mana. Not even a strand of fiber or a hint of ashes was left. The jacket was *magically* gone without a trace.

Glenn rubbed his temples, grappling with a growing headache.

"That's a little disappointing," he sighed in frustration. "Where the hell did it go? Can magic reduce atoms to nothingness?"

Questions... So many questions. Hey, at least you could get rid of bodies or the like with that spell! Diamanes cackled. Glenn shrugged him off, doubting he'd ever want to use that sort of magic.

Crafting a functional cleaning spell was proving to be more challenging than he had anticipated. He cast one last despondent glance at the spot his coat was previously before heaving another sigh of disappointment.

You know, I did notice a few Fixers going around shirtless. Even though you don't have the same massive muscles as they did, it should still be fine, right?

"I don't think I have a choice anyway..."

Glenn steeled himself and stood. He wanted to check out the Library, and he had the afternoon free to do so. After all, he wasn't going to take a contract while looking like a barbarian. He chose to use the opportunity to fill in his knowledge blanks.

Yeah, reading some more about spell crafting would be nice. And I guess it couldn't hurt for some leads to unlock my Third Circle. Just so you shut up about it, Diamanes.

You can lead a dumb horse to water, but you can't make him drink. Diamanes laughed mockingly.

Ignoring the insult, Glenn left his room only to find himself face to face with his neighbor. She wore a white hooded robe that concealed her figure. The hood fell low over her deep, marine blue eyes and raven-black hair.

No, this can't be a coincidence anymore. Glenn almost blurted out loud, incredulously.

Oh, oh. Maybe fate pulled you together—seeing how often you cross paths with your usually-mint-scented friend, Diamanes quipped.

The woman stared at Glenn defiantly, and he returned her stare with the same intensity. An awkward silence hung between them for a few seconds before Minty wordlessly retreated into her dorm, locking the door behind her.

Puzzled, Glenn lingered for a moment before continuing onwards. *Talk about weird...*

Diamanes snickered, offering no further commentary.

After walking for a few minutes, he arrived in front of the Library. He entered with assured steps, trying not to show how out of place he felt. He approached the counter, where a seemingly bored man was playing with a pen.

"Excuse me, where can I find the history section?" Glenn asked politely.

The librarian pointed in a rather lackluster manner, sparing no energy on additional words. Glenn nodded before proceeding to the indicated section. The word 'History' was prominently displayed on the bookshelf, housing an extensive collection.

The shelf towered at least five meters high, highlighting the Library's extravagant scale. Glenn gazed upwards, noticing a skylight in the glass ceiling, which bathed the area in natural light.

Shaking his head in disbelief at the opulence of the Cleaner's Workshop, Glenn sifted through the shelves in search of a compelling title. Something peculiar soon caught his attention—a majority of the books were written by someone named Exan. Intrigued, he selected a few of the author's works.

Among them were *Munirp and its Legends*, *Magiconomicon: 7th Edition*, and *The Bestiary*. Those hefty tomes promised to fill the gaps in his knowledge. Choosing an unoccupied desk, Glenn made himself comfortable—opting to begin with *Munirp and its Legends*, as it was the shortest one comparatively.

Glenn flipped through the pages lazily, unable to concentrate on the text. He had never been much for history, be it on Earth or in this world. Legends were a bit more interesting, but they weren't his main focus.

Thankfully, an old man in the corner of the Library was doing a lesson for a bunch of muscular warriors about a certain First King.

"The Founder of King's Rise, Builder of the Four Gates, and First User of the Fallen Pieces reigned for a thousand years... That is who you all have to thank for the existence of this city, and for your peaceful life today!" stated the old man with a clap, waking up half the warriors from their naps.

Glenn shook his head and snorted. *The First King ruled for a thousand years? What the hell is that nonsensical lifespan? And what are all those titles?*

It's honestly a bit disappointing. You'd think that a guy living for a thousand years would have the time to conquer the entire planet, but it seemed like he calmed himself after uniting Munirp. Diamanes clicked his tongue judgmentally.

Glenn's eyes widened in indignation. *That's already quite the feat, honestly!*

Why are you getting angry? It's not even your king?

I don't know, I just feel like he's worth respect. Glenn shrugged.

Tsk, tsk. That's probably not the full story. No matter how well-written history is, the pen is always held by the victor.

"Now, now, listen to the tale of Comte Noir and the War of Four Fronts!" The old man cleared his throat and launched into another lecture.

Glenn listened without a word, familiarizing himself with this world's mythos. He would rather have that instead of reading a few kilograms worth of legends. Not that he wouldn't like doing so, but more because time was of the essence.

Once the old man was eventually done with his lesson, Glenn opened *Magiconomicon: 7th Edition.*

Thankfully, Diamanes kept silent, letting his host read in peace. Myths were nice, but practical knowledge about magic was much better.

"Alright..." Glenn stretched as he closed the book. He had identified a few key points. He was about to pick another tome when suddenly one of the muscular guys sat in front of him, flexing his pectorals.

Great, more bare-chested perverts... Diamanes sighed.

"Can I help you?" Glenn raised an eyebrow at the tough-looking man.

The latter's gaze went from Glenn to the volume he was holding, the Magiconomicon. Finally, he joined his hands together and bowed.

"Brother. Can you tell me what's in that book? I can't read, and I'm supposed to learn its contents."

Glenn blinked. "How did you recognize it then?"

The warrior stared back proudly. "I remember the drawing on the cover, haha!"

I don't even know what to say. Glenn chuckled. "Sure, why not?"

"First, Mana isn't of the same density everywhere. High-density zones have lots of Rifts and are easier to practice magic in, like King's Rise. Low-density zones are filled with natural beasts belonging to the area's ecosystem."

Funnily enough, they mentioned the Ink Dunes as an example.

Glenn rubbed his chin. *Maybe it's because of the density of Mana in the Ink Dunes that Sahro is incredibly focused on Aura, even though he should have access to Mana too from what I understand.*

Skip, skip. Let's be done with these explanations already! exclaimed Diamanes, bored out of his mind.

Glenn cleared his throat and continued educating his surprise student.

"The second point... Mages are separated into nine ranks depending on their number of Circles. One Circle makes you a Beginner Initiate, two an Advanced Initiate, and three a True Initiate. After that, it's Magi, Expert Magi, and Archmagi."

"Above that is the domain of Rulers. The Seventh Circle is a Newborn Ruler, the Eighth Circle a True Ruler, and the Ninth Circle an Ancient Ruler."

Glenn had even found an excellent quote from Exan to describe the difference between each realm of power.

A True Initiate can replace an entire squadron of bowmen. An Archmagi can destroy a city. And an Ancient Ruler should be able to destroy a continent, even though I never saw such power myself.

"The evaluation of Aura ranks is done with a similar system—separated into nine ranks: Novice, Squire, Knight, Grand Chevalier, Crusader, and Saint. Then it's the same for the Ruler stage. Exan didn't explain how to use it, though, because he was only a Mage, after all."

The burly warrior nodded frantically, drinking Glenn's words.

"As for the matter of breaking through to the Third Circle and beyond, Exan only gave a hint."

It will happen, or it will not.

So fucking helpful... Glenn thought to himself dejectedly.

"There are also different schools of magic. Most Mages practice the School of Words. A few words in Ancient Tongue, a sufficient amount of Mana, and *ta-da*, your spell is ready. There is also the School of Runes, which is practiced by those aspiring to create magic equipment and artifacts."

As Exan noted:

Everyone is laughing at those guys until they bring out big-ass magic rifles and cannons.

"Of course, that damned old fogey didn't teach me any of those," Glenn muttered, slightly pissed off. The warrior shrugged dismissively.

"There is one last 'common' school—the one my master taught me— called the Draconic School. It is an immensely complicated path, named that way because it was originally intended for use by *actual dragons.*"

Dragons! The thought baffled Glenn. *Did the old man indulge in a few too many magic mushrooms?*

"Dragons!" gasped the warrior, his fists clenching the edge of the table tightly. "That's prey worthy of me!"

Glenn blinked at the excited man and chose to ignore him.

"The Draconic School traces its origins back to Sevirox, a dragon who personally instructed his sole human friend, the First King. He was an incredibly important component of the First King's strength, and perhaps the only reason he managed to unite Munirp."

Oddly, history remembers the dragon's name and not the king's. Oh well, remarked Diamanes casually.

"The Draconic School grants the unique ability to use one's Mana Heart's specialty to create incredibly powerful spells. But there are a few stipulations. Students can *only* use their specialty and are forced to rely on the School of Words to cast spells with different affinities. Additionally, it also has the drawback of requiring immense Mana capacity, intellectual capability on par with a dragon, and extensive, madman-level training"

"That sounds too difficult." The Muscle-man frowned. "Aura is much simpler! Just cut through the enemies! Haha!"

It was undoubtedly a potent method since users of the Draconic School could face other Mages of higher rank—usually an unthinkable feat, from what Glenn gathered. To quote Exan:

It's the path for geniuses and insane bastards.

Glenn sighed. *Too bad I'm no genius or madman.*

Are you sure about what you're saying? Diamanes inquired.

Glenn managed a wry smile. *Yes, I'm pretty sure I'm not a genius, Diamanes. But thanks for the compliment nonetheless.*

No, I meant you're sure you're not actually insane.

The young man's smile disappeared, and he cleared his throat.

"There we go. That's everything I learned from that book. Want to try reading it?" Glenn held the Magiconomicon in the warrior's direction. The latter gazed at the book with terror and hurriedly shook his head.

"No, no. Thank you, brother, but I refuse to touch this item of torture. Thank you for the lesson!" The warrior suddenly stood and exited the Library, flexing his muscles on the way.

Curious character, remarked Diamanes.

I couldn't agree more.

Glenn chuckled and flipped through *The Bestiary*, making a note of all the more dangerous creatures, only to stop at the very last page. His jaw dropped. There, written in bold, black ink, was a phrase in a familiar language.

English.

Not the Common Tongue of this world, but genuine English.

Wait, what? You're not the only Fallen One? What a surprise, Diamanes mocked Glenn's astonishment.

It has been exactly fifty years since I found myself stranded in this world. I've tried everything. I've forgotten most of the English and need my journals to help write this damned language. Common Tongue is so much simpler now... I thought I was stronger and more special than the rest and that I could do everything I wanted. A young man's dream of some sort...

Glenn's eyes trembled with bewilderment as he continued reading, his face paling with each word. "No..."

Written with a trembling, tired hand, that line was the nail in the coffin.

There's no hope. I can't go back. No one can.

Glenn gritted his teeth and hurriedly opened the previous books he read to their very last pages, finding other messages in English.

"What the fuck do you mean, Exan? What does it mean that *no one can go back*?" he hissed.

The *Magiconomicon: 7th Edition* message was a little longer.

Well, it's been forty-five years now. I wonder if writing all this bullshit serves a purpose. Hah! Those stupid nobles think I've hidden some kind of treasure in these texts since I'm putting one at the end of each book. But no, it's just my place to vent, haha. I think I'm going mad. But! There is still hope. I can still try to access Earth. I'm way stronger now. I'll keep you updated, dear readers.

The line ceased abruptly. Glenn rubbed his eyes, struggling to comprehend the revelation. There was another person like him in this world—well, at least there had been. Glenn did not know the book's age or whether Exan was still alive. Regardless, he couldn't help but hope for the latter.

He turned his attention to the third book, *Munirp and its Legends*. Once again, a few lines in English graced the last page.

Well, what's to say? Sixty years. I also celebrated my 75th birthday three months ago. I never thought things would go so fast. Luna helped a lot. The fact that I gave up that time also helped. This was only a fool's enterprise. Anyway, I'm happy now. I have a life. Everything is well.

Glenn closed the book, leaning back in his chair as he swallowed audibly.

"That guy..." he muttered as he buried his face in his hands. "That guy spent sixty years in this world, and still couldn't find a way back? Shit..."

What am I supposed to do now?

Chapter 49

EXPLORING THE MYSTERIES OF EXAN

Glenn leaned his head against the chair's backrest. He looked at the light passing through the glass ceiling with a blank expression, feeling as if his strength had left him. People walked past him, throwing judgmental stares as he groaned.

He covered his eyes with his hand. Exan seemed to be sure that escaping this world was impossible, and he had more than sixty years to try.

So you're going to give up just because you read some shit that this guy might have made up? Diamanes tried to rile him, to no avail.

It was as if Glenn was empty of everything—motivation and soul alike.

You can still check out that guy's other entries. Get some information, at least, Diamanes recommended.

Glenn nodded slowly, his determination returning at an equally slow pace.

"This... this is disheartening," Glenn admitted.

He didn't move for another minute before clenching his teeth and straightening himself up.

"No use in losing all hope," he mumbled. "I might as well try to prove Exan wrong."

He stood and went back to the history section, searching for more books written by the fellow interplanetary expat, but sadly, most were copies of the ones he already read.

He only found one book that he hadn't checked out called *Studies of Munirp's Population: 4th Edition*. Standing in front of the bookshelf, he opened it, reading the few usual lines of English.

Today is a grand day. I married Luna! Well, I originally planned to make a harem as any reincarnation protagonist worth this salt should do. But no woman in this cursed land comes to my Luna. It's been twenty years that I've been living in Munirp, and still, no fellow countryman of mine has come to visit. I am not starting to despair, but I might begin to have doubts. Please, if you read this, you have to give me a sign that you exist, alright?

Glenn turned the page and confirmed that there was no other special text.

"And how do I do that, dear Exan?" He said as he closed the book and brought it back to the table.

Diamanes snorted. ***Oh, I have an idea. What about... visiting him, or sending a letter? He can become your new pen pal.***

Glenn scoffed, looking at his bandaged hand with indignation.

Alright big brain, mind telling me his address so I can do that?

Diamanes remained silent, as Glenn had expected.

Now stop taking me for an idiot and start giving me some good ideas.

He shook his head while turning the pages. Suddenly, his eyes froze, reading a line embroidered on the back cover.

A malicious voice resounded in his mind, ***Well, well, well. 'Royal Library's director, Exan'. Ask, and you shall receive. Don't you think that might be the address you wanted, my dear moron?***

Glenn pushed through his embarrassment and ignored the entity, instead choosing to concentrate on reading Exan's books.

Shame on you... Shame on you... Diamanes' voice echoed in his mind.

Glenn hid his face in his hands, sighing heavily. After exhaling his distress and recovering his bearings, he concentrated once again.

Once he was done with each book, he knew he had to send a message written in English to the Royal Library to contact Exan.

If there even is a way to send mail up there. I can't even get into the Bourgeoisie! Still. Maybe it's a shot in the dark, but it has a tiny chance of working. If I could get the help of a fellow... What do I call someone in my situation? An Earthling? Yeah, I could receive the help of a fellow Earthling, which is nothing to sneeze at.

When he finally raised his eyes from the books, Glenn noticed that the Library was bathed in the dim light of the setting sun. He had spent the whole afternoon immersed in his studies, trying to understand magic better. He stretched on his chair, letting out a tired moan.

Today had been especially tiring. Reading was surprisingly more mentally draining than he remembered. Perhaps it was because he was focusing on academic lessons instead of the fantasy novels he was used to back on Earth.

He stood, returning the books to their original places on the shelves. Glenn paused as he looked at his wrist, a habit from his old life. However, he still had no watch.

I wonder if watches exist in this world. And if so, where can I find one... Glenn pondered, his curiosity undiminished. With that thought in mind, he exited the Library. There were still a few people reading, but much fewer than when he initially entered.

"Let's try sending a letter to that Exan guy first... The Cleaner's Workshop should know how to handle that, right?" Glenn muttered before leaving for the Main Hall.

The weird, probably-robotic female employees were there, serving Fixers and customers alike with their machine-like smiles.

Glenn's turn eventually arrived, and he was welcomed by Alisson's bright smile.

"Sir Glenn, how can I help you? Do you wish to accept another contract?"

Glenn shook his head and pushed forwards a letter he hurriedly scribbled in English during the wait. "No, nothing like that. I'd like to know if the Workshop can send a letter to the Royal Library?"

Alisson stared at him for a moment, unblinking. Glenn stared back awkwardly, unsure of how to react.

"I apologize, Sir Glenn, but I'm almost certain that any Royal institutions are situated in the upper region of King's Rise." Alisson bowed her head apologetically. "Communication between each stratum is practically impossible due to strict regulations."

"Is that so? Alright..."

Alisson made an apologetic expression. "Can I help you with anything else?"

"No, no. It's fine..." sighed Glenn.

Of course it couldn't be so simple as sending a damn letter. Why do they even regulate the information between social classes? Fuck...

Haha, the day luck is on your side is nowhere near! laughed Diamanes.

Glenn walked away in the Dormitory's direction, crestfallen. He intended to check if Sahro was there.

Who knows what that idiot has been doing after being left alone for a whole afternoon?

Entering the building, he bumped into someone, a sense of déjà vu washing over him. He turned to face a robed figure. An awkward few seconds passed before Glenn pointed his finger at them.

"You..."

A blur appeared before his eyes, the tip of a dagger dangerously close to his throat. Glenn didn't even dare to swallow, fearing the sharp blade.

The scent of mint touched Glenn's nostrils as Minty removed her hood and revealed deep, marine blue eyes. He struggled to keep his gaze averted from her alluring figure, an internal battle raging within him.

Damn, you really are a pervert, commented Diamanes.

No, I don't want to look, alright!

Glenn raised his hands in the air as a sign of peace. He used the occasion to study the face of the mysterious lady. She had pristine, white skin with no defects, and a straight, symmetrical nose. Her luscious lips were red, and she clenched her white teeth.

Minty glanced around with a suspicious gaze before muttering something between those pearly whites.

"Who sent you?"

Glenn's eyes widened, realizing that it was the second time such a situation had occurred. First, Redan, and now this beautiful stranger. *Do I have the looks of a spy or something?*

He slowly pushed the knife away from his throat. "No, who sent *you*?"

Minty froze for a moment, confused. "What? What do you mean?"

Glenn dusted off his shoulders and shrugged. "Do you think you're the only one who can act mysteriously?"

The woman blinked, unable to respond before she sheathed her dagger and turned away. Glenn frowned and grabbed her shoulder.

"Are you maybe following me?" he asked, before shaking his head dejectedly. "Sorry, but I'm not interested in these kinds of relationships. And seriously, stalkers are creepy."

Minty pinched Glenn's hand as if it were a piece of trash.

"Disgusting. Leave me alone." She reeled back as Glenn's lips curved upwards.

He stepped past her and headed upstairs, satisfied.

"That look of confusion was…" He grinned widely. "Perfect. She seemed completely lost. I almost laughed out loud in her face."

Diamanes sighed, not bothering to comment.

On the way to the Silver floor, Glenn passed Bronze. He threw a curious glance inside. Those were shared rooms, with dozens of beds crammed together that offered no privacy whatsoever.

Glenn was grateful he had achieved Silver rank right away, sparing him the grind.

He eventually arrived in front of Sahro's room and knocked three times. He waited for a response, but there was none. Concerned, he knocked once again.

The door suddenly opened, revealing the Black Heir's distressed face. He was only wearing pants—showing off his dark skin and perfect muscles. Glenn couldn't help but notice the fear in Sahro's eyes as he looked over his shoulder in fright.

"Glenn. Glenn, help me!" Sahro muttered, freezing when he heard a giggle from behind.

Glenn chuckled and patted his friend on the back. "What's going on? You're also rocking the topless style?"

The Black Heir hurriedly ran behind Glenn, hiding from whatever monster lurked inside his dorm.

Glenn offered him a thumbs-up and a wide smile. "Sorry, I don't want to bother you. I'll leave you to it!"

He laughed as he went for the door to his room, only for Sahro to hold him back with a dark expression. Tears welled in the Black Heir's eyes.

"You have to get me out of here, Glenn. Please!"

Glenn let out a bewildered laugh. He opened the door and allowed Sahro refuge, casting one last glance at the Black Heir's dorm before shaking his head.

"Well, well, well. It seems like the grand Sahro finally met his match. Haha!"

Sahro held his head in his hands. He turned towards his companion, fear in his eyes.

"What is wrong with those human women? I felt…" He shivered. "I felt like prey under the claws of a powerful predator!"

Glenn threw his head back, laughing loudly. *Well, that felt good.*

"I'm glad you're enjoying life, Sahro. Haha!"

Chapter 50

THE FIRST LEAD

Glenn wiped his tears of laughter, his eyes fixed on his dejected comrade. Sahro's sullen expression made it impossible for him to contain his amusement.

"Well, who warned me about all the racism in King's Rise?" Glenn quipped, a mischievous glint in his eye.

Sahro shot him a glare but remained silent. Seeing Sahro's dark mood, Glenn clapped his hands, redirecting his comrade's gaze.

"So, how did this happen?"

Sahro rubbed his neck, recounting the day's events.

"Well, since you left me to fend for myself, I decided to take on another contract. We need money, so I figured taking on as many jobs as possible would be the fastest way to get it."

Glenn nodded in agreement, seeing the logic in Sahro's decision.

"So, I picked one from the Silver rank that paid the most. Everything seemed normal at first. I had to eliminate a Rift in a sewing workshop."

"I went there, after enduring the creepy attendant to grab my contract, of course. The shop wasn't far from Central Street, so it only took me five minutes to arrive."

Sahro paused, his hands fidgeting nervously before he continued. "As soon as I stepped into the shop, I could sense something was off. The human women inside kept eyeing me like I was a piece of meat—as if they wanted to eat me alive…"

Glenn's eyebrows shot up in incomprehension. "Didn't you receive similar stares back at the Black Heir's camp?"

Sahro froze, his eyes wavering slightly. Slowly, he shook his head, his voice filled with dejection. "I… I was always an outsider there. Only Giselle and Redan talked to me. The others looked at me as if I were a disgrace to their existence."

Glenn's smile vanished, replaced by a solemn expression.

"Probably because you're mixed-race, huh?" remarked Diamanes.

Both Glenn and Sahro froze, their attention drawn to the cocky entity in Glenn's left hand, its bandages loosening to reveal a red tongue.

"What?" Diamanes chuckled mockingly. **"You know of my existence now. No need for me to hide when you're around, Sahro, the half Black Heir and half *human*."**

Sahro's face darkened, and he reached for his sword, only to find it missing.

Glenn waved his hands in front of Sahro defensively. "Don't get angry at him; it's useless."

Sahro stood, cracking his knuckles, his face contorted with anger. "Well, maybe he'll change his mind if I rough him up a little."

Glenn's face paled. "Uhh, no? It's still my hand, so, no? Please?"

Sahro cast one last menacing look at the mischievous hand before returning to the bed, exhaling deeply as he continued his story.

"Where was I? Right, so, under the predatory gaze of the women in the shop, I ventured into their atelier. It was filled with mannequins, and it sent shivers down my spine. I spotted the Rift as soon as I walked in."

He glanced fearfully at the wall that separated them from the faint echoes of giggles in his room.

"It was a smaller Rift, maybe the size of my head. I thought I couldn't locate the enemies. That's when the mannequins attacked."

Glenn grimaced in response. "Ugh, creepy."

Sahro nodded in agreement, and even Diamanes chimed in, "**Yeah, for real.**"

Glenn shot a glance at the entity, hesitating for a moment before tightening the bandages to muffle it.

Sahro continued with his tale.

"So, after I decapitated the dummies, it became clear that a weird creature with tentacles controlled their wooden bodies. But I finally managed to get the job done. The problem was, my clothes were in tatters after the fight. It was inevitable. I was outnumbered and without support. I had to take some hits. After sealing the Rift, the women practically pounced on me."

Sahro shivered, wrapping his arms around himself.

"They started saying the strangest things and forced me to try on clothes for them. I had no choice; they wouldn't sign the contract otherwise. They even followed me to the Dormitory and pulled me into my room. That's when you arrived and saved me."

Glenn nodded, his smile returning as he placed a supportive hand on Sahro's shoulder.

"Sahro, welcome to the world of being *hot*."

The Black Heir furrowed his brow and touched his forehead.

"I don't think I am, though." He paused and his expression darkened. "Do you think I've been cursed with a fire spell or something?"

Glenn stood there, dumbfounded, rolling his eyes before letting out a sigh.

"Did they explain why they were so fixated on... 'eating' you?"

Sahro frowned and then paled as realization dawned on him.

"Don't tell me... humans eat Black Heirs?"

Glenn facepalmed, exasperated. "It's a metaphor... Just forget about it."

Sahro rubbed his chin, a fearful expression on his face. "That's why they were trying to bite me..."

Glenn stared at Diamanes, exchanging mental incredulous glances.

"**What the fu—**" Diamanes began before Sahro cut him off.

"They did say something interesting. They mentioned that it was only the second time a Black Heir visited their shop, even though the first came with a noble," he said while rubbing his chin.

Glenn paused, the gears in his mind slowly clicking together.

"Wait, the second one? There was *another* Black Heir at that workshop? Who came with a noble?"

"Yeah? Those clothes didn't look cheap whatsoever, so I don't know—"

Glenn gasped and hurriedly stood up from his bed. "Holy shit."

He dashed out of his room, stopping on the doorstep. He turned back and grinned widely at Sahro's incomprehension.

"Sahro, that Black Heir you're speaking of... What are the chances that he's Callum, Giselle's grandson?"

The Black Heir gasped. Glenn ran inside Sahro's room without knocking. He stumbled upon two young, attractive women—both practically naked and lying on Sahro's bed. He froze for a second, looked down at his bare chest, and coughed.

One woman had a heart-shaped face with blue eyes, fair skin, and a warm smile. And the other had a more angular visage, with similar bright eyes, tanned skin, and a confident demeanor.

They both had blond hair—one curly while the other straight. They weren't at the level of the mysterious Minty but still quite beautiful nonetheless.

He coughed. "'kay, sorry girls, but Sahro isn't coming back. So I'd advise you both to get your clothes on."

The curly-haired woman jumped out of the bed and walked up to him. She passed her finger on his back, the feeling sending a shiver down his spine.

Well, well, well. Look at that. He left Sahro to enjoy the two hungry ladies to himself! Diamanes laughed wickedly, killing any desire that had tried to flare up.

"Hmm... It's too bad about Sahro, but I'm sure we'd both be satisfied with you..." the woman whispered.

Glenn stepped out of her reach. "Once again, sorry. Maybe another day, alright?"

The woman pouted, her friend already dressing up. Glenn turned and waited patiently with his arms crossed, wondering what would have happened if Diamanes wasn't here to *ruin his life*.

Oh, come on. Don't tell me you're against someone watching you during the act!

Glenn clenched his teeth and somehow managed to shut the voice up.

"You can turn, it's fine," the woman said with a disappointed tone.

Glenn sighed. "You see, my friend Sahro isn't exactly used to so much... proximity. So I fear he might have gotten a bit scared. Don't worry, you're both very attractive."

His words made a red tint appear on the girls' cheeks.

"Anyway, I have some questions for you, if you don't mind?"

The girls nodded, giggling.

"You said that my friend was the second Black Heir you met? Could you tell me more about the first one?"

They looked at each other before answering.

"Well, the first one was with Sir Howard. He comes occasionally with his soldiers and servants."

The curly-haired girl fiddled with her hands, a weird smile on her face. "They come for the Harvest. The Baron wouldn't visit the Fringe if it wasn't for that."

The straight-haired girl whispered into Glenn's ear. "No one likes him. No one likes nobles in general. But that guy is particularly disgusting."

Glenn stepped back as his suspicions were confirmed. It wasn't as hard as he thought to find Baron Howard. He was surprised that the noble had kept the Black Heir for so long though. He was half-expecting to find Callum's dead body lying in a trench. The real question now was: how in hell were they going to free Callum?

His thoughts were interrupted by the women closing in on him, a hungry look in their eyes. Gulping, he swiftly left the dorm, leaving the girls giggling as he returned to his room.

He locked the door behind him and sighed in relief; he was free from those ravenous beasts. Sahro was sitting on his bed, looking at him inquisitively, yet unsurprised.

Glenn took a deep breath. He grinned widely.

"I was right. I found Callum and Baron Howard."

Chapter 51

PLANNING THE PLAN

Glenn and Sahro settled onto the cold, hard ground of Glenn's room—their eyes locked in a silent exchange. In front of them, the Howard Family ring lay, its golden glint almost mocking their predicament.

"So, what's the plan?" Sahro asked, his eyebrows furrowed and his arms crossed.

Glenn's gaze shifted from Sahro to the ring, lost in thought. Finding Callum so soon felt surreal. They had no actual confirmation whether that Black Heir under the Baron's command was indeed Callum, though. Perhaps it was another Black Heir that had been captured and sold to Howard.

Glenn rubbed his chin. "First, we need information. Send word to the Black Heirs that we found a trail. I'm sure Giselle would be overjoyed to hear that we already have some news."

Sahro nodded slowly. "The message will take a week to arrive, but I suppose it doesn't matter?"

Glenn pointed at the ring. "No, it's just to keep Giselle up to date. We won't need their support since I have this."

"Will that ring be enough to trade for Callum's life?"

Glenn chuckled and patted his dimensional pouch. "I got it off the Baron's son, Jefferson Howard. I also have his diary. I think it shouldn't be too complicated to agree to a simple exchange."

Sahro's expression hardened. "What if he asks to see his son? What will you tell him?"

Glenn sighed. "I'll improvise. We're not strong enough to attack a Baron and survive. And I don't know about you, but I'm not a stealth expert, so we can forget about infiltrating wherever he lives and extracting Callum." He paused. "Negotiation seems like our best shot at getting Callum back."

The Black Heir grunted, "And you're sure this servant is Giselle's grandson?"

Glenn shook his head. "Not entirely, but I'd say at least ninety-five percent. We just need to wait for the Harvest, whatever that is."

I bet my thumb it's just a dumb name for tax day, cackled Diamanes.

Or what about that trial out in the Golden Fields—the one with all of those creepy scarecrows? I could ask that farmer, Carys.

He glanced at the window and watched as the sun settled down, leaving space for the twin moons.

Glenn stood and dusted off his pants. "Tomorrow, you'll gather information on what the public thinks of Baron Howard. Get a sense of his reputation, when he was last here, what he likes to do when he comes to the Northern Town—things like that. Collect as much gossip as you can while doing contracts. We still need funds."

"And what about you?"

Glenn grinned, his smile strangely similar to Diamanes'. "I'm going to find out whether it's really Callum or not. And get new clothes. Do you want me to pass along an order for you?"

Sahro looked down, still topless, and shook his head.

"Don't worry. My clothes are a bit special. Even if they're tattered today, they'll be fine tomorrow."

Glenn shrugged. "Your choice, your loss." A rumble escaped his gut, forcing a grimace out of him. "How about we grab a bite to eat first?"

Sahro laughed until his stomach grumbled too. He shot a thumbs-up.

* * *

Glenn looked at the 'Closed' sign in front of him. The last time he came to the Armory, he almost lost his soul. Thanks to his own recklessness, yes, but still.

He entered, Rusty nowhere in sight. He had no idea of how the matter with the Seed of Darkness ended up, but hopefully, it was positive for him and negative for the Thorns Church. The more organizations he rallied to his side to fight those sick cultists, the better.

Unless... Glenn's heart skipped a beat as he thought of a terrible possibility. *They wouldn't be colluding with the Thorns Church, would they?*

The Cleaner's Workshop does practice a suspicious kind of magic, commented Diamanes.

You are not reassuring me, replied Glenn with a hint of annoyance.

Good, because that wasn't my aim at all.

The stone chest that contained the Night Silk sat alongside the wall, a strange light shining from it. Curious, Glenn approached the container. A single white particle flew from it, floating strangely in the air before landing on Glenn. The coffer suddenly unlocked itself and opened, revealing its contents.

A small piece of paper rested on top of a pile of classy-looking, folded clothes, reading, "*You can change in the back. I also included some gloves since I saw you bandaging your hand.*"

Excited like a child receiving a Christmas present, he picked up the stone chest—barely struggling—and took it to the storeroom. He ignored the weird contraptions in there and quickly changed.

A full-length bronze mirror stood conveniently in one corner. Glenn gasped as he stared at his appearance. He had changed quite a lot, and he dared to say that he was damned handsome. *If I was already attractive before, now I have heaven-defying looks!*

Just listen to him... Diamanes sighed, desperate.

Glenn ignored him and straightened his clothes, smiling from ear to ear. He wore a black, elegant waistcoat paired with a crisp, white shirt and a black tie. He rolled up his sleeves, giving off a relaxed vibe. A leather belt with a steel buckle cinched his black trousers.

His hair had transformed from its original chestnut shade into a deep black, save for a single strand that had turned pristine white. His eyes, now predominantly blue, featured a subtle purple tint in his left eye and green in the right.

"Can't I just cut that strand of white hair off?" Glenn mumbled as he held the intruder in his perfectly black hair. *Even that mint-scented psychopath lady would be jealous of my hair now.*

Don't worry too much. It's just a side effect of almost losing your soul. It should go away in a few weeks, Diamanes said casually.

To complete his ensemble, he donned black leather gloves, concealing most of the purple skin on his left hand.

Glenn still didn't have any hair growing on his chin or under his nose, but he was fine with that. His face was handsome enough without a beard.

"When the hell will you stop admiring yourself and start doing something interesting? I'm not even hoping for excitement. Just something interesting, please," Diamanes begged.

Glenn clapped his hands, grinning widely. "Well, about that. I've got the perfect place to show off— Er... Try out my new clothes!"

"I heard the 'show off' part, you know?"

"I'm sure you heard wrong. Let's get going!"

* * *

Half an hour later, he was standing in front of the Golden Fields, observing the farmers at work. The golden color of the wheat shone in his eyes as he watched the scenery, trying to find Carys.

His hand acted as a visor against the burning sun. And after a few minutes, he spotted a man with a straw hat.

"Well, I almost didn't recognize you!" Carys yelled from afar.

The farmer came to meet him under the guise of a quick water break, a happy but puzzled look on his face.

"Wow, those are some really good-looking clothes. They suit you!"

"Thanks, I just got them."

Carys shook Glenn's extended hand before wiping sweat from his forehead. The unending drone of cicadas surrounded them, accompanied by the crushing summer heat.

"What can I do for you?"

Glenn cleared his throat. "I had a few questions to ask you about the Northern Town. Do you know anything about the Harvest? I heard that term quite a few times. Is it a tax day?"

Carys froze. A bead of sweat trickled down his cheek as he swallowed with difficulty. The farmer glanced around fearfully before forcing a laugh out.

"Hmm... The Harvest..." Carys pushed down on his straw hat. "It's not something I can explain easily. There's a place, a discrete one. The Frosty Beer. I know the owner; he's trustworthy."

Glenn raised an alerted eyebrow. *What the— Why is he so terrified of it? Shit, I'm even starting to get goosebumps!*

"Alright, alright..." Glenn nodded slowly before whispering, "It's not dangerous to speak of it, is it?"

Carys' expression hardened, and he shook his head. "No, it's not. If you only want to consider it a *tax day*, at least."

"Carys, get the hell back to work, you lazy bastard!" yelled a foreman further in the field.

The farmer adjusted the position of his straw hat.

"I still have work until dusk, so let's meet once night falls, alright?"

"Sure, I'll be there. Thank you, Carys."

He bid the farmer farewell and headed towards the Northern Town. Something moved at the periphery of vision, startling him. He felt a shiver down his back and glanced at the fields, staring at a lone scarecrow standing in the middle of the crops. Glenn straightened his tie before hurriedly leaving the farmland.

Anyway, that's one task done. That Harvest seems ominous, but that's just the case with every lead I find. I can save all of those worries for the evening, at least. In the meantime... Should I finally take a look at the Magi Brotherhood?

He willed the recommendation plate from his soul, and it appeared in a white cloud of particles.

As if reacting to his thought, a sudden nudge in his mind made him want to infuse mana into the plate, summoning a small blue orb in the air. The orb moved towards the Northern Village, waiting for Glenn to follow it.

The young man obliged, not even surprised anymore. He was finally getting used to all this magic.

"Here goes nothing, I suppose..." he muttered.

Chapter 52

NO MUSHROOM NEEDED

Glenn stared at the unassuming hut, perplexed by the disappearance of the guiding orb. A sense of unease crept over him, and he couldn't help but question the choices that had led him to this moment.

With hesitant determination, he knocked on the wooden door, fearing it might crumble under his touch. Time stood still as he waited, and no response came. Steeling himself, he carefully pushed the door open, a creaking sound resonating through the shabby structure.

"Er, hello?" His voice trailed off as he ventured further into the dimly lit room.

He took a few more hesitant steps. A beam of light shot from the recommendation plate toward the floor, where a small stone pedestal emerged. There was a convenient rectangular slot carved on top of it.

Silently, Glenn placed the plate into the slot, and a strange, mystical sound emanated from the pedestal. An overwhelming wave of nausea washed over him. The world warped. When he finally opened his eyes, the urge to vomit prevented him from assessing his surroundings.

He somehow spotted a bin nearby and hurriedly ran to it, falling to his knees and puking. After he recovered his senses, Glenn wiped his mouth and cautiously looked up, realizing that he wasn't in the shabby hut anymore.

Glenn stood in the center of an awe-inspiring hall fit for titans, carved in white and black marble and lined with gold and silver. His gaze rose to a ceiling that simply wasn't there—replaced by a starry sky.

The hall was bustling with activity—be it individuals walking, running, flying, or floating. A speeding object in his peripheral vision forced him to duck. His eyes widened when he discovered that it was a broom autonomously cleaning the floor.

Glenn examined the marble, watching in awe as it changed color to a white, crystal-like composition.

W-What the hell is this place? There are… so many enchantments. I almost feel like I'm drowning! Diamanes exclaimed.

"Holy fuck…"

He stepped away from the trash can, his gaze darting around in disbelief. There were flying books and mages riding winged or scaled beasts while donning cliché wizard robes. He even saw a man flying with heavy plate armor, unbothered by the steel's weight.

He paused next to a group of scholars deeply engrossed in discussion.

"Maybe if we try using *Concalo* alongside *Saxeus* and *Nitens*, we might be able to create gold!" one of the men in the group proposed.

Another man shook his head and crossed his arms. "Sir Olinca already tried that formula, but he only managed to expend all his Mana for nothing. No, I say we try with *Aes* and *Lucrum*, maybe that'll summon gold…"

Glenn scoffed and turned away. "How nonsensical… If it was possible, gold wouldn't be worth anything. Why bother using it as a currency then?"

A sudden nudge from the recommendation plate drew his attention. It lit up with a strange pattern. In a matter of seconds, a stranger cloaked in a blue hooded robe materialized before him.

"Glenn, is that right? Please follow me," the cloaked figure said with an androgynous voice.

Glenn nodded hesitantly and followed the hooded guide as they traversed a labyrinth of inexplicable phenomena. Even though they had been standing in the middle of the hall just a second ago, their surroundings shifted, and they arrived at a formidable door constructed of red and green metal.

The cloaked figure halted and opened it. "Please enter."

Inside, he found an imposing chamber with ten massive chairs arranged in a half-moon formation. The ground featured an intricate compass rose; the north arrow pointed towards the chairs and the south indicated the door they had just come through. Glenn walked to the center of the compass and looked up at the seats, confused and excited at the same time.

An old man's voice emanated from one of them, although the occupant remained concealed behind a peculiar veil.

"Glenn, an Advanced Initiate, was recommended for a Savant position by Tom Delora. Shall we have a vote? Who here wishes to accept the young Mage?" the voice inquired.

A brief silence hung in the air before the old man's voice resounded in the vast chamber once again. "And who rejects him?"

Another pause ensued before a wooden hammer struck a board, creating a resounding echo.

"Glenn, Advanced Initiate, has been accepted for the Savant position. Next ordeal."

Glenn felt himself being magically pulled towards the door while the heavy metal gates closed. He stood out in the hall for a few moments, bewildered.

"What the fuck was that even for?" he asked in confusion.

Weird. I couldn't find anything out either... commented Diamanes.

"So that's it?"

"Hi, Glenn!" a cheerful voice chimed in from behind him.

He turned to see his interlocutor, a friendly girl with an appearance concealed under a hooded robe.

What's with these Mages and their robes, for real? Glenn wondered.

The girl extended a small hand towards him, and Glenn shook it—still grappling with his bewilderment.

"I'm your handler for today. Welcome to the Magi Brotherhood! I'll be showing you around and explaining what being a Savant means."

Glenn nodded, his gaze briefly returning to where the metal doors had been, now replaced by a stone wall. He attempted to shake off his confusion before focusing on his guide.

"Nice to meet you, miss…"

She smiled. Well, Glenn guessed that she did. "Nirva Dalum. Nice to meet you too! Let's start the visit, shall we?"

She then walked in small but hurried steps. Glenn didn't have an issue following her just by making large strides. The path seemed to warp as they arrived in a training ground, where Mages cast spells at target dummies.

Glenn watched a man shoot a literal laser from his eyes, destroying one of the steel targets before writing something in a notebook with a disappointed look. Before Glenn could inquire about the nature of the spell, Nirva spoke.

"This room is the Savant Room. It's where Mages invent and try out new spells. There is an unlimited supply of targets, and the surroundings will distort in function of your need. Don't ask me how it works. That's above my pay grade."

She stepped aside as a bird-shaped thunderbolt flew past her.

"Of course, it might be a little dangerous to work in such conditions, but we believe that the threat of death helps Mages create more potent spells. Great pressure produces diamonds, as they say."

She nodded towards a Mage that was playing with a ball of magma before handing Glenn a little, black stone shaped like a diamond.

"You just have to put this in your recommendation plate, and it will give you limited access to the warping magic of the Magi Brotherhood Headquarters. You can come back here to the Savant Ground at any time."

Glenn could only nod, casting a fearful gaze at a Mage running from a giant sphere of malevolent darkness.

Did I just land in an asylum?

Glenn held the black stone above his recommendation plate. He wondered where to place it when the gem suddenly made the decision for him, encrusting itself into a corner.

"You can summon a terminal anywhere here to input knowledge—be it spells, rune combinations, efficiency against certain types of creatures, et cetera, et cetera…"

"Depending on the quality of the information, you'll receive credits—which are the currency here. Don't bother trying to buy it with gold, it won't work. The only way to earn credits is to contribute, so…" She smiled under her hood. "Contribute, okay? That's the whole crux of the Savant position."

She was about to step back but exclaimed, "Oh, and of course, if you want to leave, you just have to infuse Mana into your recommendation plate with the idea of leaving. You'll get transported to the last beacon you used. If you want to come back here, it's the same process."

She rubbed her tiny hands together before clapping them.

"Well, it has been a pleasure. On those words, have a good day!"

She then suddenly warped out of existence, leaving a bewildered Glenn alone in the middle of magical explosions.

"Why is every handler in such a hurry every time? First Sir Reginald, and now this Nirva Dalum."

Diamanes made a puking sound in his mind.

What's up with you?

The entity answered weakly, ***I don't know. This place gives me nausea. There is simply too much magic; you're walking through layers and layers of different spells. Give it a glance with Mana Sight and you're done!***

Glenn shook his head. This place was insane—so insane these past few minutes felt like a fever dream.

What if it is? Glenn pressed his hand against his forehead, but it didn't feel warmer than usual. *Well, then. What should I do now?*

Chapter 53

THE SAVANT GROUND

Glenn crossed his arms, a little confused and curious at the same time. "First things first, I might as well record all the magical data I collected so far. What did she mean by 'terminal'?" he mumbled inquisitively.

As soon as the word left his mouth, a stone pedestal holding a book surged out of the ground.

He blinked and approached it. *They sure do love stone pedestals here.*

Glenn flipped through the book's pages, finding a summary. There were multiple sections, but all of them were crossed out except for the Spell Creation category. He flipped further, only to realize that the rest of the tome was empty.

What kind of magic is this? Glenn smiled in awe. *Diamanes, any idea how all this works?*

The entity groaned, ***Don't talk to me. I'll sleep for now. This place is horrible. Wake me up when you're out of this... this hellhole.***

Glenn laughed and shrugged it off before going through the book's spells. They were all relatively simple: Magic Arrow, Light, Fire Spark, and so forth.

He looked at the description of Magic Arrow, curious.

Spell: Magic Arrow, provided by the Magi Brotherhood

Description: The Magic Arrow spell manifests as a luminous, translucent arrow, typically taking on a vibrant hue that corresponds to the caster's magical affinity.

Usage: Magic Arrow can be employed as a ranged attack, capable of striking opponents with precision from a distance. It can pierce through physical defenses and enchantments of an inferior level and is extremely simple to use and learn.

Formula: *Proiectum + Penetrabile + Accuratio*

Mana Usage: Very low / Beginner Initiate friendly

Credit Cost: Free

Glenn nodded in understanding. "It's so systematic. It's honestly impressive. It looks like anyone can use these, as long as they have Mana."

He looked at his hands. "Should I try it out?"

After speaking, a target dummy appeared fifty meters away, ready to be shot down.

Glenn snorted. "How convenient."

Glenn channeled his Mana while reading the words on the pedestal. *"Projectum, penetrabile, accuratio."*

A blurry arrow appeared in front of him, struggling to manifest itself. Glenn aimed at the dummy, fueling the arrow with Mana to maintain it. It was a strange and new feeling. He was still in control of the spell, but it felt rigid. It didn't look like there was a way to modify the range of the spell or its power. Even putting more Mana into it seemed to end up as a waste. It was very different from when he used Draconic School spells—like Magic Bullet or Implosion.

He flicked his finger, and the arrow flew away—piercing through the air with a sharp whistle. The arrow landed straight in the center of the dummy's head, perforating it before disappearing in a flash of blue Mana.

"Huh." Glenn couldn't help but look at his hands in amusement. "That was really easy. I just need to say the words, channel Mana, and I'm done. Crazy."

He quickly swiped through the available spells, hungry to try more combinations. *What would happen if I changed the order of the formula for Magic Arrow? Wasn't that something that could make a wholly different spell?*

Glenn's lips curved upwards as he wondered what could be possible with the School of Words. His Mana reserve had barely been used by the Magic Arrow, and he certainly intended to learn the rest of the provided spells—at least until his body wouldn't let him cast another.

Don't forget you have to meet Carys at nightfall, Diamanes reminded him with a tired voice.

Glenn blinked and grimaced. "Ah, yeah, I did plan that. Could I have a—?"

A huge clock suddenly appeared next to him. Cute drawings depicted dawn, midday, and evening. The clock hand pointed a little past noon.

"Should be around 1:30 p.m.," he grumbled.

That gave him a short yet considerable amount of time to experiment. If his Mana reserve allowed him to do so, of course. He picked another interesting spell and quickly read it.

Spell: Light, provided by the Magi Brotherhood.

Description: The Light spell manifests as a white ball of light.

Usage: It can be used to shine light in dark places. Probably the simplest spell in the world.

Formula: *Lux*

Mana Usage: Insignificant / Can be charged with Mana for more potency

Credit Cost: Free

"Nice..." Glenn laughed before extending his palm outwards. "*Lux!*"

A ball of light appeared above Glenn. He didn't really understand the underlying principles behind magic, but he still loved it. He stopped his Mana from channeling into the sphere, letting it quickly vanish.

"So I can control its existence with my Mana. Seeing what's written in the Mana Usage column, that probably means I can also send more Mana than the bare minimum." He concluded, before repeating, "*Lux!*"

The ball of light appeared once more, but this time, he tried to send more Mana. The result was a ball of light so bright it blinded him. Satisfied with the results, he read through the other spells.

Spell: Fire Spark, provided by the Magi Brotherhood.

Description: The Fire Spark spell summons a small flame the size of a thumb.

Usage: Can be used to light objects on fire or simply illuminate one's surroundings. It's a simple utility spell that always comes in handy.

Formula: *Ignis*

Mana Usage: Charging it with Mana only allows for an increased duration.

Credit Cost: Free

"That would have been a nice spell to know back when I was freezing to death, naked, and trying to make a fire with a flint and a sword," muttered Glenn as he extended his hand once again.

"*Ignis!*"

A small flame floated above his gloved palm, burning with real heat. Glenn could feel it despite the leather. He cut off the Mana supply of the spell and watched as the fire was snuffed out.

"Nice. Next one..." His eyes widened when he discovered the name of the next spell.

> **Spell:** Cleaning Touch, provided by the Magi Brotherhood
>
> **Description:** The Cleaning Touch allows you to get rid of filth anywhere.
>
> **Usage:** Can be used to clean dirty weapons and armor, or even sanitize wounds. Practical, even more so when you don't have a maid to wash your belongings.
>
> **Formula:** *Mundare*
>
> **Mana Usage:** Insignificant / Overcharging with Mana might cause complications.
>
> **Credit Cost:** Free

"Shit, that's exactly the spell I tried to create yesterday... *Mundare!*"

His hand shone with a light hue, but nothing happened.

He looked around and quickly found debris left by another Savant's spell. Placing his hand over the dirty spot, he watched as the light consumed the filth. He chuckled and cut off the Mana supply.

Hmm... I clearly don't understand how the formulas work, besides the fact that I'm saying a word and it summons a spell. Maybe I should try to recreate a Magic Bullet using a formula.

His logic was simple. This way, he could contribute to the spell repository and gain access to new and more intricate spells. Also, if he managed to understand the School of Words system, perhaps he'd be able to reverse-engineer their spells.

Powered by this idea, he looked through the terminal to find an explanation of the words in the magic formulas. There it was with a hefty explanation in a language called the Ancient Tongue, which came from an ancient civilization that was powerful but fell mysteriously, blah blah blah. What interested Glenn were the words that could be used as the basis for his Magic Bullet.

The first word should be Proiectum, meaning Projectile in Ancient Tongue. The second wouldn't be Penetrabile which means piercing, but instead, Angor which is supposed to mean pressure. I just have to add Accuratio for the precision, and it should work!

Glenn asked the Savant Room for a new dummy, and it warped into existence while he was channeling his Mana.

"Proiectum, angor, accuratio!"

He sent Mana into his spell, excited about the idea of understanding a new magic system. His excitement quickly turned into dread. What appeared was a weird, fluctuating hand possessing eight fingers that rushed at the dummy with an anguished scream before bursting into a death rattle. Glenn stared dumbfounded at the result before checking the terminal to understand the mistake he had made.

Soon, he found out the source of the problem. Words in the Ancient Tongue often had specific connotations. *Angor* indeed meant pressure but in the sense of suffocation, distress, and torment. *Accuratio* could also mean carefulness, explaining why the spell took on the shape of a hand. Or not. This system was more complicated than it looked.

All in all, Glenn gained a new spell. Yes, he had no idea what its use was, sure. But still, great shit.

The weird-ass ominous magic hand didn't consume a lot of his Mana. If he had to put it quantitatively, it would be around five Magic Bullets. Glenn sighed, noticing the time. It was already 2:30 p.m.

This was going to be a short afternoon; he could feel it.

Spell: Weird-Ass Ominous Magic Hand, provided by Glenn.

Description: Summon an ominous-looking hand with eight fingers that screams in pain while flying at a designed target.

Usage : Intimidation? I don't know, figure it out yourself.

Formula : *Proiectum + Angor + Accuratio*

Mana Usage: Very Low

Credit Cost: Owned

Disclaimer: The Magi Brotherhood would like to remind every Savant that the description of spells are by the contributors themselves. We do not endorse opinions stated by the authors. Kind regards.

Chapter 54

NEVER OVEREAT

"Hahaha! I got it!" Glenn yelled.

"His eyes were bloodshot as he pumped his fist victoriously at a target dummy with a small hole pierced through its head. He hurried back to the terminal, his pen flying on the paper as he excitedly wrote the file on his Magic Bullet.

Spell: Enhanced Magic Bullet, provided by Glenn.

Description: An invisible thumb-sized projectile that emits a sound when fired.

Usage: An invisible and potent alternative to Magic Arrow, with increased speed and perforation capabilities.

Formula: *Proiectum + Velox + Destructum*

Mana Usage: Thrice the Mana of a Magic Arrow / Beginner Initiate friendly

Credit Cost: Owned

It wasn't precisely the same versatile Mana Bullet that he could conjure with the Draconic School, but it was the closest he could get to it. As a bonus, it was more powerful than the original! Of course, it came with the annoying restriction of having to shout the words for the formula. But in exchange, he gained more power, more speed, and... Well, a better spell in concept.

After recording the results, the ink soaked into the paper, and the book suddenly closed. It reopened seconds later, displaying the page for Enhanced Magic Bullet. The Magi Brotherhood had accepted his formula like it did before for his Weird-Ass Ominous Magic Hand.

He quickly returned to the book's summary, a little disappointed when he saw that he still only had access to the Spell Creation section.

Glenn flipped back more out of habit than anything, smiling in surprise when he found new spells to be studied. Strangely, only the names, descriptions, and usage were available. The formulas and their Mana usage remained hidden. It also seemed like it was restricted to Beginner Initiate level spells—which ultimately didn't matter as it was all Glenn could use for now, excluding his Implosion. *What rank is my Implosion anyway?*

"How the hell am I supposed to unlock these... Ah." The second he asked that question, numbers appeared next to each spell—fluctuating between ten and fifty, but never more.

"That should be the price, I suppose... How many credits do I have, then?"

A number appeared in the upper right corner of the terminal, displaying fifty credits. Above that was his name, Glenn, as well as a picture of his face. There was also his Circle rank, showing the Second Circle.

"There certainly are a lot of mechanics to this. It's pretty fun to research spells!"

He glanced through the repository, wondering if he should learn one of them when a weak voice rasped. ***Glenn... Get me out of here, or I'm going to...***

Diamanes? What's wrong?!

"Damn it all!"

A whirlwind suddenly appeared in Glenn's left hand that absorbed the fabric of reality itself. Glenn felt a sudden surge of information arriving in his mind—messy pieces of spells and enchantments, formulas and their runes—mixing into a fever-inducing dance.

When he regained his senses, he was lying on his back. His vision blurred. Standing up carefully, he noticed Savant Ground contorting, inspiring awe and fear. It seemed like a Rift was about to spawn at any moment, or that something was about to explode.

Without thinking twice about it, Glenn summoned his recommendation plate. Space warped and twisted, and the familiar feeling of his body being pulled and pushed in every direction accompanied him as he teleported out of the Magi Brotherhood Headquarters.

He landed back in the shabby hut—a runic circle shining under his feet. He stumbled forwards and plopped against the cold, stone wall.

The dim glow coming from the dirty window informed him that dusk had yet to fall. He breathed out, an uneasy feeling in his gut. Looking at his left hand, he discovered in astonishment that it was shining with a purple light under the leather glove and bandages.

"Diamanes, what the hell is going on?!"

"Buuurrrppp!"

"Are you serious?"

"I didn't have a choice, alright?" Diamanes tried to defend himself.

Glenn took off his glove, staring at his hand with a deadpan expression. Diamanes' black tongue moistened his lips.

"Listen, how can I explain this… You remember burgers?"

Glenn nodded hesitantly.

"Well, imagine there is one in front of you, looking tasty—so much you just want to take a bite."

Even though he doubted he would find a burger in this world, Glenn *could* imagine. *Huh, that's an idea. Cooking burgers in another world.*

"If you see a mountain of burgers, it might look daunting, but you'd still want to take a bite of them. Since they look so delicious, right?"

Glenn shrugged. "So? You're saying what just happened was you took a bite out of the spell mountain in the Savant Ground?"

Diamanes wriggled his mouth before answering. **"Well, no. It was more like I was drowning in that mountain of burgers, and my only choice was to eat my way out."**

Glenn let out a short laugh. "What kind of explanation is that?"

Just as he was about to mock Diamanes, a painful headache stopped him. A deafening sound hissed, and strange voices whispered beyond the veil. Listening to them only made the agony worse, so he tried to shut them up by plugging his ears.

After a minute of groaning, the noise calmed, disappearing into the distance. Glenn pushed himself up and held himself against the wall while rubbing his temples.

"What—"

Glenn coughed heavily and bent over to expunge the lump blocking his throat. He witnessed in silent fright as a red clot of blood landed on the floor, wriggling as if it was alive. Reflexively, he stomped on the clump until he was sure it wouldn't move.

"I... I think there's something wrong with me. *Cough...*" noticed Glenn, wiping his mouth and staring at the blood on his hand.

"I'll say this just in case, but it's not my fault," Diamanes warned in a grim voice.

Glenn put on his glove and left the shabby hut as the sun set. He groaned and strode towards the Golden Fields.

"Shit... Why now? I still have to meet Carys at the Frosty Beer..."

He tried to push through it, thinking about Giselle's mission. *I can't waste time on a damned headache!*

Out of breath, Glenn took a break. He leaned on his knees, his stomach bloated. He shook the feeling off, intending to honor his meeting with the farmer.

After stumbling for a while, he finally arrived in front of the Frosty Beer—a not-so-glamorous establishment that gave him a strange sense of déjà vu.

It looked hastily built, with cheap brown paint and secondhand tiles. The tavern was a bit of a letdown compared to the Auberge, but at least it wouldn't be teeming with druggies and Thorns Church chumps. Hopefully. He pushed the saloon doors open, the feeling of déjà vu reinforced.

Guided by his gut, he turned towards the counter. His eyes widened. The barman was someone he knew—someone he thought he would never meet again.

"Who's that? Wait, young master?!" The bartender gasped in shock. "It's me, Winston! Do you remember me?"

Glenn chuckled in disbelief. "How could I not? I almost died because of your fire staff!"

Winston guided Glenn to an isolated table and brought a small barrel of ale. He slammed two mugs in front of the young man.

"I can't believe you're alive, honestly," Winston admitted as he emptied his tankard in one gulp. "When the Thorns Church sets their eyes on someone, that someone disappears forever. Almost every time."

Glenn grimaced, staring at the ale distrustfully. His searing headache showed no signs of calming down.

"Well, I probably am the only one who ever escaped that prison. How come you were working with them, though?" he asked, wondering whether he should trust the bartender.

After all, the latter had a stash of Moongrass and held an establishment right in front of the Thorns Church. If that wasn't suspicious, he didn't know what was.

Winston spat out his ale in shock. "Me? Me?!"

He slammed his mug on the table and took out a golden bracelet. "I'm a proud member of the Gold Church and a loyal contributor!" The bartender scowled. "The only reason I was *working* with those insane cultists was to make sure my family wouldn't be in danger. I had no choice!"

Glenn reeled back in a placating manner, his hands raised. "Alright, alright. I believe you. And family, you say?"

Winston paused before suddenly adopting a warm smile. "Yes, yes! Do you want to meet them?" Without even giving Glenn a chance to reply, he sprang up from his seat and darted off. "Give me a second. I'll present you to my wife and daughters!"

Glenn chuckled and leaned back, using the opportunity to empty his mug of ale into Winston's. Someone suddenly patted him on the shoulder, startling him.

"I see you've started without me, Glenn," Carys said with a chuckle as he sat in Winston's seat.

Glenn smiled. "As I said, it's on me. Thanks again for that day with the scarecrows. If you hadn't told me to stay on the road, I might have joined the skulls and bones in the ditches!"

Carys paled and crossed his hands worriedly. "D-Don't joke about that, Glenn! I've seen how you fight. You're a Mage, aren't you?"

Glenn shrugged. "How is that impressive? Anyone can have a Convergence with the Magic Identification Bureau, can't they?"

The farmer blinked and slowly removed his straw hat. "Glenn..." He spoke in disbelief. "Don't you know it's extremely expensive to learn magic?"

Glenn opened his mouth, but Carys stopped him. "I'm not talking about the Convergence, Glenn. I'm talking about learning to use magic."

He opened his palm and muttered something silently. A small pool of water appeared, trembling for a few seconds before destabilizing and falling apart. "I only know a few spells, yet I got my Convergence a decade ago. Books on magic are expensive and extremely rare. And I'm not even mentioning how difficult it is to learn."

Glenn blinked in incomprehension. "But what about the Cleaners or the Magi Brotherhood?"

Carys chuckled, incredulous. "What about them? They're the ones who control the magic market, and the reason books on the subject are expensive. They keep all their knowledge for members of their organization and promising individuals!"

Glenn nodded, slowly understanding. That's the moment Winston chose to appear, his expecting wife and daughters following him with happy smiles. They all thanked Glenn as if he was their savior. Winston joined the discussion after his families were done expressing their gratitude and making him uncomfortable.

"I know I've already thanked you for this, young master, but..." Winston looked at Glenn with tear-filled eyes. "This inn, the Frosted Beer... I built it with the gold you gave me. Our son is due soon, and without it, my family and I would still be stuck outside the walls, worrying about those damned cultists."

Glenn laughed awkwardly. "Y-Yes, don't mention it."

Winston took a big swig of his beer and chuckled happily. "And to top it all off, ever since the Auberge collapsed, everyone's been coming to my establishment! Business is booming, haha!"

"So, Carys, what's up with that Harvest?" Glenn asked as he pushed away Winston's fourth attempt at refilling his mug.

The bartender's cheery smile faded.

Carys' face darkened as he gazed into his ale. "The Harvest... It's an old tradition from the age of the First King. It used to be the way that the Northern Town thanked the throne for protecting them. The villagers would cultivate the Golden Fields and offer a sizable part of the yield to the kingdom."

Glenn frowned. "But that changed, didn't it?"

"Indeed." Carys nodded. "The food market is strictly controlled by the Gold Church, who forces the price to stay below or above a certain threshold. The Harvest still happens now, though... led by Baron Howard."

He gazed into the distance. "It began some time ago. Every year, the Baron would come down to the Northern Town and take his share of whatever he wanted—be it money, resources, or…" He clenched his fist tightly and hissed, "people."

Glenn crossed his arms. "I see. He's basically a tyrant."

Carys sneered dejectedly. "No, he's just a thieving murderer. And whenever someone tries to stand up to him… It never ends well for them."

Winston emptying his mug. "Alright!" he shouted. "Let's not ruin the mood any further. Drink, my friends!"

Unfazed, Carys continued. "That Baron Howard is a fiend. A *real* fiend. You want to know the darkest bit about him, Glenn?"

Carys took another swig of his ale, his voice growing lower. "He deals with dark magic that isn't meant for mortal men. Deep beneath his manor, there's a chamber where he conducts twisted experiments."

Glenn's eyes widened.

"He's been dabbling with the Thorns Church. When the Harvest comes, he takes citizens as he pleases, and you know how they end up? Monsters. Soulless monsters who abide by their master's every order, feasting on humans like beasts. And he can steal their souls, binding them to himself."

Glenn's expression turned grave. "And nobody does anything about him? That's insane."

Carys nodded solemnly. "He's a noble. That's *why*! Nothing but death awaits anyone foolish enough to stand against him. But ever since he took my sweet Anita from me, I can't…"

The farmer peered into his ale. He pondered for a moment, grinding his teeth. Then suddenly, he slammed his mug on the table.

"Glenn… Why do you care about the Harvest so much? Anyone who isn't a resident leaves while it happens anyway."

Glenn scratched his chin, hesitating. He glanced at Winston, who had carefully pushed the barrel of beer away, wearing a serious face.

"Listen… Baron Howard captured someone, and I need to save him," Glenn said slowly. "And I have something the Baron may want to… trade with me to get him back."

The inn became completely silent. Glenn felt a shiver crawl up his spine. Every customer stared at him, their hands resting on hilts and handles.

"All of these folks are people who lost someone to him. Husbands, wives, children, parents... the Baron spares no one." Carys stabbed the table with a knife.

Oh-ho, I like this plot! Hey, prepare the guillotine, Glenn! It's time to Robespierre the Baron!

"I said most folks go out of town during the Harvest, but can you guess why some remain despite the risk? Despite the threat of being taken away, transformed into a *bloodsucker* who'll kill even his own family?" Carys looked at the silent crowd and pressed his palm against his chest. "Because this is *our* home! The one we poured blood, sweat, and passion into! The place where our ancestors rest!"

"Aye!" shouted the inn's patrons in chorus.

"What kind of men would we be if we gave up on our homes? On our honor? Our pride!" Carys raised his fist in the air. "Fuck that! The Baron may rob us, but he'll never manage to steal the soul of this town!"

"Aye!"

"So, Glenn." Carys glanced at his interlocutor. "I'd like to propose a deal with you."

Glenn crossed his arms, the corner of his lips curving upwards in a manner strangely similar to Diamanes. "I'm listening."

"We have a lot of fighters. Lots of strong, capable men. None are Mages or Aura knights, but we have numbers for ourselves. We only need someone to subdue the Baron's guard and take care of his thralls."

The farmer poked his finger in Glenn's chest. "And I want you to handle that. Whatever idea you had, *trading* with the Baron, it won't work." Carys grinned wickedly as he pulled his knife out of the table. "In King's Rise, it's eat or be eaten. Which do you want to be, Glenn?"

The young man leaned back in his chair, his eyes going from one revolutionary to the other. There were many strong men, as Carys said, but also women, grandparents, and even kids. They all had that same look on their faces, that same desperate pride.

The most dangerous creation of any society is the man who has nothing to lose, quoted Diamanes with a cackle.

Glenn looked at his mug, full of untouched ale. *A rebellion...* Little by little, a large grin crept up his face.

"What kind of man would I be if I refused after such a speech?"

Carys laughed broadly as he shook Glenn's hand. "We'll be counting on you, Glenn! With you, we will finally be able to oppose the Baron. You'll be our spearhead!"

Glenn rubbed his chin curiously. "I wonder, though, I'm sure there are other people stronger than me. Why not ask them? The Cleaner's Workshop is filled with mercenaries who would accept such a mission. Or what about the Church of Onnea?"

The farmer shook his head. "The Cleaner's Workshop has a non-interference clause. That's the only reason they have a monopoly over the Fringe's mercenary business. They can't accept requests like that. Similarly, the Church is bound to the Crown. And..." Carys grimaced. "We need to be careful of moles."

"Moles?" Glenn chuckled. "And what makes you think I'm not one?"

Carys clicked his tongue. "Someone who doesn't know the rules of the Golden Fields and had no idea what the Harvest was? If you're an informant for the Baron, I'll gladly eat my scythe!"

Glenn coughed. "Shaming strangers, huh?"

The farmer patted his shoulder. "Thank you for accepting, Glenn. I knew you were a good guy right when I met you."

I think that's a lie, considering how he thought you were a noble back then. Oof, and on that note...

* * *

Glenn and Carys discussed the plan further. It took a few hours before Glenn eventually left the Frosty Beer, his blood boiling with excitement.

In theory, the rebellion was quite simple. Carys and his rebels would take care of the Baron's foot soldiers, delaying them as much as possible while Glenn subdued the elite fighters.

Using their numbers to their advantage, Carys' revolutionaries were confident they could get rid of the grunts without too much complication, as long as nothing came along to interrupt them.

I'll be honest, I think I needed a breath of fresh air... mumbled Diamanes.

The whole operation would rely on Glenn's strength, but the latter wasn't too worried. With the help of Diamanes and his Magellanic Clouds, he would be able to fend off a thrall or two easily.

And I also have Sahro to count on. Yeah, it really could work, couldn't it? At worst, I can just reverse-kidnap Callum and run away.

I don't want to ruin your fun Glenn, but—Hmpf! Diamanes winced, but Glenn was too excited to catch on.

"Never in my entire life would I have guessed that I'd be part of a revolution! Can you believe that, Diamanes?" said Glenn with an awed chuckle.

Diamanes grunted painfully. ***Glenn, you might want to find a discreet spot. I feel like I'm going to throw up sometime soon...***

Wait, what do you mean 'throw up'? That's my thing! he exclaimed.

He took a shortcut through a dark alley hidden between two rows of houses. The searing headache that plagued Glenn returned full throttle.

"This sucks..." Glenn sighed as he held his head and leaned against the house.

He glanced at the sky worriedly, muttering through his teeth, "Looks like it's about to rain sometime soon."

As he removed the glove, Diamanes gurgled.

"You're scaring me, Diamanes. What's going on—"

He gasped as a wave of power surged through his left hand; the terrible headache amplified to incredible heights. He grabbed his head and groaned loudly in pain, falling to his knees. The world around him started to twist and turn into a warped version of reality. In a way, he felt something similar to what he had peered into the Seed of Darkness and almost lost his soul.

Through his fever, he noticed a robed man closing in on him, a sword in his hand. Glenn shouted for him to stop, but his voice couldn't leave his throat.

He held up his left hand in one last desperate attempt to halt the figure. The stranger lunged at him before Glenn felt an immense power escape his palm.

A warping sound echoed, as well as some disgusting flesh noises. Glenn heaved with difficulty as the headache faded. He forced himself to look up and observed in horror as the robed man quickly turned inhuman. His flesh became slimy and covered in writhing tentacles akin to worms. And his face grew a mass of black tendrils and eyes that seemed to defy human comprehension.

Glenn felt a primal fear grip his soul as the creature stepped towards him, a strange sound coming from its mouth. It took another step as Glenn tentatively summoned a Magic Bullet. Suddenly, the monster collapsed, its tendrils squirming desperately before transforming into ash.

Soon enough, the only remains were a robe and a longsword.

Chapter 55.

STALKERS

Glenn panted on his knees, drenched in cold sweat. His trembling eyes fixed on the pile of ashes in front of him, his thoughts racing as it struggled to come up with an explanation.

"Did…" He froze and looked at his hands in horror. "Did I just kill someone?"

The grotesque image of the squirming, dying figure imprinted in his mind. He stumbled back, falling into the mud with tears welling up in his eyes.

"Glenn, give me a break and breathe. The guy had a sword. I'm pretty sure he wasn't a barber giving out free haircuts," Diamanes commented weakly, his voice somewhat ethereal.

Thunder exploded in the sky as if the Gods were angry at Glenn's actions. He breathed in and out and slapped his face.

Once his mind was finally back in the right place, Glenn crouched next to the remains of the man he killed, intending to at least figure out his identity. He picked up the robe and winced, a smell of sweat, squid, and blood coming off it. He patted the cloth to search for hidden pockets but couldn't find anything.

The longsword seemed to be a standard one too. There were no engravings, be it on the pommel or the blade. He finally glanced at the pile of ashes, his heart in a wrench, but he steeled himself.

He hesitated for a few seconds, but then a gust of wind chose for him and thrust the ashes into his face. Glenn fell back and retched as he spat out the remains of his accidental victim.

A shining gleam caught his attention. It was a broken, purple ring that gave off a malevolent aura. He felt like he had already seen that ring before...

At the Auberge? Wait. The Thorns Church?

Every sign pointed to that damned sect. His guilt melted away like snow in the sun, and he grinned.

"Well, well, well, isn't that a strange coincidence..." he muttered as he tightly clenched the broken trinket.

He was no fool. He knew it wasn't by chance that one of those cultist bastards found him in an alley. Those creeps were back on his trail, and they probably intended to make him pay for stealing the Seed of Darkness.

"*Ignis.*" A small flame appeared on his finger as he conjured a Fire Spark.

The robe burned, leaving nothing but ashes. He then carefully stashed the purple ring in his dimensional pouch, making sure no part of his skin came into contact with it. He had seen how the Church of Onnea behaved in front of those objects, and he intended to be at least as careful as them.

Once he made sure that nothing was left, he headed back to the Cleaner's Workshop, grinning wickedly. He believed he deserved a good, long night of Meditative rest, and he wasn't going to get on this creepy street.

He stopped as he felt a cold sensation in his neck. As he pressed his finger on it, he discovered moisture. He looked up and winced.

It was raining.

Glenn rushed back to the Workshop, thinking that he would deal with Diamanes' outburst when he was somewhere warm and comfortable. He ran back to his room, making a pit stop by the baths, which—after thinking for not so long—was probably Glenn's favorite facility. That and the Dining Hall.

He cleaned his clothes with a quick Cleaning Touch and went back to his dorm. He collapsed on his bed and sighed heavily.

It was strange when he thought back on it. A few months ago, he was just a normal student trying to survive through university, but now... He had to kill to survive. An amalgam of unfortunate druggies, overgrown rats, cultists... Taking a life was as easy as breathing in this world.

"And I don't feel guilty whatsoever." Glenn realized as he stared at the ceiling blankly.

"Well, stop whining like a bitch. We need to cook, alright?" Diamanes quickly stopped his rumination. **"There are a lot of things that need explanations, so you'll be guilt-tripping yourself a little later."**

Glenn dismissed his morbid thoughts. Be it Diamanes' burger mountain crisis, the living clump of blood he spat out, or the Lovecraftian abomination that just *died*, it had all been quite disturbing.

"Another Monday." Diamanes yawned. **"Now, considering Mr. I-Burst-Into-Tentacles-And-Died appears to be from the Thorns Church, does it confirm they can transform people into monsters at will?"**

Glenn paused. "That's... a good question. It's not the first time someone transformed into a monster because of them. I don't think it was intentional, though, considering how he first came at me with a sword and died right after transforming."

"Perhaps my... hmm, *vomit* accelerated the process, and something went wrong because of that?" suggested Diamanes.

"Maybe." Glenn retrieved the broken purple ring. "This must have played a part too."

"Hey, what if that ring is the catalyst for the transformation, but I broke it from my purge? After all, it's very similar to what the Auberge's abomination dropped after it died," realized Diamanes.

Glenn rubbed his chin as the jigsaw puzzle started to piece itself together. The more he thought about it, the more it did make sense. And the Thorns Church was a prison full of monsters that were once humans... He suddenly froze as he realized what that could mean.

"Are they creating those rings to force artificial Corrupted Ones?" he muttered in awe. *If that's true... then the Thorns Church is even more of a threat than we thought.*

Still, Glenn felt a bit better that he was able to put words to matters he couldn't understand before. Knowing what plagued him made Glenn fear it less. After all, now that he knew the sources of his issues, he could probably find a way to take care of them, right? He sighed and sank deeply into his comfortable mattress.

"All I know is, my headache is gone, and another cultist is dead. All in all, quite the positive outcome, don't you think?"

"Any outcome that isn't *death* or corruption is positive," grumbled Diamanes. **"And I'm almost certain that the headache was a lingering effect from peeking inside the Seed of Darkness. I managed to purge some of its influence, but..."** He paused and clicked his tongue. **"You still have a creepy green eye and that ridiculous strand of white hair."**

Glenn played absentmindedly with said strand, pondering. "While we're at it, is there anything we forgot?"

"You did. You never asked what I did to the Rift," Diamanes replied in a matter-of-fact tone.

"You just ate it, didn't you?" Glenn answered as if it was evident.

Diamanes paused, taken aback. **"Well... Yes, but don't you care what that means for you?"**

"Come on, enlighten me." Glenn groaned.

"Well, me eating a Rift reinforces your body temporarily. That's why your eyesight got better."

Glenn scoffed, "Oh, great! That means if I want a slight buff to see only *a little better*, I need to absorb a goddamn Rift." He shook his head dejectedly. "Sorry, I don't exactly feel moved to tears."

Diamanes remained silent as his host laughed. With some peace of mind, Glenn took off his clothes as he put himself to bed—every grim thought about him killing someone displaced in another part of his brain.

He would deal with that later. Right now, he needed some sleep. After all, it was raining. He always slept better when it was raining.

* * *

Glenn tossed and turned, struggling to fall asleep. Each time he closed his eyes, he saw the robed figure squirming in pain as they morphed into some kind of cosmic horror.

Finally, he had enough, and he stood up from his bed. He yawned and moved towards the window, noticing that the two moons were high in the sky. But something was wrong. Terribly so. The sky... seemed purple. The same shade as his left hand. Glancing down the streets, he discovered a hazy, green fog.

He rubbed his eyes, only to discover that he wasn't in his room anymore. While trying to cast a spell defensively, he learned he couldn't muster any Mana. He was standing in a wheat field, ominous mist surrounding him, and a purple sky pushing him down. His body trembled uncontrollably, fluctuating between hot and cold.

Suddenly, his heart started thumping out of his chest. As he turned back, he saw a strange figure approach him, a longsword in his hand.

Glenn held his hands out in a pitiful manner, but the stranger only came closer to him, brandishing his sword. Thorns crawled under his feet, and he emanated a malevolent aura. Powerless to resist, Glenn could only watch in agonized terror as the robed figure unveiled its face—a grotesque visage composed of writhing, black tendrils resembling worms.

At last, the figure impaled Glenn's chest—driving the blade to its hilt—while murmuring incomprehensible incantations. Amidst the torment, one word pierced through the chaos: Paradox.

Gasping for breath, Glenn snapped awake, drenched in sweat. He clutched his chest, half-expecting to find the blade's cruel mark. But it was nothing more than a haunting nightmare.

Or so he thought.

His gaze shifted to his pectoral, and dread overcame him as he discovered a new tattoo etched above his heart.

"Oh, not another one," he groaned in exasperation, his eyes fixated on the intricate design—a circle of thorns, very reminiscent of the... *No.*

"Diamanes, how did I end up with this shit?"

"Come on, let me sleep a bit more..."

"Diamanes!"

The hand jerked himself awake. **"What is so important you dare wake me from my slumber?"**

"This!"

Glenn pointed a finger at the thorns circle.

Diamanes let out an exasperated sigh. **"That's a curse. Good luck with that."**

Glenn squeezed his possessed hand.

"What?! What do you mean by a curse? Like the silence curse that stopped me from speaking? What are the effects of this one?"

Diamanes mumbled something unintelligible, prompting Glenn to shake his hand with renewed urgency.

"Alright! Alright," Diamanes grumbled in surrender. **"You're Marked, which means they can find you—anywhere and anytime."**

The young man paled, quickly putting his clothes on.

"Damn it. Of course I would be cursed with a damned tracker. Because magical trackers just exist!"

He rubbed the fatigue off his face and prepared to exit his room, but Diamanes stopped him.

"Relax," Diamanes advised with a rare note of reassurance in his voice. **"You're safer here. This workshop is protected by Fixers and Cleaners and fortified with wards. They won't find you easily."**

Indeed, the Cleaner's Workshop was as good as a fortress. And since he had a tracker, running away was useless.

"Diamanes, can you remove it?"

His hand smacked his lips thoughtfully. **"Sure, but you won't be able to use it. Don't want to use yourself as bait, huh?"**

Glenn shook his head negatively in silence.

Diamanes snorted. **"Yeah, just put me over the mark."**

A minute later, the curse was gone, leaving Glenn relieved. No way in hell would he go back to that damned cell in the Thorns Church prison. And if he had to fight them, he'd rather do it once he was strong enough to shoulder that choice. Because he didn't consider himself strong at all right now.

"Shit, I really should stop trying to sleep normally. If I'm going to fall into these shitty nightmares every time, what's the point?" he mumbled in horror. "I hope this is the last I see them for a while."

"Next time, I'll be the one hunting *them*," Glenn swore hatefully.

He paused and scoffed at himself. "But for now, let's just Meditate and slowly get stronger. I'm impatient for this day to be over."

Chapter 56

FASTEST TRIAL EVER

Glenn stared at the ceiling, contemplating the tasks ahead. During his conversation with Carys, he learned that Baron Howard was likely making an appearance in the next three days. Soon, he'd finally have the chance to unmask the Black Heir in his service and see if he was Giselle's grandson.

Despite the farmer's suggestion to use his brawn, he trusted his brain. He'd need to smooth-talk the Baron's guards—a task that could prove either straightforward or challenging, depending on the effectiveness of the Howard family ring. If nothing else, that endeavor would provide an opportunity to assess the Baron's security measures and determine the feasibility of rescuing Callum safely.

There was a reasonable chance of success, especially with Sahro's assistance. And if Howard truly was the monster the townsfolk talked him up to be, taking a legion of thralls head on was less than ideal.

Glenn planned to meet Sahro for lunch in a few hours at the Dining Hall. He hoped his comrade managed to gather some useful information about the noble in the meantime.

Until then, he needed to grow stronger—and do so rapidly. He had to dedicate more time to the Savant Ground, expanding his repertoire of spells and aiming for the Third Circle. Achieving the status of a True Initiate would undoubtedly bolster his abilities, a necessity if he found himself pitted against the Thorns Church.

And that confrontation was inevitable. With the Mark now upon him, fleeing was no longer an option.

"If push comes to shove, hopefully Giselle will keep her promise," he muttered.

Glancing through the grimy window, he noticed that the sun had begun its ascent, casting a gentle veil of orange morning light over the town. He had not rested at all, thanks to the cursed affliction.

With a sigh, he rose from his bed and began dressing himself. As he readied to leave, he couldn't help but yearn for a comforting cup of coffee. *Sadly, that divine nectar doesn't seem to exist in this world. I'll have to look into it when I have the time.*

When he swung open his door, his fatigued eyes were greeted by the unexpected sight of Sir Reginald standing in the corridor, absently twirling his mustache.

Wait, how long has he been there? Glenn wondered.

The gentleman gracefully tipped his top hat, offering a slight bow. "Hello, Mr. Glenn. I shall require your presence to accompany me."

Glenn's eyebrows arched in surprise. *Could it be related to the Seed of Darkness?*

He didn't have much time to ponder as the Cleaner briskly set off, compelling Glenn to hurriedly follow. Exiting the Dormitory and entering a designated 'Cleaners Only' area, they arrived in a vast chamber that bore an uncanny resemblance to...

A courtroom? Am I on trial?

There were Cleaners everywhere, be it in the stands, or on the bench as judges. Glenn was welcomed with worried whispers and careful glances. He recognized Mary, as well as the two members of the Delora family: Tom, the tiny robed figure and the bald Tak.

He looked up, discovering that the Cleaner directing the assembly was Kane, the Manager of the Cleaner's Workshop. Glenn searched for Rusty Stoneheart, but he didn't manage to find him in the audience.

The resounding thud of a wooden gavel struck the table, silencing all the murmurs in an instant and startling Glenn. He cautiously advanced, gazing at Kane with a quizzical expression. An empty lectern awaited him, presumably intended for his use as no one else appeared to be present.

Kane massaged his ass-shaped chin thoughtfully before heaving a weary sigh.

"Our apologies to you, Mr. Glenn," he began, his eyes reflecting fatigue, "but this couldn't wait any longer. We received the results of the item you gave us, and it, sadly, is indeed a Seed of Darkness. It has been taken care of—in a place and way that's of no concern to you."

Kane leaned forwards. "Now, what we need to ascertain is precisely how you came to possess that cursed artifact."

"Well, it's a rather lengthy tale. Are you certain you want me to tell you everything right now?"

Kane nodded solemnly, and Glenn responded with a nonchalant shrug. "So be it then."

Without a shred of hesitation, he recounted the story of how he got abducted—not even bothering to lie about why they attacked him. He destroyed their stash of drugs, was kidnapped, and then tortured for two months. He only escaped thanks to his incredible survival skills and luck... and totally not thanks to the intervention of a certain evil entity living in his left hand. During his escape, he picked up that Seed of Darkness, hoping to cause enough chaos, which succeeded. And now he was here.

Kane's countenance grew somber. He stood from the bench and left for a corner of the courtroom where he convened with his fellow judges.

Sir Reginald motioned for Glenn to follow him, guiding him outside.

"Sir Reginald, what's going to happen now?" Glenn asked.

The gentleman froze, his hand placed on his top hat. Then he simply left without a word.

"Shit is going down, huh?" Glenn muttered, staring at the back of the gentleman shrinking in the corridor.

"Hgn, what?" Diamanes groaned in displeasure.

"Go back to sleep, idiot," Glenn responded in a dry tone.

Diamanes obliged, leaving Glenn alone with his thoughts. He decided to use the early morning to practice his spells in the Savant Ground. Since Diamanes was asleep, he wouldn't have to 'eat his way out' of a burger mountain.

He departed from the confines of the Cleaner's Workshop and traversed the labyrinthine lanes of the Northern Town. At this early hour, he encountered few individuals apart from the diligent farmers embarking on their workday.

When he entered the humble shack, he summoned his key. 'Key' seemed far more practical of a name compared to the cumbersome 'recommendation plate', so he settled on that.

After the intricate twists and turns of the teleportation process, he materialized in the main lobby of the Magi Brotherhood. To his surprise, the area was teeming with activity—mirroring the bustling ambiance of his previous visit. It appeared that Mages were impervious to weariness, a testament to the efficacy of Meditation.

He used his key to enter the Savant Ground and quickly went to work. First, he attempted to create a magic shield using the Draconic School methods. Defense summoned instantly would be ten times more useful than a defense summoned too late because he had to yell some power words.

He thought of a strong and sturdy shield that could block anything. Stronger than stone or metal. He channeled his Mana, summoning a thick armament in the air that towered over him.

His Mana left his body at an abnormal rate. He slowed down the flow and discovered that, instead of simply disappearing, the heavy shield crashed into the ground as if it were made out of actual matter. Curious, he tried to pick up the magical guard, finding it manageable but still quite hard. It wasn't very ergonomic to hold, having no grip or strap—just a huge chunk of Mana that could block incoming attacks.

Or well, its defensive capabilities remain to be seen.

"Can I get something to attack this shield?" As soon as he asked for it, a fireball flew out of nowhere towards him.

He struggled to raise the shield and block the attack. The impact was light, and Glenn didn't even feel the heat of the flame. He examined the armament, seeing no apparent damage. His Mana had been consumed slightly, but nothing too incredible. He cut off the flow of the spell, evaluating his creation.

He could summon a very resilient—and very heavy— magic shield. The issue was getting it to float in the air. That required way more Mana than was feasible to expend. But he wasn't finished brainstorming.

Rethinking the design, he tried for something thinner and more refined. He imagined a tapered design with sturdy enarmes. He channeled his Mana once more, summoning a kite shield.

It was smaller than its giant counterpart, but it was easier to handle and could be strapped to his arm. He could also make it float a little, even if it wasn't cost-effective in terms of Mana. He decided to name this version of the Portable Shield, and the other the Magic Wall. He could summon the Magic Wall to cover his back, and the Portable Shield for more precise shots. With this, his defense was bolstered pretty well.

Now, he had to invest some time trying to learn buffing spells. Glenn felt like it was oddly video-game-like to summon a buff. *How does it work? In a game, a buff augments certain stats or skills. But how would I do that in reality? A speed buff could almost be considered like time magic. But what would a strength buff do? Make my muscles stronger somehow?*

He summoned the terminal, intending to check if any spells could augment one's power. After flipping through a few pages, he discovered something similar to what he was looking for.

Spell: Blood Surge, provided by Azenoir

Description: The Blood Surge spell accelerates blood circulation within the recipient's body.

Usage: Blood Surge temporarily enhances the physical capabilities of the target, encompassing strength, agility, and reaction times. Additionally, it expedites the natural healing process, mitigates the onset of fatigue, and results in heightened mental acuity, alertness, and cognitive functions.

Caution: Excessive use can be fatal for individuals with underlying heart conditions, and may lead to dehydration, blood clots, and other cardiovascular injuries.

Formula: ???

Mana Usage: ???

Credit Cost: 100 *(Owned credits: 50)*

Glenn gasped. *That's balance-breaking! OP! It buffs the entire body! Well, the risk of dying might look a bit bad, but the creator probably went overkill with the warning.*

He looked for the cost, his eyes widening in shock. One hundred credits?! He thought there were no spells above fifty! And fifty was all he had! Damn it!

"Why the hell is it so expensive?" he complained, letting go of the terminal.

That was the perfect spell too! Well, now that I have an idea thanks to the description, perhaps I could try to replicate it in the Draconic School way.

He tried to imagine his blood flow accelerating, pulled by Mana. He concentrated, entering a state of Meditation accidentally. In front of him, he saw his body—his veins highlighted in red. He tried controlling Mana delicately to help the blood run faster, but he soon ran into an issue. It was *impossible* to control Mana with such precision. Well, he didn't know about better Mages, but it was impossible for him, that's for sure.

Glenn sighed, leaving his magic buff idea for later. Now was the time to get to the even cooler part. The offensive spells. Glenn's first goal was to fuse Arcane Auger and Magic Bullet, creating a small, drilling bullet.

The process was straightforward—creating the bullet and channeling his Mana into it until it spun. Before long, he summoned his first Drilling Bullet.

"Ahh, it feels good to have something work exactly like I want it to!" exclaimed Glenn.

He then asked the Savant Ground for a target, and it happily obliged. A steel dummy appeared thirty meters away. Without waiting, he shot his Drilling Bullet. The projectile penetrated the steel easily before disappearing into a cloud of Mana only a few centimeters deep. Glenn strained his eyes, doubting the efficiency of his spell.

"The Drilling Bullet is probably great against armored opponents while the Magic Bullet can tear through flesh, like those fat rats back at the bakery."

The only downside was that it consumed double the Mana of Magic Bullet, but it wasn't a lot anyway.

Good improvements all around! He then tried to think of one last spell— one to use if he was surrounded by a lot of enemies, like in the Golden Fields and its army of creepy scarecrows. *Maybe a fireball would do the trick?*

Glenn didn't waste any time, imagining a fiery, destructive ball. He channeled his Mana and... nothing happened. Creasing his eyebrows, he focused on the image in his head. But no matter how hard he tried, nothing would happen. He was just throwing Mana away.

Glenn grimaced before trying another spell. He imagined a simple directed shockwave. With the concept in mind, he channeled his Mana, witnessing in silence as he blasted a dummy a few meters away.

Why can I do this spell and not the other? What's different? Is it because I tried to use an element—fire in this case—to create a fireball?

Glenn shook his head. He could summon a Fire Spark without any issue using the School of Words.

Wait. Could I do the same thing with just my thoughts?

Glenn concentrated, imagining a little flame burning on top of his finger. He channeled his Mana and... once again, nothing happened.

He groaned in confusion. *Why won't it work?!*

Chapter 57

BROTHER KHAN, TELL ME A STORY!

Glenn stared at his fingertip, hoping for a flicker of flame. But once more, he felt like a fool as his Mana dissipated without a spark.

Frustration gnawed at him; he couldn't grasp the elusive rules governing elemental spells. He experimented with ice, wind, and earth—nothing worked.

He sat on the floor, pondering his predicament. Both Redan's tutelage and Exan's writings taught him that Draconic School spells were linked to one's Mana Heart. But what did that mean if his Heart took on the shape of a celestial body?

"Fire is the combustion of oxygen," Glenn mumbled, his chin resting on his hand. "Maybe I need to envision oxygen burning? But no, it doesn't make sense..." He frowned. "I doubt they know about atoms and molecules in this world. So how?"

Glenn began to Meditate, diving into his Mana Heart and gazing at the Magellanic Clouds—his source of magic. He knew it held explosive potential with Implosion, but he hadn't delved further into it. Implosion had been more the product of luck and enlightenment, instead of an expected result.

Redan's Mana Heart resembled a spear made of white ice, and he was proficient with ice magic. Glenn needed to create spells using the Magellanic Clouds' power. *What would my proficiency even be? Cool exploding shit?*

Glenn suddenly understood Redan's confusion when he saw his Mana Heart. Indeed, he had his work cut out for him. He tried to recall the knowledge he had on the Magellanic Clouds. He never was an expert on heavenly bodies; the name had only been given to him in a strange, enlightening way.

The Magellanic Clouds were two dwarf galaxies containing billions of stars and vast amounts of cosmic materials. If he used that as an explanation of his Mana Heart's power, that meant it contained immense and nearly limitless magical potential. Nonetheless, he didn't feel as if he had unlimited power. When he used Implosion, he fell instantly into a short coma, and he didn't want to imagine what would happen with even stronger spells.

Am I fated to be a one pump chump?

No, he refused to accept that. Glenn resolved to create a new spell harnessing his Mana Heart's power.

"Give me some steel dummies!" Glenn requested from the Savant Ground, gritting his teeth.

With utmost care, he visualized the Clouds descending and conserved his Mana. As the spell formed, his consumption rate surged. The dummies crashed to the dirt, crushed by the force of his new spell. Beads of sweat trickled down as he struggled to halt its momentum, but it was too late. His Mana flowed uncontrollably, fueling the gravity spell.

"Damn it!"

Glenn finally managed to cut off the flow while he gasped for air. He had succeeded in not using every last drop of his Mana, but he was left without enough to even summon a Magic Bullet.

I'm just lucky I didn't lose consciousness like last time. He sighed.

If steel dummies buckled under the pressure of his gravity spell, he was certain that humans would be in for a world of hurt. Plus, it was good for crowd-control if he managed to tweak the settings.

Maybe a wider range with less power. Or instead, I concentrate it in one spot to crush a single target. He shivered, not willing to imagine the aftermath.

That would be a bloody mess. That's all I'm saying, Diamanes suddenly commented while yawning.

Glenn shook his head, recognizing that his practice session had concluded with the awakening of his demonic hand. He glanced at the Savant Ground, slowly coming to terms with the fact that he was going to need more Mana before truly diving into his Mana Heart's specialty.

He infused his remaining Mana into his key with the intent to leave the Magi Brotherhood HQ. After reappearing in the shabby hut and exiting, he realized that most of the morning had passed, leaving about an hour until his lunch meeting with Sahro.

Strolling through the Northern Town's streets, he stopped by Hearts Bakery. When he arrived, he found an intriguing sight: a long queue outside the shop. The tantalizing aroma of freshly baked bread wafted through the air, causing Glenn's stomach to rumble. He joined the line, patiently waiting his turn.

The shopkeepers efficiently served customers, and Glenn eventually reached the front doors. A petite woman rushed around the counter, her face beaming when she noticed Glenn.

"Mrs. Laurence," Glenn greeted her, eyeing the shelves piled high with steaming loaves.

She wiped her brow. "Hello, Mr. Glenn! I hope Mr. Sahro is doing well. I apologize for the wait. As you can see, we have quite a crowd today. What can I get for you?"

Glenn smiled and pointed at one of the baguettes. Mrs. Laurence swiftly packaged it and handed it to Glenn, who accepted it gratefully.

"Two coppers! Come on, chop, chop!"

Glenn chuckled and paid. He left the bakery, clutching the warm loaf under his arm. Business appeared to be thriving for Mrs. Laurence. He tore off a small piece of bread and savored its crispy exterior. A few more bites confirmed its deliciousness.

As he wandered the Northern Town's streets, he lost track of his surroundings and found himself in a tranquil park surrounded by greenery.

It was almost as if he had been transported into the middle of a forest. People relaxed on benches to the singing of birds or strolled by lush gardens of sweet-smelling flowers.

As Glenn followed the trail, he discovered a huge church situated at the center of the park—supported by two ancient, towering trees that served as its foundation. Green moss covered the stone walls and wrapped around the stained-glass windows that depicted a benevolent woman shining light on her followers.

Curious, Glenn entered the church. Instead of the solemn silence he expected, priests eagerly chatted with citizens who came to share their worries. A soothing feeling washed over Glenn as he stepped inside, calming his heart and mind.

Although, Diamanes couldn't help but complain. *I almost feel like I'm going to transform into holy light. Why did you come here exactly?*

Glenn shrugged off Diamanes' protests. *Maybe they offer discounts on exorcisms.*

Glenn explored the church, admiring its architecture while ignoring the entity's curses of indignation. A well of light cast a spotlight on a massive statue of a beautiful woman wearing a benevolent smile, mirroring the stained glass.

A young priest carrying a hefty book approached Glenn with a polite demeanor. His slender frame and good looks could have graced the pages of a magazine on Earth.

"Do you need help, young man?"

Glenn adjusted his tie. "I'm just visiting, thanks. Is this the Church of Onnea?"

The priest smiled. "Indeed. Are you not from here?"

Glenn shook his head, prompting the priest to continue.

"Do you want me to tell you the story of the Church? If you have the time, of course," asked the young priest.

Glenn shrugged. "Well, why not... Uh, mister?"

The priest bowed. "I'm Brother Khan. But you can call me what you like."

He invited Glenn to sit on a nearby bench, opening a book with a silver scale on the cover. He coughed before starting his explanation.

"Our religion is dedicated to the Dame of Harmony, the Mother of Eternal Balance—Goddess Onnea. We're the ones who push back against the forces of darkness, restoring order in this chaotic world. We're heavily invested in world peace, and due to that, have one of the most powerful religious forces in the world. Almost comparable to warring religions," Brother Khan proudly explained.

The Dame of Harmony and the Mother of Eternal Balance... What grand titles, thought Glenn.

The young priest continued. "We're based in every region of Munirp, but our headquarters are in the Holy Grounds in Westeria. It's another country that has been blessed by the Dame of Harmony and the holy land for us believers of Onnea."

"Our goddess appeared in a time of war and apocalypse, before the First King. She, along with the other six Primordial Gods, protected our world, sealing it away from the evil entities beyond. This was the Epoch of the Gods." The priest sighed.

"Even today, after thousands and thousands of years, marks of those terrible battles still plague our world."

Glenn's eyebrows rose as he held out his hand in question. "Wait, is the Moon Rift one of those marks?"

The priest tilted his head. "Well, some think that it is. Some think that its origin is something else entirely. The issue is that all records from before the Epoch of the Gods are gone, so no one knows."

Glenn rubbed his chin thoughtfully. "Who were the six other Gods?"

The priest smiled and flipped through the pages of his book, opening it to some illustrations. He pointed to a drawing of a golden, eastern dragon sleeping on a gigantic mountain of gold.

"There's the Order of Plutus, or the Gold Church, who venerate the Lord of the Merchants—the Emperor of Greed as some call him. It's... a peculiar religion, oriented towards gaining wealth."

I think I'd like that religion, thought Glenn. *Wasn't Winston a follower of the Gold Church?*

"They are the ones who hold the most money in this world. Banks, loan companies, merchants associations... Each of them is linked to the Gold Church in one way or another."

He then flipped to a page showing a shadow wielding a scythe. The drawing was exceptionally dark, obscuring any details.

"Then there is the Cult of Nergal, the Underworld Church that venerates the Reaper of Souls. It's a very mysterious religion. There are little records of them—legends of their believers appearing on battlefields and gathering corpses before disappearing strangely."

Glenn frowned. "If there are so few records, how do people know they exist?"

Brother Khan shrugged. "Who knows? Even with such little information about them, every major governing body accepts their existence."

He flipped the page once again, showing a faceless man covered in thorns and lashes. Brother Khan grimaced but continued his explanation.

"You probably heard of them with the recent events surrounding the Auberge. That's the Thorns Church. A religion venerating the God of Pain, Epinos. Its members are fanatical, and apt to... *proselytize* the vulnerable. We at the Church of Onnea have a particular distaste for their kind. They aren't present in King's Rise, thankfully, but perhaps you saw their church outside the Frozen Gate."

Glenn nodded painfully. The young priest quickly turned over the page, uneasy when seeing the illustration of Epinos.

"Originally, the Thorns Church wasn't like this. There are records proving that it was a church of pardon. But during the Epoch of the Gods, the religion became a masochistic cult."

"Bastards..." Glenn blurted out before looking away from Brother Khan's confused gaze.

The latter shook his head and then pointed at a new drawing showing a wounded, muscular man roaring. His leather armor was torn, and he held a sword and an axe in his hands. He stood on a pile of bodies in a bloody, macabre scene.

"That's the Brotherhood of Iron Blood, venerating the Father of War. The central tenet of the Brotherhood is martial honor. Honor triumphs over all, in their eyes, encouraging their believers to uphold a strict code of ethics in combat. The Brotherhood traditionally forges their own weapons, bounding them to themselves in an ancient, divine ritual."

Glenn whistled, impressed. "They sound like real badasses."

Brother Khan smiled gently. "They are. There is a branch in the Military District outside the city, as well as the Western Town. I think they want to build one in the Northern Town too."

He flipped the page, letting Glenn discover yet another illustration. An elderly figure with a long, flowing beard and hair as white as snow wore a robe adorned with intricate runes. He floated above a library, holding a radiant crystal orb in one hand and a tome in the other.

"This is the Divine Sage, the Keeper of Arcane and Ruler of Magic. They are a peculiar God, as they don't have an actual religion."

Glenn's brows creased. *A God without a religion? There's something wrong with that sentence.*

"Instead," continued Brother Khan, "they introduced the foundations of what is known today as the Magi Brotherhood during the Epoch of the Gods."

Glenn gasped. "What? I'm part of the Magi Brotherhood, and I wasn't even aware of that!"

Brother Khan laughed. "It's not surprising. The Magi Brotherhood is, as envisioned by the Divine Sage, a place to learn and trade magic—pushing its developments further. Not to revere a God."

He turned the page, revealing the seventh God. Only, the paper was blank.

Glenn looked at the priest quizzically. "Weren't there seven Primordial Gods?"

Brother Khan rubbed his head, smiling awkwardly. "Well, I can understand your confusion. The seventh God, uhm, *died*."

Glenn's eyes widened. *A God can die?*

The priest raised his hands helplessly. "The records state the presence of a seventh God. But there is no reference to their name, their principles, or their believers. It's as if they disappeared completely. We know they were here, but we don't know what they did."

Glenn sighed, looking at the stained glass. His gaze suddenly shook, seeing the sun high in the sky. He stood up, flustered.

"Damnit, I forgot Sahro. I'm sorry, Brother Khan, this was a fascinating history lesson, but I need to go now!"

The priest bowed. "Do come again, and may the Goddess Onnea watch over you."

The Goddess watching over me... Glenn chuckled in awe. *These Gods are probably real, considering the supernatural powers priests wield... I wonder if there's a way to meet them. Maybe they know something about what brought me to this world.*

Chapter 58

DAMNED MOSQUITOES

Glenn held his chin, carefully rubbing the swollen spot that would soon become a bruise. Sahro sat opposite him, glaring in frustration.

"Bastard, I ate seven whole chickens in the time it took you to get here!"

"What? You pig, you ate seven *entire* chickens? Are you mad?" Glenn exclaimed in awe.

They were in the bustling Dining Hall, their plates filled to the brim as they exchanged words, each punctuated by bites and sips.

Glenn shook his head as his eyes widened. "Do you have a black hole for a stomach? How can you eat seven chickens and order another damn steak?!"

"I'm a warrior. I need a lot of food! And what the hell is a black hole, anyway?" Sahro blurted out as he pointed his knife at his friend.

"It's something that even your idiocy can't fill! Crazy, right?!"

"Who's the idiot? Not even the Thorns Church bastards are as stupid as you, Glenn!"

Both of them slapped down their chicken wings, locking eyes defiantly. Glenn finally sighed, surrendering. They had more pressing matters, like rescuing Callum.

Glenn cleaned his hands with *Mundare,* a soft light consuming the dirt on his fingers. Now that he had access to utility magic like Cleaning Touch, he planned to make full use of it.

"So, what have you learned?" Glenn asked.

Sahro wiped his face with a disposable napkin like a normal person before coughing. "Everyone."

Glenn looked at him quizzically. "Everyone what?"

Sahro leaned forwards, supporting his chin. "Every villager I spoke to hates Baron Howard. Every *single* one of them despises him."

Glenn frowned. "I gathered as much. There is literally a rebellion broiling, and we're going to be part of it."

Sahro blinked. "Sorry, what?"

Glenn cleared his throat before briefly explaining Carys' plan, Baron Howard transforming his kidnapped victims into beastly servants, and the citizens' grudge against him.

"Hmm... So we won't be alone fighting him. Good." Sahro nodded slowly. "From what I understood, the main line of defense between us and the Baron are his soldiers. Cruel low-ranked soldiers who love to make the townspeople's lives harder."

Glenn rubbed his chin. He didn't exactly have a great measure of how strong Aura users were—aside from his few bouts with Sahro—but it couldn't be good if every enemy fighter possessed it.

"Low-ranked how?"

Sahro rapped his knuckles on the table. "The bottom of the barrel. Stronger than normal people, but not even ten of them would be able to take one of you. And I'm not even talking about myself."

"Hmm... Which means Carys' help does have some use. Excellent. What else?"

The Black Heir's expression hardened, and he crossed his arms. "The Baron has a personal guard, Stormblade. A knight wearing dark armor. Nobody's seen his face, like nobody's ever seen the Baron without him. He's our main target, according to your rebel friend's plan."

Glenn pointed his fork at the Black Heir. "Careful. Don't forget there are those... *thralls* to be wary of. Carys couldn't tell me much about them, but they'll certainly be dangerous—and our burden to take care of."

Sahro spat on the ground, a look of disgust on his face. "Damned *eubayd!*" Sahro sneered. "There were Mages like that in the Ink Dunes. Giselle told me about them. Monsters weren't the biggest threat—they were!"

"They would kidnap our people for their bloody rituals," Sahro continued, his voice full of anger. "They weren't Black Heirs, nor humans, but they shared the same physiology. Their skin was pale white, as if they never saw the sun. And their eyes glowed in the dark like red rubies."

Glenn choked on the cider. *There's no way. There were vampires in the Ink Dunes?*

"Sahro, do they only appear at night? Any legends of them drinking blood? Transforming into bats?"

Sahro fell from his chair. "You know about them?"

Glenn chuckled with a hint of despair, hiding his face in his hands. "Damn this world... From what I know, these *eubayd* of yours are called vampires, and Baron Howard is one of them."

"Vampires?"

Glenn explained, "Immortal beings with human appearances who avoid the sun to prevent incineration. They feed on the blood of most living beings, but more often on humanoids. I'm not sure if that's what they're called in this region, but that's what we named them in my country."

The Black Heir crossed his arms.

"Are they just sun-averse leeches?"

Glenn shook his head seriously. "If my knowledge is accurate, vampires are immortal—using blood as their source of power. They can control blood with dark magic and can transform others into vampires. They're weak to silver and garlic."

"Garlic?" Sahro raised an eyebrow.

First, no coffee and now no garlic bread? This place really is Hell.

"Yeah, never mind that. It'll be better for us both if we spend our time sharpening our blades. Ah, and he might have a connection to the Thorns Church, so keep that in mind."

"When is he returning to the Northern Town?"

"Soon. Could be a few days. It depends on our luck, I suppose. But the more I learn about him, the more I feel like we need to be prepared."

Sahro stood, placing his hands on the table. "I'll try to get more contracts and gather information. If we need silver weapons, we'll need a lot more money."

Glenn cracked his neck. "I'll search the Library for information on vampires. Let's meet at my place tonight."

* * *

Glenn entered the maze of bookshelves, seeking a tome by Exan. He had taken a liking to his fellow Earthling, and even if he couldn't contact him directly, Exan stood as a reminder that *home* was still out there.

Glenn quickly flipped through *The Bestiary* to find a section on humanoid monsters. He skimmed through the various entries, each accompanied by vivid illustrations. His eyes froze when he recognized a creature.

__Ghouls__ are creatures of death. They often linger on battlefields where corpses are numerous. Otherwise, they remain nestled underground, hanging in hundreds around their Ghoul Mother. They're scavengers but will still attack living beings without any hesitation.

You kill one of these little bastards, and a hundred of them swarm your ass, pulled by the smell of their dead colleague. You can quickly get overwhelmed by them, even though they are pretty weak atrocities.

A drawing of a humanoid creature with a face replaced by a gigantic mouth full of teeth waited for him on the next page.

"So that was a ghoul. I suppose I should be happy that I fled the scene quickly back then..." Glenn muttered, holding his stomach.

Something was strange, though. Exan mentioned that killing one ghoul was enough to bait the rest of the swarm, and yet...

Was I just incredibly lucky, or did something protect me? pondered Glenn as he thought back to his temporary healing ability and whatever allowed him to understand languages in this world. *I doubt Exan would make such bold claims if he wasn't certain.*

The memory of him getting eaten alive was still very fresh in his mind. He turned the page, wishing to not reminisce.

Finally, he found the information he sought. Glenn winced while he read.

***Vampires** are immortal, humanoid creatures, often as smart as they are wicked. They use blood as the source of their power and are able to transform those who drink their blood into a thrall.*

It is said that they're the product of a curse, which is why they burn under the touch of the sun and react adversely to silver. Uneducated people might think they're also weak to garlic, but all that would do is give a vampire bad breath. And if you eat it, garlic would only season your blood, so don't. At least, not to protect yourself from vampires.

They're not all bad, but some are on the extremist side—wishing to dominate humans to use as food stock. They are excellent fighters, excellent Mages, and to top it all off, often have absurdly powerful regeneration.

Glenn leaned back in his chair, sighing in tiredness. Indeed, vampires were *vampires*, which meant probable trouble for him and Sahro. Perhaps the Baron was a bloodsucker who kept Callum around as an occasional snack.

Glenn then blemished, thinking of another possibility. *What if the Baron made Callum into a thrall?*

That thought sent a shiver down his spine. Glenn shook his head, not wanting to dwell on the idea. After all, there were numerous accounts of the Baron moving about in daylight, often accompanied by his Black Heir. He likely wasn't a vampire but some sort of Mage with access to the vile tactics the Thorns Church used.

He returned the tome to its shelf and was about to leave the Library when he noticed a smaller book a row below, titled *The Fringe's Traditions.* Glenn's eyes brightened, and he hurriedly seized it.

"This has to contain some information about the Harvest," muttered Glenn, hopefully.

It's nice to hope. Ugh, it looks old. And look at all that dust! This is the Cleaner's Workshop, and yet it's dirtier than a teenager's bedroom! complained Diamine's.

Glenn ignored him as he flipped through the pages.

"The Harvest... Ah!" Glenn smiled as he found what he was looking for.

The Northern Town, as well as all three other cardinal towns, were built to assure a steady and stable stream of food supplies to the Crown. In exchange, they would receive the protection of the Watchers—elite troops who guard the walls of King's Rise.

Out of gratitude for the security given to them by the Crown, the towns created a tradition: **The Harvest.** *Periodically, a large amount of resources—be it food, weapons, or workforce—would be sent to the upper stratum of King's Rise. A noble of the Bourgeoisie is chosen to watch over this process and ensure that just enough resources are taken from the villagers.*

This tradition is the foundation of the good relationship between the Fringe, the Bourgeoisie, the Court, and the Crown.

Glenn closed the book, puzzled.

And then corruption swept over the land and turned it into a blood harvest. The end, muttered Diamanes.

Glenn stored the book back in its place and headed for the Library's exit. At the doorway, he encountered a familiar woman playing with a knife.

"Ms. Mary? Can I help you?"

The attractive Cleaner wore a broad grin as she sheathed her knife. "No, but I can help *you*."

Glenn regarded her with a hint of suspicion as she handed him a letter.

Hey kiddo, I couldn't help but notice ya had a stupidly strong body and a stupid brain to use it. So my friend here's gonna help teach you. Better listen to her carefully!

—Redan.

P.S. Don't try to reply—It's a one-way message. I'm out of town by now anyway.

Glenn looked back at Mary. "Uhm, are you the one who's going to train me, Ms. Mary?"

Mary's grin grew wider, taking on an almost predatory quality. She nodded slowly, her gaze scanning him up and down.

Oh, lucky you. Yet another teacher that's here to salvage the mess that you are, mocked Diamanes.

Glenn could only sigh in response. *At least I'll have a beautiful woman training me. That has to count for something, right? Right?*

Chapter 59

MY BODY IS READY

Glenn followed Mary as she led him to the Training Hall. It had been converted into a vast, open space with sparring rings, obstacle courses, and climbing walls. Wooden swords, spears, and more lined the weapon racks, alongside training dummies.

They entered one of the empty combat circles, and Mary pointed to the rack.

"Pick a weapon and come at me. No magic—just the sweat and sinew of combat. I'm here to teach you the art of melee fighting, got it?"

Glenn swallowed hard, his heart beating like a snare roll. He selected a wooden sword, the weight of it heavier than he'd anticipated. It felt like a lead bat. Not that it bothered him; it was still quite light for his abnormal body.

He positioned himself before Mary, his grip on the hilt tightening. Mary, unarmed but oozing confidence, didn't flinch. Glenn knew he was in for a bruising. Memories of his previous humiliation at her hands gnawed at him. Yet, he was determined to try.

With a burst of adrenaline, he lunged at her, the sword cleaving the air with a resounding whoosh. Mary sidestepped effortlessly, a taunting smirk gracing her lips. She beckoned him to try again, her eyes gleaming with challenge. Glenn, his temper simmering, attempted a flurry of slashes. He then aimed a thrust at her, only to have it deftly dodged as she cocked her head with a mocking expression.

"Was that an attack? My apologies. I must've missed it."

Even though he was trying his best not to get riled up, Glenn still got a little annoyed at his opponent toying with him. He dashed at her, cutting his sword in a wide, crescent movement, but she ducked under the blade effortlessly.

Without losing a second, Glenn continued his assault and feinted a kick, only to punch her with all he had. Mary smirked and swiftly used Glenn's momentum to throw him on the ground.

Mary loomed over him while dusting off her hands. "Oh, nice try using your fist. Perhaps that would have worked against the weakest of thugs. Too bad I ain't one, right?"

Glenn scrambled to his feet, gritting his teeth as he scanned the arena for his lost sword. His frustration mounted as he clenched his jaw. Mary nonchalantly tossed the wooden sword to him, and he snatched it midair.

Just as he grasped the hilt, a shoe filled his vision, and a fierce kick landed on his face, propelling him backwards. The hit stung, but it was Glenn's pride that suffered the most.

"Shit, am I really that bad of a fighter?"

With a groan, he glanced upwards, only to find Mary preparing another kick—this time targeting his most vulnerable spot. He rolled away just in time and held up his sword—ready to block the next assault. Yet, to his astonishment, Mary had vanished.

"Where is she?" Glenn mumbled before his legs swept out from under him, and he thudded onto the ground with a thundering crash.

Glenn coughed and forced himself up, locking eyes with Mary, who regarded him with disappointment.

"I thought you'd be more of... something, considering the old man sent you my way. But you're not what I expected." She sighed, stretching her limbs casually.

Glenn seized the opportunity, launching himself at Mary and hurling the wooden sword towards her and preparing for a tackle. *Hitting a woman isn't gentleman like? Who cares!*

Success seemed imminent as his arms closed around Mary's waist. But before he knew it, his body soared over her head. Glenn slammed into the mat, a cloud of dust billowing around him. He coughed, the breath pulled out of his lungs. He stumbled on his feet when a heavy object suddenly collided with his skull, sending him sprawling once more.

Struggling to open his eyes, Glenn realized the world was shaking. He could even discern a star or two through the blurry haze.

"Well, at least you've got stamina," a voice remarked, though Glenn only caught half the words through the ringing in his ears.

Glenn clutched his head as he gradually regained his senses. The fog in front of his eyes dissipated, replaced by another shoe hurtling towards his face. He rolled aside just in time to avoid it, springing to his feet as quickly as his battered body allowed. Though not exhausted—as his enhanced body afforded him formidable stamina—he still felt helplessly outmatched.

Mary watched him patiently, a smile playing on her lips. He raised his hands in surrender, mentally exhausted by the beating.

"I... I give up!" he heaved, a trickle of blood running down his chin.

The woman's sly smile turned devilish for a second before disappearing, making Glenn doubt his eyes. She closed on him and grabbed Glenn by the shoulders.

"You're sure?"

Glenn nodded. *My pride suffered enough. Even my supposedly abnormal body feels like it has been beaten to a pulp.*

Mary grinned wickedly. "But I don't want to stop?"

Huh?

Thump!

Glenn bent in two, holding his belly. His breath had been brusquely cut, and air refused to return to his lungs. He felt like he was about to puke.

"Shit! *Cough, bleurgh!*"

Glenn threw up a bit of his lunch, falling to his knees. *How is it possible for a hit to hurt so much?! It's almost as terrible as getting impaled by a spear.*

Wait. His eyes regained their focus, as he understood one thing. *Almost as terrible? No way! This isn't even close to some of the other shit I've been through!*

What was happening wasn't the worst thing that hurt him. This... This was great compared to the pain of ingesting Beast Blood every day for two months or getting eaten alive. A walk in the park! Just a rough massage! He forced himself back up, a grin decorating his face. He took one deep breath after another as he wiped the vomit off his chin.

Glenn struggled to raise his wooden sword. With resignation not an option, he lunged at Mary, a roar of rage escaping him. He thrust and threw his entire body into each attack. Blood rushed through his veins, his heart pounding with adrenaline. He absorbed every blow he suffered with grim determination. His attacks, though futile, were relentless.

"Argh! Damn it!" he bellowed.

He pressed on, his body battered but unwavering—even as none of his strikes found their mark. Mary's eyes gleamed, her grin replaced by a knowing smile as she observed Glenn's unyielding spirit.

But then, Glenn's body suddenly went limp.

No... I... I can still fight! he thought desperately.

A voice sighed in his mind. **She hit one of your vital points. Enjoy the sweet nap. See you in a few!**

Glenn crumpled to the ground, his body battered and bruised. Mary looked down at him with a weary expression, shaking her head. She fetched a bucket of water before kneeling by the unconscious young man.

"*Sigh.* I've got my work cut out for me."

She emptied the bucket on Glenn's head, jolting him awake. He made a resigned expression as he pushed himself up, standing on two wobbly legs and keeping up an equally wobbly guard. His wooden sword was lying a few meters away, but Glenn gave up on it. *It's not like it's helping me anyway.*

Mary overturned the bucket and used it as a seat. She stared at the weary Glenn with a smile.

Glenn stepped forwards hesitantly. "Is... Is it over?"

The woman crossed her legs. "Me humiliating you? Yes, for now."

Glenn breathed out in relief, plopping back down on the sparring mat. His whole body ached like hell, but he still had fight left in him. Having a supernatural physique allowed him to have enhanced strength and stamina but didn't block the pain.

The woman clasped her hands together, an innocent expression on her face. "So, from my observations, I can guess a few things. You have a really stupidly strong body, but you've never fought once in your life, have you? You've probably never held a weapon ever, and now you mainly rely on magic to fight even though you have such perfect constitution."

Glenn chuckled painfully. There was nothing he could deny. He understood why Redan sent Mary to train him. But why did it have to be so brutally painful?

Mary put on a curious expression, a finger on her chin. "I think they call it the Heavenly Body in the Eastern Countries. It's pretty rare, but it's often given to geniuses. Too bad you're far from being one."

Glenn shrugged, impervious to the provocation. He moaned in pain as he sat himself up, locking eyes with Mary. "So what now?"

The woman stood from her makeshift seat, heading towards the weapon rack. She picked up a spear and threw it next to him.

"Try attacking me with that." Upon seeing the despaired expression of her student, she let out a short laugh. "Don't worry. I'm not fighting back this time. It's simply to check your affinity with weapons."

Glenn sighed in relief, using the spear to help himself to his feet. He held it awkwardly, taking a bit of time before finally getting comfortable. Despite being made of wood, it strangely weighed a ton. He took a breath before lunging forwards, trying to skewer the Cleaner, only to be mocked by her effortless dodges.

In frustration, he hurled the spear at her, throwing it as if it was a javelin. She simply stared at the projectile landing meters away from her, a judging expression in her eyes.

Glenn approached the weapon rack himself. He chose a one-handed mace, hoping to crush the woman's head, even if he knew there was no way it would happen.

Still, it was good to dream. He hesitated to pick a shield as a secondary weapon but decided against it; Mary was fast enough to get behind him any time. A shield would only slow him down.

Instead, he picked a machete. *Perhaps with two weapons, I'll get different results.*

* * *

Glenn held his face in frustration. He had tried everything—short swords, longswords, spears, scythes, war hammers, and morningstars— literally every weapon possible, but nothing made a scratch on Mary's fair skin. He plopped onto the ground, wiping the sweat off his forehead.

"Well, look on the bright side! You're equally shit at everything, which means you can only improve!" Mary cheered, her mocking words hurting the dispirited Glenn.

He rested against the wall, glancing at the numerous weapons abandoned on the training ground. He didn't have an affinity for any weapons, sadly. Perhaps he was destined to fight using spells and ranged attacks. He shook his head, refusing to accept such a result. It would be way more practical if he could use both.

"As I see it, the only solution would be to train your body to handle as many movements as possible," said Mary.

"Better to be a jack of all trades and know how to defend yourself rather than lose our time trying to make you a swordmaster."

Mary selected the largest, heaviest, and longest sword she could find from the rack, alongside a simple shortsword.

"Since you have no affinity," she began, "I'll train both your body and your technique. A spear would be simpler to learn, but a sword is more versatile."

Glenn arched an eyebrow, genuinely curious.

"Since your body is already so unnaturally strong, it's going to be hard to train it using common methods. This stupidly huge piece of garbage is going to strain your muscles, and use some that you never even knew existed."

With an effortless flick of her wrist, she tossed the greatsword to him. Glenn barely managed to catch it, nearly dropping it due to its colossal weight. It must have weighed around fifteen kilograms and stood at an impressive two and a half meters. Crafted from oak wood, it bore holes in the 'blade', revealing its leaden core—the source of its considerable weight.

"In addition," Mary continued, "if you can learn to handle this monstrosity, you'll become proficient with any lighter weapons as a bonus."

Glenn inspected the unwieldy greatsword, and on the hilt, he noticed an engraving that read, 'The Fool's Trainer'.

Huh. Really adding insult to injury.

He gave the weapon a few experimental swings, struggling to control the behemoth. Though fifteen kilograms didn't seem heavy for him, the awkward size was working against him, making it feel ten times as cumbersome.

Glenn glanced at Mary and then back at The Fool's Trainer. "Wait, am I supposed to spar with you using this?" he inquired, a bead of sweat forming on his brow.

The woman sneered before shaking her head. "No, I'll teach you some moves, and you'll practice them until I say otherwise."

Glenn's gaze shifted to the wooden shortsword. "And what about this? Why did you bring that out?"

Mary's smile grew predatory once more. "Oh, that's for sparring with me, of course! Did you think I was done with you?"

Glenn's face drained of color as he sighed, mentally preparing himself for the ordeal ahead. *It's all for my own good*, he reminded himself.

Damn it.

* * *

As Glenn stared at the sky, his thoughts drifted back to his past on Earth, recalling simpler times when his only concerns revolved around grades and career aspirations. He was able to fool with his friends and have time with girls. Now... Well, now he felt like dying would be quicker than what he was doing.

He had an inkling that he was only one step away from the afterlife after this torture of a training session.

Glenn lay sprawled on the grass of the Nexus, his body aching in every conceivable place—every breath a reminder of his pain. His hands were blistered, and his eye, swollen from a brutal hit, barely allowed him to see. Even his bouts with Sahro hadn't left him in such a pitiful state.

But that wasn't the worst of it. Oh, no. The worst part was that it wasn't a one time thing. Mary wasn't done with him. They had to meet every afternoon—daily—starting from today.

The Fool's Trainer's weight lingered in his hands, its relentless swings ingrained in his muscle memory. He must have swung that monstrous blade a thousand times, and with each failure, he endured a punishing blow from Mary.

Nevertheless, Glenn felt a measure of satisfaction. With each passing day, he sensed his strength growing and his understanding of Mana deepening. He was inching closer to the Third Circle. It wouldn't be long before he became a True Initiate. In addition, perhaps in a few weeks, he would be able to defend himself in melee, becoming the epitome of a magic swordsman... or whatever his strange build was called.

So, when are you planning to take action? Diamanes mused, his boredom evident in his tone. ***You know, do something genuinely useful?***

I'll do exactly that when that damned Baron arrives in the Northern Town. Right now, I'll use this time to build my strength. Isn't that exactly what you wanted? Glenn answered tiredly, a little annoyed at the lack of sympathy that Diamanes showed to him.

I want you to get to the Third Circle, not just watch as you get beaten up. It's quite entertaining, don't get me wrong. But you know, it does get tiring at some point.

Well, all in due time, Diamanes. Right now, my priority is on trying to survive Mary's training and improve my magic. Carys told us the Baron could come anytime soon. I need to get as strong as possible before that.

Glenn closed the subject, straining himself to stand up. "Argh... Fuck..."

After a few painful seconds, he managed to leave the Nexus, heading for the Dining Hall. He mindlessly paid a silver coin to the canteen worker and picked up his tray. The meal consisted of a slice of roasted boar meat, a platter of root vegetables, and a mushroom dipping sauce. A freshly baked bread roll sat in the corner of his plate.

Finding a seat at the closest table, he ate his dinner slowly—each bite reminding him of his strenuous training.

He frowned at the heavy scent of mint. *What a weird seasoning to pair with boar meat.*

After giving up on a slightly too big piece of meat, Glenn raised his eyes from his meal. He jumped in surprise when he noticed Minty.

"Wow."

"What are you doing here?" she asked in a dry tone.

"Eating?" Glenn answered by reflex before shaking his head. "No, what are *you* doing here? Can you stop stalking me?"

Minty leaned back, a disgusted expression on her face. "What? Me stalking you? You're the one following me everywhere!"

Glenn scoffed, taking the bottle of cider from his dimensional pouch. He served himself a cup, ignoring her glares.

"I don't even know who you are. Who cares about a whacko who likes to perfume herself in mint, anyway?"

Minty's face turned red, but she quickly managed to regain her composure. "Well, I'm sure even mint is better than the mix of blood, sweat, and tears that's coming off you."

Diamanes sighed, mentally face-palming. ***Why do you have to mess with everyone you meet, you dumb—***

"Sorry if the scent of *effort* displeases you. I guess you must not have smelled it a lot," Glenn countered.

Minty froze and grabbed her belly in shock. "Oh, didn't it come to your pitiful little mind that maybe I can exercise effort without looking like I just got run over by a car?" She leaned on the table oppressively, her face as red as a tomato.

"Yeah, I figured you've never taken physical classes—" Glenn paused.

"Wait." He slowly placed his fork and knife beside his plate before wiping his mouth.

No, I probably heard it wrong. Still.

"You... What did you say?" he asked gravely.

The lady blinked before sighing in frustration. She waved her hand dismissively.

"What, did I offend you? Oh, I am so sorry," she mocked.

"Car," he blurted out.

Minty froze. "What?"

"You said 'ran over by a car', right?"

"Uh, yes? Ran over by a cart, yes? Are you deaf in addition to being stupid?"

Glenn stood silent, not answering the provocation. Minty shrugged before leaving.

Diamanes hesitantly chimed in, ***Uh, what was that?***

Glenn shook his head, breathing out in disappointment.

I have a strange suspicion that she might be from Earth like me. Either way, she knows way more than she's letting on.

Diamanes smacked his lips, uninterested. **So what if she is? That wouldn't have changed anything.**

Glenn rubbed his face thoughtfully. *Maybe, but it would have felt good to meet another person like me. I don't know if I'll ever encounter Exan, but if we aren't the only ones then...*

The young man slowly finished his plate, disheartened, before heading back to the Dormitory. The night was about to fall. The training session with Mary had taken most of his time and energy.

He arrived in front of his room and found Sahro waiting beside his door. The Black Heir restrained a chuckle before bursting into laughter, holding his stomach and pointing a finger at Glenn's bruised face.

"Hahaha, look at you!" Sahro proceeded to mock him for at least a dozen minutes, which Glenn endured patiently before they finally headed into his room.

Glenn sighed. "I've confirmed the abilities of vampires, and it doesn't look good."

"*Eubayd!*" Sahro spat.

Glenn waved his hand. "Well, don't worry, they're only excellent fighters, Mages, and tacticians, in addition to being very old. Well, we can hope that the Baron is a newborn or something."

Sahro winced. "About that. There's something you should know."

Glenn looked at him with a puzzled expression. "What?"

The Black Heir sighed. "From what I've heard, he's always strolling around while hiding under an umbrella. Same for the Black Heir that accompanies him."

Glenn's mouth opened, but no sound escaped from it.

Damn it. The Black Heir too? Does that mean... Shit. This is the worst-case scenario.

Chapter 60

KILLJOY

Glenn was sitting on his bed, concentrating on his Meditation. He could feel his body healing itself, the aches and wounds from his sparring with Mary disappearing slowly. Opening his eyes, he bathed in the morning light. He stretched before sighing.

If Carys was correct, the Baron could show up as soon as today. He had no time to waste. He spent the entire morning working on his spells in the Magi Brotherhood and then stopped at an inn. Maybe *someone* would know when exactly the Baron was going to arrive.

One thing that surprised him was the apparent shortage of Fiery Spirit, the alcohol that knocked him down a few months ago.

"I heard that you can only find some in the Bourgeoisie and beyond now!" a mercenary at his table exclaimed before filling up his mouth with a piece of meat.

"What happened? I drank some outside of King's Rise three months ago!"

The mercenary shrugged but was pushed aside by one of his colleagues.

"Fiery Spirit is produced mainly in the Southern Continent, but there was a small production in a village near Still Peak... Palancar was the name."

"I heard that during the last Moon Rift, something destroyed the village and burned all its surroundings. It's basically a no man's land! As for the Southern Continent, caravans stopped coming for a few months now."

He looked left and right before pulling a suspicious-looking bottle from his backpack.

"This is one of the last bottles, but I can give you a price if you want."

Glenn froze, dumbfounded. He refused the offer and kept eating. The mercenary's explanation made something click in his mind, and he remembered the explosion he witnessed from atop the Still Peak—a small village endangered by a huge, flaming object. Glenn frowned. *Was that Palancar?*

A vaguely familiar woman joined their table, a grim expression on her face.

Her colleague asked in worry, "What's wrong, Marina? I haven't seen a look like that on your face since you let that undead bear eat your prized axe!"

Marina sighed and served herself a huge jug of ale. She drank around one liter of it before slamming her mug on the table. "Prepare yourself. I've heard that *he* is coming soon."

The faces of everyone turned dark—one mercenary even spitting on the ground, a hateful expression on his face. Glenn didn't struggle to understand who *he was*. Baron Howard was on his way to the Northern Town.

"How soon are we talking?" Glenn asked.

Marina shrugged. "My friend in the Watchers told me that he left his home in the Bourgeoisie yesterday. I'd say at the earliest, tomorrow. But feel free to pray for him to arrive later."

Glenn crossed his fingers in front of him. Two of the mercenaries stood and left, bidding the rest of the patrons good luck. Only Glenn and Marina remained.

Glenn turned to her. "What are you going to do?"

Marina half-heartedly finished eating a chicken wing and wiped her hands on her pants.

"It's already my third Harvest; I'm getting used to it. If you're not a citizen, I suggest you leave town. It does no good to be around during a Harvest."

Glenn nodded, silently taking in the advice.

* * *

On the way back to the Cleaner's Workshop, Glenn decided to stop by Hearts Bakery. The atmosphere was heavy in the empty streets of the Northern Town.

His heart tightened. He couldn't help but worry about the kind baker.

"What the hell is going to happen?" Glenn muttered.

He finally arrived at Rampart Street. There was no queue for delicious bread, and Mrs. Laurence was closing the shutters of her shop. She froze when she saw him, grabbed him by the arm, and pulled him inside. After throwing a glance out the window, she turned towards him, an angry and worried look on her face.

Glenn clenched his teeth. *Why does she look so much like my mom? Why am I so worried about this stranger?*

"What are you doing here? Don't you know the Harvest is coming?"

"I'm actually new to the Northern Town. It'll be my first Harvest."

The woman's face paled, and she grabbed Glenn's shoulders.

"You should leave town with your companion for a while. The Baron isn't kind to newcomers or Black Heirs. What did you come here for anyway?"

Glenn smiled awkwardly, feeling his guts wrenching inside him. Each passing second reinforced the anxiety he felt about this Harvest.

"I came for your cider, Mrs. Laurence. I fear I did become addicted!"

Mrs. Laurence shook her head. She offered a bottle to Glenn. "Here. Now go quickly, find your friend, and get out of here!"

She pushed him out of the shop, not even letting Glenn pay for the bottle. She clenched her teeth worriedly before adding, "My fool of a husband has been colluding with those delusional farmers. No rebellion will bring back our lost son."

"Please... be safe." The baker gave him one last sad smile before slamming her door shut. Glenn slipped a silver coin under her welcome mat.

I didn't know Mrs. Laurence also lost something to the Baron. Damn it...

He headed back to the Cleaner's Workshop, meeting a dispirited Sahro sitting on a bench alone.

"What are you doing here?"

Sahro sighed. "My contract got canceled, *again.* All they talk about is the Harvest."

Glenn winced and invited the Black Heir to follow. He quickly explained what he learned from the inn.

"Are you also getting anxious? My palms are sweaty like never before." Sahro asked, his face grim.

"I don't know what to expect, but maybe it's better if you don't show yourself. I heard he doesn't like Black Heirs."

Sahro tightened his shemagh around his face in answer, pulling the cloth up to his nose and leaving only his eyes exposed.

They entered the Workshop, silence their only host. The main lobby was empty, only the three attendants waiting at the counter, smiling as if everything was normal.

The duo arrived in the Training Hall, discovering that it was as empty as the lobby. Mary was waiting in one of the rings, sharpening her knife with a lost look. She raised her head as they approached.

"Oh, you brought your boyfriend? How cute!" she mocked, sizing Sahro up and down.

Glenn didn't react.

"What do you gentlemen say we do a light sparring to shake off the tension?" She stared down the two men like they were prey.

Sahro happily accepted before Glenn could refuse. "With pleasure. I didn't train today, so it'll be perfect!"

Glenn facepalmed, knowing exactly what was going to happen. He scraped his feet against the ground as he unwillingly picked up the Fool's

Trainer. He knew he would probably never hit Mary with it, but at least that would train his muscles a little.

Sahro judged Glenn's choice of weapon before taking off his shemagh and picking up a curved sword. Mary took two daggers, twirling them in her hands.

After a brief staredown, they threw themselves at each other. It seemed as if Sahro had initially planned to fight the two at once, but he soon didn't have a choice but to ally with Glenn to fight off Mary's relentless attacks.

Mary, Mary, Mary! Diamanes encouraged in Glenn's mind, clearly choosing to bet on the winning side.

Glenn inhaled, contracting his muscles before hurling his sword horizontally, cleaving the air in two. He used the momentum of the sword to pull it back effortlessly on his shoulder. He wasn't proficient with such a move, so he only managed to strain his muscles while not even hitting Mary.

The woman smiled devilishly as she dashed in between the two fighters, slashing at their legs and arms. Glenn could only endure it while Sahro avoided or blocked most of them. Nonetheless, the two men were pushed back by the beautiful woman, who was dancing on the training mat.

Glenn suddenly threw his sword at Mary before dashing behind her and shooting a Magic Bullet at her back. He tried to use the opportunity to slash at the woman, but he only received a heavy hit to his skull as punishment, making him fall face first.

"No magic in our fights!" she exclaimed, dashing back towards Sahro.

The Black Heir fought admirably, but after a not-so-short exchange, his sword flew from his hands, and the tip of Mary's wooden dagger pressed against his neck. Glenn panted as he pushed himself onto his feet.

The fight had indeed taken some stress off his shoulders, and the heavy mood reigning in the Northern town seemed to have a lesser effect on him. Mary chuckled before stretching with a satisfied expression.

"Well, that felt good. You should come and spar with us more often, Mister..."

"Sahro," the Black Heir said.

The Cleaner smiled. "Pleased to meet you, Sahro. I'm Mary, Glenn's teacher."

She made one of her overly gracious bows. Suddenly, the sky turned dark, and a rumbling sound echoed through the Workshop.

Mary's smile disappeared. "No way... He's already here?"

She turned towards the two young men, a sad look on her face. "Good luck."

On those words, she swiftly ran. Glenn and Sahro stared at each other, both panting from the short spar.

Haha, finally it's time for the revolution! The guillotine, Glenn, the guillotine, I said!

Only Diamanes was excited. Glenn sighed deeply.

Only the Gods know what will happen next.

Chapter 61

TRADING ONE'S LIFE

Sahro swiftly covered his skin with his shemagh while Glenn stashed the Howard family ring in his dimensional pouch, ready to be retrieved at a moment's notice.

"Did you order the silver-coated weapons?" he asked with a sense of urgency in his voice.

The Black Heir shook his head. "I had planned to do it this evening after gathering as much money as I could from the contracts."

Glenn winced, his gaze locked on the darkened sky, which hung over them with an ominous weight. His gut told him to run, but he couldn't do that. He and Sahro had a mission to accomplish, and he had given his word to Giselle.

The duo left the Training Hall, heading for the highest point of the Cleaner's Workshop—the Observatory.

As they arrived, they noticed a few figures standing in contemplative silence, their attention directed towards the ramparts of the Fringe. Glenn joined them, acknowledging the presence of the mysterious Minty and the mercenary Marina.

Together, they silently observed the scene as a deep rumbling shook the entire Northern Town. Gradually, two massive gates controlling access to the Bourgeoisie swung open, exuding a foreboding aura. The faces of those around them bore the weight of the moment. After what felt like an eternity, the gates revealed what lay beyond.

Another town unfolded before their eyes, an abundance of brass and copper in its architecture casting a warm, golden hue that was both captivating and unsettling. Bronze-clad knights emerged from the gates, escorting an ostentatiously decorated carriage.

Two huge, brass-plated horses pulled the vehicle, followed by a procession of maids on foot. If all this splendor was merely for a Baron, Glenn could scarcely imagine the wealth held by the Counts, Dukes, and the King himself.

Marina spat on the ground, a dark expression on her face.

"Here it comes," she mumbled, her eyes fixed on the ornate carriage.

They watched as the parade made its way towards a massive mansion a few minutes from the Northern Town, and their view gradually obscured. The duo chose to leave the observatory, heading down the stairs.

Sahro rubbed his neck, his expression contemplative. "The mission is going to be... much more challenging than I had anticipated."

Glenn mirrored his friend's dismay, rubbing the bridge of his nose as he attempted to calculate the number of bronze-clad knights they had seen. *At least fifty? And that doesn't include the servants and maids accompanying the procession. Then there is Stormblade, the formidable enforcer at the Baron's disposal.*

Facing such overwhelming forces alone was an almost insurmountable task. Thankfully, he wasn't alone. Glenn sighed. Although he possessed the Howard family ring as a potential solution to trade for Callum, it remained uncertain whether the Baron would take the deal.

And if he didn't... *Well, I guess all of my training was for this moment.*

They roamed the corridors of the Cleaner's Workshop in silence, eventually leaving the building. The streets of the Northern Town were eerily deserted, almost as if it was a ghost town.

The pair headed to the Frosty Beer, finding Carys and a few hundred men and women ready to fight for their freedom. Armed with knives, smithing hammers and even rakes, they looked as determined as when Carys first gave his speech. The farmer was strapped in leather armor, a scythe resting against his shoulder.

Winston cleaned a glass as he watched over the revolutionaries' preparations. Somehow, his tavern had become the main headquarters of the rebellion.

"You came," Carys acknowledged before glancing at Sahro. "And that must be that famous companion of yours, the Black Swordsman."

Sahro raised a confused eyebrow, unaware of the moniker. Carys extended his hand.

"All help is welcome. Thank you."

The Black Heir shook Carys' hand with a smirk. "I'm doing this for myself, not you. Don't fool yourself."

Carys scoffed and exhaled heavily.

"We will be counting on you two."

Glenn clenched his sword's pommel. Suddenly, everyone's lives weighed on his shoulders. Failure wasn't an option.

"We will follow you." Carys stood. "Please, be the spearhead of the revolution."

A grin appeared on Glenn's face, the perfect mask to hide his worries.

"How can I refuse when you asked so nicely?" he turned to the inn's exit and muttered under his breath, ignoring Diamanes' laughter.

"Time to overthrow a tyrant."

* * *

The revolutionaries' steps in the paved streets of the Northern Town echoed with a silent rumble. Not a word was exchanged—not a glance, not a sigh. Men and women united toward one goal.

Freedom.

Glenn and Sahro stood at the vanguard, their weapons unsheathed. The Black Heir was tense but also wore an excited smile, his fingers tightly wrapped around the hilt of his sword. Glenn could almost sense his companion's lust for battle.

They led the group to the outskirts of the village, where the Baron's mansion stood. The bronze knights had set up camp across the plains, their tents proudly displaying the Howard family emblem, a peacock with fanned feathers. Torches surrounded the entire camp—beacons for the villagers' hatred.

Carys turned back to his people and silently raised his scythe. The villagers imitated him, the silent show sending a shiver down Glenn's spine. He smiled confidently, chasing away his anxiousness.

We definitely have a chance. I'll save Callum, complete the deal with Giselle, and get rid of the Thorns Church. Heh. Do you think Brother Khan is praying for me right now?

There's no point in relying on Gods. Diamanes laughed mockingly. **You have skills, spells, allies—and even me!**

Glenn grinned. *Yeah, you're right. None of those have failed me before.*

"Okay, so, I'll go ahead first and request an audience with the Baron," Glenn said. "If I don't return in—"

The farmer shook his head. "We don't negotiate with monsters."

Carys exhaled slowly before pointing at the enemy camp. All at once, the revolutionaries rushed forwards, emboldened by the flames of liberty.

What? Oh, come on! At least let me try my plan!

The drowsy knights on watch couldn't believe their eyes as a hundred villagers charged the camp. A soldier reached for a horn at his waist, intending to sound the alarm, but a curved blade cleanly sliced through his throat, silencing him.

Unfortunately, footsteps echoed through the camp. The bronze soldiers scrambled to their feet, grabbing weapons and helmets hurriedly.

"Attack! It's an attack!" someone yelled.

Sahro dashed between the tents, running for Howard's mansion. Glenn exhaled heavily, steeling himself before following his companion.

They ignored the knights on their way, sprinting through mud. There was a steel gate blocking their way, but they didn't stop. Glenn channeled an Arcane Auger. The spell flew and pierced through the lock effortlessly. Sahro kicked the gate open, his sword covered in crimson Aura.

Behind them, the soldiers and revolutionaries' screams mixed in a bloody chaos. A few tents went up in flames, spreading to the fields.

Glenn and Sahro stormed inside the mansion, ignoring the terrified servants along the way.

"I'll check the upper floor!" shouted Glenn as he dashed up the stairs. Sahro didn't reply as he ran through the hallway.

They had multiple objectives, but the most important was still to bring Callum back. It didn't matter how much Glenn enjoyed the idea of a revolution, nothing mattered if he couldn't bring Giselle's grandson home.

Glenn kicked open one door after the other. Dusty guest rooms, storage rooms, and even more rooms—but no sight of a Black Heir or a *vampire*. He did notice countless portraits of the Baron's lineage on the walls. Glenn's gaze settled on one particular painting, his curiosity piqued.

He retrieved the wanted poster that had long been tucked away in his dimensional pouch, comparing it to the portrait titled *The Howards*. The eldest figure, a stern-looking man, proudly wore the Howard family crest on his vest—his angular face and jet-black hair marking him as the patriarch. An imposing madame with an ostentatious red dress and ample bosom, presumably the Baron's wife, clung to her husband's arm. Positioned between them were two young adults: a man and a woman.

The young man bore an uncanny resemblance to the face on the wanted poster—blond hair, the same prideful stance, and black attire that matched the garments Glenn had found. It could only be Jefferson Howard. Yet, the person assumed to be his sister lacked a face, as if it had been deliberately erased from the painting.

What a nice-looking family! Glenn thought sarcastically.

Yeah, I'm not sure you have time to dwell on a random painting, Diamanes commented. *Then again, what are a few villagers' lives worth compared to art?*

Glenn grimaced, ignoring the entity's voice. He almost started to doubt whether the Baron even came to the Northern Town when he suddenly entered an old office.

Plush couches beckoned from every corner, and a well-stocked bar adorned the back wall—a testament to the Baron's indulgences. A man sat at the far end of the room, his large leather chair a symbol of authority. He shared the same features as the portrait but older, his pallor ghostly and his frame emaciated. Behind him, thick curtains had been drawn to allow the moonlight inside.

I bet he's our Baron. Oh-ho, it's going to be disastrous, isn't it? muttered Diamanes, failing to discourage his host.

An imposing figure stood two meters tall beside him, clad in coal-black steel. *Stormblade.*

"A rebellion..." Baron Howard pressed his fingers against the side of his head.

Glenn raised his sword carefully as he stepped into the room.

"Howard!" he barked. "Give me that Black Heir you kidnapped twenty years ago, and I'll tell you the fate of your son. I might even convince the revolutionaries to let you leave alive!"

The Baron raised a curious eyebrow. "My... son?" He turned to Stormblade with a frown. "Didn't he die outside King's Rise? The fool..."

Glenn's heart skipped a beat. Howard didn't give a single fuck about his son. With a swift motion, Glenn threw Jefferson's ring and journal onto the Baron's desk.

"He's still alive!" Glenn lied through his teeth. "And we have him! Free Callum, and we'll give your son back to you."

The Baron slowly picked up Jefferson's ring, looking at it silently.

"You want to see... Callum, is that right? Well..." He rang a bell for a servant, who promptly came out of a dark corner to serve his master a drink.

The young man's forehead was marked with a distinctive white pattern. He had blue eyes, black-red hair, and most importantly, black skin. He bore a strong resemblance to Giselle—a scrawny, younger male version of the proud Black Heir leader.

A wry smile tugged at Glenn's lips. *That's Callum. There's no way he isn't her grandson.*

The Baron sipped on his cup before tilting his head in the servant's direction.

"Tell me, Callum. Do you wish to go with this man, or would you rather stay here serving me?"

Callum bowed, his face expressionless. "Of course, my duty is with you, master."

Glenn's features hardened, and he stabbed his sword into the floor. "This wasn't a request. I'm taking him with me, whether he likes it or not!"

Yep, it's either that or Giselle throws me back at the Thorns Church. And no way I'm letting that happen.

The Baron raised his hand, and Glenn's senses tingled with impending danger. "My son is dead. You wouldn't have his diary nor his ring otherwise. After all, he was instructed to keep his ring in his dimensional pouch at all times."

He smiled from ear to the other, revealing two sharp fangs. His breath was fetid, exuding a putrid odor that filled the room.

Glenn's blood froze in his veins. The Baron crossed his arms and slowly shook his head.

"What a disappointment... No worse than his sister," he grunted.

The Baron suddenly closed his fist on the ring and crushed it, dropping the bent metal on his desk. Jefferson's journal suffered the same fate.

"Nonetheless." The Baron's lips curved upward slightly. "What an interesting twist of fate. Maybe I should thank the idiot for sending you my way. I'll play with you, sure."

In a swift motion, Glenn lunged forwards, evading Stormblade's grasp. He rolled to his feet, his instincts sharpened by the imminent threat. Without hesitation, he sprinted towards the windows, his heart pounding.

Glenn unleashed a Magic Bullet that shattered the glass into a thousand glinting shards and leapt onto the ledge. As he looked back, Callum's expression remained impassive.

"May the Harvest commence," the Baron murmured darkly.

With unwavering resolve, Glenn jumped from the third-story mansion, the ground hurtling with great speed.

This couldn't have gone worse, Diamanes remarked.

"No shit!" Glenn hissed through his clenched teeth as he braced for impact.

Chapter 62

THE HARVEST

Glenn rolled forwards to disperse kinetic energy. His knees felt like they were on the brink of breaking, but he stood nonetheless. The servants in the garden looked at him with half-surprised, half-amused expressions. Glenn didn't spare them another glance and dashed for the manor's exit.

Wait, servants in the garden? It's the middle of the night.

Glenn spun on his feet just in time to deflect a sharp shovel away from his neck. A servant with bright red eyes grinned ominously, sharp fangs peeking out of his mouth.

"Thralls..." Glenn silently cursed as his Mana swirled around him.

In one instant, the servant pointed his shovel at him. In another, his head exploded thanks to a Magic Bullet. The thrall fell to the ground, lifeless.

Hey, at least there's one positive! You're doing the work Carys asked of you! cackled Diamanes without a care.

The expression of the other servants—no, *thralls*—twisted. They raised their gardening tools and circled him.

Glenn held his breath as he dodged a pitchfork, parried a pair of shears, and endured the cold bite of a trowel in his arm. He kicked one of the thralls away before stabbing another in the stomach. Without looking, he let go of his sword and crouched to dodge another shovel attack, punching the last vampire in the chin. He grabbed the monster's head and slammed it on the floor.

The thrall coughed out a lump of blood, his eyes rolling in their sockets. Glenn flinched as shears pierced him in the back. He spun forwards and pushed himself up, gasping for air.

He wasn't the only one who stood.

The thrall he stabbed slowly pulled the sword out of his stomach, grinning wickedly. Another servant licked her shears while she rose. Her neck bent at a weird angle.

The only thrall that wasn't moving was the one Glenn had decapitated.

Glenn winced as he held his wounds. "Shit. The Walking Dead logic, then. Fuck me…"

Mana swirled around his hands as the thralls lunged at him. Magic Bullets whistled through the air, piercing the monsters. He managed to blow one's head off and another's leg, but the female servant dodged his attacks.

She jumped on him silently, aiming for his throat. Glenn blocked with his arms, his flesh lacerated. He hurriedly dove away, grabbing his sword from the ground, but it was too late. The thrall's shears aimed for his heart when, suddenly, a scythe cut through her arm.

The female servant looked up in disbelief, grabbing the blade helplessly. Carys grunted as he sliced off her limb.

"You alright, Glenn? Where's Sahro?" asked the revolutionary leader.

Glenn winced and stood by himself. "I-I'm fine. I've endured worse. Sahro is still inside—"

Carys' face paled as he stared at the female thrall. "Anita?"

Glenn's heart tightened. Carys looked at his wife, tears welling up in his eyes. Anita was indifferent, her wounds already healing. She clenched her shears once more.

"I'll take care of her," said Glenn, but Carys pushed him aside.

He clenched his scythe firmly and smiled sadly at his comrade. "Please."

No words were needed. Glenn rushed away as Anita jumped at her husband. Carys' scythe stabbed her directly in the neck, decapitating her on the spot.

After a few minutes, the revolutionary leader returned to Glenn's side, his eyes bloodshot.

"Let's keep going," he hissed. "This isn't over until we have the Baron's head on a spike!"

Glenn reached for Carys' arm. "Wait, no, he's stronger than we—"

Carys didn't listen as he ran back towards the manor's entrance, fighting the soldiers along the trail. Glenn cursed and tried to run after him, but the mansion's wall suddenly exploded. Sahro flew through the air, crimson Aura covering his flickering sword.

Stormblade stepped out of the debris, his greatsword glowing with a turquoise gleam.

"Sahro!"

Glenn shot multiple Magic Bullets at the dark knight, but he endured them without flinching. The spells simply exploded against his armor without denting it.

As Glenn dashed for Sahro, he found him unconscious. His temple bled profusely.

Oh, yeah, that doesn't look too good. And not to worry you, but the tables seemed to have turned for the rest of your fast friend, Diamanes warned.

Glenn glanced one last time at Stormblade before picking up the Black Heir and running away. Baron Howard watched from the height of the manor's steps, smirking.

Dashing through the burning encampments, Glenn coughed out his lungs. The Black Heir was surprisingly light, but that was no saving grace when the odds were so miserably stacked against him.

Soldiers lay in the mud, their throats slit and hearts pierced. But for each dead guard, there were five times as many dead villagers. Glenn's heart tightened.

They had been slaughtered. The whole operation was a complete, utter failure. Bronze knights pierced through corpses with their halberds, ensuring their deaths. Many laughed maniacally, raising their weapons towards the clouded moons' light. Their crazed voices covered the roaring flames devouring the encampment.

"It has begun!"

"Harvest!"

"Harvest! Hahaha!"

They marched past the burning tents with little care. Nonetheless, Glenn wasn't going to let go of the opportunity to escape—that was for sure.

He eventually reached the edge of the camp, hidden behind a supply cart as the knights roared. Another villager screamed for aid. Glenn cursed and almost went to help him, but the weight of his comrade in his back stopped him at the last moment.

Well, it happens, you know. You shouldn't torture yourself too much. Our lives—Sahro not included—are much more important than those simple villagers. Diamanes' cold voice rang in Glenn's head like an admission of guilt.

The young man dashed through the wheat fields.

A dark figure suddenly appeared in front of him—his long, ominous greatsword drawn. The tip dragged against the ground, making an eerie whine as it dug across the mud.

"Stormblade!" Glenn blurted out, his Mana swirling madly around his hands.

"We usually take prisoners for the Baron to have fun with. But you killed too many of his precious thralls. Prepare to die," the knight declared with a raspy voice, his sword gleaming.

Glenn threw Sahro into the wheat and held his own sword straight in front of him.

The black knight lunged forwards, his dark cape fluttering. His boots dug through the mud as his sword tried to cleave Glenn in two. The latter side-stepped it, the blade cutting the air an inch away from his face.

He shot an Arcane Auger at Stormblade's chest, but the knight sliced through it with one swift movement. The shock of the blast still forced him to take a step back, but...

It's not even half as effective as I hoped it would be. Glenn's fingers tightened on his sword's hilt as he charged at his enemy.

He hadn't learned as much as he could have under Mary, but one thing he did understand was to never squander an advantage. Glenn shot three more Magic Bullets, accurately aiming for the knight's helmet. The latter dodged the first two shots and deflected the last one, only to watch helplessly as the tip of Glenn's sword stabbed him in the chest.

Or at least tried to.

Glenn's blade ricocheted against the steel, deflected as if the attack was meaningless. The knight laughed and kicked Glenn away, throwing him to the ground. Glenn rolled away, breathless. He pushed himself up and coughed out a lump of mud. There was a boot imprint on his waist from the might of the attack.

"Trying to rebel against a noble with that strength?" Stormblade scoffed as he raised his sword once more. "Pathetic."

Turquoise Aura covered the blade as he stabbed into the dirt. Glenn didn't let that display impress him and shot a flurry of Drilling Bullets. But alas, the spells dissipated as soon as they touched the steel.

The knight raised his weapon high before cleaving down. Glenn hurriedly jumped to the side, only for his eyes to widen in horror.

Shit, it was a feint! Stormblade shoulder-bashed him. Glenn flew like a ragdoll, his lungs burning for air.

He took a raspy breath, only to see the heavy, black blade falling towards his face. He threw himself aside, watching in shock as a huge portion of the Golden Fields disappeared. The ground ruptured.

"*Cough,* Damn it!"

Blood gushed out of his cheek. He panted as he concentrated on summoning his Arcane Auger.

The one-meter-wide drill made a buzzing sound as he jerked it forwards. The knight side-stepped it, letting the spell graze on his breastplate before hitting Glenn with his pommel.

The latter fell to his knees, his head ringing, only to hurriedly put up a Magic Wall. The greatsword crashed on his defenses, a loud clang echoing between the two fighters. The Magic Wall creaked weakly before exploding in a flurry of deep blue particles. The second Glenn recovered his senses, he retreated from the sword's reach.

"*Proiectum, Velox, Destructum!*"

An Enhanced Magic Bullet left his hand and hit the knight in the chest, knocking him back. He fell to one knee, looking at his armor in an almost confused manner.

Glenn dashed forwards and pressed his hand against the knight's chest. He glared up at the empty eyes under the black helmet.

"Let's see if your armor can block this!" he roared as he channeled almost the totality of his Mana into an Implosion.

The armor caved in with a loud creak, and in a blinding flash, the knight flew back a dozen meters. Glenn was thrown away from the recoil, his arm jerking in an awkward position. Adrenaline pumped through his veins as he heaved with difficulty.

The knight didn't stand up.

"Fuck..." Glenn gasped as he held his broken arm.

He hurriedly retrieved Sahro from the field. While running away with his friend on his back, he ignored the pain and exhaustion. He tossed his sword into his dimensional pouch, forced to admit that it had been less than effective. *I busted my ass practicing melee combat for nothing!*

I don't see why it surprises you. You had what, two days of training? Diamanes mocked.

"Very helpful as always Diamanes," Glenn grunted as he ran towards the Northern Town.

When he eventually arrived in the streets, the bronze knights had begun their march, yelling "Harvest!" in a macabre rhythm. He entered an unlit street and leaned against a wall, gasping for air. His shoulder ached, but he forced himself to continue.

He checked the roofs and clicked his tongue. "We'd be safer up there."

After a quick exhale, he propelled himself up the wall with the strength of his legs. Sahro's head bobbed from side to side limply.

It's moments like these that I'm almost thankful for getting tortured in that prison, Glenn thought sarcastically as he lay against the tiles while gazing at the starless sky.

A few minutes later, the bronze knights marched through the alley, torches in their hands. They entered each house, leaving with citizens and coin pouches. Glenn carefully watched from over the ledge, trying to understand what the soldiers wanted to accomplish.

Soon enough, a dozen people had been pulled from their homes and dragged towards the town square.

Glenn leaned back, wincing. Mrs. Laurence was right. He should have left town while he still could. He was not strong enough to deal with the Baron's forces. If he struggled that badly against his *escort*, how strong would Howard —*a vampire*— actually be?

"This whole revolution was doomed to fail from the start..." he winced dejectedly, holding his broken arm.

Sahro grunted, cracking his eyes open.

"Fuck... Did I lose? Shit! I lost, didn't I?" he mumbled in disbelief.

Glenn sat up with a grimace of pain. "How good are you at first aid?" He pointed his chin at his arm.

Sahro gave him an expert look. "It's only dislocated. I'll put it back, but clench your teeth. It'll hurt like a bitch."

Glenn snorted. "Do it. We can't afford to waste time."

Without a shred of hesitation, Sahro snapped Glenn's bone back in place.

Glenn hissed, the pain ringing through his entire body. He shook it off, his eyes gleaming with determination.

"I made a promise, and I'm keeping it," he muttered as he forced himself up. Baron Howard was dying tonight, and he was going to make sure of it.

Sahro nodded slowly, agreeing. The two exchanged one last glance before looking over the town. Numerous groups headed for the square.

The duo quickly planned their routes over the rooftops, jumping from house to house and following the trail of torches. A few minutes later, they arrived at their objective, panting and hurting. A procession of bronze knights and civilians gathered in a large plaza that had once hosted market stalls.

A bonfire burned at the center and Baron Howard stood in front of it. His hands were clasped behind his back, Callum standing right beside him. Glenn grimaced when he saw the Black Heir but quickly gasped in surprise when he noticed the figure next him. Stormblade simply stood there, silently.

"How the fuck is he?" Glenn blurted out.

"Great question! I think there might be a *little more* under that armor than we initially thought," Diamanes mumbled.

The villagers had resigned faces. Some cried, but none had the will to fight their fate. They all knew the revolution had failed.

The Baron suddenly coughed lightly.

"My dear denizens." Howard smiled, warmly opening his arms. "How happy am I to see you once again—to share with you the pleasure of this long-lasting tradition, the Harvest!"

Glenn strained his eyes as he took cover in the shadows.

"Do forgive my early arrival, but I assure you all that it's best if we begin the *festivities* in a timely manner."

He turned to the group of terrified denizens and grinned wickedly. "Today, I shall announce the three chosen ones who will ascend to the Bourgeoisie!"

The Baron walked towards the crowd. Knights and denizens alike parted. Glenn's eyes widened as he recognized Liam among them.

"What is he doing here—?" Glenn mumbled. *I have a bad feeling about this.*

The Baron paused in front of a bald man, placing his hand graciously on his head.

"Hmm... Not the best potential, but you'll do nicely. You are?"

"Garin, sir!" the bald man answered, his eyes resolute.

Howard smiled before turning towards another person in the crowd, a woman with a bulging stomach. Glenn's eyes almost popped out of their sockets. *Isn't she Winston's wife? Damn it!*

The Baron gave a warm smile to her.

"You shall be the second, dear..."

"Ma—Marie, sir," she said, shaking in her shoes.

Howard stroked her hair and gave a sign to the knights beside him, his smile unchanging. The knights grabbed Winston's wife, her expression confused and fearful.

"My... My Lord?" she asked, her voice trembling.

The Baron turned towards her, a puzzled expression on his face. "What, my dear?"

She slowly glanced left and right, her movements jerky. The Baron nodded, and one of the knights punched her in the belly—forcing her to her knees.

Glenn's pupils dilated. He jumped off the building without a second thought, dashing through the crowd. Sahro closely followed him, his sword glimmering with a crimson Aura. They charged the two knights when a heavy weight suddenly crashed over them. They collapsed to the floor, their chins pushed against the cold tiles.

"My, oh my. Look at that! Aren't you the *spearheads* of this ridiculous revolution?" The Baron mocked as he towered over them.

Stormblade had a knee pressed against each of them. His murky Aura had flared up, rendering their struggles useless.

Spearheads? Glenn's eyes widened. The only one who called them that was Carys.

A mole, Diamanes stated in a dark tone.

The Baron turned back to Marie, his smile evil in the light of the brazier. Fearful gasps came from the crowd, but the knights quickly calmed them down with a nudge of their halberds. Glenn's eyes locked on the Baron.

"I'm bringing *you* to ascend with me." Howard poked his finger at the woman's belly. "But I never said *it* could come with you."

Winston's wife cried, her screams soon muffled as the knights pummeled her stomach restlessly. The Baron's grin only widened. He raised his hand, finally putting a stop to the horror. The knights released the woman, letting her fall to the ground.

Her tears stopped, and her expression turned blank. "My... My baby..."

"You fucking monster!" Glenn spat through his teeth, anger painting his face red.

The Baron raised an eyebrow. "Monster?"

He crouched in front of Glenn as his smile faded, replaced by pure, evil hatred. "You little *fuck*. You dare stand up to me? To show yourself in front of a *noble* and believe you're righteous?"

He pressed his foot against Glenn's face, crushing him under the sole of his boot.

"You're pigs. Prey to be slaughtered," hissed the Baron. "I'm the butcher."

"But... you're pretty special pigs, aren't you? I'll fatten you up and wait for you to bite me again. The day you do..." He licked his lips hungrily. "I'll eat you whole. But for now..."

The Baron opened his arm in a warm gesture.

"My friends, I know you're all *dying* of curiosity to know who the third chosen one will be!"

The Baron gave a smile to the horrified crowd, his eyes stopping on a scrawny kid.

"I've heard of a boy who survived the machinations of the Thorns Church! I think he deserves that honor more than anyone else, doesn't he?"

Howard grinned. "Liam, please join us."

Liam walked out of the crowd, his clenched fists trembling. His eyes, on the other hand, were unwavering, emboldened with a resolve of steel.

Diamanes clicked his tongue. ***He's targeting those around you.***

Glenn bit on his lips until they bled.

Nothing was going according to plan.

Nothing.

Chapter 63

THE SOUND OF SILENCE

Glenn's eyes locked with Howard's, his fists clenched. Beside him, similarly crushed under Stormblade's knee, Sahro was trying to push himself up without success. The Baron grinned widely before suddenly sighing.

"Of course, there's an even *grander* hero among us today. Who hasn't heard of the newly minted Fixer who helped kill the monstrous being that appeared in the Auberge?"

Howard clutched Liam's neck, his fake smile as sharp as a blade.

"I can understand if you wish to stay here among these... peasants." His smile disappeared, replaced by a cold, calculative face.

"You have skills, Glenn, and *potential*. You even managed to hurt Sir Stormblade!" Howard said as he turned towards the black knight. "It'd be such a waste to let you rot in the Fringe. The Bourgeoisie would offer you so much more, and you'd just have to, well, serve me for life."

Baron Howard whispered in Glenn's ear, "Isn't that a *deal*?"

"Go fuck yourself, you vulture!" Glenn spat.

The Baron blinked before carefully wiping his face with a handkerchief.

"I see. If you'd rather not come, I won't force you. It's your loss. But hey, at least someone else will benefit from it, right?" Howard patted Liam's back. The kid nodded frantically.

I need a solution. Diamanes, can you take away Stormblade's strength? Any advice?

Diamanes cleared his throat. ***I'd need direct contact with him, and it's not even guaranteed your body would be able to handle it. I think he just toyed with you earlier. There's a shroud over his actual power. I have no idea how strong he truly is.***

Glenn pressed his forehead against the pavement, cursing silently. Baron Howard's intentions with Liam were clear.

Goddamn it. He's telling me he's going to kill the kid, and I can't do anything!

His Mana flared up, responding to his emotions. He managed to lift himself up slightly. Stormblade grunted and shoved his face back onto the stone, his steel gauntlet clenching Glenn like a puppet.

The Baron shrugged. "That's your choice. But just *imagine* how *good* his life will be—once he ascends!"

"Aren't you *jealous* of that?" Howard hissed like a snake.

Glenn foamed at the mouth, his entire body struggling against Stormblade. Not that it changed anything.

Liam looked at Glenn, his resolute eyes contrasting with the terror his body seemed to feel. It was as if he was saying, 'Don't worry about me'.

That kid... Diamanes mumbled with a rare, impressed tone. ***He thinks he's paying back a debt.***

Baron Howard shook his head and sighed. "Too bad. I am certain you would have made a fine replacement for my fool of a son. Well, I'll have to be satisfied with these three then..."

Glenn could only watch as the Baron turned away, the bronze knights following him as they carried the 'chosen ones' along. Glenn's eyes emptied of emotions, blank and soulless.

But suddenly, the Baron stopped, his procession imitating him.

"Ah, I almost forgot!"

He snapped for his knights, who drug three bodies from a shrouded alley. Glenn's heart skipped a beat.

"My dear denizens, you might be aware of the failed attempt at rebellion that happened earlier. My loyal soldiers captured the important figures of the revolution!"

The Baron smiled while eyeing the three naked bodies covered in lashes and punctures.

"It is my responsibility as a noble to protect this town from troublemakers, so... I got rid of them!"

"No, no, no!" Glenn felt the world spin, his breath taken away.

The Baron flicked his fingers, and the three bodies flew up, animated by a strange magic. Bolts of red crucified them against the walls.

Those three corpses hanging like meat were people he knew. Tears blurred his vision. The first person was the friendly bartender who had two daughters and a wife—a wife taken away by the Baron.

The second...

Glenn lowered his eyes to the ground, struggling to breathe. The second victim was the first person he met when he entered the Fringe—the smiling farmer who worked hard every day under the sun in the Golden Fields, and who tried to fight for his people's freedom. His hat hung on his chest, crumpled and covered in blood.

Glenn headbutted the pavement. The third was a strong, petite woman with a round face and figure. Her practical glasses were half-embedded in her previously rosy cheeks. She would never bake another delicious loaf of bread or offer any more bottles of cider. Her smile was the closest Glenn came to seeing his mother's face again. And she was dead because of him.

They all died because of him. Because he accepted to lend his *pitiful* strength to a cause doomed to fail from the start. Blood flowed from the cracks of Glenn's hands. He had pierced his skin from clenching too tightly.

The Baron left the square laughing aloud. His procession's chuckles echoed in the Northern Town, accentuated by the sound of dripping blood.

Glenn couldn't see or hear anything anymore. He had the image of the three victims burned into his vision. Even if he closed his eyes, he could only see them—their empty stares.

"This... This is all my..." Tears stopped him from speaking.

Church bells rang ominously, announcing the coming dawn. As the sound reverberated, the denizens finally left the plaza. A few headed to the bloody street where the three bodies had been unceremoniously left to rot.

Stormblade, who still held Glenn and Sahro, laughed wickedly as he listened to the crowd's wails. Glenn couldn't listen. The only thing he could hear was a loud, disturbing command.

KILL! KILL HIM! SLAUGHTER HIM! DESTROY HIM!

That wasn't Diamanes' voice. No... It was his own, exploding in his mind. Glenn's Mana surged in one last desperate attempt. His eyes were bloodshot as he channeled his Mana for the strongest Implosion he could muster.

Stormblade's sneer was the last thing Glenn heard before the world finally went black.

* * *

Shing!

Glenn held his head in his hands, a painful headache seizing him. He felt a thick bump on his nape.

"What the hell happened?" he mused, his eyes unfocused.

Shing!

"Stormblade's knocked out," a man's voice responded dejectedly from beside his bed.

Glenn turned, discovering Sahro at his bedside, sharpening his sword.

Shing!

That's... the weird sound...

Glenn tried to collect his thoughts. A heavy silence instilled itself in the room.

His left was bare, but Diamanes remained quiet. A few minutes passed without anyone saying anything.

"What... What happened?"

The Black Heir sighed. "The Baron already went back to the Bourgeoisie."

He paused. "The three... were buried this morning. The town is working again as if nothing happened. Hearts Bakery is gone. The kid who worked with Mrs. Laurence said he'll still be staying there a while. A shoemaker offered to buy the building and give him a job."

He coughed a little before continuing. "Winston's daughters are taking over the Frosty Beer. His legacy lives on... in some sense."

Glenn slowly got out of bed. He still had his clothes on. He touched his cheek where Stormblade sliced him. A crust had formed.

That'll leave a mark... he thought absently. "What about Carys' family?"

Sahro shook his head. "He was alone. And after the failed revolution, nobody wants to speak of him anymore."

Glenn lowered his gaze. "I see... A sad end for a sad life..."

Sahro stood from his chair, looking hesitantly at Glenn.

"I'll be in my room. Just... Tell me if you need something."

Glenn nodded, his mind raging with thoughts.

After Sahro left, he headed for the small, dirty window. The streets bustled with activity once again.

"That was a really bad day," he said aloud.

His eyes closed as he bathed in the sunlight. Finally, a teardrop fell, and then another one, and another...

"Damn it."

* * *

Glenn stood alone in the Training Hall in the middle of a sparring ring. He swung Fool's Trainer without stopping, sweat pearling from his forehead. It had been at least three hours since he started. His body hurt everywhere, and his hands were full of bleeding blisters. But he kept swinging, restlessly. He couldn't train his Mana. Hell, he couldn't even enter Meditation. So he did the only thing he could. Swing a sword.

Swing!

With each swing, Glenn felt his muscles strain, asking desperately for rest. But Glenn continued, his gaze unchanging.

Swing!

In his eyes, the corpses hung, covered in blood and wounds.

Swing!

Winston.

Swing!

Carys.

Swing!

And Mrs. Laurence.

Swing!

His helplessness.

Swing!

His lack of strength.

Swing!

He couldn't accept it, but it was done. All because he was too weak to fight off the damned Baron and his goons.

Swing!

Rage distorted his vision as he swung again, and again, and again. His left hand glowed slightly, the purple skin creeping up his arm inch by inch.

Swing!

That was the only thing he could do right now. The only thing he could think of. His eyes were resolute and his determination as strong as steel. He could already imagine the road in front of him. Paved in blood and iron. But he didn't care. He would get stronger. Infinitely stronger. So much that he would be able to crush Howard like the bug he was. And he'd get back to Earth, free from the horrors of this world.

He would let nothing stop him.

Nothing.

End of Book One

<u>*Blood Moon*</u>

Extra Chapter

"THINGS COULD HAVE BEEN WORSE."

Glenn drew a deep breath and called out to the sky in a strained whisper.

"Status!"

"System!"

"Inventory? No? Nothing?"

A blue window suddenly appeared before his eyes, shining with a light of hope. Glenn's heart missed a beat, and he pumped his fist into the air with great happiness.

Fuck yeah! I knew I wasn't alone.

He took a moment to still his breath, calming his excitement, and carefully read the blue window's contents.

"Hmm..." His eyes darted over the screen. "Alright, that's what I was expecting."

Glenn sighed and clenched his sword tightly. Killing monsters to level up, unlocking skills, and eventually defeating the big bad guy in the sky so he could rule the world.

"That still means I need to return to this place..." He shuddered as he turned toward the battlefield, which was teeming with more of these ghoulish creatures.

He shook his head and lightly slapped his cheek. Getting stronger was the first step to survival. And if killing those ghouls meant getting stronger, then he better get to it.

Determined, Glenn strode back to the plain covered in corpses, sword in hand.

A few minutes later, he died.

* * *

Glenn held his breath as he reached out for the white crystal. He pressed his palm against it, trembling as he felt a pulse of power run through his body.

The sensation was indescribable, a divine blessing which he couldn't get enough of.

"Ah! Wait, no!"

Glenn turned to ashes, joining the pitiful pile of Jefferson Howard's remains.

"Ah, man. I really thought he was the one. Welp, time to wait another hundred years, I s'pose."

* * *

Glenn felt his heart beat loudly in his chest. In a sleek, metallic frame, its body was divided into two distinctive sections—a ten-centimeter-long barrel and a handle grip. On the side of the cannon, engraved in small letters, was 'Smith and Wesson .38.' He flipped the gun over, finding 'Springfield, Massachusetts, 1899' written on the other side.

Diamanes, I—I can feel it!

What the fuck?

The young man raised the gun in front of him, a bald eagle suddenly landing on his shoulder out of nowhere.

"Time to bring freedom and democracy!"

* * *

Sahro tapped lightly on Glenn's shoulder, his expression grave as he nodded towards the clerks. They tossed their hair back at the same time, mimicking Alisson's motions in a mechanical manner.

Glenn rubbed his eyes, wondering if he perhaps had seen wrong. The next second, the two clerks leaned back and stretched *in unison*, sending a shiver down his spine. He tensed and exchanged a concerned glance with Sahro.

The latter whispered discreetly, "It didn't happen only once. They seem... connected."

"What the hell?" Glenn muttered in awe. *Diamanes, any idea what they are?*

"Hmm..." Diamanes groaned hesitantly. **"I... I honestly don't know. Maybe it's because I woke up not that long ago, but I can't tell."** The entity gasped in realization. **"I know! Try saying this..."**

Glenn looked at his left hand dubiously. "M-Magical girls, assemble?"

The Cleaner's Workshop's lights suddenly dimmed, shining only on the three female clerks.

"Alisson!"

Bang!

"Dana!"

Bang!

"Mina!"

Bang!

They struck the lamest of poses as magical particles surrounded them.

"Together, we are the Cleaner's Fairies!"

Glenn and Sahro politely applauded them.

ACKNOWLEDGEMENTS

Thank you for reading!

I hope you enjoyed the ride. It's only the beginning of Glenn's ~~torture~~ adventure, and Onnea knows it won't be a walk in the park.

If you want to help, or really enjoyed the book, or both, please, leave a review! (Or you'll end up with Diamanes stuck in your hand. Your choice.)

Guylhann

Thank you for reading a MoonQuill® original novel. More exciting stories can be found at www.moonquill.com.

We would greatly appreciate it if you would take a moment to leave a review. Each one helps the author and supports their ability to continue writing fantastic books for everyone to enjoy!

If you're looking for more great books to read, join our mailing list by scanning the QR code below. You'll get few ebooks for free!